27 APRIL 1999

RICHARD

- BUYING BOOKS? THAT'S O
SCOTS MYTH DISPELLED; I BET
YOU'D WEAR Y-FRONTS BENEATH YUK
KILT, TOO!

BEST WISHES

Steve

NO REHEARSAL

Steve Keeling

MINERVA PRESS

ATLANTA LONDON SYDNEY

ISBN 0 75410 398 6

First Published 1999 by
MINERVA PRESS
315–317 Regent Street
London W1R 7YB

Printed in Great Britain for Minerva Press

NO REHEARSAL

Or are they?

For Sophie with love.
Whenever and wherever you are.

Acknowledgements

This, along with a preface, is the bit of any book that no occasional reader really seems to read; and as a result, you're perhaps sometimes lucky enough to find words that the author couldn't bring themselves to include in the main text like 'bum' and 'knickers', or even the odd 'poo', but thought that they could slip in somewhere unnoticed. Well, sod that; I've included them all in the main text, so if you're easily titillated, read the entire story.

Who should I openly thank? More to the point, *should* I openly thank at all? Well, 'yes' is the answer to that one, and the more folk I do, the more will read this particular page, I suppose. It goes without saying that there have been many influences upon me, the resultant cocktail of which has lead to the creation of the ensuing tale. The following, however, have had more than their fair input over recent months, and it is they who deserve special acknowledgement. My thanks, therefore, extend to:

Mum and Dad – both individually and collectively, whose actions some time in 1967 led indirectly to this book, and whose love, guidance and support have been unerring. Your knowledge of the Brownies and of electrics (or is that 'electric Brownies'?) was invaluable.

My grandparents – without them, Irene and Gordon wouldn't have been able to meet...

Sophie Eleanor – you're what life's all about, and always with me.

Joanne, David and Christine – keeping the flag flying in foreign parts, and always a dormant inspiration.

Charlotte – for putting up with me for so long on the trip that provided the spark of an idea. Is there any lemon vodka left?

Alan, Debbie and Emily for support when it mattered most, the escape of boating and the oft-unwitting sounding board for many a crazy thought. Here's to cracking cheese and Anal Nevets!

Mike and Donna – without whose Sainsbury's shuttle I'd have probably starved, and co-writers' enthusiasm I'd have dried. Madge, for being a great mate and a whizz with the photocopier. Mike and Margaret, Jules and Linda, and Bob too for hospitality above and beyond the call of friendship. Andy, for regular pints in the Twilight Zone. Mick, Steve P, Paul and Lee for the sessions scaling from the unique to the bizarre. Ian, David, Malcolm and the gang at the 'Social' Club – there's no such thing as 'no hope'.

Ellen – never good, but always careful. Steve M – for whom listening is an occupation and *twenty questions* his favourite game; and who will, I'm sure, one day finish his apprenticeship. And not forgetting Jean – nothing short of a martyr.

Eric and Audrey – your initial success spurred the dream for more words.

Trevor Kelk, English teacher whose elucidation of the subject instilled a corrupted admiration of the language. And more so, for not giving me detention when, in 1983, I laughed at Ramsay Isaacs' efforts to clear his propelling pencil, when from the rear it looked like one hell of a masturbation technique. And how could I omit Ramsay Isaacs – for brightening up the duller moments in English lessons (I've got to say, Trevor, there were one or two).

Matthew Clark, without whom, the inspirations and writings would never have been possible. Never look back.

Gill Impey and the 'Team', for making the HTV weather so... interesting and accurate. To Jordans for 'Frusli' – the best chewy snack bars under one hundred and fifty calories. Not forgetting too, whoever you are, for producing Sainsbury's and Safeway's pure unsweetened orange juice – I could bath in the stuff.

In assistance with the content of the transcript, thanks to Graham Sharpe of William Hill who assures me he's never played football for Everton. For related legal issues, Tod Merson and Peter Cooke (who to the best of my knowledge has never met Dudley Moore) – both of Bevan Ashford; and regarding medical matters, thanks to St James Medical Centre, Taunton, and the British Epilepsy Association for their essential advice. Details for contacting the British Epilepsy Association may be found at the rear of this book.

Of course, sincere thanks to all at Minerva Press for being daft enough to say 'yes' in the first place, and for the assistance in getting these words on to this page and in front of this eager reader looking for author recognition.

Apologies specifically to Mike J, for not being able to include a sexually hyperactive market analyst-type character – a very specific genre I fear, and unlike Somerset, Lancashire isn't brimming with them; and more generally to anyone not mentioned by name that has had an influence, great or small, on this endeavour. There are so many, and I thank each and every one of you.

To those of you either not mentioned, or who haven't had an influence on me yet, my heartfelt thanks for reading

– you'll find six bums, thirteen knickers and seven poos if you continue.

To everybody, I hope you enjoy.

SK, Taunton, some time 1997

'Nothing Lasts Forever, Not Even Your Troubles'

Anon

I T WASN'T THE fact that she didn't like his taste in music that much. Some of it was all right; the older stuff was a bit off the wall for her though. She wasn't into jazz, or the blues. Come to think of it, she'd never heard him listen to it either. It must have been a phase he'd gone through once, perhaps when she'd popped out to swap homework notes with a friend.

No, it wasn't that at all. Liz wished she could fade into the background, away from the condolatory eyes. She didn't particularly want any of the belongings he'd left her, especially the Fats Waller album – even if he was the 'Clown Prince of Jazz'. What she really wanted, more than anything, was her big brother to be back here with them. She missed Edward so much and, being selfish, didn't know how she was going to manage with her exams now that her ever-willing revision aid was gone.

The reading was soon concluded, and the small and silent gathering moved towards the oak door; distinguishable from the rest of the panelled room, thought Mrs Beech, only by virtue of its immaculately polished handle and hinges. I'll be buggered if I'd find the time to Brasso them, she thought, with pity for the poor soul who had to.

The unexpected voice from behind offering hotpot and a nice cuppa made her jump. Arrangements had been made days ago that they would all return to the Mallory house once proceedings were over in town.

Emma Beech had never cared for him. He was a snob of the first order, even now. 'Forgotten his roots,' as her mother would say. His wife, though, was different. She was the real source of their money and while she very much knew it, you wouldn't have thought it of her. She was the sort from whom Emma would accept hotpot and tea.

'Come on, Dan,' she ushered. 'Don't light that thing in here,' pointing at a 'No Smoking' sign on the wall as he tried to roll a cigarette in the main doorway to Harman, Harman and Quirk. 'Get a spurt on, or that bloody man'll insist that we go with them.'

'Don't know what all the fuss is, woman,' he choked through the plume of smoke that the tobacco was now emitting. 'He's a decent enough sort. Underneath.'

'Just move on quickly you great lump, the taxi'll be here soon.'

As the minicab drew up to the kerb, Emma bundled her husband into the rear seat just as Mr and Mrs Adrian Mallory reached the doorway and bade their farewells to Samuel Harman, the senior partner of the practice. He was a short man, with thinning grey hair and one of those suits that could only be from a tailor specialist in clothing for the legal trade. His round spectacles glinted in the springtime sunshine as he craned his neck to study the much taller Mr Mallory's face and, being dazzled by the brilliance of the light, returned his focus towards the man's wife.

'Many thanks, Sam,' she offered her gloved hand.

'My dear Valerie,' the old acquaintance began. She cringed. No one had called her Valerie since her wedding day. 'It has been a great pleasure to see you again, though the circumstances are most regrettable,' he continued. 'How is your father?'

'The old bugger's just fine, unfortunately,' was what she wanted to say; but a mere, 'He's very well, thank you,' was all that those within earshot were to hear.

'Then please give him my kindest regards,' the man fixed her with a practised smile. 'And of course, the same to your charming mother.'

Val watched her daughter disappear out of sight, on foot towards the busy town centre. 'It's been hard on our Liz,' she said; apparently to nobody as, unbeknown to her, Adrian had marched at a pace up the incline towards Chapel Street and the Range Rover. 'And us,' she told his back glumly.

'Bent Lane, Ash Norton please,' the woman in the rear seat instructed.

The driver turned. 'You wanna go through town?'

'Whatever's the shortest route,' replied Emma; her new hat was now firmly in her lap having been thwarted in its attempts to go it alone, taking its own chance at escape from Adrian Mallory by cartwheeling down Winston Square towards the park in the gusty winds. 'This hat's ruined,' she cussed. 'Ruined it is.'

'Don't fret, Em,' said a puff of smoke next to her.

'Sorry mate, I'm asthmatic. Can't smoke in here,' protested the driver, who clearly hadn't shaved that morning, his five o'clock shadow resembling a midnight blackout.

The growing cloud spluttered something about 'hell fire' and the 'waste of another cigarette', as a hand appeared from somewhere within to wind down the window ejecting the Rizzla and its tightly packed contents from the vehicle.

'Dan!' his wife snapped. 'Behave like a human being, please, for me. Today's been hard enough on all of us, and we've still got to break bread with Ed's parents.'

'Aye, p'raps Aide's got a peace pipe I'll be allowed to smoke,' a cheeky grin appeared. They laughed; or at least showed their teeth and made a noise, noticed the driver, who was beginning to relax now that the air was clearing and his inhaler had taken effect. Joining the back of a queue of traffic that he knew wouldn't move for some time, he settled down for a wait.

'*Must* you do that?' pleaded the female passenger. For the third time in as many minutes, the driver, whose identity card on the dash board named him as Roger Pickering, was true to his name and removed a foreign body from his pitted nose. Each was carefully rolled between thumb and forefinger and sent, without concern, flying into the outer atmosphere through the sunroof of his aged and well-worn Datsun Laurel.

'Sorry missus – hayfever,' he explained, believing his actions justified.

'Just 'ow long do you expect us to be sat in this 'ere jam?' Dan demanded, craving a cigarette, not for the first time.

'Dunno, probably...' he paused to study the ear wax expertly extracted with the nail of his forefinger, '...probably another half hour or so.'

'But it's been that long already,' protested Dan, trying hard not to study the man's prize.

'Well, mate, it was you that wanted to go the shortest route, and this *is* the shortest route. If you wanted speed, well that's diff'rent. We'd have followed that Range Rover down Pitt Street and out by the athletics track, that way.' A jerking thumb still bearing squashed wax gestured behind a ducking Emma. 'Can't really turn round now. One way system y'see.'

The hotpot was in danger of becoming a solid mass when the exasperated Beech family finally arrived at Wingate Farm, nearly an hour after leaving the solicitors.

'It's a ten minute drive, where the hell have they been, for Christ's sake?' seethed the host.

'How am I supposed to know?' Val sighed. 'Just take it easy, smile, and do try to be nice, dear,' she told him, knowing that the latter would be most difficult for him.

Poor Adrian, she pondered. For some reason, it seemed he was always trying to prove that he wore the trousers in this household. She didn't know why, it was a self-inflicted task; but she supposed that since their chance meeting at the station some thirty-odd years ago, he wanted to show that he was worthy or something.

Of course he had nothing to prove, even though her father had warned her that 'Bounders and laggards like him are just praying to find gems like you, my girl.' What tripe! Which century were we in for God's sake? He was the man she loved and had since they first clapped eyes on each other. So what if he wasn't loaded?

She'd dismissed, years ago, the terrible arguments that upset the Quirk family home; the threats of disinheritance from her father, and her teenage counter threats. She could laugh about it all now, but how could Dad have been so irrational? Did he *really* believe that Adrian knew of her circumstances when he stepped off the London train, straight into the crowd of screaming teenagers, blissfully unaware of the identities of the four mop-haired young men behind him?

Her idols had faded when she'd felt her legs weaken and buckle. Her next vision was a dreamy one of the fresh-faced and smiling young traveller, as she recovered her senses on a railway bench, just the two of them on that now empty platform.

'Are you all right darling? Darling?' he was saying.

She looked at him with a warm smile.

Adrian waved his open palm in front of her face. 'Wakey

wakey, darling, they're at the door.'

'Come on in, come on. You look exhausted,' welcomed the still-beautiful but now lined face of the lady of the farm. Farm by name, but not in reality. It was an old farmhouse that had been bought in the early eighties, when dilapidated properties were being snapped up as future 'des-res' homes. Val had designed the upgraded layout and furnished it in her own style, bringing out the traditional character that befitted such a period building. 'We were wondering where you'd got to,' she told them, not seeking explanations.

'Sorry we're late,' apologised Emma.

'Some idiot in a taxi practising nasal surgery,' continued her partner, 'took us through the town centre, knowing damn well that there were roadworks,' his arms waved expressively. 'Over an hour we've been sat there like a couple of dummies, and I couldn't even have a fag! Do you mind?'

The air filled with the smell of phosphorous upon the shake of Val's head, and Dan sighed with affection for his nicotine dosage.

'Oh yes, the improvements to Church Street. They are a bother, aren't they, Adrian?' Val looked encouragingly at him. 'You should have come with us, shouldn't they?' she tried desperately to drag her husband into the conversation.

'Yes,' he attempted, poorly. 'Absolutely.'

They quickly sat to dine; once a salvaged dinner of what resembled a meaty sort of *pommes de terre mâché* (no one but Val could be sure that it was, as billed, hotpot), red cabbage and plenty of strong tea had been consumed, the group of four retired to the spacious living room.

The farmhouse restoration had been worth every penny, thought Emma, admiring the beamed ceiling with carefully-stencilled motifs off-setting the antique wood; the walk-in fireplace with its inglenook of local stone, and not overdone brassware.

The pictures, simple originals, were of a rural theme; while the large sash windows revealed the rolling Lancashire countryside that Emma had for so long appreciated from afar on the southern side of the town, but had only recently seen close up, despite living so close all her life.

Adrian offered the guests a seat on the large settee that arced away from the bookcase by the doorway, towards the oversized television in the opposite corner. Emma sat, and immediately lolled into Dan, his weight absorbing the comfort buffer in the plush furniture. 'You're a puddin', Beech!' she cried, caving sideways. Her subsidence complete, her eyes fell on a colourful picture postcard resting on the mahogany dresser opposite.

Val's gaze followed that of her friend and fell on the same. 'Ah, that was the last one they sent. Have you still got yours, Emma?' she asked in a vain attempt to start up some form of flowing conversation.

'Yes, all of them,' Emma nodded, struggling to sit herself upright. 'How they ever saw anything beats me. Seems they spent all their time writing to us oldies.'

'Speak for yourself!' snorted her cushion, his rough pointed finger jabbing her in the ribs. 'Don't include the present company in your "oldies" observations. Some of us are still in our prime *and* under forty, remember.'

Silence fell, the relevance of his words dawning. 'We've got to let them go,' he added in reluctant tones. 'Life goes on, and we've all to be strong.' A single tear appeared from nowhere to betray his feelings, leaving its glistening trail swerving downwards towards his chin.

Val shifted in her seat, needing to avoid yet another awkward silence, or she herself would be joining Dan in the tears. 'I've got the rest in a little box that Edward once brought back from a school trip to the Lakes,' she bravely continued.

'Yes,' Emma inhaled deeply to stay calm. 'I keep ours in a Black Magic box by the sewing machine,' as if its whereabouts were essential.

Adrian had said little all day, and this banal chatter was not helping his unsettled mind. He was too emotional about the whole thing and had seen Dr Ahmad only three days earlier. He'd wanted to see Dr Ainsworth, his normal GP, but as he was on holiday he would have to swallow his pride and, without telling anyone, see the locum 'witch' doctor who had subsequently prescribed something to help him relax.

He thought it was time for a helper and, rising, excused himself. Sensing the moment to be right, his guests rose together with him. Thanking their companions for their hospitality, they left the house in further silence, without draining their after-dinner drinks.

They turned left out of the gate, and walked the one hundred yards or so to the bus stop in time to see the number 151 come over the brow of the hill, and stop in front of their outstretched arms.

'Two for the station please,' a somewhat subdued Emma asked the driver.

'Come on, luv, it'll be all right,' assured Dan, putting his arm around her. 'Hey, that lad had some wit, didn't he?' He tried a cheery approach. 'Gonna be some cremation next week with the music he's chosen for 'imself. I liked the idea of The Crazy World of Arthur Brown!'

She didn't respond.

'Wonder if they'll scatter the ashes to Bob Dylan?' he quipped.

'What?' She was in no mood for his games, her expression sullen.

'Scatter the ashes to Bob Dylan. "Blowin' in the Wind",' he laughed half-heartedly, suddenly realising that Emma wasn't amused by his tact.

'I just hope she's there, Dan,' she told him with forlorn hope. 'For her own sake as much as his.'

Neither spoke again that evening.

★

It was some time since the reading of Edward's Will. As a young man of nineteen, he didn't have a great deal to leave anybody. Not material objects perhaps, mused his mother, but many happy memories.

She wandered around his bedroom. It was still his bedroom, though she had sought agreement from Adrian that it shouldn't become a shrine. Adrian had agreed, but was still distanced, she thought. He had loved his son dearly and had suddenly aged since the young man's untimely death, nearly five months ago.

Val missed Edward with agony. He was still there in his room. His scent and taste – he had decorated the room just before leaving England on what he'd theatrically described as his 'studies at the University of Life'. The smell of fresh paint had long gone, but the brush marks where the cheap bristle brushes had shed their unwanted numbers were still evident. So, too, was the patch of ceiling that he had completely missed. Just like his father, she thought fondly.

She smiled, remembering the fights Edward and Liz had fought over the room each should have when the house had been ready to move into. Hell, that was thirteen, or was it fourteen years ago now? It must only have been thirteen; Liz was a very forward three years at the time – a fact not missed by her Grandpa Quirk.

She glanced at the badly photocopied note that had brought her to the room:

1st ASH NORTON CUB SCOUTS

Tumble with your jumble

Please fill a bin liner with that unwanted
jumble and help the aged this winter

Bags will be collected on Friday 8th August
Jumble sale at All Saint's Church
Saturday 9th August, 10 a.m. – 3 p.m.
All Welcome

Please give generously

The 1st Ash Norton pack had been Ed's pride and joy, especially during 1986 when he was made up to 'Sixer'. Akela, or Mrs Adams as she was out of woggle, had been keen to tell Val over coffee the week before his promotion how Edward's helpfulness and determination to succeed, while sometimes overbearing, made him the only real candidate for the vacant position, now that Andrew Norris had moved to Clitheroe and had transferred to 2nd St Mary's there.

She stood, glowing at the thought as if it were yesterday. She let time pass, staring into space, pride oozing from every pore. How can I have outlived my baby? That's just not fair. She began to cry, the tears blurring her vision of the countryside through the large bay window that still bore the 'I've been a Monkey at Belle Vue Zoo' and Blackpool Pleasure Beach stickers from years ago. That great big world that he'd gone to see. He'd seen only a fraction and now would see no more. How she wished she could take his place now and give him a second chance, perhaps to make amends for something, though she knew not what.

'You okay, Mum?' The quiet enquiring voice broke the silence. Val wiped her face with the back of her hand, marking her cheek with her signet ring, the first gift Adrian had given her.

'Hey Mum, what are you up to in here?' asked her daughter with a caring smile. 'Apart, that is, from cutting up your face?'

The only one who hasn't really gone to pieces, thought her mother. 'Oh, I'm just digging out a few things for Ed's cubs. You don't think he'll mind, do you?'

'He's gone, Mum,' she wrapped her arms around her mother. 'You won't mind, will ya?' she asked the ceiling. 'Or should it be that way?' Her gaze fell towards her feet.

The trace of a smile appeared on her mother's face. With the ruffle of the girl's long blonde hair, and a gentle rub of the facial scratches, the elder woman nodded at the chest of drawers. 'Come on, cheeky chops, help your old mum fill some bags.'

At the same time, Emma Beech was using her day off work to clear the remaining boxes from the room once occupied by her only child. How she missed her daughter, who had become her best friend over recent years, as they had grown closer during, ironically enough, the youngster's time away at college.

'How strange that time apart draws you so much closer,' the girl had once said whilst at home on holiday. How true that was, even though she had been talking about the dog at the time.

Emma brought to mind with a wry smile how she had come to blows with her new husband, and was determined not to have her first child named after his fantasy girl of the time. 'Have you ever heard anything so stupid, Mother?' she'd asked the worldly-wise grandparent. 'Sandie! Of all the names he could choose!' she stormed. 'He says not, but I know it's after his bloody barefoot pin-up. What does he think I am, an idiot?'

'Well, it is 1975 dear, and that sort of name is in vogue. Isn't it?' It was the sort of comment Emma could have expected to hear from her mother-in-law, but surely not her own flesh and blood.

A couple of days later, there was agreement when Dan (named, he was proud to say, after his own father's comic book hero) had come up with a surprisingly beautiful name; and at 10.30 a.m. on Sunday November 22nd, 1975, baby Olivia (can't-agree-a-middle-name-so-there-won't-be-one) Beech was christened at St James Church, Hulton.

By 5.45 p.m., however, a proud and drunken father had told of the inspiration for his suggestion, and it was only the vicar's insistence that it was now too late to change the child's name that eventually calmed Grandma Newton, and brought an astounded Emma back to her senses.

'Thank God she wasn't a boy,' was all she could finally say, pointing with disdain at Dan slumped senseless in a corner with a bowl of salted peanuts fallen in his lap. 'I couldn't have lived with myself, bringing another one of him into the world.'

'Yeah,' agreed the godfather facetiously. 'Daughter of a Beech is bad enough.'

Three years later, any upset over the name had long since given way to resignation, and Emma even began to think of it as an inspired choice, following a rare trip to the Odeon cinema, where its origin featured in the hit musical film of the day.

She looked at the posters of that same musical on the wall.

Now, more than twenty-one years later what had it all been about? She would rather have had her Sandie Beech than this endless cloudy day. The doctors had picked up on Edward Mallory's illness, and could only come to one conclusion about the accident. Olivia hadn't had a boyfriend, well, not a proper one at any rate, before Ed and now... She stopped herself. There was no point in raking that one over again, it would serve no purpose.

The last boxes needed to be sorted out, and anything left over was to be sent to the hospital charities. Olivia's note had said she wanted it that way.

At the bottom of the box, marked in Olivia's own hand 'Private Things', and under a whole host of birthday cards, Christmas greetings and letters – all addressed to her Durham flat – Emma found a large hard-backed and spiral-bound notepad. Had it not been for the nature of the box contents, the pad would have been merely thrown away with the other 'sundry rubbish' as Olivia had obtusely described it.

She was curious and flicked it open.

'What've you got there, Mother?'

'Oh, it seems to be Edward's travelling diary.'

'Let's have a look then!' Liz grabbed for the notes.

'Don't be a ghoul!' Val's reprimand. 'No, it should be disposed of as appropriate to your brother's privacy.'

'Get lost. You surely don't mean that nonsense.'

'Oh, yes I do!' Assured conviction in her voice. 'We've not seen this, okay?'

Liz reluctantly agreed, but knew that curiosity would surely get the better of her inquisitive mother.

'Hello, Val?... Yes, hi... I'm fine thanks, how are you?... Oh, that's good... Did she? Clever girl! I always knew she had it in her... Oh? Yes, yes I'd like that. What time?...

Suits me fine. I'll see you then. Bye.'

'Do you ever get a word in?' asked Dan with a smirk. 'Only we always seem to pay for the privilege of her getting things off her chest.'

'Oh shut up, you,' Emma bashed him with the newspaper. 'Are you going to do something useful today, or will you just be getting under my feet?'

'I'm on holiday!' he protested.

'No, dear, industrial action is normally referred to as "a strike". Isn't there a picket line or something that you can join?'

'I could stand outside the letter box by the chippy if you want,' replied the postman. 'But then your ladies might think you've sent me out to sell my body.'

'There's plenty of it, Mister, why not try?' she laughed. She wanted desperately to be able to see Val Mallory without too many questions from her husband. He wasn't the sort to let the minor details of life get in the way, but nevertheless, she could do without any interrogation today.

She glanced at her watch; it said 11.30. She had two hours. Dan would want feeding, and if she didn't make him wash the dishes, she could perhaps get him out of the house somehow. 'Tell you what,' she suggested wistfully, 'I'll make us an early lunch then you can go and play on your steam train this afternoon. It's a nice day, get some sunshine to all that muscle,' she added, squeezing a handful of his side belly.

'Gerroff!' His feigned hurt.

'Whatsamadder?' The other hand pinching his round cheek. 'Doesn't chudgy-pudge want to play choo-choos today?'

'Only if I can toot the whistle,' he scowled.

That's him sorted, she thought. Poor lamb. If gullibility were a disease, he'd be in quarantine.

After his meat and potato pies – soaked in gravy with a healthy helping of mushy peas – Dan set off for the old railway goods shed where he and his fellow volunteers were designing and building a scale model railway for a local children's hospice.

'It keeps him occupied,' Emma told the window as she waved him off with a loving smile. 'Be back for eight,' she called aloud.

With a thumbs-up in acceptance, he turned and sauntered towards the main road.

She turned to the mantelpiece, only to find the clock had stopped. Another curse in its general direction. The blessed thing was always on the blink. She scoured the kitchen drawer for a fresh battery. It was in such a state, she could hardly find anything. String. One elastic band, green. A penknife. One paper clip, complete with strange hairs and ball of fluff. Microwave oven leaflet – 'Installation Instructions'. Better keep it just in case. Birthday candles – one green and white stripes part used, one red and white stripes unused. One battery! Wrong size. Marker pen lid. Bicycle clips; one, two, three? One burnt metal thing. A pencil sharpener. Spare keys. Oh look! That's where the dog's vaccination certificate went. Pity we've buried him. Sewing kit. Sellotape. Marker pen without lid. Piece of cardboard with torn edge. Pinking shears. At last!

She replaced the battery and returned to the kitchen to check the time on the oven clock. 'Damn and blast!' She had just twenty minutes to get ready. Val was never late.

On Radio Two, Jimmy Young was wrapping up his show as she switched off the car radio and inserted a cassette. A little Cliff Richard before arriving in Hulton. She was late. She hated being late, and prided herself in *never* being late. Those infernal so-called improvements to the centre of town. She crossed the Ribble over the old bridge, and took what was once the main Liverpool road, up the hill and on for a further mile or so. She noticed that the newsagent on the corner had closed and been replaced by a bookmaker's. She supposed her husband had been personally involved in its transition. He was once full of his small empire, but hardly spoke of it now. This was a new shop, though, so things must be going well enough.

She continued along the main road, slowing only for the pedestrian lights and allowing an elderly couple to cross long after the green man had changed to his halting red friend. The butcher's had gone too. She thought back to the last time she'd been along this way, in daylight, anyway. It must have been the first time she'd met Emma and Dan. That's right, Olivia had invited her and Adrian to join Edward that Sunday, and they had all enjoyed home-made sponge cake on the patio. How *did* Emma find the time to work and keep that house going? Oh yes, Adrian had dropped one of the tea plates and although he said not, the look on Daniel's face had confirmed that it was indeed part of their best set that was now in a dozen pieces.

So lost in her thoughts was she, that she missed the tight turning for Parkland Drive and had to turn around. Reversing into a gateless driveway, she stalled. The old man tending to his garden saw it his duty to advise Val to restart the engine.

'Thank you,' she waved with a tolerant half-smile.

'Now put it into gear and get your biting point,' the aged instructor advised. 'You know, clutch and accelerator in harmony.'

'Yes, thank you,' she waved again. 'Bloody man!' she mumbled.

He moved to the pavement and, checking in either direction, noted an oncoming motorcycle. 'Hold it!' his upright palm on outstretched arm directed. 'Wait a minute, motorbike coming. Almost there. Come on... come on... come on... *Stop!*'

She pressed hard on the brake. 'All I need,' she muttered. Get out of the way, you blithering idiot and I might see where I'm going.

'There's a car coming,' the old man mouthed, as though she needed to lip-read.

The motorist passed, and before her guide could make further comment, Val sped her smart new Rover 200 past the gardener, and left him in a storm of gravel.

'No gratitude, these women drivers,' he told his freshly-trimmed privet.

'Hello!' called Emma from the living-room window. Turning her wave into a sweep of the arm, she motioned her visitor to come around the side of the house to the front door.

'What's the time?' asked Val as the door opened.

'Almost ten to,' replied Emma without needing to look at her watch.

'Bloody man,' she tutted. 'I'm sorry I'm late. Let's get going,' Val suggested. 'I've something I want to put to you.'

'Me to you, too. It's been bothering me.'

The journey took them away from town and quickly into the surrounding agricultural area. 'Few animals out this way,' observed Val.

'Arable around here. Plenty of spuds and carrots but few burgers and chops,' replied Emma, pleased with her knowledge. 'It's the next left, and then we're only half a mile away,' she directed. 'I could murder a coffee.'

Once a clearing in the traffic allowed, the hatchback turned right into Allerdale Nurseries, a favourite Sunday haunt of the Beech family.

'They do a lovely toasted teacake in here,' Emma tempted her senses.

'I'm on a diet, Emma,' Val advised, downcast. 'Strictly cream cakes, I'm afraid.'

They giggled like schoolgirls, linking arms and huddling into the brick and glass building, through the pet accessories and barbecue furniture, straight towards the café.

'Over there,' pointed Emma. 'In the conservatory, by the trellis,' she told the waitress who had offered to serve their cream eclair and horn of plenty to the table. As the pair collected a tray brimming with cups, saucers, teapots and cutlery, they plotted a route to their prized table and reached it just as an elderly lady deposited her tired-looking feather hat on one chair, and her rather large and equally tired-looking posterior on another.

'I'm sorry,' said Emma, 'but this is our table.'

'No it's not, I've been sat here for five minutes while Ellie's getting the tea.'

'You don't understand, we've given this table number to the waitress who'll be serving our refreshments here,' Val returned.

'If you've got yours, you'd better find a free table dear, so's it doesn't go cold,' the years of experience advised. 'I can't just jump up, my bones won't stand it. I'm old, you know.'

'Don't we just?' muttered Val.

'Come on,' suggested Emma, touching her companion's arm. 'There's only one table left, look – over there by the till.'

'What *is it* about old age?' asked Val as they reached their new table.

'Over here!' a gesticulating Emma shouted to the waitress who could have sworn that neither lady who had ordered the cakes was wearing a peacock before.

'I've told Liz to shoot me before I get to that stage,' continued Val, lying. She'd told Edward to do the dirty deed only a day before his death.

Her face told Emma she was quickly drifting far away. Perhaps Elizabeth's GCSE results might bring her round, thought Emma. 'Wonderful news of Lizzy's. Four As, two Bs and a C, was it? Who does she get her brains from?'

Val snapped back to the present. 'Oh Christ, definitely her father! But for pity's sake don't tell him I said so. It'll ruin years of educating him that I'm the brains,' she smiled. 'Anyway, your go first. You said you had something that was bothering you.'

Emma took a deep breath and scanned the room. There was only one face she knew, but couldn't really place it, so she felt free to talk on that score. The café was busy, and there were plenty of people close by which made her wary that what she had to say could, if she went into detail, be juicy conversation for someone's dinner table that evening. She decided to press on regardless.

'It's something I found. A book. Well, notepad actually, but book.'

'Buried treasure?'

'No. Well, I don't think it will quite lead to buried treasure, but it's treasure to me,' Emma admitted. 'It's a journal of Olivia's.'

Val's chewing motion ground to a halt. 'Like a diary you mean?'

'Yes. Journal, diary, whatever. It seems to start a couple of years ago at about the time she and Edward met.'

'And?'

'Well, I know she's not here to, well you know, to object I suppose, but it's private, isn't it?'

'Her diary?'

'Yes, I feel like I'm abusing her privacy or something if I read it.'

'Oh, Emma,' Val wiped the cream from her lips. 'How long have you been worrying about this?'

'I was clearing away the rest of her things last Thursday and, well, since then,' she shrugged, 'I've not wanted to mention it to Dan.'

'That's strange, you know. I was sorting out a few things with Lizzy for a jumble last week, and I came across a similar thing. Edward's of course, not Olivia's,' she smiled, not knowing if the light-hearted approach would be appropriate. She knew first hand the pain that her recently-found friend was suffering, but at least she had a second child to carry on for. A brief and stunted smile returned across the table. It hadn't really been appropriate.

'You must either dispose of it without opening it again, or if you're looking for clues she may have left and you think you can face it, you'd better read it,' Val advised. 'Whatever you decide to do, you must tell Dan,' she stressed, realising that the eclair now took second place.

'I can't stand not knowing why she did it,' sobbed Emma. In the awkwardness of their conversation, the café now seemed unnaturally hushed, and Val was aware of at least three interested parties on table nine who had frozen their own animated discussions to concentrate on what the ladies by the check-out were themselves deliberating.

'Don't upset yourself,' Val offered a tissue from her handbag. 'We'll drink up and have a wander around the shrubs, eh?' and half turning away, added, 'Away from flapping ears.'

Table nine erupted into heated debate on the current changeable climate, and the poor quality of strawberries this year.

Once outside, the sunshine warmed Emma through as they walked slowly towards the flowering perennials section at the far end of the site.

'I'm sorry,' she said.

Val linked her arm through that of her friend. 'Don't be sorry. It's only been a few months,' she offered. 'Adrian and I are finding it difficult too, but we at least know why Edward died. We're here for you, the pair of you. All four of us need each other, Emma,' a tear welled in her eye. 'We do need each other.'

'Do you know, it's been five months and six days.' A vague mother sat on a rosewood bench, the orange tag spinning '£249' in the breeze. The tears suddenly flowed. 'Why did she do it Val? Why? She has so much in front of her. Why did she leave us like that?'

Emma's weeping became uncontrollable. She had not been able to cry until now. She had sobbed a little, but now her heart was pounding. Her stomach felt wrenched, and her lungs couldn't offer adequate oxygen to her shaking body. Oblivious to the staring customers that passed by, Val held her until her breathing had steadied and she was able to sit up, if only hunched, herself. They sat for a while in silence, Emma slowly tearing strips off a tissue.

'I've got to know why, Val,' vehement determination in Emma's words. 'I can't go on like this. I've got to read it,' she eventually ventured. 'Like you say, it might reveal something that might help.'

They had been there for thirty-five minutes. Emma felt like a great weight had been lifted from her shoulders, as the sheer relief that she had finally been able to share her frustrations and hurt dawned. 'I like this bench,' she surprised Val. 'I'll order one,' she concluded pragmatically.

'Yes, it is nice, isn't it?' agreed Val, looking around at the bench beneath her for the first time, her eyebrows still raised.

'Come along, Mrs M.' Emma rose. 'Let's have a good look around now we're here,' and she continued along the bark-covered pathway towards the sign marked 'Evergreens'.

Amazing woman, admired Val, double pacing to catch up. 'Wait for me!'

'Why Valerie,' Emma stopped and turned. 'I do believe that your eclair has weighed you down,' she teased.

Having scoured the premises, the two found that there

was now little room left in their low-level trolley to safely place a second tray of pansies. Val decided that she would carry them to avoid damage, and, supporting them with the palm of her hand, steadied the black plastic with the other. 'Are you all right with that trolley?' she asked Emma, watching her wayward attempts to steer. 'You seem to be having fun.'

'I'll manage, but don't enter me for "Supermarket Sweep",' was the last she would say before swinging the wheeled weapon into a concrete donkey, decapitating it and breaking its leg in a single blow. 'Shit!' she cursed.

'...And I'd like to order one of the rosewood benches please,' Emma advised the assistant with the broom, as if it would erase her error.

'Which one?' the youngster asked. 'There's three designs.'

'The two-seater with the scrolled back please.'

'Eight weeks,' said the boy without emotion or explanation.

'What is?'

'It'll be eight weeks.'

Was she missing something? 'What will?'

'Do you want the bench or what?'

'Yes, of course I do.'

'Eight weeks then, the order.'

'Oh, I see. Right,' his meaning finally becoming clear.

'Pay in advance.'

'Fine,' she reached for her purse.

'Today.'

'Young man,' interjected Val. 'Do you wish to sell this lady some garden furniture?'

The assistant looked perplexed. 'Yeah,' he ventured, suddenly chewing on imaginary gum.

'Then for God's sake, say what you mean and be polite about it,' she hissed.

The youth appeared hurt. 'Today... please... then,' he shrugged.

Val looked skyward. 'Blood and sand!'

'That will be fine; do you take Switch?' asked Emma.

'Pay at the till,' he told her, and noticing Val's glare, quickly added: 'Please... madam.'

'What did you have to tell me?' Emma asked, as their homeward journey took them past the school that Olivia attended as a small child. 'I seem to have hogged the day, I'm sorry.'

'Oh, nothing of importance,' Val fibbed. She knew now what she should do with her own treasure.

'What the...?' Dan's gaze didn't leave the garden as he walked up the driveway and opened the door. 'I'm home!' he shouted.

'Hi, love,' a call came from the distance.

'Em? Where are you?'

'Up here,' the stairway revealed. 'Hang on, I'm coming down.'

He heard the footsteps tread lightly across the floorboards in what sounded to be Olivia's room, and on to the landing as the loose board by their bedroom door groaned. She was halfway down the stairs when she saw only his shoes.

'Get them off now!' a horrified shriek demanded as she continued her decent. 'Outside. Go on, outside now. And the overalls, get 'em off!'

'But I've nowt underneath,' he protested, pointing to his waist.

'I don't care! Give the neighbours a thrill, go on, off! I don't want your oily mess all over the house.'

He removed the steel-capped boots outside, and stepped in again to take off the overalls on the doormat. 'Em? Why is there a headless horse in the garden?'

'Oh, has it dropped off again?' she sighed.

'The head has, yes. But what is it doing in our garden? It's dreadful.'

'Long story, Casey Jones,' she chuckled. 'And it's a donkey, if you don't mind.'

He grabbed a towel off the basket of linen in the hallway that his wife had minutes before brought in from the rotary drier in the back garden, and, wrapping it around his waist, stepped outside again and wandered around the front of the property.

'But its leg's wonky, too!' he shouted with disbelief. 'How long before we win the bet?'

Inside the house, she smiled. 'Get back in here, you fool, before they lock you up as a flasher.'

His towel started to slip as he stepped back over the threshold and he struggled to keep himself covered.

'Phwoar!' Emma mocked from the kitchen doorway. 'Who needs the Chippendales, eh? Give us a look!'

'It'll cost ya,' he laughed, making his way upstairs to the bathroom still fighting to cover his modesty.

'You've got fifteen minutes before it's on the table,' she hollered after him. 'And just look at that bum!'

Over dinner, she told her husband of the previous week's discovery, of the indecision and her afternoon with Val. He listened, unsure of what to say. Like Emma, he had not been able to cry, but then real men don't cry, he would tell himself. He had found it extremely difficult being strong for Emma. She was a strong individual in her own right, who had forced herself to get back to her job at the travel agents. The multitudes of memories he had were so vivid as any father's would be. Why were the happy ones only snippets of smiles and not the full incident, like the bad?

His mind flashed back to a phone call. One he'd sooner forget. 'Hello?' he heard his voice saying.

'Mr Beech, it's Margaret Platt from next door. I think you should come home right away. It's your Olivia.'

He saw himself dropping the parcel that had delayed the start of his second delivery round that day – a Monday. Into the car he jumped, his throat dry, his heart beating faster than he had ever known before. The barrier at the sorting office was slow to rise. He recalled the desperation as it jolted upwards and the lack of concern when he wrongly anticipated its speed and drove into it, clipping the car's front wing. He felt sick. All the traffic lights conspired to delay him. Had this town bought a job lot? Please let everything be all right. Mrs Platt was an old woman who'd have you believe the Martians had landed if a firework fell into her back garden, but it wasn't bonfire night; had they really landed this time?

In the present, he could hear his wife's words, but they weren't registering. He was engrossed in that day. The start of some building works in town. The long crawl over the bridge and up the hill towards home. A large motorbike with huge panniers, evidently in a hurry too, overtaking the slow moving traffic on the wrong side of the road. The bloody pedestrian lights – on red and no one crossing. The nausea was unbearable. His head was thumping. A siren somewhere around him; was it an alarm? The cyclist making a right-hand turn, slowing the traffic further. The eventual tight left into Parkland Drive. The motorbike outside number thirty-nine? His house! His heart was in his mouth. He abandoned the car behind the vehicle that had blocked the drive. The front door was locked. He fumbled for his keys once more and opened it. He ran into the house, senses numb. Where were they? Where is everyone? He was shouting for Olivia, Emma, anybody? He dashed upstairs – no one. The open bedroom window revealed movement in the back garden. He flew down the stairs and out of the open back door to see the body on the grass. Oh God. He saw Maggie Platt, who turned and rose to face him. The medic moved away to use a radio, revealing a leg, lifeless in the sun.

'Dad!' he could hear his Precious, his little girl. He was confused, she appeared from the garage. 'I'm sorry,' she blurted. 'He crawled under my deckchair and it collapsed on top of him and there was a crunching noise,' her shocked rambling continued. 'There was no real need for you to come. I'm *really* sorry.'

'She was so upset Mr Beech,' a defiant neighbour struck first, feeling Dan's glare. 'The only thing I could think of was to call you, your Emma being away an' all.'

'There's nothing that can be done,' the vet explained to a tearful Olivia. 'I'm afraid Samson's suffered a broken neck, Miss.'

'Dan? You with me, luv?' asked Emma with a touch of his arm. 'What's the matter?'

'Oh,' he sighed. 'Reliving a nightmare with a dog,' he replied blankly into space. Facing towards her, he apologised. 'What was it you were saying?'

'Nothing. It can wait,' she stroked his hand. 'I love you.'

'I know,' he smiled, 'and I do you.' He stood and told her where he was going. 'Won't be long,' he promised.

Emma had never heard Dan weep so freely before, and even the twice flushing of the toilet could not disguise his anguish. She took their dirty dishes to the kitchen, and removing the dog's redundant vaccination papers from the drawer, threw them along with the waste chicken bones into the swing top bin.

'Where's your mum, Samson?' she asked. 'Where is she, eh?'

M ONDAY 10TH JUNE – Day 1: Today's the day! After all the organisation and excitement, we're finally on our way. It's now almost midnight and we've been in the air for almost an hour and forty five. Ed's tucking his way through my meal as well as his own. It looks revolting. How can these airlines make potato look so unappetising? It is potato, isn't it? Yuck! Heaven help his stomach!

Well Diary, what's happened today then? Ed arrived at our house this morning at about 11 and told me off for the amount of clothes I'd packed. Great start! Okay, so there was a suitcase and the rucksack, and we did say that we were travelling light, I suppose. I had to leave all sorts behind – I thought that we might be able to dress up at least once in six weeks, but he said a definite 'no' to the high heels. I do love it when he's firm. Ooh Diary, that's rude!

So, I'm down to the backpack and a holdall for hand luggage and if you hang on a minute, I'm going to get my CD player and listen to some music – this stuff on channel 8 is hopeless.

There we are. Sheryl Crow, much better. Now, Mum drove us to the station and the train eventually got us into Euston by 4.30. Oh God. That man on the train! He must have been forty if he was a day and his mother was waving him off at the station. When the train started, she began to run along, waving and he was waving back! Ed told me off again for laughing, but I couldn't help it. I hope narky pants isn't going to be bossy all the time.

'You were right, love,' Dan shouted to the silhouette that was busily tidying the kitchen. 'I've reached the bit about their trip in the diary – they've not even left England yet and she was being a little sod!'

Anyway, Mummy's Boy decides he's going to have a cup of coffee from the man with the trolley, and settles down to read. It's only when we get to Wigan that he realises he's heading south instead of north, panics, knocks his cup all over his book and the old biddy next to him, and pulls the emergency cord! The train grinds to a halt, there's railway people running everywhere and he's going to pieces because his first edition book of God-knows-what is covered in Brazil's finest blend. Twenty minutes later, we're back on the move with MB safely off the train and heading north, no doubt via the Transport Police office. Even guzzle guts next to me had to laugh at that one, but Diary, you had to be there I suppose. Well you were, I know, but you weren't open, were you?

From Euston, we took the Underground black line down to where they have the theatre ticket thingy (but we didn't leave the tube station), and went on the blue line like a couple of sardines out to Heathrow and Terminal 4. How can those people travel like that day in, day out? Is that a sad life or what? It's bad enough when you've to stand up on the Corporation bus all the way home, and that's only a few miles.

We were quite early checking in, but we've found ourselves on the back row without binoculars to see the film. I can't work out the listings in the magazine.

Oh good! The stewardess has just brought me another bottle of red wine. I'll be sozzled before we reach Bangkok. His Lordship's got his eye on the bimbo serving the other side. I'll kick him in a minute.

The film's either Three Weddings, A Christening and A Carol Service or that other one with Kevin Costner. It doesn't really matter, we can't see it anyway. There he goes, ogling again! Shall we kick him now, Diary?

'Poor lad. How did he ever manage with that lass of ours?'

It's now 4.27 a.m. on Tuesday, so I suppose that this should be day two really. I can't sleep. Ed's snoring his head off. I wish I had a tape recorder, he swears he doesn't snore! Just like he swears he doesn't fancy the blonde in the uniform. No doubt I'll have lots of opportunity to find out about the snoring now, Diary. Do you think he's going to be able to control himself? He says it's okay that we don't, but I'm not sure if all this time together won't be too much for him. As long as we keep talking – that's the main thing. Keep his mind off my eggs.

'Oh Christ! Bet his balls were blue weren't they?' Dan chuckled.

'What's that?' The distant voice.

'Your daughter,' he called. 'Tease of the year. You were never too proud about your "eggs" in your youth were you?'

'We didn't have chickens, only Fluffy pussy.'

Dan's uncontrolled laughter strained his bladder. 'Like I say,' he howled, 'never too proud.'

Tuesday 11th June – Day 2: Arrive at Bangkok for a couple of days to be met by Meedej waving a 'Mallory/Beech' sign. I wonder if that's Mr Meedej or Meedej Somebody? Anyway, he's a very nice man who doesn't mince his words like he minces along the arrivals hall. What a nightmare getting to the city! The traffic is chock-a-block and exhaust fumes fill the air. It's so hot! I can hardly breathe in this transfer car, and the driver says we can't wind the windows down or else the air-conditioning won't work. Meedej tells us all about the evening pleasures of the area known as Pat Phong. Ed wanted to know if that was something to do with cow shit but no one laughed, probably because they didn't understand it! I under-stood it, just didn't laugh. We've booked a city tour for tomorrow morning to see the wonders of Thailand. We'll be picked up at 7.30 a.m. from the hotel lobby. Great! This is a holiday?

The hotel lift carpet tells us it's Tuesday. Time for a snooze I think. I'm knackered.

6.50 p.m. and I've been asleep for just under two hours. I feel rough. Ed's been wide awake reading up on the area, but can't work out where in the city we are. We should have bought a Berlitz guide or something but I'm not all that bothered about seeing much here. It's filthy. We've both got grumbling tummies, so we've chosen to dine in a select establishment this evening – the Tivoli Coffee Shop in the reception area. Oh yes, a 24 hour café, what more can you ask for? An all night Italian diner serving American style burgers in Thailand. Update after grub I think!

Well Diary, Ed's in the bathroom so I'll keep you up to date. Thai food is very nice. We had some black bean something with noodley stuff and lots of half cooked vegetables. Sounds odd but delicious. Then we've been for a walk along this main road – the traffic's not half as bad now as it was. Perhaps that's because it's gone midnight! There's lots of dogs and common people, and very little to see really. I'm ready for bed like never before. I'm not sure I'll be able to get up in the morning for an early tour. This is our first night together. We've never spent 24 hours completely alone together before and this is a record! I think I'll keep my knickers on.

'I've had enough of this,' Dan snapped the book shut. 'You'd better read it yourself Em, it'll make more sense to you. It's all women's logic – knickers on and common people. I'm off to bed.'

'Night then,' she wished. 'Oh, what time's the alarm set for?'

'Three,' preceded his kiss.

'Okay, sleep tight. Tomorrow I'll tell you all about cellulite and the Change,' Emma grinned and donned her glasses. She read for herself the latest of Olivia's journal. Both she and Dan had learned much of their daughter from the pages now resting in her lap. Although Olivia had confided in Emma a great deal, there was a lot of detail to be gleaned, and Emma felt ever more hopeful that there would be something mentioned that would set their minds at rest. Deep down, she knew her daughter would be fine, but the uncertainty was crippling.

The following day, Emma was back to work with her usual gusto.

Shut up, won't you? Stupid tart, she thought. The incessant female voice was disturbing her concentration.

She enjoyed meeting people, but now found the work somewhat repetitive. She had always maintained that once you'd got over the first excitement of booking a holiday or arranging a tour to some exotic location, you'd much rather be going to these places than sending someone else there. It was a kind of resentment. But then, when it came to going away herself, she couldn't be bothered to try and convince Dan that the Caribbean was a better idea than Spain; he'd miss his 'proper' food. Not that paella was proper food. Anyway, he'd burn himself on day one and be a nightmare to live with until he got home. And of course, he hated flying. No, all in all it was better to do what they would both enjoy.

She had been given the chance to go on what the manager had called 'an educational' to Jersey the month before. She fancied the trip but as she wanted to go with Dan at some time, she passed up the offer and it went instead to Sharon, and it was Sharon who was now in full and vociferous flow.

When Sharon was in this state, an almost daily occurrence, no one listened. She was the youngest of the full-time staff and would dress accordingly. She was the one in full make-up who appeared to use a full hairspray canister to control a single wayward strand; with one too many blouse buttons undone, and a bra that made Anthony, the work experience boy, stare in admiration.

Emma was caught unawares, having made the mistake of re-entering the office just as Sharon had taken a rare pause for breath, and did not realise that the ensuing words were still part of a much greater monologue. She regretted listening immediately, but now her ears felt compelled to take notice, even though the rest of her body was trying to focus on other things.

'...And I said "You sauce, you!" But 'e just carried on. Ooh, an' weren't 'e a dish 'n all.'

'Sharon,' the manager sighed. 'If you've nothing to do, would you please show Anthony how to do something?' he asked, coming to everybody's rescue and making the teenager's day. Both he and Sharon blushed, but for different reasons.

The relieved office resumed its business. A local doctor was looking for the cheapest flights to Delhi, and two youngsters were deliberating whether the coach would be comfortable enough for a twenty-four hour trip to Spain, or if they should fly for the first time. A young mother waited for her husband who was buying his foreign currency for a business trip; her baby, showing the first signs of hunger, began to cry.

'How old is he?' asked Emma looking up from her paperwork with a gentle smile.

'Sixteen weeks tomorrow,' the proud mum beamed back. 'It's time for his feed, do you mind?'

'No, luvvy,' Emma's head shook. 'You carry on.'

It was unfortunate that the woman should begin to un-button her denim shirt as Anthony, already enjoying his task because Sharon had set it, came back into the shop carrying an armful of the latest summer brochures. Craning his neck in an 'I'm-not-trying-to-look-but-is-she-really-going-to-get-her-boob-out?' way, the youth stopped in his tracks and gawped.

'Anthony, do those need to go out?' asked Emma, already knowing the answer.

'Yes, I'm just deciding where they should go,' he replied, his gaze still fixed on the nuzzling infant's mouth.

'Well, would you like to have a think over here?' Because they don't go there, you little pervert! she suppressed.

The baby was only in need of elevenses and rejected his mother, leaving her offering her nipple between fore and middle finger to the elements while she coaxed him to take more.

'Anthony. Here.' Emma's authoritative tone ordered half under her breath. 'Right now!'

He approached. 'Did you see that?' The boy shook his head in amazement. 'In public too. She's got her knockers out in the shop, Emma!'

She turned him violently away from view. 'Behave for God's sake!' She shook his arm. 'The lady is feeding her baby and she doesn't need you thinking there's a queue! Snap out of it.'

'Sorry,' he sighed, putting the brochures down and beginning to sort them by tour company. 'But I bet you never got 'em out in a shop in your day,' he added ruefully.

'He needs hormone treatment, I swear,' she told Dan that evening at the dinner table. 'One minute he's ogling some poor woman trying to feed her baby, then the next, he's announcing that Sharon's going to the cinema with him tonight.'

'Fast worker, eh?' noted her husband, casting his mind back to his teens.

'Fast worker? I'm sure lads were never like that in our

day. You weren't anyway. Were you?'

'Had me moments,' his face glowed.

'Like when, Daniel Beech?'

'I remember a cute little chick with her Aladdin Sane make-up and glitter pants who never objected if I...'

'Hold it there, Buster!' she didn't need reminding. 'Okay, so he's only a man, is that what you're saying?'

'A bit red-blooded by the sounds of things, but he's normal,' Dan's observation. 'Just needs to learn a few tricks on sideways glancing and shoelace tying p'raps,' he smirked.

'All the bloody same, aren't you? Lazy buggers from birth. Take far too long to come out in the first place, then spend the rest of your lives trying to get back in!'

'Is that an offer?'

'No it isn't an offer, you filthy animal. Finish your tea and then you can wash up.'

He stood and stacked a few plates before adding his half empty mug of tea and heading for the door, trying desperately not to laugh aloud.

'Then you can have a cold shower!' she shouted after him with a feigned annoyance.

Out of sight, he thought for a moment. 'What film were they going to see?' he called.

'Haven't a clue,' the reply from the dinner table. 'Why's that?' a tone of suspicion entering Emma's voice.

'Could have caught them on the way in and given him a few pointers!'

'He'll get enough of them, don't you worry,' Emma assured him with certainty. 'Sharon knows what she's doing.'

'Ah, of course,' Dan mocked. 'It's the fella that's the beastie, isn't it? Women are pure sugar and spice. Poor lad.'

For whatever strange reason she couldn't pinpoint, thought association took Emma from Sharon devouring

Anthony, to Olivia's diary. She had a little time before her television programme started, so moved over to the settee with her cup, took up the page where she left off, and continued to read.

Wednesday 12th June – Day 3: Carpet says it's Wednesday, but I've lost all track of time already. It's the Grand Palace Tour day, and what a day. After a buffet breakfast, Meedej met us nice and early and, after having our sunglasses steam up as the heat hits your previously air-conditioned face, we crashed, literally, into the mini bus. Meedej seemed disappointed that we didn't go to Pat Phong last night. Perhaps he was on stage at some joint and thought we might have sampled his good-time antics – who knows? We promised that we'd go tonight. He's told Ed all about the women who may not be women, so he's a bit worried now!

Collected an older Asian couple on the way to the rendezvous (big word, Ollie!) point. They're over from Britain on the return leg of an Australia trip, but I think they were working over there or on a conference visit or something, so they didn't have a lot to say. After picking them up, we went to a big modern hotel with a river jetty to wait for another couple joining us by boat. It's so busy on the roads that it's quicker for them to get here on the smelly Chao Phraya river.

When they finally get here, they're obviously fresh-weds! They're both flashing shiny rings and keep playing with them. They're both as white as flour (says the pot) and are all lovey-dovey. Ahh! It soon turns out that she wears the trousers – well, what must have been thirty denier tights actually – in this weather? It's thirty-five degrees if it's freezing, and she's in high heels and tights. Hmmmm. Perfect for a city tour, love!

We're not allowed to wear shorts on this trip because of the Palace, so we're both in jeans that soon get a bit sweaty around the you-know-where's and Ed's complaining that his boxer shorts are chaffing his bits. He's been walking like John Wayne all day!

It's now 1 p.m. and I'm going to try and have a poo. I've not had one since I left home and I feel bloated. Ed's complaining that he can only fart and gives his visits to the loo marks out of ten for 'pooability'. Wherever did I find such a charmer Diary?

10.45 p.m. Hooray! I've had two poos – only tiny rabbit-dropping type ones, but I'm sure a proper one is just around the corner. We've just come in from a strange night out. To see what Meedej was going on about, we took a tuk tuk (or is that fuk fuk? It's a three-wheeler taxi thing anyway) to Pat Pongo. It's just like the open market in town really with T-shirts and watches all over the place. We've bought some wooden bookends that look really good but they're a bit big. There's not much space in the rucksacks anyway, and I think that that's just been filled! Ed's eyes were out on stalks at some of the bodies on show. Men coming out of bars with menus, I thought we'd have a bite to eat but it turns out that the menu is for bites on you, or licks on you or anything that you're willing to pay for – if you're a bloke of course! Didn't see Meedej. Perhaps it's his night off. Anyway, risked life and limb to get back here by fuk fuk and now it's bed time. Neither of us is used to the time difference yet, and tomorrow it'll get even worse. Bangkok's an experience but I'm glad we're leaving.

Ed's asked if he can read you, Diary. No, he can't! Good night.

Thursday 13th June – Day 4: More hoorays! We're going today! Slept soundly until eleven this morning and went down to the Italian in reception to eat. I wanted a photo of a tuk fuk (I can't remember what it's really called now!) so we went out for a quick lungful of fumes, got the photo and dashed back. Ed had a five out of ten this morning he tells me, but I've struggled to reach the scale. What I wouldn't do to have a good trump.

Sent the first lot of postcards but knowing the way international postage works, they'll be home after us.

Sweetie guide met us back at the hotel lobby with Grumpy the driver, and we joined the queue of traffic to get to the airport. Why are there so many cars in this place? It's terrible. Eventually at the airport, Meedej helped us with our bags and I thought he was going to give Ed a smacker on the lips. So did Ed, I think that's why he suddenly needed the loo. Yes, I've just asked him, and he thought he was going to do a ten out of ten there and then in the concourse! Poor lamb, and him having one of his clumsy, forgetful days too.

We're at the airport now waiting for the BA flight to Sydney. There was some trouble over security tapes on our bags (or at least the lack of them) but my man got that sorted out. He's reading at the moment – never seen him read before, have you Diary? I'm going to buy a drink, so more later.

God, this flight's noisy! Why won't anyone try to sleep? More inedible plastic food and supposed tea, and I'm hungry. Ed gave me that look, you know, the 'I'm not going to say anything but I'll raise my eyebrows in disgust' look, when I asked a girl sitting alone on the centre aisle if she'd swap with us so that I could lie out across three centre seats and rest my head on Edward Cushion. She swapped without a word but Ed's making sure I know she looks uncomfortable. She could have said 'no' couldn't she? We left Bangkok at 5.30 p.m. local time and get into Sydney at half-past five in the morning! Oh, why do we do it? It's a nine-hour flight and I can't sleep. Diary, let's pester Ed, he's reading again and I can see right up his nose from here.

We're agreed that nothing can be as bad on this trip as Bangkok. I can't wait to get to Australia. Ed's never met Viv and I've not seen her since she left work to move out here. I hope she's at the airport to meet us. She always was a dizzy one, and if she's got to be there for 5.30 in the morning, then there's even less chance of us meeting! Only just under four hours to go now, so I suppose it's approaching 2 a.m. in Sydney. I'd better get some sleep I suppose. I'm thirsty. Diary, tell Ed to press that attendant button and get us a glass of water.

Oh Lord! He's at it again. Admiring the tanned dark-head that *brought the water now. Is it my fault? She's only a glorified waitress, what's she got going for her? Okay, she's got a lovely figure. Cow. But she's lacking in the tits department isn't she? You need a bit of padding don't you, dearie? Hmm? You're using some? That's nice, love. Oh, now he's pretending to be asleep since she's gone. I see! Dreaming about her now I suppose. I CAN'T SLEEP! What's on the screen, Diary? Some film, is it? Let's give it a go.*

'Sorry, love, what's that?'

'I said, "Do you want to watch *The Street*?"' Dan repeated. 'It's on in a second.'

'Oh, yes please. Is the kettle on again?'

Dan pointed to a steaming cup of coffee that rested next to her elbow. 'You were miles away,' he said.

'Somewhere over Indonesia I think,' she laughed as she changed glasses so that she could focus on the television. 'My eyes are getting worse,' she frowned. 'I think it's the screens at work.'

'No, chuck,' Dan disagreed, 'it's your age.' He ducked the flying *Radio Times* in vain, as it caught him under his protective raised arm. 'I'm a victim, I am. A victim of domestic abuse and a dominant wife!'

'Shut ya face and watch you daft 'apeth,' she told him in the direction of the television.

During the commercial break, an idea struck Dan. 'Why don't we contact that homeless magazine, *The Big Mag* or whatever.'

'*The Big Issue*?'

'Aye, that's the one. Ollie was always buying it, wasn't she?' he remembered. 'If she still does and they have her details in there, we may get a call from her. What do you think?'

'Worth a thought,' Emma replied. 'But we don't know where she is, do we?'

'Exactly,' shrugged Dan.

'No, I mean she took her passport and cleared her savings, didn't she? She might not be in Britain. But if she is, and she still does, yes – good idea,' Emma nodded thoughtfully. 'I'll buy a copy on my way in tomorrow and we'll see what can be done, eh?'

Sharon and Anthony arrived at the shop together the next morning, with his attire looking rather on the casual side, though he was wearing a tie – the only real stipulation for the male members of staff since the uniform was made optional a couple of years before.

Emma pondered on the current state of her long time employer. The company had gone downhill fast over recent years. Mere children were running shops. She was lucky in the sense that David, her manager, was one of the brighter and more mature amongst his peers, many of whom seemed to lack basic knowledge of life, let alone the business they were moulding the future of.

'Morning, you two!' she called to the approaching colleagues, watching David unlock the door from the inside. 'Had a good time?'

Anthony flushed.

'Brilliant!' exclaimed his companion. 'Went to see a film then on to the pub down by the docks, didn't we, tiger?'

'Er, yeah. Down by the docks,' he repeated, quite nervous of the attention he found himself getting.

Once inside, Sharon entered her talking mode and Emma turned her brain to 'mute', scouring the publication sold to her by the young man with a black mongrel which had been hungrily cleaning its rather bulbous genitalia on the corner of Cheapside. It must just be the pride and joy for the male of any animal, she'd thought, as she handed over the one pound coin and waved dismissively at the suggestion of change.

Allowing her ears to tune into the conversation that Sharon was having with herself, she learned that Tony, as he was somehow now referred to, had missed his last bus home and, not having adequate funds to cover a taxi, had stayed over at Sharon's flat.

Anthony, who was opening the mail, appeared to have taken on a shade of crimson and his mouth bore neither a look of disdain nor a smile; it was a kind of wavy line. It was a look that would subsequently reappear when Sharon began to tell any fresh ears of the previous night's goings on.

It was a busy Friday morning, lightened only by a pantomime horse and a Postman Pat who came into the shop collecting for famine relief.

Postman Pat seemed a little worse for wear and apart from regularly slapping the pantomime horse's hind quarters and shouting 'Yee – har' as only a postman with a huge nose and a voice that comes from chest height can, he did insist upon waving repeatedly at Emma. No one would hazard a guess how much money was prised from the shop, as most of the customers stood in a state of fear of the latex nose, or in utter amusement, without touching their purses or wallets.

The entertainment had subsided when Anthony approached. 'Emma. What do I do with all the old files?' he asked.

'Sharon busy?' she enquired, peering around the junior towards the young lady in question.

'No, I thought I'd ask you if that's okay.'

'It's fine by me. Just a bit too much to handle, is she?'

An embarrassed half-smile appeared. 'Well, I didn't realise women could be like that.'

'You're safe with me, Tony, take a seat for a moment,' she said, wondering if she should pat his knee when he did and really give him a fright.

'Anthony,' he corrected. 'I'll stand if it's all the same. Tell you the truth, I'm a bit sore today. You know,' he nodded downwards.

'Ahh. You do whatever's best,' Emma suggested sympathetically, 'but come with me and we'll sort out the "historics" as we call them.'

'What, the over thirties?' Anthony attempted a joke as she led him towards the rear office.

Emma laughed; threatening to make the 'cheeky sod' run if he didn't watch out.

Emma was enjoying her work for the first time in weeks. Occasionally she liked to do something useful in the office; a little different from the norm. Normally, she'd take herself off and defrost the staffroom fridge, or clear out the brochure cupboards of all the outdated issues. Since a stream of work placement and casual labour staff had been taken on, though, this type of job was catered for and as the senior in the shop, she was left to concentrate on the serious side of the travel trade – the customer.

'There's one here too thick to fold properly, Emma, what do we do with that?' asked Anthony.

'Let's have a look,' Emma stretched out her arm to allow the document to be passed over.

'In the name of Beech,' he offered. 'Two travellers.'

Emma's heart skipped. She was stunned for a moment and didn't know quite how she felt. Was she elated or was she distraught? She wasn't at all sure. She took the file from his hands and looked at her own handwriting on the cover. The full itinerary was there. All the documentation pinned to the rear of the buff lead sheet. The file was thick. There had been a lot of planning involved; most of which had been done by Edward and Olivia. Edward mainly, Olivia didn't have a great head for detail.

'Thanks,' she finally managed. 'Leave this one out for the moment, I think I may need it.'

'Got a wobbly table leg, have you?' asked the unwitting assistant.

'Something like that,' she replied with a forced smile, pulling herself together and placing the file behind her in the doorway of the staff room.

'Emma!' a distant voice called. 'Phone.'

'You carry on as you are for the moment, Anthony,' she told him, pulling herself up off the lino floor with the aid of a low shelf. 'I'll be back in a moment.'

She dealt with the call in her usual efficient manner, and no more than five minutes after taking the receiver, she had calmed down the agitated traveller, taken the details of his baggage loss, and set the wheels in motion for an insurance claim. Returning to the rear of the office, she heard the unmistakable tones of Sharon.

'...It's a shame. She doesn't know where she is. Just left a note and cleared off when 'er boyfriend died in some funny 'ow-do-ya-do.'

'All finished, Anthony?' Emma shouted around the doorway in warning that she was approaching and the couple should let their conversation cease.

'Oh, Emma. I was just telling Tony about your Olivia. Have you heard anything?' asked Sharon with the brazen tact of granite.

'No, Sharon, we've not,' she seethed. 'But I'm sure you'll be the first to know. That way it'll save me and Dan telling anyone else, won't it?' Emma concluded with malevolent inference. 'Anthony,' she stressed his name, 'would you mind finishing this yourself? I've got plenty to do and I know you're quite capable of managing.' Looking towards Sharon, she added: 'On your own.'

'Are you all right, Emma?' asked David, placing the Beech booking file on her desk. 'I heard raised voices and unless my maths are really bad, my two and two have made four,' he said.

'Your maths are fine,' Emma confirmed, picking up the papers. 'Just fine,' she added vaguely.

'Look, it's lunchtime,' he suggested. 'Take your break and forget this place for an hour or so. Go and spoil yourself around the shops.'

She collected her thoughts and handbag and left the shop. The air outside didn't make her glasses steam up as Olivia's had, despite the shop being air conditioned. 'I need a bloody good holiday,' she muttered, and headed off towards Marks and Spencer to select something for that evening's meal.

Passing the card shop and turning right into the shopping centre, she wondered what she should do with the birthday card that she had bought and saved especially for her daughter's birthday in just over seven weeks' time. She hoped that it could be written and received at the appropriate time. It was Dan's birthday soon, too. I'll be married to a forty-something, she thought. I'm getting old.

She reached her goal and taking a wire basket from the stack, took the first aisle – frozen foods. She reasoned with herself that she could put the frozen stuffs in the freezer compartment of the fridge at work for the afternoon, and get home in good time before they'd completely defrosted. Not that it would matter if they'd thawed.

'Not home-made pie tonight then?' a jocular voice whispered into her ear. 'Skiving off, Missus?' asked Dan.

'Is that a question or a confession?' she asked with a snooty air.

'Question. I'm on round sixteen today, Madam. The entire High Street, through to the Guild Hall and round to the Centre. Just checking the quality of the chocolate bars as I go,' he proclaimed.

'And will you eat your tea, Podge?' she asked, poking his stomach.

'Why, such compliments,' he patted his paunch. 'This is the sweet you can eat between meals and given that it's only just gone midday, I think I'll manage my tea. Don't you?' he said, waving a chocolate-covered coconut bar.

'Make sure you do, now that your little secret's out!' she warned. 'Hey, how are you fixed for taking time off?'

'What now?'

'No, for holidays.'

'Oh, and I thought my luck was in with the lady bearing frozen peas,' he glanced towards her basket.

'Dan, I'm being serious.'

'Oh, well if we're being serious, it shouldn't be too much of a problem. I'll have to check the list mind.'

'Right,' Emma said. 'You check the list for late September, early October and I'll see what I can get hold of in the sunshine. Make it a fortnight if you can.'

'What about Olivia's birthday?' he asked.

'She can come too if she wants.'

'Emma! Be reasonable,' Dan protested, not knowing how she could be so flippant.

'I am being,' she defended. 'If she's back, she can come with us. Call it a welcome home, happy holiday, oh, and big four-oh celebration.'

'Well, don't get your hopes up will you?' Dan suggested. 'Look, I've got to go. See you later, about six?'

'Around then,' she nodded. 'Give us a kiss for Christmas.'

They kissed off balance and clashed noses like amateurs. Then, without another word, they went their separate ways. Him towards the exit and High Street, her towards the chilled food for yoghurt and cottage cheese.

After a hectic, if not tedious afternoon, Emma arrived home to be greeted with a proper kiss. She liked Dan working the early shift, it meant that she wasn't coming home to an empty house – something she hadn't quite got used to. What she hadn't yet taught him was the true function of the kitchen; and that if he used the right bits of metal and plastic, combined a few contents of packets, tins and containers, he would in fact be the creator of what he knew and loved as 'tea'. This concept, though, was still somewhat of an enigma to Dan, who preferred to stay hungry or pick at biscuits than try to get to grips with the recipe for beans on toast.

She was now ready for the weekend, although she was working on the Saturday. This was always the odd day of the week, when those out shopping had run out of conversation with their partners and decided that a visit to the travel agents would be a good way to kill a few hours. Alternatively, a visit would help shelter those waiting for the hourly bus to Southport or Manchester from the elements. It was rare that she enjoyed working a Saturday, but it was the one day when the entire staff worked for a common good. The feeling of 'us' and 'them' was strong, and the unspoken bond that joined them in their desire to survive the day and close the door at five o'clock was tangible.

The typical Saturday enquiry would be the archetypal time-waster, as she saw it. Most would refer to that week's holiday programmes on the BBC or ITV, and of those, the obscure week of pony trekking up an Icelandic glacier with only three days' rations would always be tops.

But that was tomorrow. For now, she would set about preparing yet another meal. Noticing that Dan was settling down for a sleep in front of the television, she reached for her shoulder bag and realised that she had completely forgotten her lunchtime purchases which would still be filling the freezer compartment at work. With a curse, she reached deep into the bag to retrieve her purse and, extracting a crumpled ten pound note, headed for the living room.

'Come on lazy bones!' she shouted, kicking the sole of his foot. 'Do you fancy chips or pizza?'

'Eh?' the sleepy reply from Dan as with the back of his sleeve, he wiped a stream of dribble from his rounded chin.

'Chips or pizza?' she repeated. 'I've forgotten the stuff from Marks 'n' Sparks. Be a love and nip out for something, will you?'

With reluctance he agreed, and, putting on his coat before heading off for the Italian takeaway, grumbled something about how he always got the exciting jobs when *Goals Extra* was on.

Emma wondered what excitement was these days, and decided that to get a few people together for Dan's birthday might be one way to spice up their existence.

'HERE, LIZ? ISN'T this the Olivia that used to go out with your brother?' said the girl, offering the latest copy of *The Big Issue* and pointing to a picture of Olivia Beech.

'Yes it is!' the astonished friend stared as she took the magazine to study it closely. 'What's it say?'

It was her first day at the town's leading tertiary college where she was to learn Business Management for two years. She and her mother had visited the college the week before to register Elizabeth on the course, and today was what the Principal called 'Reconnaissance Day' or 'R Day' for short. It was meant as a gentle introduction to the new surroundings before the serious work started the next day. What in reality it boiled down to, was a great deal of time spent sitting twiddling thumbs and catching up with friends, not seen for anything up to ten weeks since finishing exams and leaving school in the early summer.

Liz studied the page closely. The appeal was from Mr and Mrs Beech who, it said, were worried for her safety and would like nothing more than for her to contact either them or a friend to say she was safe and well. Her own mother and father were also mentioned, so why, she wondered, wasn't she aware of this before?

Edward came vividly to mind, and she was painfully reminded of how she missed him so much. The whole family had grown to live with the hurt, though Dad was still very upset and hadn't wanted anyone to read Edward's diary in his presence. Out of his way, Liz and Val could do whatever they thought best, but he became quite disturbed if they flaunted anything to do with his son. Liz had explained to her grandfather some weeks previously how it was that the whole family were having to learn how to live with each other again. She thought that communications were good, though, and was somewhat upset that she had been kept in the dark about the publication now back with Carole, its owner.

Carole had spent most of the summer with Liz, and had learned to allow her friend as much space as she needed when she became maudlin, knowing that a full-scale tantrum could follow if not handled correctly. 'Talk about light blue touch paper and run,' she'd once told her own mother.

The pair had been friends since their first day at infant school together, though Carole had, according to Liz, gone through a funny patch when she met Dave and forgot that telephone lines ran into Wingate Farm as well as out. It was only the messy break-up of Carole and Dave – she'd caught him with his tongue exploring Paul Vicker's tonsils at her own birthday party – which had temporarily put her off the male of the species (she couldn't bring herself to call him a man after all), and brought her back to Liz at about the time of Edward's demise in March.

Right now, they were sat in the college refectory along with many other freshers, wondering for just how long they were going to be needed on their first day. Surely, Carole had reasoned while eyeing up a chisel-featured hunk, everyone could go home once they'd done three laps of the technical block.

'Why do you think 'Livia took off like that?' she asked, re-reading the piece entitled 'Missing, Can You Help?'

'I really don't know. I do know that she was distraught when Ed died – she probably just flipped!' replied Liz, trying not to show her real concern for the girl she'd always hoped might become part of the family one day. 'I'll see if Mum knows any more tonight,' she added with dual purpose.

'And how's my clever girl's first day at college been?' asked Val as a now bored Liz opened the bottom half of the split back door, and entered the kitchen where her mother was busily sewing curtains.

'Oh, you know,' shrugged the girl.

'Do I? That's probably why I asked. Yes, in fact I know exactly what you did and how you did it. I was only asking to expend some more of my boundless energy, wasn't I, kettle?' she responded sarcastically, turning towards the large metal pot sitting on the Aga that her daughter had leant against.

'Yes, Mother,' the teenager rolled her eyes in exasperation. 'Thank you for asking. I had a boring day, sitting around reading magazines and appeals to find Olivia Beech.'

'Olivia? What sort of appeals?'

'The one Mr and Mrs Beech put in *The Big Issue* with you and Dad – that's what sort,' she said, pointing at the picture in the borrowed magazine and thrusting it towards the elder.

'It *was* a good idea,' Val smiled. 'Oh look, your father and me are mentioned! Well, we are worried too.'

'Oh, and I'm not?'

'Liz, dear. Nobody thinks that,' her mother explained. 'I'm sure you weren't meant to be excluded. Emma said she'd contacted Missing Persons only a couple of weeks ago – they must think that Olivia's case is in need of high-lighting. They're having a rough time and they need all the support they can get right now. They know you miss her too and you're bound to be worried.'

'Yeah, great!' Liz moaned. 'Olivia'll think I don't give a toss, though, if she reads it.'

'Stop that now, you little madam!' reprimanded Val. 'Just buck up your ideas, lady. You're not the only one with troubles.'

'I know, Mum. I'm sorry. It's just when Carole showed this to me, I looked a right pillock not knowing anything about it. I just thought you'd not told me.'

'Well this is the first I know of it too, so don't go shouting at me, all right?' her voice moving up a pitch. 'Now,' she calmed herself, 'do you want a brew or are you just going to stand there with a face like a wet weekend?'

'Please. Hey, where's Ed's diary?' she rummaged underneath the almost complete landing curtains. 'I bet you've finished it and I'm only a few days in.'

'It's not under there. Try my bedside cabinet. I've put a Joanna Trollope cover over it so I can read it in bed with your father there!' she confessed, raising her hand to a mock-horrified open mouth.

Liz took her cup of milky tea and settled down in the big single-seater in the corner of the sitting room by the fireplace. It was only half past four. The tutors had seen enough of the new intake for one day, and had sent everybody home with instructions to be back bright and early tomorrow to start their student lives in earnest. She calculated that she could read uninterrupted for some time before her father returned home from the office, and before her Weight Watchers frozen meal would be prepared by Mum.

Flicking through, she saw that her mother had not read too far ahead of her and so, returning to the pages she had already covered, found the spot where she was to pick up the tale.

D. 5 – Fri 14 June: Arrived in Sydney a little earlier than scheduled – 5.20 a.m., to be met by this bloody mental woman! Christ was she on something, or what? I'd tried to sleep on the flight but Livvy kept pestering. One minute she's having a go because I'm admiring the stewardess, the next I can't cuddle her because it makes her uncomfortable. There was a lot of noise on the plane and as neither of us got much sleep, we were both knackered by the time we reached Australia.

Anyway, Viv the mad woman keeps us talking in a coffee bar in Arrivals for nearly three hours while she catches up on all the gossip from Livvy. I'm sat there like a prat, trying to add bits where I can and be funny about it – both of which are difficult when you can't remember the last time you've slept properly. It turns out that the place where we're supposed to be sleeping tonight/today (Viv's flat), is shared with half a dozen others, and everybody is moving out tomorrow as they're all going off travelling the country before heading back to Britain. She tells us that we're still welcome to join them and stay tonight and tomorrow night – she's only moving out on Sunday.

So, after Viv going to the ladies to nick three toilet rolls (they've been using magazines since yesterday morning), I wonder just what we're going to find when we arrive in Bondi Beach where this flat is located.

We all pile into a taxi and ask for Bondi and off we toddle. I'm in the front seat with an immigrant taxi driver of what I'd safely say was Asian persuasion. From the back, our hostess is telling Livvy in less than subtle tones how everyone in the city is great, but no one takes any notice of the blacks.

Well, I'm getting a bit wary that this guy's gonna kill us or something, but he just kept his mouth shut and glared at the back seat through the mirror.

Halfway there, it starts to rain a bit. Ten minutes later, it's absolutely pissing down and this is our welcome to Bondi Beach!

Luckily, I've got some Aussie dollars because no one else has enough to cover the fare when we arrive at the flat. Entering the flat itself was something I don't think I'll ever forget! God, squatter's rights prevail! There were no beds at all. The settee was two cushions on three upturned crates, and the carpet was sticky underfoot. There was no way I was staying there any longer than I needed to, and decided to go for a walk – suddenly not tired at all.

Livvy and Viv stay in to try and sleep, so I'm in Australia – the other side of the world on my own, and the rain's coming down like stair rods. Went to the beach and it's a bit of a let down! Bondi-Super-Mare it should be called! There were plenty of folk jogging and walking dogs – all wrapped up in their winter woollies, and here am I in a pair of piggin' shorts and flip flops!

Had a McDonald's at about ten o'clock (breakfast) to kill a bit of time, and knocked around the pavilion-type thing for ages watching a film crew make an advert or something. This poor little girl had to walk up and down the prom in a big coat and wellies with a brolly that wasn't protecting a great deal from the elements. Various muscle-bound 'hunks' joined her for different takes. These were wearing very little – shorts and T-shirts. Hey! Maybe it was some kind of pervert ring. God, I hope she's all right!

No, it must be okay. One of them was being mobbed by on-lookers when he'd finished, and he asked me if I wanted his autograph as so many others had. 'Why?' says I sarcastically, 'do you want mine?' It might have helped if I'd known who he was, but he didn't want my scribble, so he could stick his up his ego!

Got back to the flat at about 1 p.m. to find that Livvy was worried about me. Ahh! She hadn't slept a wink and had been chatting to Viv. Livvy suggested we go for a walk. Christ alive! I've just traipsed all round Bondi for three hours plus, nearly taken a bus into the city thinking she'll be asleep for hours, and when I get back, she wants to drag me out in the rain again for something to eat. Anything not to stay in the flat though, so out we go.

First stop, McDonald's for lunch (Livvy's breakfast unless she'd eaten some of Sydney Airport's toilet tissue beforehand, of course).

Livvy said she didn't want to stop in Bondi, it was too far out of the city, she said. True, it's not so easy just to wander down to the

Harbour Bridge. Had it been summer here, it might have been a different story with round-breasted tanned bodies, with bums like cherries, sprawled everywhere (and the women might have been a bit tasty too!).

Went back to the flat to explain to Viv that we were moving on and to collect our bags. She understood and we agreed to meet up the following night in Sydney city – at The Fringe. This isn't a hairdressers apparently, it's a bar on Oxford Street.

A taxi driver with the instruction 'take us to a hotel in the city that's not too expensive', took us to the city end of Oxford Street and a place called The Koala. The rate was a hell of a lot more than the $16 we could have paid in a hostel, but what the hell? We're here for eight days so let's get Australia off to a good start. Okay, let's have a stab at getting Australia off to a good second start after one false one!

It's now 8 p.m., we've had a wander around Hyde Park nearby, and I'm ready for bed. Livvy's farting around with the TV and wants to know when 'The Price is Right' is on again. How should I know? I hope we can have a proper night together. She's not taken her knickers off yet, maybe tonight. I bloody well hope so!

D. 6 – Sat 15 June: 6 a.m. I'm wide awake and have been since two! We've been nattering for hours and Livvy's trying to get some sleep again, but I can't even try. Well, Willy nearly got inside them briefs earlier but not quite. At least she's happy to rub-a-dub-dub, and I'm allowed to do anything else but the full thing, so it's not all bad I suppose. She looks lovely lying there with her eyes screwed tight. When she's asleep, she'll start to whistle, but swears blind she makes not a sound when she's sleeping. I can't make out why she insists on wearing her knickers in bed, though. They're ever so strange, these women.

I'm going to get up now, have a shower, and get dressed. Today's the first full day in Australia and I can't wait to see Sydney.

Okay, it's 3 a.m. Sunday now but as my body doesn't know what the hell is going on, it's still Day 6. What a day! Had the shower, got dressed etc. Woke Livvy who must have rounded up all the local dogs with the instructions she's unwittingly whistled, and she managed to be ready in no time (must be a record of some sorts!). Had breakfast – if you can call it that – in the hotel restaurant. Knowing that we'd be at it all day (I wish), we decided to have the full works. You get the fruit juice, cereals, toast, Danish pastries and fresh fruit along with a cooked – or should that be electrocuted? – breakfast of fossilised bacon, 'bashed' brown, the hardest sausage seen outside of an X-rated movie, and so called scrambled egg. The one saving grace was the cinnamon toast that amply made up for the slop and burn they have the nerve to call 'English Breakfast'.

The weather has been mixed today, but generally better than yesterday. We set off from the hotel and could see the cityscape straight away. Over Hyde Park, you can see a big tower that someone called Centrepoint. Lots of photos on the walk as we decided to head for the Harbour Bridge and more importantly, the Opera House.

Followed the road signs for Harbour Bridge – a quite sensible way of doing things without a proper map we considered – but soon found out that we were going far out of our way, and through a rather run-down part of town. The clincher came when the footpath stopped and the road turned into an underpass. We'd decided to double back and head up a grassy hill towards a huge sculpture of a burnt match when a young man approached and, pointing in the direction that we'd just come from, asked in a broad Liverpool accent, 'Is that the way to the Harbour Bridge?' Livvy said 'yes' before I had chance to open my mouth, and he duly thanked us and sauntered off that way.

We ran up the hill to put as much distance between him and us as possible and puffing at the top, she turned to tell the empty hillside that it is the right way – if you're in a car! She's a cheeky bugger sometimes. Fancy treating a Brit like that. Even if he was a Scouser!

My bet that the old building to the right was a museum proved to be correct which pissed Livvy off. She hates my logic. If only she realised that I only make predictions that are most likely to be true, she wouldn't get so het up. But then again, it wouldn't be so much fun! I also suggested that if the church opposite was a cathedral, we'd be near the red light district – I've often noticed that they go hand in hand for some reason. Weird professions to be linked. Vicars and tarts parties all year round though!

Anyway, agreeing to return to see the museum one day this week, we headed off down the other side of the hill and crossed a bridge over the road we'd been following. Just at the other side is a large park gate and we went through for a look. There, some twenty yards in, was a map and it told us that we would come out right at Sydney Opera House! Follow your nose and you'll always get there, as Dad would say.

The park turned out to be the Royal Botanic Gardens and even though it's autumn, going on winter here, they still look really nice. Our first Kookaburra swooped over us and crapped on Livvy's arm. Oh, did I cry or what? It was a lovely slime of white, blue, green and black and all she could do was scream! It was like glue trying to get it off, and it stunk like hell. Half a dozen tissues and a dose of perfume afterwards, we were back en route to the Opera House with Livvy shooting me nasty looks because I'd laughed. The more she glared, the more I laughed. She saw the funny side eventually, when we sat on a bench to find a drink from the bag, and I put my hand in a fresh dose of Kookaburra glue lurking on the arm rest. We're as warped as each other.

The first sight of the Opera House was amazing. The waterside footpath took us alongside the gardens while allowing a clear view of the bay, and it just came into view all of a sudden. It's huge and breathtaking. A picture was a must, so we set up the camera on the waterside wall, and Livvy stood in view while I lined up the shot to use the timer so we could both be in the photo.

Pressing the button, I didn't realise that it only gave me nine seconds before taking the photo, four of which had already gone. Dashing to get in the frame, I turned halfway just as it flashed.

The second attempt was more successful, although a skateboarder's dog did manage to cock its leg just in front of us as the shutter closed. God only knows what they'll come out like!

Walking around the Opera House is a little bit of an anticlimax after the initial 'Wow!' It's got white floor tiles on its roof and is quite dated when you're up close, but it has been around for quite a few years now so what can you expect? From the Opera House, there's a brilliant view of the Harbour Bridge. An American couple asked if Livvy'd take their photo against the backdrop of the Bridge, and they did the same for us.

Had a humungous cappuccino on the lower concourse and wrote a load of postcards while Livvy went to see if there's a show we could catch at some time in the week. It turned out that the ballet was sold out, and the only tickets for Taming of the Shrew were at the back and half a king's ransom to boot. The saving grace was that The Cranberries were on in town on Monday.

From the Opera House, we went around Circular Quay to the Coca-Cola Museum. That's probably the cheapest gallon of Diet Coke I've ever had, at $4 to get in and as many free samples as your stomach can hold before you drown or die of flatulence. The history of Coke gets on your wick after a few minutes, though.

From there, round the Quay to the restaurants by the ferry terminals. Lots of pictures here of the Opera House and Harbour Bridge, and then in-land again to find the Sydney Entertainment Centre (or SEC as the locals call it) where The Cranberries are to play. Went through the shopping area in the heart of town and decided to take a ride on the monorail which would take us right there.

Once on the monorail, we realised that we'd got on only one stop away from our destination but it was the wrong side of the anticlockwise trip, so we went all the way round to travel all of eight hundred yards! It's a nice trip anyway, so it gave us a chance to rest our weary legs and plan the next stage of our assault on Sydney.

Having flown through the city and passed over Darling Harbour (must have a proper look at that), we arrived at the Entertainment Centre. The box office was a sod to find and the timings on the door *told us that we were twenty minutes too late to gain access. Through the smoked glass, however, we could see that there was a woman behind the counter and pushing the door open, we asked if we could still buy tickets. The woman turned out to be a bloke with long hair and an extremely spotty face who said yes we could. Two now tired Poms gave a sigh of relief and asked how much for two tickets for The Cranberries. 'They've cancelled,' came the reply with a smug grin that must have popped a succulent zit or two when the skin went taut. Apparently, one of the band had injured themselves, so they've either flown back to Ireland or are soaking up the sunshine in some far-flung isle. Never mind! Plenty of other things to do. I'm not too bothered and I know Livvy was only wanting to go to a show for the sake of going, so nothing lost really.*

Next door to the SEC is Paddy's Market, a rich assortment of leather and plastic souvenirs intermingled with the obligatory woollen cushion covers bearing varying degrees of likeness to koalas, kangaroos and emu. Olympic Sydney 2000 merchandise adorns alternate stalls but you can never tell if it's the real thing or rip-off stuff. Hell, they beat Manchester to the bid, so I'll be damned if I wear any of it, anyway.

Livvy bought a couple of cuddly toys and a sun hat straight out of Thunderbirds, and we headed back towards Circular Quay via Chinatown to see if we could get on a boat tour of the harbour. Chinatown is lively enough and, quite remarkably, crammed with Orientals of tourist and resident nature. It doesn't seem to be too big and we were soon back into the main shopping area, past the monorail station that we first used and heading south towards the ferry terminals.

Livvy's still having trouble with her solids being too solid, so we spent a while at the Circular Quay loos while she strained her way to disappointment. By the time she returned, I was ready for a sleep rather than a boat trip, and lo and behold, we were too late for a trip anyway.

Rather than walking, we took a bus back to Oxford Street, which dropped us almost opposite the hotel, and outside a strange looking café bar which neither of us had noticed in the morning. It's sign was a ♂ (do you call that a Mars symbol?) with another above and joining, sort of ♂ ♂. The place next door but one was a bit weird looking too, with pink triangles in the window and lots of bald-headed mannequins wearing bondage gear and little else.

At the hotel, I started to wonder if we were in the red light district. Or is that hope? I was too tired anyway to think about it, and made the mistake of lying down to rest. That was about four thirty this afternoon, and lucky Livvy set the alarm because it woke us both at half seven. Bearing in mind we're meeting Viv at eight in an unknown bar somewhere on Oxford Street (length also unknown), there's a bit of a dash to get up, have a shower each (shared one for a change! Phwoar!) and get out. It took us less than twenty minutes to be out of the room and legging it up the street, away from the direction of the city.

We weren't talking too much, just trying to keep a look out for The Fringe and walking as fast as we could. It soon dawned on me that this was no ordinary part of town. Every other shop or business premises had names suggesting sex – both the act and certainly dubiety of individual's preferences, perversion, or a combination of both. Livvy eventually asked if I'd noticed anything out of the ordinary, to which I had to be honest and say I was more than a little aware that we were perhaps not like those around us when it came to bedtime!

Continuing our hurry, Livvy said she'd ask Viv about the area. The Fringe must be about half a mile away from the hotel and we arrived at exactly 8 p.m., but there was no Viv. She arrived about ten minutes later and within a further five, we knew that Oxford Street is Australia's gay capital. Ah! Each unto their own is what I say, and at least now we know.

I'm bushed, I'll continue tomorrow (today). 'This is Edwina Mallory for Diary at 4.10 a.m., Sydney!'

It's now tomorrow, but to finish yesterday off: Had an Indian meal with Viv after a few beers in the bar, then walked down to Kings

Cross – the proper sleaze area. Didn't see too much of the stuff you'd expect, but I doubt I'd have survived without a slap from Lady Penelope if we had. We did both look agog and almost wet ourselves at one talc-white arse that wobbled in bottomless leather trousers though. And I thought cellulite was a mobile phone network for infrequent users!

Lots of beer at Kings Cross and a taxi back to the hotel to arrive at a little before three. Viv's off on her travels from tomorrow and we've arranged to meet up on Friday 5 July, twelve noon at a café called Le Mignon, Airlie Beach in the Whitsundays.

D.7 – Sun 16 June: Okay, covered from midnight to four thirty this morning already. It's now Sunday night 8.25 p.m., we're in the room and Sabrina with Harrison Ford and Julia Ormond is on TV. Today, rather unsurprisingly, was slower but nonetheless, pretty eventful!

Got up at 8.30 a.m. and had breakfast (no cooked from now on). Livvy's poo problems continue, so she huffed and puffed for twenty minutes before bursting into tears. I suggested that we get her some tablets to loosen the blockage – she's not been for well over a week now which can't be healthy. She just blubbered and nodded.

We decided to go to Taronga Zoo which means a ferry from Circular Quay, so we walked down to the Quay and just had time to buy some fart-start pills before jumping aboard the ferry waiting to leave.

The packet from the pharmacy gives a suggested dosage of two tablets initially, followed by one every four hours if there's no improvement. Livvy, in desperation, shoved four down her neck on the ferry, and as I've only reached a seven or eight so far, I decided I'd have just the one to see if it would give me a ten.

Twenty minutes later, we arrived at the zoo and took the bus up the hill to the main gate. First stop – toilets to see if Livvy's medication's worked. No joy. Nothing. Not a peep of a poop. Next stop – the koala cuddle and then onto the wallabies and 'roos. We can't have been there more than half an hour before Livvy suddenly wants the lavvy. The nearest one is by the elephants – about five hundred yards away, so off we go. By the time we'd reached the ladies, Livvy's cross-legged and half running.

It was when the Keeper came round for the second time and asked me if there was a problem that I became aware how long she'd been in the loo. I'm not sure if the bloke believed me when I told him of Livvy's previously low crap count, but at least he didn't cart me off as a peeping Tom.

Eventually, she came out looking flushed and exhausted. 'Did you manage?' was all that I could think to say as she staggered towards me. She'd done a great fart apparently and that had been it. Then, as she rose to leave, the gurgles started and she'd spent the next half hour shitting a gut load.

Well, at least we can celebrate that, can't we? Her only problem was the greaseproof paper they call toilet roll. It doesn't do to smear when you could really do with some absorbency, does it? Anyhow, on we go to see the monkeys, sea lions and birds, plotting our route by the lavatory facilities that may be needed. Just past the monkey enclosure – some two hundred yards from more toilets, she starts again. Now, we're caught halfway between two lots of loos and we decide to venture to fresh porcelain. This time, we're running from the first gurgle.

It was refreshing for me to hear different noises from my girl as she sat on the loo. Recently, I've almost had to put on my CD headphones to block out the grunts and groans emanating from behind closed doors and through plasterboard walls. Victoria Falls sprung to mind on this occasion, as outside from the picnic table at which I sat, we – that is me and the Aussie family lunching there, could tell when the latest avalanche had struck. Perhaps it was the 'Ahhhhh's' of relief that accompanied each that gave it away. I can't think why the family were suddenly not very hungry.

Anyway, that's when Livvy decided she was exhausted (hardly surprising really), and we headed back towards the cable car which would take us all the way down to the ferry jetty, taking in as much of the zoo as we could along the way. The cable car was a bit of a *worry. It wasn't that we'd both watched TV footage of three cars coming down with a bump from over three hundred feet in Switzerland last winter, more that Livvy thought she was going to shit herself just as the doors had closed behind us. She reckoned that even if she'd have been wearing tights, they wouldn't have stopped much! What a pleasant thought.*

Back to the hotel by ferry to Circular Quay then a bus that again dropped us outside Bondage Bonanza or whatever it's called.

What's happening in the film? Oh surprise, surprise! Sabrina's not an ugly duckling after all. Phwoar! Actually, she's a bit tasty! I'm going to sleep.

'So what is it with Joanna Trollope and the women in this house?' Adrian enquired, poking the back of the book with his forefinger as if it were a specimen of highly contaminated substance.

'Oh, er,' his startled daughter stammered. 'Well, it's a good read Dad,' she explained letting the pages fall into her chest.

'Must be,' he replied. 'I've been watching you for a couple of minutes, giggling away.'

'Like I say, good read,' she said with regained confidence. 'You want to try it some time.'

Adrian turned with a thoughtful wink and retreated to the kitchen to sample the sauce bubbling away on the Aga top. He wished he could stay at home all day, reading or gardening but there was a business to keep solvent and that was proving to be an uphill battle at the moment. He rummaged in his jacket pocket and found the tablets. They were helping no end and he wondered what he would have been like without them. Probably in a straightjacket. Edward's death was the last straw and he was just about coming to terms with it. It didn't help that his wife and remaining daughter had seemed to battle on without too much trouble. They were great, he told himself. They even pretended to be reading some novel when it's that diary, he smiled inwardly. That was the first smile that wasn't forced in a long time. In went the Prozac and, with a grimace and shake of the head, he felt he could relax.

Moments later, a kiss and welcoming hug from his wife told him that it was now time to forget the business for a while, and start working on something far more important – his family.

'Well then?' Carole placed the returned magazine in her sports backpack the following morning. 'What's the goss?'

'I'm a spoilt bitch, but then you knew that anyway,' Liz sulked. 'Mum says it's nothing to do with her or Olivia's parents. They've no control over who gets their face in your mag, so I go off the deep end for no real reason and make myself look a proper Charlie.'

'So nothing new then?' Carole asked. 'On Olivia, I mean.'

'Not on Olivia no, but I've been catching up on bro', and it sounds like they were having a scream. Australia's full of lesbians you know.'

'Oh gross!' Carole screwed up her face in horror, reminded of her earlier disturbing discovery. 'I couldn't do it with another woman. Could you?'

'Oh I don't know. I always thought your arse was quite cute in the showers. Pity you've no tits to speak of,' Liz teased her friend with the cheekiest smirk she could summon. 'Come on then,' she suddenly grabbed Carole's waist, 'Let's see what I can find. Give us a grope!'

'Piss off!' the blushing girl moved free. 'If I didn't know you better…!'

'If you knew me any better sweetie, we would be!'

'What the hell's got into you today?' shrieked Carole. 'Are you desperate for a shag or something?'

'Offering?'

'Stop... it,' she smacked Liz's arm with every syllable, 'right... now!'

Liz blew a kiss. 'You're just playing hard to get.'

'I think you need a good seeing-to my girl,' Carole wagged her finger authoritatively, and gave one last good-natured blow across the cheek. 'And not from me!' she added with a sideways glance.

'I love it when you're dominant,' Liz baited. 'But I take it you're refusing my advances. Okay,' her hands rested on her rocking hips, 'I'll just have to jump on the next man that comes around the corner then, won't I? That'll make you jealous.'

A rather conscientious looking student in tweed sports jacket, his white socks revealed by too-short grey flannel trousers, was the next to appear from behind the main building. Liz thought better of asking if he'd get his kit off, and considered the threat null and void.

Carole whistled. 'Elizabeth here wants to jump on you!' she yelled.

'You bitch!' Liz hissed through clenched teeth.

'Oh, really?' stammered the horrified youth leaping backwards, his glasses falling to the ground.

Carole dashed to help him pick them up. 'She's had her eye on you,' she whispered with a provoking wink, and skipped a teasing bound back to her seething friend.

Val appeared pleased that her daughter was no longer gay. She couldn't recall knowing it in the first place, but felt assured that the likelihood of grandchildren was not completely extinguished. What she couldn't understand was why Liz had to tell her in the queue at Sainsbury's delicatessen. She had never considered this to be the place to discuss vital statistics, let alone the preference of partner gender, and certainly not with her daughter.

'And when did you decide this?' she nonchalantly

enquired, trying to sound as if it was a normal topic of conversation in case anyone listening in thought otherwise.

'Tuesday,' Elizabeth replied without deliberation. 'I was winding up Carole, and for a moment she thought I wasn't kidding. Hey! You don't mind that I'm not a lesbian, do you Mum?' she added with concern.

'Why ever should I?' her mother replied, motioning to the assistant that she had ticket number seventy-one. 'What would you like for sandwiches next week?'

'Ham' was the reply, and they watched the assistant slice off half a pound of the farmhouse variety, bag and weigh it when Liz asked if they'd not got any of that wafer thin stuff that she normally had?

The assistant gave her the sort of glare reserved only for special occasions – someone stealing the last cubicle in the pub toilets when she was desperate; that same person leaving a warm sweaty seat and nasty smell; and customers who mucked her around over their choice of cold meats. Her nose pin glinted under the intense store lighting, and her closely cropped black hair was barely visible under the floppy white cap that jauntily adorned her apex. Liz defiantly whispered the odds to her mother on the probability of the girl being 'that way', and looking skyward, Val wondered whatever in her life could go awry next?

T HE TELEPHONE RANG again and Emma tried desperately to reach it. She was soaking wet from the bath that she had been promising herself all week. This was the first full weekend she had been able to enjoy in a long time and, as yet, nothing had gone right. First, Dan's electrician mate, Jack, had taken a look at the faulty wall socket by the cooker and condemned it there and then; suggesting that a stroll through Baghdad shouting, 'Saddam's a raving queen!' was slightly safer. He'd be calling back tomorrow and told Emma to use any other socket but that one. 'But it's the only one the kettle and toaster reach!' she'd protested in vain.

Then, no sooner had he gone, she'd dropped the kettle into the washing-up bowl and broken the three mugs that were soaking. While clearing away that mess, the grill had made charcoal of the currant teacakes she'd fancied for breakfast. Now, it was her towel that wouldn't hold, and she cursed her cleavage. Why did boobs capitulate to gravity faster than any other part? Except of course for buttocks. Boobs and buttocks – what was their problem? She picked up the receiver and yelled a desperate 'Hello' to a dialling tone. Too late.

She dripped back up the stairs and eased herself back into the comfortable bubbly water. It didn't feel as nice as before, but never mind. She closed her eyes and drifted away once more. Only a fortnight until their holidays. A package she'd persuaded the sales rep from one of the cruise lines to come up with – three days in the autumn sun cruising off the Canary Islands and a further seven on Madeira, from whence the cruise commenced. Ten whole days to themselves, away from the travel agency and hassles.

Within seconds of her mind reaching foreign shores, the doorbell was ringing. It surely wasn't Dan, he was playing trains. Anyway, he had a key. She shouted for the caller to 'Sod off' with all the silence she could muster, and closed her eyes once more. It rang again, this time for longer. She stood and angrily towelled herself before reaching for her dressing gown. She realised with annoyed mutterings that it was on the washing line, having been in with the towel wash earlier. She borrowed Dan's, which was far too short, but the material lacking in length was more than made up for in wrap. She stomped down the stairs again, her hair still matted and soaking, and opened the door.

There stood a smartly dressed young man with a face fresh enough, she observed, never to have been touched by a razor blade. 'Good afternoon,' he over-stressed. 'Have you ever wished you had more time on your hands? Time to do the things you want to do? Well, wish no—' The door slammed in his face.

As she staggered back up to the bathroom, the letterbox opened and the hallway echoed to the sound of his mildly displeased voice. 'Well fuck you, then, you lazy cow! Not dressed at this time?'

Defeated, Emma pulled the plug out of the bath, began to swill away the suds and faced the array of chores which had to be done before Dan returned. Dust and vacuum, mend the hem on the bedroom curtain, do the ironing. She wondered what miracle the expressive young man had been selling that would give her the time to do the things she wanted to do. A P45 from the travel agents, she concluded,

would be the only thing that could fit the bill. Perhaps the
correct six numbers for tonight's Lottery draw would be
better.

The volunteers were making steady progress at the goods
shed, and Bill had set up a sweepstake. Bill always seemed
to run a book or have a bet on anything and everything, but
would not, on principle, buy a ticket for the National
Lottery. He would choose six numbers, but refused to buy
a ticket. What a fortune he wouldn't win if theirs ever
completely matched his.

This sweepstake was on the month and day (or nearest,
though not after) that the engine would be up and running
for no less than ten yards. What Bill hadn't told anyone, and
they in turn had not realised, was that as it was he who was
'finding' the track on which the locomotive would run, he
could more or less be guaranteed to win. He was last to
choose, and, handing over his ten pound wager, unsurprisingly ensured that his date was the latest.

Dan enjoyed the time spent with the engine. While he
and Emma were working at different times, it occupied his
time. He didn't like being away at the shed while Emma
was off work, they both worked too hard during the week
not to spend their carefully synchronised days off together.
Today had been a cock-up. He had thought that Emma
hadn't been able to get the day and so agreed to do a shift
with the lads. The project had been going well, mainly
because half of the group had been striking on and off for
seven weeks, and most of that time had been dedicated to
the restoration. Now they were all back to work properly,
and the project had taken on its usual ad hoc timing.

Emma had been okay about the double booking, though
he knew it would cost him in her choice of restaurant for
that evening. Taxi fares were astronomical too, but what the
hell? Even if they still had the car, he wouldn't have driven

on a night out like this. He even fancied his chances for a bit more than a cuddle afterwards. In fact, he almost considered checking the odds with Bill, as that would be money well staked.

Walking home, Dan made a conscious decision to educate himself a little better before the evening's delights and, not wishing to appear ignorant amongst those of his age, called upon a younger and, in Dan's opinion, most likely to know about women's things.

"Ere John,' he said, slapping the acquaintance barely twenty years of age and covered in grease. 'You're a man of the world, aren't you?'

'Me? Sure am!' he replied, a glow of pride covering his acned face, which Dan read as 'Go on, Pops, ask me anything.'

'Well, you seem the kinda bloke who'd be, what do they call it? Who'd be in touch, aye that's right, in touch wi' women.'

John's glow positively sizzled. He felt good. He, John Wright, was going to be asked, asked by an older fella too, about 'women's things'. What a day! What he didn't know wasn't worth tuppence.

'What's your understanding of cunnilingus?' continued Dan.

John's face changed ever so slightly. What he didn't know, he'd bluff. 'Cunnilingus? Well, one thing for sure Dan, you don't want that! No sir-ee! Best thing for that is special talc after a bath or shower. Just you nip the bugger before it all gets outta control.'

Dan looked puzzled. 'So you *nip* then?'

'Too right, matey. Nip it quick. Won't know what's hit it,' he continued with confidence. 'Anything else?'

'No, not really, I don't think,' Dan replied thoughtfully. He couldn't see how Emma would find him nipping her a turn-on – especially down there, but you hear about these folk who tie each other up and use whips and leather. She'd said that was her wildest fantasy, though. God, how you think you know someone and then they completely surprise you. 'Oh, where'd you get this talc then, John?'

'Down the chemist's,' his bravado now completely out of control. 'They should have it.'

Thanking his new-found tutor, Dan turned left into Parkland Drive and with a spring in his step, approached the driveway with anticipation and apprehension.

He entered the house and smiled at his wife. In fact, he smiled at his wife's backside as she delved deep into the under-stairs cupboard for a replacement vacuum cleaner bag, the existing one in shreds on the floor amidst a pile of dust and fluff.

'One of those days, eh?' he asked, patting the round seat.

Emma, not in the mood for being touched, turned and faced Dan with an harassed and exasperated flush, her hair messily covering her face. 'Sod off, why don't you?' she yelled, bashing him about his head with a plastic carrier bag filled with yet more screwed up bags, all waiting to be reused. 'I've bloody well had enough!' she screamed.

Watching her storm up the stairs, Dan deduced that it had indeed been one of those days, and thought that perhaps his luck wouldn't be in tonight after all. He headed for the safety of the kitchen, and the comfort of a nice cuppa. Fresh tea bag, a drop of milk in a china mug. Where's the one with the cow on it? Oh well, cats it is. Fill the kettle and plug it in...

As she lay on the bed with a pillow over her face, Emma first thought that the bang she'd heard was a part of her brain exploding in all the frustration. Then, in terror, she remembered. Running down the stairs she saw Dan slumped, eyes closed in a heap against the kitchen door which itself was hanging off its hinges. 'Oh Jesus, Dan.

Don't use the kettle there!'

His hair was vertical, and the lump that was fast forming on his head reminded her of a cartoon injury. All he needed was the little birdies and stars around his head to complete the scene. She found a pulse and grabbed the phone. By the time the ambulance had arrived, he'd regained his senses but the paramedic insisted he go with them for a thorough check-up. The gash on his head obviously needed stitches and he couldn't feel his right arm, his hand moulded in the form of the plug.

The ambulance pulled away with blue lights flashing though silenced sirens, with Emma to follow on in a taxi when she'd got herself together.

'The poor guy's delirious,' the medic told the driver as they headed for the hospital. 'All he can say is, "No cunnilingus talc tonight then, Em".'

The telephone rang, and a cheerful Valerie launched into flowery greeting.

'I'm sorry, Val,' Emma interrupted, 'Dan's just blown himself up and I've got to get off to the Royal as soon as I can. I've got to call a cab, so if you don't mind…'

'Blown up?' Val yelled. 'Oh Emma, I'm so sorry. He'll be all right though? Silly question! Yes, I'll get off the phone and you call a cab right now. No, I'll come and pick you up. No, that means I'll drive past the hospital to get to you which is a waste of time, so you get a taxi and… Emma? Are you there? Emma? It's gone dead, Adrian. Come on – the Royal, and be quick about it.'

The taxi arrived within minutes, too early for Emma. She hurriedly put a few essentials in a holdall for Dan and ran downstairs to open the door. Pyjamas! she realised. Oh Lord, he never wore them. What the hell, she thought, these nurses have seen it all before. Anyway, there'd be a gown or something that they'd let him use.

'You okay, love?' asked the small, bespectacled driver as the ashen-faced woman appeared at the door. She only nodded, pulling the door closed behind her with a slamming bang. 'That your phone ringing?' he asked, straining to listen through the wooden door.

'It'll have to wait,' she replied. 'They'll call back. Come on,' she told him, pointing to the blue Vauxhall chariot. 'Better get wer skates on.'

Miles away, a frustrated young woman was anxious to get a reply from home, but no one had answered all day.

While Adrian was parking the Range Rover, Val paced the reception of the Royal's Accident and Emergency unit waiting for Emma to arrive. Dan was inside already, and there was a lot of the general brisk activity that a Saturday evening brings upon these places.

Val had never had to visit this hospital in the ten years that it had been open. She studied the surroundings and felt fortunate that she was able to afford private care. There were no stained glass windows in this reception. Nor a coffee percolator. She'd have to make do with the machine.

Adrian scurried through the crowds of dressing-gown clad in-patients standing by the door with their cigarettes and roll-ups, and allowed the automatic doors to open before striding confidently towards the reception desk in search of his wife.

'Adrian!' he heard from his left. 'Have you got a twenty pence piece?' she asked as he approached.

'What for?'

'A coffee. I've only got a bit of change and they won't break a ten pound note over there,' gesturing towards the receptionists who were desperately wrestling with an early evening drunk, who was dressed as Postman Pat and shouting, 'You can't operate on Jess without my written consent!'

'Here you are, dear,' Adrian handed over a handful of loose change. 'Thank God for medical insurance, eh?'

'That's just what I was thinking as you walked in,' Val nodded. 'Couldn't they give him a tranquilliser or something?'

Pat though, was still highly charged. '...But I'm tellin' ya Jess is in BUPA. She's not just any old moggy, she's a bloody mega star!'

Adrian suddenly felt quite ill and in desperate need of a tablet.

The dirty blue taxi drew to a stop beside a crowd of half-dressed smokers, and Emma hurriedly paid her fare. Forcing through those who were obviously trying to either freeze or smoke themselves to death, despite the best efforts of the medical staff inside to add time to their days above ground, she dashed into the crowded reception to be greeted by Val. Adrian, it transpired, had taken charge and would be checking on the latest – when he'd returned from the Gents.

'Thanks for being here, Val,' Emma sobbed. 'It's my fault. I didn't tell him about the socket, and I was so nasty to him when he came home.'

Val's calming words didn't pacify Emma who stopped a passing nurse and asked how Dan was. The nurse pointed her in the direction of the reception, suggesting that they would be best able to assist.

She strode over the legs of a now very subdued Pat. So subdued in fact, that his Latex nose was bent double as he lay slumped against the snack dispenser.

Yee – har, she thought, unemotionally.

The receptionist phoned through to the treatment area to find that Dan was still being attended to and that yes, it would be possible for Mrs Beech to see her husband if she wanted to go through now. Emma returned to her companions to tell them that she was going to see the patient, and to thank them again for their moral support.

'We'll wait,' Adrian told her, 'and take you home when you're ready.'

'That's very kind,' she replied, allowing her feelings towards him mellow a little. Perhaps he wasn't such a prick after all.

A porter escorted Emma through to the bay, where she found Dan surrounded by two nurses and a third female in a white coat looking over a chart. 'How's the wounded soldier?' she asked timidly.

'Ah, Mrs Beech?' the doctor turned, 'Hello, come in,' she beckoned. 'He'll be fine. Won't you, Flash?' she nudged the man on the bed.

He was lapping up the attention. One nurse attended to the wound on his head that had just been stitched; the other, an auxiliary, tidied away the remains of discarded dressings. His moaned response made all four women laugh.

'Typical bloke, aren't you?' accused the nurse applying gauze. 'Surprised us that you even knew where to find the kitchen!'

If he moaned again, it would either dig him in deeper or finally gain some sympathy. Their mocking told him he should have kept quiet.

'Now then, you, we've got to get upstairs for observation,' said the second nurse helping him off the bed. 'We need this bed and there's no time for malingerers.'

'They're keeping me in overnight, Em,' he told his wife who had guessed as much. 'I need a fag.' He looked a sight. His hair was still a mess, his head was swollen and bruised from the knock, and the dressing over the stitches was already showing the first signs of blood seepage.

'Well you can't have one!' she replied. 'I've brought you

some things but there's nothing for you to smoke, nor to wear in bed.' The heavy bag was lifted into view.

'That's okay,' he replied wearily, shuffling his hunched body towards the curtain. 'I'll just wear a smile.'

'No you'll damn well not! I'm not having you flashing your bits at all and sundry.'

'No, Mr Beech,' added the nurse, pulling the drape to one side, 'mixed wards, you see. Don't want you frightening some old dear with a dodgy ticker now, do we?'

'Mixed?' he shot upright. 'What d'ya mean mixed?' The thought alarming him.

'Relax, Mr Beech,' the nurse gently guided him towards the waiting wheelchair. 'We've had to make cuts and so in low risk areas such as observation; we have double beds to save on linen. You don't mind sharing with a lady, surely?' her innocent eyes questioned. 'It has a double benefit to the hospital,' she continued, 'we find it also keeps Maternity busy enough to avoid closure,' she winked at Emma, who by now had found a huge grin.

'I'm not bloody well sh—!' he looked wary. "Ere, are you having me on, young lady?' he chuckled, catching sight of the nurse's facial twitch, though it made his head feel like it had just hit the doorway again.

'Of course, she is,' smiled his wife. 'They only have you sharing beds with men! Look, I'll see you on to the ward and then get back if you don't mind. It'll give you some rest.'

Ward Eight was busy, and there were few staff available for Emma to ask what should be done about collection and so on, so she kissed Dan softly on the cheek, told him she loved him and apologised for not warning him about Jack's incomplete work.

Making sure he was settled into a bed of his own, she found the ward sister in her office and had a brief chat to warn them not to give him prunes, unless of course, they were going to keep him in isolation with a toilet of his own. Ignoring the lift and opting for the stairs, she made her way back to the A and E reception, where she found Val and Adrian sat quite defensively in a corner, nervously watching the procession of drunks and victims trouping through the doors.

'How is he?' they both arose and asked together when Emma approached.

'Oh, they're keeping him in overnight to keep an eye on him,' she told them. 'I've got to phone in the morning to see how he's gone on, but they don't foresee any problems really. Just a precaution, they say.'

'You two ready, then?' Adrian was worrying about the paintwork on his vehicle. They made for the door and, with the car park fee paid, they were on their way. It was getting quite late and they were all desperately tired.

'I'm glad to be out of that place,' voiced Adrian over his shoulder to the passengers in the back seat.

'Not a nice experience, is it?' agreed Val. 'Fancy having to work there, poor things.'

Emma sat in silence. She was worried about Dan, but also unsettled at the idea of Olivia being caught up somewhere like that. Alone, late at night, in need of medical treatment – it didn't bear thinking about. Beyond her thoughts, Val and Adrian were chattering away, oblivious to Emma's quiet. It was Olivia's birthday in just under three weeks, and she herself suddenly felt quite lonely.

It was almost nine o'clock when the Mallorys had seen her indoors and headed back towards the other side of town. A flick of the light switch had no effect – the hall would not illuminate, and she remembered the violent bang of electricity meeting Dan's hand. The fuse box would need attention, and, finding a torch from the garage, Emma changed the fuses that had blown. Although she was tired, she couldn't face going to bed and tried to busy herself. There was still the pile of dust and waste from the vacuum cleaner bag standing proud in the hallway, a single footprint of an ambulance man clearly imprinted. It could wait. She propped the kitchen door up against its frame and went to make herself a coffee. Ah, no she wouldn't. A whisky would have to do.

With a large tumbler, heavy on whisky and light on soda, in hand, she flopped down into the easy chair by the living room window. She liked that chair, although rarely got the chance to enjoy its comfort. It didn't offer a good view of the television set and anyway, the remote control was on the TV itself so she wouldn't be switching it on.

She lethargically flicked through the magazines that lay on the table beside her. None took her fancy, especially as all but one was Dan's railway or model-making publications. The other was *The Big Issue* which featured Olivia's photograph, and she'd read that from cover to cover more than once.

She decided though to root out Olivia's diary and read parts again. It fell open at:

Monday 17th June – Day 8: Well Diary, woke at five this morning desperate for the loo. I can't go on shitting like this. I spoilt yesterday's trip to the zoo and want to see so much more than the hotel bathroom. Fingers crossed (and sphincter tight), I've not been again since – although it is only nine o'clock. We've just had breakfast and have decided to go on a helicopter ride around the harbour this morning, since we missed the boat trip we were going to do on Saturday. More later, I'd better see if there's been a fast-track of breakfast through my bowels before we set off.

Well Diary, it's just gone 8.45 p.m. and what a day we've had! Brilliant! The weather was a bit cloudy when we set off for Circle Quay or whatever it's called, but by the time we'd walked there via

Hyde Park and the Anzac Memorial (where Mr Narky shouted at me for lounging on the Memorial – too disrespectful nar-de-nar-de-nark), the sun was out and we had clear blue skies overhead. The leaflet on the helicopter rides told us to go to the tour office at the Quay, and the girl there phoned to book for us.

Because it was short notice and there was only the two of us, they offered us a trip up to the Blue Mountains for an extra $80 each instead of the additional $200 that it should be. What were we going to say, Diary? 'Oh sorry! We don't want a day trip for forty quid more than a twenty minute flight!' Think not, somehow!

Half an hour later, we're being picked up and taken to the airport where we fly from. When we've been through the checks with the pilot (John), up we go for the tour around the harbour – me in the passenger seat at the front and Ed in the back. What views! Going over the Opera House and Harbour Bridge was breathtaking.

Then up the Parramatta River, over the site for the 2000 Olympics (an old oil terminal or something) and on to the Blue Mountains, so called because of the blue haze that the eucalyptus trees give off. It started to get really misty the higher up we went, and John had to plot a zigzag route through the mist and mountain peaks. We were so close to the ridges it was amazing!

Eventually we landed at a homestead by a creek on the very edge of the National Park where we had a huge plate of meat (literally) and salad, and veggies, and – you name it. A group of Japanese had been driven up to the mountains to be flown back. We were to be driven back to Sydney via the Three Sisters – three enormous rocks that have some story attached to them I've no doubt – probably some bloke put a chastity belt on each of his three daughters and each gnawed through the other's so they could have it away with the woodcutter's son, and the father came back and found out so turned them all to stone because he loved them so much. Or it could be something far-fetched, of course, Diary.

Anyway, there was so much mist around, we couldn't see the Old Slags so we stopped for the toilet and carried on. Garth, the driver, was funny. He had us in stitches telling us about the in-breeding in the outback towns. How there's a population of 150, and 148 of them have the same surname and no one speaks to the other two. How your son could also be your cousin, and where 'safe sex' meant that there were at least two people watching you doing it.

Back in Sydney, Garth dropped us off at The Rocks by Ken Done's shop, and it started to rain really hard. Did a bit of shopping there and got some pressies for Mum and Dad, a sweatshirt (though I prefer the one Ed got for himself so we might nick it off him, eh, Diary?) and some more postcards.

Took the bus back to Oxford Street where Ed gawped into his favourite kinky outfit shop opposite the hotel and here we are. Neither of us fancied anything to eat and Ed fell fast asleep. The best news though is that I've not needed the loo anything like as much today, which is a good job when you've had to sit for forty-five minutes in a helicopter.

Ah Diary, look at Ed. Isn't he peaceful? He's finished his book already and now he's a tired boy. He's a love really. I know he wants me to sit on his chopper for forty-five minutes but what should I do? Not tonight. Clean knickers on, I think. Good night, Diary.

I swear I don't know where she's got this attitude from! thought Emma.

Tuesday 18th June – Day 9: I wrote this tomorrow, Diary, because there wasn't chance last night, but I'll write it like it was last night so that it reads like yesterday. But it's tomorrow. Anyway, here goes.

Completely barmy! Must be her father's genes.

Bright and sunny today – all day! Chance to wear the new sun hat that Ed takes the piss out of so much. Walked back into the city and went up the Sydney Tower at Centrepoint. I felt a bit giddy at the top and had to go and sit down in the middle – I thought that I was going to fall out of the place. Ed insisted on taking my photo against the Sydney city backdrop – heartless bastard. I couldn't get down from there fast enough.

As the weather was so nice, we strolled down to where other than Circular Quay, and bought lunch at The Rocks. These sandwiches would have fed an army and they were yummy. Wrote another six postcards by the waterside at C. Quay while Ed watched the world go by. Hmm. More like watched the women go by, Diary! There were one or two brave souls baring a little more than knees today.

He took the piss out of me because I'd written 'Boticanal Gardens' on a postcard home. I suppose it was funny considering the botty problems I've had this week (all cleared up now – whoooppeeee).

The weather has just been so good – the whole place looks completely different. Wandering back through the Botty Canal Gardens was lovely and we've just lazed on the grass.

Had a Chinese meal on Oxford Street at a BYO place (Oh, Diary! BYO is Bring Your Own booze! Don't you know anything after almost a week here?) We bought a couple of bottles of wine and had a really good time. First time we've felt anything like pissed. Came back to the hotel and (this is why you were put away for the night, Diary, to save your sensitive eyes) finally bonked. Well, it was sort of bonking. His willy wouldn't work too well because he'd had too much to drink he said, but we giggled a lot and it felt all right. I think I love him, Diary – that's why I suggested we should do it. You know me, Diary, I'm not one of them stone slappers in the mountains. Don't just drop 'em for any old knob.

Good girl! Oh bugger, where am I? '…any old knob.'

I think he loves me too. He's my best friend – better even than you, Diary.

Ahh that's lovely. I'm going to cry.

…and I know that he's waited a hell of a long time for that

moment. I want to do it now. He's still asleep seeing as we're still getting used to the time difference, and it's almost 8 a.m. I'm going to say 'Bye' now Diary, and wake him up with a surprise. I'll see you later.

Emma decided to call it a night, having felt assured that Olivia was happy when she scribed her recollections of the events. Edward was the sort of boy that you don't mind your daughter bringing home. In fact, he was the type you dream will accompany your daughter. He'd proved his maturity by putting up with Olivia's funny ways. He was 'a love' as Ollie had called him, and Emma shuddered, feeling a wave of emotion crash over her. For one moment, she was Olivia. She felt the anguish of losing a lover, a best friend and confidante all at once. Such special friends are rare to find, and Emma felt a touch envious that she had never felt that close to anyone – not even to Dan, whom she loved with all her heart. In that moment, she warmed too. Warmed at the thought that Olivia was safe. She didn't know where, but her instincts told her so.

The next morning, Jack was guiltily running fresh cable to the offending socket. 'I *am* sorry, Emma. I should've isolated it properly yesterd'y.'

She shrugged. 'It's not your fault, Jack,' she told him. 'I've been on at him to get this place re-wired for ages, but he'd sooner go play trains. He might do something about it now.'

He finished the job and repaired the door for Emma. 'Tell 'im I'm *really* sorry, won't you?' he begged of her before dashing off to play pub-league football for The Rat and Drainpipe's five-a-side team. He was late already.

Emma had only a short walk to the bus stop. It had the makings of a bright day and she made the effort to enjoy all around her. The first signs of autumn were appearing. She did like autumn – crisp leaves a hundred shades of rich brown and gold, fallen and blowing on dewy ground. She admired the chestnut tree across the road. Soon the local children would be throwing sticks and old shoes high up into its branches to dislodge this year's prize cheggy.

Turning onto the main road, she waved to Mrs Solomon carrying Mindy, her Jack Russell terrier. Mindy wasn't afraid to take on the deranged barking of the Rottweiler kept chained in all weathers to the garage wall by the strange biker couple who lived opposite Parkland Drive's tight opening, but her owner was. Mrs Solomon was the lady who, in every community it seems, had always lived in the same house which, despite its long-term neglect, never looked any worse for wear. The paint on her house had been peeling for as long as anyone could care to remember, and she flatly refused any assistance in rectifying the fallen perimeter fencing. The house and garden had always been Mr Solomon's pride and passion until he passed away, berating Nasser and his plans for the Middle East. That's just how he'd wanted to go, his surviving widow would tell Emma many years later at the street party held in celebration of Charles and Diana's wedding.

They mouthed 'hello's to one another, and carried on their respective ways – Emma to the bus stop, and the old lady to chat to an equally old man, vigorously clipping the air above his neatly trimmed privet.

The Sunday buses were not as frequent as other days, and it was a while before Emma's enjoyment of her surroundings was interrupted by the number 120 pulling alongside with the 'per-shish' of pneumatic brakes.

Taking her seat for the ride into the bus station, she pictured Dan, badly shaken, with his hair stuck on end. She could begin to see the funny side of the whole thing now, but thought better of telling her husband that. Not just yet, anyway. That was powder to keep dry for a special occasion.

A change to Corporation services at the station took Emma the ten minute trip to the hospital. Using the stairway, its sterile odour reminding her she must buy a new toilet brush, she made her way back to the ward where she had kissed goodbye to Dan only the night before.

The staff had changed shifts, but Emma soon found someone to give her the latest on the patient.

'Oh yes, he's fine,' said the staff nurse. 'He's obviously had a shock, but there's no long-term damage. In fact, he's been pestering the other patients and all the staff for a cigarette since long before breakfast rounds.'

'That's Dan all right,' smiled Emma, pleased that she wasn't going to be facing trial by jury. 'Can I go and see him now?'

'Take him,' replied the nurse. 'Please!' she added, hiding her Marlboros deep inside her desk drawer.

Emma wandered towards the bay of four beds where Dan had spent the night, and could hear his voice from some distance. Seeing his wife turning the corner, he looked forlornly at her and croaked a pitiful greeting.

'Don't give me that, you great lummox,' a distinct lack of sympathy accompanied her voice. 'Come on, up you jump. Get these on, we're going home,' she tossed the holdall of clean clothes from under the bed on to the mattress beside him.

'Home, Em? I'm not well enough for that, am I, nurse?' he pleaded with a tall brunette who, Emma noticed, wouldn't require a Wonderbra or a corset.

'Stop showing off and get changed,' Emma scowled.

'You be a good boy, Mr Beech and do as you're told,' said the nurse, drawing the curtains around his bed with a friendly 'don't worry – they're all the same' expression for Emma.

'Dan, you're blushing!' his wife teased.

'I don't like you showing me up like that, luv,' he frowned. 'I was only kidding about the bed bath.'

'She's young enough to be your daughter, you dirty old bugger. I hope you've not been embarrassing yourself whilst... What do you mean, bed bath?'

'*Touché*, Mrs Beech!' he laughed. 'Mixed beds: 1, Bed baths: 1!' his head throbbed, but it was worth her reaction. 'Now get me outta here,' he grabbed her wrist, 'before I rip yer clothes off and 'ave you here and now, you little vixen.'

She looked disbelieving. 'Well, the shock's not short circuited the theory. Do you think it'll improve the practical?' she kissed his cheek and patted his lap. 'Get your pants on, Romeo, and control yourself, we've a bus to catch,' she stood to allow him to dress. 'Oh, and before I forget; Jack says watch what you're doing next time!'

As they made their way down the ward, bidding their farewells to complete strangers and their visitors, Dan noticed a familiar face.

'Na then, Jimmy. What you doin' in 'ere?' he quizzed, approaching the older man laid on his side on a bed.

'I've made a fool of mi sen again, lad. Fell over last night, I did,' he replied. 'Hello, Mrs B,' he added, peering round Dan with a smile towards Emma.

'Oh, hello,' she offered politely.

'Em, this is Jimmy. Jimmy this is Emma – the missus,' Dan introduced.

'Aye, we've met before,' Jimmy smiled again.

'I'm sorry, I don't remember,' she struggled to recall. 'Nice to see you again, anyway, then Jimmy.'

All three froze in awkward silence, waiting for someone else to continue the conversation. 'Well, gotta go, mate,' Dan finally chirped. 'I'm off for a decent cuppa.'

'I could do wi' a chat Dan,' the man's desperately pained plea faltered.

'Aye, no problem. I'd better get goin' now, but I'll catch up with ya soon, eh?'

The patient looked disappointed.

'You be good now,' Dan tapped the bed, leaning sideways towards the man, 'and stick to the orange juice!' he whispered. He straightened, and turning Emma away towards the exit, waved his goodbye.

'Where on earth do you know him from?' Emma asked as they reached the lift.

'Work,' Dan mouthed knowingly with a long slow nod, like an old mill-hand to her friend amidst the intense noise. 'He's a bit of a one on the quiet, is our Jimmy.'

'Shan't ask!' Emma whispered, mocking Dan's manner as the doors of the lift opened and they stepped inside. 'If you're wanting a cuppa,' she thought aloud watching the doors close behind them, 'we'd better stop off somewhere that sells a kettle on a Sunday.'

They found a catalogue store open in the town and decided upon a cordless design which, they reasoned, was less likely to blow up if dropped in the sink and later plugged into a badly earthed socket. After a short wait for the bus outside the shopping centre, they were almost home. Turning into their driveway they saw a well-dressed middle-aged lady in tweed suit and flat-soled leather shoes, the style advertised in Sunday newspaper supplements balanced on someone's finger tip, post a note through the letter box.

The woman turned to leave and noticed the couple watching her from a distance. 'Mr and Mrs Beech?' she enquired.

'Yes,' they both replied, now approaching.

'I have some news. Can we perhaps step inside for a moment?'

THE ROOM WAS cold and decoration sparse. She waited impatiently by the pay phone. Mrs McMahon said she'd let her know by six and it was almost a quarter-past. She chewed the already frayed skin around her thumb nail, staring at the handset, willing it to ring as she had been doing for the last hour.

The suspense was adding to her chill. The heavy evening sky closed in, and the late September light was strong enough only to cast a glow around the aluminium-framed window, the rest of the room starved of its presence. She was too anxious to be concerned about the light switch. What purpose would it serve? It wouldn't make that phone ring, would it?

She stood and moved to the window. The road below was full of bustle. The clouds burst their grey mass, and the resulting downpour made people in the street run for cover, cars wipe their greasy screens with worn out wipers, and the pavement dance and dazzle in reflective colour splashes. It was over as quickly as it had come, but few bodies returned to the street save a young boy on his bicycle. He weaved in and out of the fresh puddles, his heavily-pregnant mother chasing after him with his coat, and his father chasing his wife with hers. She turned to take her seat once more by the telephone. Her watch said 6.21 now. Come on Mrs Mac! Where are you?

For the umpteenth time, she studied the pictures on the walls. Where, she wondered, did people actually *buy* Crying Boy? *Why* did they buy it, more to the point? On the wall by the door, the framed bowl of fruit was out of perspective. Either that's a hellish big apple or a funny coloured melon. Maybe it was a small bowl. No, the banana looks like a banana so the apple's wrong. Oh God phone, ring why don't you?

She returned to the window; the boy was wearing his coat now and pedalling for all his worth as his parents watched, arms folded against the evening elements, silently shouting warnings of unseen dangers on the road. From her vantage point, she contemplated her own future. How would she cope without someone to follow her with a coat? She watched their body language. The adults weren't communicating. They have so much together and don't seem to appreciate it. Should she shout from the window? They surely enjoyed the sight of the boy didn't they? Show it! she wanted to shout, before it's too late!

Another anxious glance at her watch told her it was half past six. She wanted a wee but decided to hold on. Crying Boy wept some more, watching her pace to the door and back again, not knowing quite what to do with herself.

When the phone finally rang, she approached it with caution. Three rings was enough to test her nerve, and she grabbed the handset, thrusting it nervously to her right ear.

'Hello?' she yelled.

'Olivia? Is that you?' The caller's familiar voice.

Tears streamed from nowhere down the girl's face. 'Mum? I love you, Mum. I'm so sorry. I'm so, so sorry,' the words tailed off into silent sobs.

'Don't worry, sweetheart. It's okay now. We've missed you *so* much. Your Dad's here, hang on won't you?'

Dan's voice was uncharacteristically gentle. 'Ollie, luv?'

'Hi Dad,' she blubbered.

'Oh Ollie, luv. Ollie,' he didn't know what to say through the emotion that overwhelmed him. 'Your Mother's blown me up, luv.'

They sat and cried, saying nothing, more than two hundred miles apart.

'Here's your Mum again,' Dan wept, passing the line back to Emma who assumed the same, speechless ecstasy.

'Olivia,' a third, calm and soothing voice took up the receiver. 'It's Jane McMahon. I think we were right, don't you?'

Olivia nodded down the phone.

'Let's get you home, eh? Your parents want to travel tonight if possible and they'll get to the hostel as fast as they can. I think it's safe to say that they're over the moon. Are you okay?'

She nodded again, the tears dripping from her reddened cheeks. She was relieved more than she'd ever thought conceivable. It was the call she'd so desperately wanted. She could start to rebuild her life again.

The volunteer stayed at number thirty-nine until she was satisfied that the parents, intoxicated on joy, were thinking rationally and had collected their thoughts sufficiently to appreciate what had happened there that afternoon. It had taken three painstaking hours to explain Olivia's fears, and to begin to prepare them for what they as individuals, and as a family, would face. Emma's initial enthusiasm to telephone the London number was soon replaced with worry and apprehension, and it had taken many uses of the new kettle before she and Dan were sufficiently composed to call.

Jane McMahon telephoned the railway station to find times of London-bound trains that evening, while Emma turned out the holdall that stood by the front door where she'd dropped it, and collected together the few items that she and Dan would need for the trip.

Dan sat in a daze, fearful he would wake up at any moment and find it all a dream. His head pounded so violently, he thought his stitches were about to split.

The last evening train was departing in only a few minutes, and with little chance of making the distance to the station, they decided to take the first one out in the morning at 6 a.m. Neither slept much that night. The fusion of excitement and fear raced through the atmosphere as they lay there holding each other in silence. 'Dan,' Emma whispered. 'Are you awake?'

'No,' his alert voice replied.

'Oh. You won't hear me tell you I love you then, will you?'

'No.'

'And you won't feel this either?' she kissed his hairy chest.

'No.'

'What about this?' she pulled gently on the hairs.

'No, try lower down though.'

'No point,' she smiled through the darkness. 'You're asleep and can't feel a thing,' she held him tighter. 'I just knew she was all right, didn't you?'

'Deep down.'

There was silence once more and he felt moisture on his chest. ''Ere, are you dribbling on me?'

She sniffed and he knew to draw her closer. 'I love you, Em,' he spoke into her hair, softly kissing her head.

They woke to the alarm at four thirty, still embraced. Dan felt nothing in his blood-starved arm, but didn't complain. Emma headed for the bathroom, while Dan phoned the sorting office to let Bill know he was signing himself off for a couple of days following the accident, and during the brief discussion, also told of the good news.

While Dan showered, Emma called for a taxi and prepared breakfast. Within the hour, the doorbell was ringing and Dan opened the door to the small frame of a man wearing round spectacles. 'Me again!' the stranger smiled as the door was opened.

'Again?' frowned Dan.

Ah, thought the caller. This was someone he'd never met before. 'Mornin'!' he tried again, noticing the woman's face he recognised, desperately trying to control her wayward hair in the hallway mirror.

Emma turned and smiled. 'Come in for a minute and meet the patient,' motioning towards Dan.

'Getting to be a regular call for me this is,' said the driver. 'I think you left this on the back seat the other night,' his outstretched arm offering a lipstick.

'Oh, I'd not even noticed it missing. Thanks.' Emma took the cosmetic as Dan looked on bewildered.

'Back seat? Other night?' he dared ask as the visitor stepped outside once more.

'Just get your coat on and into the car, Dan,' Emma ushered, knowing what was going through his mind. 'And don't worry, he's only got a little one!' she teased.

He laughed nervously. He wasn't in the mood for foolery and told her so.

'Who's kidding?' she asked, almost straight-faced.

At the station, the ticket office was empty and with their tickets bought, they headed off to platform four for the early train with a little under ten minutes to spare. The platform was surprisingly busy, Emma thought. Men in suits mainly, but there were normal folk too. A mother vainly attempting to control a toddler, the father uninterested in anything but his tabloid. An embracing couple not noticing anything or anyone around them. She wondered which was about to leave and which would be left there in the cold, grim station.

Dan needed the toilet and scurried off in the direction of

a 'Gentlemen' sign. Emma took a seat and watched those around her. A large group of the men in suits were in animated discussion about a recently announced company car policy. It had caused consternation whatever it was – something to do with diesel. She'd ask Dan when he returned.

Another group was swapping vulgar jokes, much to Emma's disgust; she couldn't hear them properly. One suit stood all alone, reading the financial section of a broadsheet, every now and again shaking his head in disbelief.

The entwined couple was still fused as Dan sauntered back with a newspaper under his arm. 'I thought we'd have the platform to ourselves, Em,' he said, taking a cold metal seat next to her.

'Mmmm. So did I,' her eyes moved from the frisky toddler and fell on Dan. 'I think we'll be talking car policy or something all the way there.'

'Car what?'

'That answers my next question,' she replied disappointed, taking the paper from under his arm and snapping it open in front of her. 'There's no one of interest here; I hope the train's better for people-watching,' she added, scanning the headlines, a tired yawn contorting her face.

The train drew up to the announcement of the 6 a.m. service to London Euston, calling at Wigan, Warrington, Crewe, Milton Keynes and London Euston, and the apprehensive travellers boarded the nearest coach which, to Dan's dismay, was not a smoker.

'I'm not having this,' he said. 'Let's find somewhere I can have a fag.'

They headed towards the rear of the train and found the smoking compartment. A single carriage of haze and fumes that even he could not contemplate.

'Bloody Nora!' he groaned to Emma, following obediently. 'I wouldn't have to light one of me own in 'ere; just breathe,' he predicted, turning around and bundling her backwards in the direction from which they'd just come. 'Back we go; I'll do without.'

Emma couldn't be annoyed. She was pleased that she wouldn't have to spend the next three hours cooped up in a smoky train, so now she led the way back along the route towards the front. The train began to pull away and Emma noticed a tearful girl on the platform, desperately running along with it. Her erstwhile Siamese twin sat just the other side of the moving window, trying not to show his feelings in front of strangers with whom he'd have to spend some considerable time.

She noticed too that the suits had all disappeared from the station and must therefore, now be aboard.

'What about here, Em?' called Dan from behind.

She recognised the scruffy suede shoes of one of the diesel men and shook her head, not stopping to explain why. She moved on to the next carriage, which was relatively empty, and certainly free of made-to-measure executive types. Finding a table, she put the holdall on the rack above and dropped down in the window seat facing forwards. Dan took the seat next to her and held his bandaged head.

'Killing me, this is!' he moaned, his eyes screwed tight. 'Bill was all right about me taking time off – he's probably running a book on how long by now.'

'Oh hell! I didn't phone David to tell him I won't be in,' realised Emma out loud.

'Don't worry, they'll survive without you for a day or two,' Dan reassured her.

'But it's his day off and I'm the only key holder today. They'll all be stranded outside at nine o'clock.'

'Oh dear,' he sympathised sarcastically. 'Let's get the driver to turn around and take us back. You can open up and we'll all be happy.'

'Dan, this is serious,' she scowled. 'I'll have to call him when we stop.'

He saw her genuine concern and became helpful. 'Don't they have a phone you can use on the train?'

'You're right, they must have. We'll ask the conductor when he checks the tickets.'

'Good. That's settled, then. Just try to relax now and enjoy the ride, will you? Get some sleep or something.'

Emma closed her eyes and, as suggested, tried to sleep while Dan read the paper. She fidgeted and twitched, and couldn't get at all comfortable in the seat. In no time they had arrived at Wigan and the carriage filled. Dan took little notice of those boarding except for a pretty blonde, well-dressed and business-looking who smiled as she asked if the seat opposite Emma was free.

Dan nodded and peered over his paper to watch her slide across the aisle seat towards her chosen spot. Her jacket parted and he noticed her ample breasts sway through a silky blouse.

Oh God, no bra, he thought. Just one of them lacy things.

'Nice day,' she said noticing Dan's gaze. 'These early starts kill me, though.'

'I'm used to them, but I know what you mean,' he replied a little guiltily, not knowing if Emma was asleep. He glanced and saw her eyes still closed. At least she wasn't snoring; he felt thankful.

'That looks like a nasty bump on your head.' The young woman pointed a well-manicured finger towards his bandage.

'I gave it to him last time he chatted someone up,' a voice from the corner said, eyes still closed tight.

Oh shit! Dan thought, but the woman laughed.

'I think I was chatting him up, actually,' she said, looking directly at Dan with another lovely smile.

Oh shit! he thought again.

She opened her slimline leather file, produced a magazine from within, and started to flick through half-heartedly. Emma's eyes closed again; a brief check on the female voice had confirmed her suspicions.

'All tickets, please,' the conductor called from the head of the carriage.

'Ask about the phone when he gets here will you, Dan?' Emma suggested.

'Phone?' enquired the woman. 'You can borrow mine if you want.'

'No thanks,' Emma looked her in the eye for the first time. Dan opened and closed his mouth like a fairground fish, waving his finger up and down as if seeking permission to prevent a certain fight.

'Tickets, please,' the conductor had reached their table.

The woman handed over hers. 'Thank you, Miss,' he said.

Dan fumbled in his pocket to find their tickets, and Emma took the opportunity to ask if there was a telephone that could be used.

'The one in the buffet car is playing up, I'm sorry to say, Madam,' he advised. The blonde smiled at the inference of Emma's age. 'At this stage, I can't let you use the mobile either, not unless it's life and death.'

'No it's not,' Dan interjected. 'Thanks anyway,' he said, handing over the tickets for punching.

Emma remained composed. She'd just get off at the next stop and call David.

'Can we take you up on your offer?' Dan asked the woman to Emma's disbelief.

'Sure Dan, just dial and press "send".' She withdrew the phone from her file and handed it to him with the broadest smile yet, revealing a row of gleaming white teeth and a soft dimple in each cheek.

'Thank you,' he accepted. 'There you are, dear,' he passed it to Emma, trying to calculate if he'd really gone too far.

She snatched it from him and dialled the number found in the back of her diary. 'Nothing's happening,' she told the woman smugly.

'Did you press "send"?'

Emma's satisfied smirk disappeared. She pressed the button and in no time, the ringing tone could be heard from the tiny earpiece.

'You go far, Dan?' Blonde asked.

Emma glared. He choked. 'Sorry?'

'Today,' she persisted. 'You going far today?'

'London. There and back. You?'

'Same. Business or pleasure?'

'Neither, really. Duty. You?'

She ran her forefinger around the fine gold necklace that off set her tanned skin. 'Both really,' she mused, mimicking his phrasing with a sparkling edge to the words. 'If you can't find pleasure in business, then it's not worth the hassle is it?'

Dan couldn't formulate a coherent answer before Emma started to speak.

'David, it's Emma. Look, I'm sorry to bother you ...oh God! I'm sorry, I didn't realise it was still so early... You sure?... Well, I'm *en route* to London. It's Olivia, we're going to pick her up, so I won't be in today if that's okay with you?... Thanks, yes it's great, isn't it? Can you keep it quiet for a day or two? I'll give you a call later to let you know how we got on... Thanks again David, and I really am sorry to wake you... Okay, bye... Bye.'

'All sorted?' Dan asked.

'All sorted,' Emma confirmed. 'Thanks for the phone,' she told the owner, passing the mobile back across the table.

'No problem,' the dimples appeared, captivating Dan. 'I'm going to the buffet car for a coffee. Anyone like anything?' the woman asked.

'No thanks, not for us,' Emma replied, Dan merely shaking his head with a diffident smile of thanks.

'Keep my seat warm, won't you?' she slid across the vacant seat once more and headed for the buffet car.

'Tart!' Emma's smarting accusation when she was safely out of earshot.

'I thought it was nice of her to let us use her phone,' Dan defended, trying not to admire her backside gliding through the automatic doorway.

'You would. I'm surprised you didn't faint with all the blood rushing away from your brain.'

'What's that supposed to mean for Christ's sake?'

'Well,' Emma's exaggerated tone began, 'what's the difference between a Wigan girl and an ironing board?' she asked with a contemptuous tilt of the head.

'You what?'

'You have trouble opening the legs of an ironing board, that's what!'

'What *on earth* are you talking about, Emma?'

'Her! Keep my seat warm, Dan. How far do you go, Dan. Come to the toilet and shag me senseless, Dan,' she mocked. 'Just you keep yourself to yourself, will you, Daniel?' she hissed through gritted teeth.

'You're making far too much of this,' he protested. 'I'm sure she's not at all like that.'

'Am I?' disbelief in her rhetoric. 'I suppose you've not noticed the ship's rivets sticking out from her chest then?'

'Are there really?' he tried to keep a straight face at the thought of her nipples, but failed and laughed in resignation. 'Look, I'm old enough to be her father, so just let it drop, eh?'

'Oh, so there *was* a rush of blood then?'

He snorted in frustration. Was she really serious? Perhaps attack was the best form of defence. 'Yeah. I got a great dongin' stiffy the minute I saw her.'

'Well then, we've got that straight,' Emma's face showed civility at last. 'So to speak,' she added hastily with a grin. 'Just behave or I'll chop it off with a *very* blunt knife!'

The woman returned with a brown bag and took her seat by the window, allowing her figure to again tantalise Dan who was looking at, rather than reading, the paper. She took out a large plastic cup, two cartons of milk and a plastic stirrer, placing them all on a serviette. She removed the lid from the cup as the train rocked, and the muffled announcement of their imminent arrival in Warrington came over the address system.

The slop of tea on to her blouse made the woman curse, and Dan stopped himself from valiantly offering to rub it down.

'That's annoying, isn't it?' Emma's compassion surprised Dan.

'Bloody nuisance!' she agreed, holding the garment away from her skin.

'Well, look on the bright side. If it'd been real silk, it'd be ruined, wouldn't it?' Emma sniped. The woman chanced a look of vitriolic indignation across the table, but remained silent. The best thing would be to rinse it through now, but the option of going see-through on a crowded train didn't appeal as a viable option. Instead, adding the milk to her tea, she cleaned up the mess as best she could and opened her magazine to detach herself from her travelling companions.

Pulling into their next station stop, the carriage filled almost to capacity and a smart young suited man came to sit opposite Dan, asking the woman by the window if the seat was occupied.

'No, please do,' she replied, patting the upholstery with

suggestive eyes.

Within minutes, the pair were chatting and Dan felt a little jealous, if not relieved that he was no longer the subject of embarrassing approaches.

Emma was bored with the window seat, and asked Dan to swap with her so that she could watch more of what was going on inside the train. There was little of interest until Crewe when a young man in casual dress boarded and stood not too far from where they sat. She noticed his kit bag and presumed he was in the forces. His conversation with any female that took his fancy was centred around himself and his physique. Granted, he appeared fit in the true sense of the word, but Emma could not believe that these girls were encouraging his conceited chit-chat. Perhaps, she pondered, the world was full of lonely people, just waiting for someone with a big enough ego to force themselves upon them.

One girl, in her early twenties Emma thought, ridiculed his arrogance and belittled him with everything she said, but he seemed to thrive on the attention. This was a new concept to Emma, and she became enthralled in the unravelling story.

Dan was dozing and Emma eavesdropping, as the young businessman on their table excused himself with a 'cup of coffee' mutter. He walked towards the front of the train, temporarily blocking Emma's view of the young service-man. She was soon aware of the woman also excusing herself, with 'the loo' being her destination, but Emma was too busy listening to the entertainment ahead to acknowledge either departure.

The train swayed violently when a north-bound train passing in the opposite direction boomed beside Dan's ear, and he woke with a loud snorting start.

'Where is everyone?' he asked, wanting to make sure he'd not made some sort of fool of himself while asleep.

'Eh?' Emma's distant reply.

'I've been dozing. Where's Wigan Girl gone?'

'Don't worry yourself, you haven't been talking in your sleep. Farting yes, talking no. She still thinks you're a stud.'

'Well, where's *he* gone?' he asked, pointing to the vacant aisle seat with disdain.

'Buffet for a coffee, I think,' Emma was still listening in to the other conversation.

'Ahhhh righhhhht,' he yawned loudly, stretching and noticing the illuminated 'Engaged' sign vanish at the head of the carriage. Should he go to the toilet now or hang on a while? He'd hang on.

He watched the young woman return down the carriage, her chest gently bobbing up and down with the motion of the train. She smiled politely as she resumed her seat, the young man returning soon after, also with a smile for Dan and Emma.

Dan looked at him from under lowered eyebrows, and wondered why he should have a trace of shirt protruding from his flies. Where, too, was his coffee? He looked at the woman, who was flushed and playing with her hair.

Bastard! he thought, and turned to look at Emma. She hadn't taken in the scene, still engrossed elsewhere. He decided against telling her, excusing himself instead and making that trip to the toilet after all.

It was a minute past nine when the train pulled into London Euston, almost on time. There had been little conversation between the occupants of the table since the Midlands. Dan and Emma were becoming more nervous about their trip as the miles piled up, and the other two hadn't said much since returning from their supposedly separate sorties.

The woman had read her magazine from cover to cover, and was now honing her taloned fingers; Zipper the Coffee Man was engrossed in a motor trade publication. Emma had become bored with the egotistical youth and reverted to fidgeting and shifting about in her seat. Dan sat and stared out of the window, wondering what to say when he saw his daughter.

The screech of the brakes and final violent judder told the travellers that they had arrived at their destination. Business cards were exchanged between the two opposite, and Emma looked at Dan with an 'I told you so!' smirk. 'Well, goodbye then,' she said to them both, as she reached up for the holdall and joined the line to alight.

'Yes, bye. Nice meeting you,' added Dan following her.

There was no audible response from either who remained seated, just smiles and nodding heads.

'She's gone off you now,' Emma whispered as they shuffled along towards the exit, their escape regularly hampered by a group of frail passengers attempting, one by one, to retrieve their heavy luggage from the rack by the door. 'I bet they're bonking before the day's out,' she predicted once they were safely on the platform.

'Perhaps they will,' Dan agreed with crooked smirk and glinting eye, pointing towards the overhead sign for taxis and guiding his wife in the direction of the blue arrow.

They asked for an Islington address and were outside the terraced house within a few minutes. Dan paid the driver while Emma stood on the kerb side, dreading knocking on the door.

From an upstairs window, they were being watched. It was more than six months since she'd seen her parents, and Olivia didn't know what she'd say when they finally came through the door. Jane McMahon had been so good since she'd agreed to call on them. In fact, everyone at the refuge had been kind and supportive, especially when it was pointed out that she'd featured in *The Big Issue*.

The callers were moving up the path and towards the door now, linking arms. She decided to go downstairs and open the door herself.

'You knock, Dan,' Emma shuddered, her nerves on edge.

He raised his hand and cautiously knocked twice. The door opened immediately and there she stood: Olivia. Her clothes, a grey sweatshirt and denim jeans, were baggy and she looked drawn and tired. Her face, her father noted, was a lot thinner than before, and there was little of her to begin with.

'Hello, sweetheart!' her mum cried, throwing her arms around the girl. Olivia said nothing, tears streaming down her face yet again. Dan stood and watched, his eyes flooding. He didn't know what to do. He awkwardly embraced them both, and there they stood on the doorstep, all holding each other. All happy. All crying. All relieved to be together again.

'There's still no reply,' Val told Adrian. 'Do you think Dan's all right?'

'I'm sure he is.' He picked up his briefcase. 'Look, I'm late for the office, I'm going to have to dash.'

'Okay. What time will you be back tonight; usual?'

'I'm at the Hulton shop this afternoon, so I might be a bit earlier,' he told her with a kiss. 'I'll see you no later than usual, anyway.'

She watched him close the door behind himself, and replaced the receiver. 'Do you want a lift today, Lizzie Mint?' she shouted up the stairs.

'Please,' the faint reply.

'Get yer skates on then, I'm going soon.'

Liz appeared at the top of the stairs and thundered down in her Dr Marten boots. 'Ready!' she shouted unnecessarily.

'What *are* you wearing?' asked her mother in a tone of disowning exigence.

'Oh shit. Val's getting old,' she sighed. 'I should have thought something was up when I got a flannelette nightie for Christmas.'

'Don't be a cheeky sod. And mind your language, I *am* still your mother.'

'Sorreee for living!' Liz's eyes flared. 'They're tights.'

'I know they're tights; what else are you wearing? More over, *not* wearing?'

'This jumper's long enough to cover me bum,' she said stretching the top to cover her knees. 'I'm wearing knickers if that's what you're worried about.'

'I should bloody well hope you are!' Val pushed her towards the door. 'Just get in the car. I despair sometimes, kid, I really do.'

They'd almost reached the college when Elizabeth asked her mum what she'd be doing during the day. She thought it best to placate her as much as possible.

'Mrs Almond's in later, so I'll be following her round with a duster I've no doubt. Apart from that, I've got to arrange the presentation for your dad and I want to see how Daniel Beech is getting on.'

'Presentation?'

'The Company presentation for the Epilepsy Association.'

'Ah, right. How's the fund-raising going?'

'Dad reckons it'll reach £25,000 by the end of the month.'

'Hell's bells!'

Val stopped the car at the rear gate to the college and pulled on the hand brake. 'He's done well, hasn't he? I hope you're proud of him,' her solemn tone almost accusing. 'It's taken a damned hard effort to make it work, and he's struggled to cope these last months.'

''Course I'm proud!' Liz defended. 'Ed would be too.'

'Yes, he *would*, wouldn't he?' she looked thoughtful.

'Now, off you go and get yourself educated young lady. And *do* make sure you don't use open tread stairs today, won't you?'

Liz growled as she got out of the car, lifting the back of her jumper to flash her knicker-covered backside in her mother's horrified face. 'Sharon Stone, eat yer heart out!'

'Where did you go wrong?' Val asked the mirror; and with a disbelieving shake of her head, she sped off towards Hulton and Parkland Drive.

There was no reply when, for the second time, Val rang on the doorbell. There was still milk by the door and the morning newspaper was hanging precariously inside from the letter box. She shoved it all the way through and moved the milk out of the direct sunlight – a habit since she was a girl.

Delving into the Rover's glove box, she found a pen and an old Sainsbury's receipt on which to write a note:

Monday 22nd. 9.30 a.m.

Hello Emma and Dan
Hope all's well and Dan's recovering nicely.
Have tried to phone but like the doorbell, no reply.
I'll try again later.
Love V x

(Milk round the back)

She popped the note through the door, and returned to the car where she sat thoughtfully for a while. Perhaps Dan was still in the Royal and Emma had gone to work, she pondered. That must be it. Yes, the milk and papers probably arrive after she leaves for the bus in the morning.

She set off for home, passing, along the main road, the betting shop that Adrian would be visiting later that afternoon. She considered making an impromptu call herself – a bit of a mystery shopper visit – but thought better of it. She didn't want to appear interfering, and wouldn't really know what she was looking for anyway. Laura Ashley was more her kind of mystery shopping, especially if it involved leaving the premises with armfuls of carrier bags.

Rather than returning directly home, Val drove to the centre of the town and parked in her usual place just off Winston Square. Taking the short walk through the wooded square, she took money from the cash point machine on the bank's side wall and continued up High Street towards the covered shopping centre that had recently sought American roots and called itself a 'Mall'. To the locals it was still the Bullring, but she supposed its Far Eastern owners knew best.

She was in search of something for Dan Beech's fortieth birthday which was only a few weeks away; having been invited by Emma to the surprise party she was throwing for him, she thought it only right that she and Adrian find him a nice gift. But what? She didn't know. There was little by way of interests to go on. You can hardly buy someone a monkey wrench or spanner for a birthday, can you? she considered. A new lighter? No, that's encouraging him to smoke. There was little point in getting him anything for a car, not since the accident all that time ago. It seemed like yesterday, though. Val felt cold and shuddered. Her mind wandered to Edward and then leapt on again to the arrangements for the presentation. She must call in at the bank and arrange for one of those over-sized cheques to be available for the photographs. Stupid woman, she censured herself. Could have done it earlier.

Her mind, now well and truly a mishmash of conflicting images, went blank and she abandoned all thoughts of finding a gift. The best option was to go home for a quiet day, via the bank. There was a fairly long queue but it didn't concern her. She swiftly reached the head of the snaking line, and moved towards counter number four when the computer-generated voice called it vacant.

She advised the clerk of her wishes, and left with the promise that she could collect one of the large cheques at any time after midday tomorrow; one would be brought out from the stores and set aside.

Back on the pavement, Val stood gazing around, not quite in control of her senses. She had the gnawing feeling that she'd not done something, or forgotten something important but couldn't think what. Still in many minds, she retraced her steps back to the car and set off for Wingate Farm, the feeling still nagging. A peaceful hour's reading would settle her, she decided, and whatever it was would soon come to her.

'Only me, Glad!' Val shouted as she opened the back door. There was no response. There should have been the sound of industrious cleaning, dusting and vacuuming but the deafening silence made her seethe. Throwing her handbag and car keys upon the large pine kitchen table, she mumbled that the 'lazy cow' would have to go. The checking of her watch confirmed that the help should still be working, and Val stormed through to the living room to make sure that there were adequate logs to lay a fire – the chilly weather was adding to her fast-frosting temper.

There, sat quite still in the corner, was Mrs Almond and, for a moment, her employer was startled.

'Oh Lord! You gave me quite a fright.' There was no acknowledgement. 'I say, you gave me a fright. Mrs Almond, are you all right?' she approached the woman. 'Glad?' She took the precariously angled cup from the woman's hand. It was quite cold despite being half full of brick-red tea.

The woman remained sat upright, eyes not blinking,

limbs relaxed.

'Bloody hellfire!' Val sighed realising the worst, patting the woman's hand and closing her eyes. 'That's all I need right now, Gladys, you daft beggar.' Val sat on the settee and put her hands to her face. Poor Gladys, only in her sixties. What on earth should she do? There *was* a sister that Mrs Almond talked of; no one else though – apart from her Arthur, but he'd passed on a while ago. And where the sister was, goodness only knew.

Calling Doctor Ainsworth's surgery, she explained her discovery to the receptionist, who sympathetically told her that the doctor was attending a management meeting that morning, but Valerie could make an appointment for Friday at 4 p.m. to see him.

'So I keep the old girl in the freezer for four days, do I?'

'I do beg your pardon?'

'Listen, luvvy. I've got one very dead cleaner occupying my daughter's favourite armchair right now, and I want to let the dearly departed keep some dignity. Please tell me what I must do to prevent me having to prop her up in your waiting room on Friday afternoon.'

'Oh, I see. She can't come into surgery then?'

Val took a long, deep breath.

'Well,' the woman continued, 'Dr Ahmad has joined us permanently now. I'll just see if he can call around when surgery closes at lunchtime. Will you hold?'

'The phone or the corpse?' Val's sarcasm seeping from every pore.

The response she received was an opening rendition of Vivaldi's *Four Seasons*, the normally soothing music linked to the surgery telephone.

'Mrs Almond?' the woman's voice returned after some minutes away.

'Mallory. Mrs Almond can't come to the phone right now.'

'Oh, Mrs Mallory. I don't seem to be able to find Mrs Almond's medical records for Dr Ahmad.'

'I doubt if she was a patient of yours,' she explained.

'Ah, I see. Can you hold?' The music returned. More time passed and Val studied Gladys's face properly for the first time. She was a pretty thing, probably a real beauty in her time, and Val regretted the awful things she'd said and thought of the hired help. She hadn't really got to know her as a person in the short time she'd been calling at the farm; only the unique way she had of cleaning the place.

'Hello, Mrs Mallory,' the voice returned. 'Dr Ahmad will come straight away. Are you at home?'

'Yes, I am,' the relief in Val's tone spoke volumes. 'Thanks, I don't think I could continue the day with her sat here like this.'

'He'll be as quick as he can, once this last patient he's seeing has gone.'

Val repeated her thanks and replaced the receiver. Now what? She should call Adrian. His mobile answered after a couple of rings, and his welcome words calmed her a little. Emotionally, she explained once more her discovery, and sensing her anxiety, he mollified her, turning the car around and telling her he was on his way home at that very moment. She felt appeased that she wouldn't have to cope alone with a doctor she didn't know, attending to a cadaver she barely knew, in the living room she cherished.

The throaty purr of the Range Rover turning on to the gravel told Val that Adrian was the first to reach the house. He was shortly at her side by the little shell of their house-keeper.

'Nice to meet you, Mrs Almond,' he told the static body. Val had to laugh. It wasn't a humorous laugh, but a nervy laugh that always seemed to appear in her mouth at the most inappropriate times.

'What's so funny?' Adrian asked, a little surprised.

'Nothing. Nothing at all,' she tried to straighten her face. 'Just seems so apt that she died so obviously skiving the job. Should I dock her wages do you think?' she managed before exploding once more into uncontrolled tittering behind fists clenched to her face.

'Hey, stop it you!' he whispered in sniggering admonishment, as if Gladys could possibly hear. 'The poor woman's croaked it, for God's sake; it's not meant to be comical.'

The sound of a second car curtailed further discussion, and both went to greet the doctor with large smiles hardly appropriate to the circumstance.

'It's not Ainsworth?' Adrian asked, straining to identify the driver, as the medic opened the door of his Volvo estate car and stood to reveal the full extent of his 5' 3" frame.

'No, it's a new chap, Ahmen or something.'

'Sounds a bit ecclesiastical Val,' he smirked. 'Isn't it Ahmad?'

'Do you know him?' she turned inquisitively to check his reaction.

He realised his mistake but didn't let it show. 'Me? No,' his head shook confidently. 'Someone at the office was talking about him some time ago. Very good with the recently expired they say,' he quipped with nonchalance.

The man approached carrying a black leather Gladstone bag and spinning his car keys OK Corral-style. 'Good day to you, Mistir Mallory,' his Pakistani dialect called cheerfully, recognising Adrian. 'Are you well?'

'Very well thank you, Doctor. Nice to meet you.' They shook hands, the smaller's understanding of his oath allowing him to be guided in the proceedings.

Val raised her eyebrows and viewed her husband through the corner of her eye. 'Misers Mallory?' he afforded Val the same courteous handshake.

'Thank you for coming so swiftly, Doctor. It's nice to

meet you.' Val echoed, uncertain of what exactly she had just witnessed.

They guided the cavalry towards his quarry, and stood back as he went about his business in an efficient manner; Val filling in as many details the doctor demanded of her as she could, while Adrian paced the room, thoughts of his own loss uppermost in his mind.

The ambulance crew stretchered the body away from the house under wraps, and secured their load before driving off into the distance towards the coroner's morgue.

'There'll be a post-mortem?' Adrian asked the doctor who was stretching to reach for his overcoat, hung high on the wrought iron wall hook.

'Oh indeed, Mistir Mallory,' he slung the coat around his shoulders. 'And may I s'gist that Misers Mallory comes to sigery very soon?'

'Sorry?' Adrian watched the man's lips in an attempt of understanding.

'Misers Mallory should comes to sigery in case of shock. Perhaps very soon.'

'Er, yes. Perhaps you're right, Doctor. I'll see what she says,' the much taller man replied, relieved he didn't mean for an autopsy. 'Oh, before I forget,' he handed the doctor a slip of paper. 'Gladys's details. Her address and so on.'

The man bowed slightly in thanks. 'Well, good day, Mistir Mallory. Please farewell to Misers Mallory.'

'I'll do just that, Doctor.' He showed the caller to his car, and bade him farewell.

Returning to the house, Adrian was proud of how well he'd coped with the situation, and realised that his medication had clearly worked. It wouldn't be long before the treatment was complete, and he could start to face situations that life was to hurl his way on his own two feet.

Val was shaking cushions and straightening curtains when Adrian entered the living room. 'Brandy?' he suggested.

'Huge one,' was her answer, not distracted from her fervent tidying.

He poured two large glasses and placed them on the table in front of the settee. Encouraging her to sit for a moment, he took his place on the roomy cushion and firmly patted the adjacent space, indicating exactly where she should retreat.

They hadn't sat together like this for longer than either could recollect. It felt nice, special and natural.

'What's brought this on?' she asked sensing his arm placed around her. 'We've not had a cuddle for ages.'

'I've been thinking it's time to get on with life. We've let too much time slip us by haven't we?' He looked her in the eye. 'I was never there for the kids when they were growing up and now, well,' he paused for thought, 'it's not too late to catch up with Liz I suppose but...'

'Good call, Buster!' Val interrupted, precluding his guilt-ridden sentence. 'Let's start anew today. Poor Gladys has made me realise that life's too short to waste,' an illustrative finger pointed to the chair of indolent demise. 'If you're not going back in this afternoon, let's sort out Edward's presentation, and then if you're serious about getting on with it, you can sit quietly and have a read.'

'Of what?'

She kissed him passionately. 'Joanna Trollope.'

D AN KNEW IT had been too good to be true. He sat stunned in the chair by the window, gazing into the middle distance. He was too young to be a grandad. Grandads were old men with flat caps and toothless smiles. They drove Austin Allegros and farted unwittingly at the dinner table. He wasn't ready for that stigma, was he? He was proud of his farts.

Emma fussed, busying herself to elude more tears. 'I'm so happy she's safe, Dan,' she told him, pulling up the cushion from behind his back and fluffing for all her worth.

'Mmm. Me too, luv,' he turned with a look of upset, yet comfort. 'Where's she now?'

'Packing her things in her room; she won't be long. The sooner we're back on that train the better I say. And don't worry,' she stuffed the cushion back behind her husband, 'we'll manage.'

He raised his eyebrows in reluctant agreement. 'Touch of the *déjà vu*'s, eh? Done it once, we'll do it again, I s'pose.'

Emma smiled. He was a gem, she thought.

'Em? Is that a grapefruit on that picture up there?' he asked, nodding to the wall. It had been bothering him for a while.

'Which one?' she asked, a little bemused and quite uninterested.

'By the door.'

'No, it looks like a melon to me,' still indifferent. 'Why?'

Shaking his head, he blew through puffed cheeks and shrugged. 'No reason.'

The door opened, and Olivia appeared with a rucksack and plastic Spar carrier bag. Neither looked particularly heavy, but Dan told her to put them down immediately; he'd carry the bags.

With a final look around the sitting room and a farewell to a couple of tired looking young women in the corridor, Olivia took the first steps back to her Northern roots and the safety of her family. With her father valiantly carrying her rucksack by one strap, and tripping over the other with almost every step, she linked arms with her mother and followed him to the kerbside. Dan hailed a roaming taxi and ordered the driver to take the three passengers the short distance to Euston. The commuting traffic extended considerably the journey time, but Emma and Olivia chatted about the recent goings-on at home and in particular, Dan's hospitalisation.

It took Dan a while to enter into the discussion but he finally contributed his version of events, and revealed with a wry smile his suspicions that Emma was plotting for the insurance pay-out. All three were in excited and animated conversation when the taxi drew to a stop beneath the station concourse, and the driver switched off the meter.

They had the best part of an hour to wait before the next service would take them back to their Lancashire home, and so headed for the fast food buffet in search of something to see them on their way.

'So,' Dan's mouthful of cheeseburger spat, 'it *is* Edward's then?'

'Dan!' Emma snapped in astonishment. 'Don't be so bloody insensitive.'

Olivia appeared upset; head bowed, silently considering her response.

'What's the big deal?' he protested. 'If it's going to happen, I'd rather it be Edward's than anyone else's. I liked the lad.'

'Leave it, Daniel,' Emma warned.

'Well, he showed great restraint from what I can see. Least he deserves is it's his,' he blundered on.

'And just what's *that* supposed to mean?' Olivia's display of anger, that her father should doubt her integrity.

'On that holiday you had. Teasing the poor sod,' Dan found himself becoming defensive.

'Dan, leave it, I said,' Emma's agitation was driving her to distraction.

'No, Mum. Let him explain,' Olivia's tone was firm. 'Who says I was?' she asked, looking him square in the face with a penetrating stare.

'You do, in that diary you wrote,' his response too quick from his mouth for the brain to stop.

'My diary? You've *read* my diary?' Olivia's astonishment clearly evident; her mouth open and eyes wide.

Dan looked to Emma, who had all but disowned him. Her scowl was uninviting. Oh, did he know he was in trouble. He knew too that he was all alone on this one, having landed both himself and Emma in the hottest water imaginable.

'Only to find you,' he appealed.

Olivia was positively infuriated. 'To *find* me?' she wheezed. 'You just thought I'd have left a map did you? Or perhaps a trail of condoms from bed to bed?' she frothed. 'Because that's what you obviously think of me; I'm just a tart.'

'Now Ollie, it's not like that,' her mother soothed. 'You must understand that we've been worried sick, and when I found your diary amongst the things you asked to be sorted, well, it was days before I opened it. Don't blame your Dad,' she held on to her daughter's hand. 'We read it because we were genuinely trying to find anything that might have led to a clue. We're sorry, but we had nothing at all to go on.'

Olivia was embarrassed. Not only had they read her innermost thoughts and feelings, but she'd put them through untold pain. She began to weep. 'I'm a selfish cow, aren't I?'

Dan wanted to agree, but Emma had thrown him one lifeline, he wasn't going to toss it back so quickly. Instead, he ate while his wife offered comfort to her sobbing daughter. He couldn't see any point in wasting good food – especially at these inflated prices. 'I'm sorry, Olivia,' he submitted, picking gherkin out of the bun. 'Me and your mum are right behind you, and I suppose it's quite exciting really; the prospect of a little 'un around the place.'

Olivia said nothing. She quietly sniffed her way through her chips, but could not face any more than one bite of the burger, shoving it instead in the direction of her father.

Checking the destination board, Emma suggested that they finish their drinks and head towards the platform to find a seat on the train. Once aboard and waiting for the train to depart, Olivia gazed out of the window into the darkness of the station. She could see her own reflection and that of her mother, silently castigating her father on the foolishness of his earlier actions. She couldn't see his reflection, he was sitting next to her; but her mother's silent 'and so you should be' suggested he truly was sorry for what he had thoughtlessly said not long before. She considered his words, and thought it only natural for them to question the identity of her unborn child's father, even though she had been going steady with Ed for yonks.

She spun her head to face them and Emma's mouthed rebuke stopped guiltily. 'Mum, Dad,' her pitch was gentle. 'I know I've put you through hell all this time, and I'm *really* sorry. I just didn't know what to do when Ed died, and I want to start over. Can we do that, please?'

''Course, luv,' smiled Dan, taking her hand.

Emma nodded violently with a smile filled with pride and release. 'It's good to have you back. Both you and your bump.'

'What time do we get in, Dad?' asked the girl.

'Just before ten, I think,' he guessed.

'Good. I'll try to sleep then if you don't mind.' She snuggled into her father's arm and soon drifted into deep slumber.

'Where's the car parked?' Olivia asked four hours later, as they walked up the steep slope and out of the station.

'There isn't a car, sweetness,' Emma told her. 'Not yet, anyway.'

Olivia looked saddened. 'Oh, I'm sorry.'

'Don't be, chuck,' Dan smiled and held her waist. 'We've managed to save up enough; there'll be one soon. Definitely one in time for Junior.' He playfully smacked her bottom and they headed for yet another taxi rank, Dan tripping over rucksack straps as he went.

The front door opened, and Emma picked up the mail and newspaper from the mat before Olivia cautiously stepped over the threshold for the first time in months. It felt strange to be back home, although so very safe. The hallway looked different somehow but it hadn't been decorated, it just looked bigger than she remembered. There was the same peeling corner of wallpaper by the lounge door where Dad hadn't put enough paste on the roll, and it wouldn't stick properly. The rug was new, she liked that. It contrasted well with the carpet. It also covered the paint spill in the middle where Dad'd kicked the tin.

'Beep beep!' her father's voice came from behind her, and she realised that she was blocking the doorway. She stepped aside and wandered into the lounge. That too hadn't changed. Had she ever been away?

The serving hatch opened from the kitchen and Emma asked if she'd like a drink before going to bed. 'You're not using the kettle, are you, Mum?' she smiled.

'I'll fill it, your father can plug it in though! Sit down for goodness sake,' she waved towards the sofa. 'Put the telly on or something if you want to. It *is* your home,' she stressed.

From her seat, Olivia heard the front door open and close almost immediately. 'Bloody kids nicking the milk again!' came grumbling from the hallway, and she observed Emma's silhouette through the glass hatch door. A satisfied smile appeared across her thin face. Oh yes, there was no doubting it. She was home.

The tea was just how she liked it – steaming hot. The milk smelt a little iffy, but never mind. The mug design was a cow chewing a daisy, and Olivia commented upon its improvement on the old, chipped mugs that she remembered. Emma recounted the tale of when and where she bought it, while Dan opened the mail.

There was nothing of much interest – a guaranteed loan facility from a credit agency in the name of Mrs D. Beech. Perhaps they were suggesting he should have a sex change and here was the wherewithal to do it. A postcard from a neighbour in Cyprus. Oh dear, their flight was delayed. That'll be Emma's fault by the time they get back. A statement from the bank – not overdrawn this month, hallelujah.

Placing the mail to one side, he lifted the newspaper to read the headlines that he'd already studied on the outward trip early that morning.

'You've dropped something, Dad,' Olivia told him from the other side of the room.

He sniffed the air. 'It's not one of mine.' He sniffed some more, 'I can't smell 'owt.'

'Don't be so disgusting!' she scolded him, bending down

to pick up the scrap of paper that lay at his feet. 'It's a receipt. Oh, hang on,' she noticed the writing on the back. 'It's a note from Val, I think!' she yelped, delighted.

'What's she say?' Emma asked, puzzled.

'She's called round and phoned but no one's been in. Huh! I know that feeling,' she muttered. 'She hopes Dad's all right and she'll call again. Oh, and she's hidden your milk round the back of the house.'

'I didn't call her either, did I?' Emma thought aloud. 'It's probably too late now, too. What time is it?'

'It's only five to eleven,' Olivia excitedly reached for the telephone. 'Let me call!'

She didn't need to look up the number. It was inscribed on her memory. She and Edward had, at one time, talked for hours daily.

Her parents looked on in admiration as she jiggled up and down waiting for a response.

'Hello Val? Who's this?' she teased. '...Yes!' she screamed and hopped around, beaming a lovely white set of teeth down the line. '...Yes, I'm here with them at home. It's so good to hear your voice. You sound a little breath-less, are you okay?... Good. How's Adrian and Liz?... Brilliant... Did she? Excellent. The clever bugger! Is she in bed?... If she's there, yes please,' she covered the mouth-piece. 'She's gone to get Liz!' she told the onlookers with glee.

'Can I have a word with Val when you're done?' asked Emma.

Olivia nodded, and her face told her parents that some-one at the other end was talking. 'It's meeee!' she yelled.

On the other side of town, the teenager was screaming her love and elation down the phone, and promised to sag off college the next day to visit Hulton instead.

'Emma wants a word, Mum,' she told Val.

The dressing-gown clad woman returned to the telephone. 'Hi, Emma! I bet you're over the moon aren't you?... Ha ha. No, I don't mind getting out of bed for news like this, don't worry about it... Oh, you know, nothing that I can tell you about now – perhaps one day! Are you at work tomorrow?... I'll see you tomorrow, then. The way Liz is jumping around here, we'll be there for breakfast. Bye, then. Oh, how's Dan?... That's good. You can fill me in when I see you... Yes, okay. See you tomorrow, then. Bye.'

Val was delighted with the news, and returned to the bedroom where Adrian was waiting patiently for her. 'What the hell was all the commotion?'

'Olivia's back home,' she smiled, removing her gown. 'Liz and me are going to see her tomorrow.'

'How marvellous! I bet they're relieved, aren't they?' he offered his open arms, admiring his wife's naked body. 'Now, where were we before we were so rudely interrupted?'

She lifted the duvet slightly and peered beneath. 'Looks like we'll have to start again from scratch.' She climbed in and held him tight to her, her hands holding his buttocks.

'Brrrr,' he shuddered. 'Your hands are ruddy cold!'

'What a day!' she laughed in awe. 'A daughter wearing bugger-all to college, a cleaner dying on me, we're halfway through the first shag we have in almost a year and the phone rings!'

He turned out the light, 'Well, don't you worry. There's nothing can stop us now.' He kissed her and rolled her on to her back, caressing her slender neck and moving slowly downwards, kissing sweetly as he went.

She was in heaven. She wanted him so badly. 'Oh God. Just screw me!' she moaned.

'Don't be so impatient,' he smooched.

'Mum!' the squeal from outside on the landing. The door burst open and light burst forth. 'Dad! Isn't it brill...?

Oh my God,' Liz retreated swiftly. 'Sorreee!' Val and Adrian crumpled into an hysterical embrace, the moment gone for good.

'Let's get away somewhere this weekend, Mr M,' she poked his chest. 'And you,' her teeth gritted, 'can bonk my brains out. If not, there's the distinct likelihood of filicide!'

He chuckled in sympathy with her frustration. 'Well, I don't normally respond to threats, *Mrs* M, but I don't want to be responsible for your inevitable arrest, so I guess you're on.'

'I'd better not be!' she punned, cupping his delicate parts and squeezing gently. 'Just you make sure your meat and veg are in full working order when I whistle.'

Breakfast was quiet at Wingate Farm. Liz, unusually not very hungry, seemed happy to study the table top while drinking her cup of coffee, while Adrian and Val said little but passed smiles and winks across the reclaimed pine surface.

'It was bloody embarrassing,' Liz told Carole on the phone. 'There's my Dad mooning at me and my Mum flat on her back – legs up, ready for it!'

'God, that's sick. Do they still do it, then, at their age?' the astounded friend asked.

Liz exhaled in wonder. 'I'm scarred for life, Caz,' she explained. 'My own parents. In our house too! Then this morning, bold as you like, they're like lovestruck kids! All kissy kissy and footsie under the table. Some people have no respect for their children, have they?'

'I'm sure mine gave up years ago,' said Carole. 'Mum was forty-three last week, they must have.' Youth reasoning.

'About last night,' Val broke the uneasy silence that accompanied them in the car. 'It's a bit awkward finding anyone in an intimate state I know, let alone your parents...'

'Aw, Mum! Do you have to?' Liz protested.

'What, be close to your father or talk about it?'

'Both.'

'Well yes, actually. It was as embarrassing for us as it was for you, and if you won't knock, you've only yourself to blame. Haven't you?' lectured the driver.

'S'pose so,' Liz shrugged. 'God it was a sight,' she chortled, seeing both the funny side and a chance to discomfort her mother a little more. 'Dad's arse up in the air, and I didn't know *you* were that supple!'

Both sat with grins on their faces for the remainder of the journey, Liz taking in the passing sights and Val concentrating on the road as best she could; her mind reliving the fleeting enjoyment of the previous night with her husband.

'What's happening with Mrs Almond then, Mum?' the funeral parlour by the dry cleaners reminding Liz of the strange tale her parents had to tell the previous afternoon.

'I'm not sure, luv. I'll try the doctor's later and see if they'll tell me anything.'

Liz thought, and studied her mother quizzically. 'How did you manage to perform last night, knowing you'd found a dead body?'

'The body we coped with,' Val giggled, 'it was our offspring that put us off. And anyway, I thought that was a closed subject?'

'It is,' Liz grinned. 'But two stiffs in one day? Can't be bad, Mother!'

Olivia was reclining on the sofa, her feet on the armrest when the doorbell rang.

'Bugger!' she cursed, not yet used to the fast swelling of her abdomen hindering her movement whenever she tried to rise.

'You'll have to watch your language with a baby in the house,' Dan warned as he went to open the door.

'Hi, Dan. How's the patient?' Val asked, air-kissing him on either cheek, and not waiting for his reply as she sped past towards the lounge, Elizabeth in hot pursuit.

'Hello, Val. Hello, Liz,' he told an empty hallway. 'I'm fine thanks. They had to sew my willy back on after a rabid dog bit it off, but apart from that…'

'What are you mumbling about?' Emma asked, coming down the stairs.

'Nothing. Come on, can't you hear they're here?' his eyes rolled towards the shrill sounds emanating from the lounge.

They entered the room to find all three women in tears, and Emma soon joined them.

'Bloody hell!' Dan groaned with a loud tut, and went to boil the kettle.

'What's this?' Liz asked, placing the palm of her hand on Olivia's stomach which had felt more than a little firm as they embraced.

'You're going to be an auntie,' she calmly replied, tears rolling down her face. 'Val,' taking her hand, 'I'm due in November, Grandma.'

Val's tears mirrored Olivia's and she stood speechless. This had to be one of the happiest moments of her life. She was coming to terms with losing her son and now, all being well of course – after all, she *never* counted her chickens – she would have a grandchild to remember him by. She hugged Olivia tight. 'Thank you,' she wept.

Liz and Emma were still exchanging tissues when Dan carefully opened the serving hatch door to check that the coast was clear for bringing in coffee.

'Get in here, Grandad,' Val ordered. 'I wanna give you a smacker!'

'Don't go away, I'll be right with ya,' he laughed, and scurried to join the delirious celebrations.

'Pucker up, sucker,' she squealed; planting a huge lipstick-covered kiss on his lips.

Over copious amounts of coffee for most, and orange juice for Olivia, all four recounted tales from recent times to the expectant mum, frequently helping each other on finer detail and the 'best bit' that was often being omitted. Olivia sat and laughed her heart out. It was so good to be home. No one had, thankfully, asked why exactly she went, or where she'd been; she wasn't ready for a full inquisition just yet. She'd prefer snippets to come out gradually when she felt able.

Edward was brought into the conversation as many times as each judged possible, and Olivia's fears that she would break down at the very mention of his name were soon quashed.

'I remember last year at Ayers Rock,' she started with a fit of giggles, 'when we set off to walk up the bloody thing and I couldn't make it past Chicken Rock...' her laughter became uncontrolled.

'Was that when he went on with all that junk in the carrier bag, and didn't realise that you'd stopped?' Liz asked. 'The daft sod!'

Olivia held her stomach, helpless, able only to nod. 'Oh Christ!' she hooted. 'Get me to the toilet, quick!'

They got her to her feet, and she dashed to avoid embarrassing herself.

'It's wonderful news, Emma!' Val said with happiness. 'You must both be so pleased.'

'It was shock enough to hear from her, let alone her little surprise when we got to London,' Dan began.

'London?' Liz enquired.

'A long story for another time, luv,' Emma assured her. 'She's safe, and that's all that matters.'

'What about your holiday and things?' Val was aiming at the surprise Emma had lined up for Daniel's birthday.

'Shit!' Emma looked at Dan in horror. 'I'd forgotten all about the holiday!'

'Don't look at me, I'd not thought about it. I'm only a fella,' he defended himself before any accusation.

'We'll just have to cancel it,' she said pursing her lips; her mind made up.

'Cancel what?' Olivia asked, returning to the room, now hushed in eager anticipation of the outcome of this unexpected dilemma facing Dan and Emma.

'Cancel what?' Emma repeated.

'Yeah, cancel what?'

'Cancel what, Dan?' she searched for help across the room.

He shook his head and raised his hands like a Parisian disputing his *pétanque* score.

'So, we've established that you're cancelling something because of me,' Olivia observed. 'Question is, what?'

'You're bloody useless, Daniel Beech!' Emma accused. 'What's this mean?' Mimicking his actions.

'It means…' doing it again, 'precisely bugger all!'

Val looked disapprovingly at Olivia's parents, and the young woman caught the expression. 'Val?' she asked with a 'somebody *please* tell me' face.

Val looked at Emma with similar countenance.

'Our holiday,' Emma said simply.

'Why?' Olivia was confused. 'Don't on my account.'

'Well, you're home now, and we don't want to go rushing off the moment you get home,' her mother replied.

'Oh, bugger off the pair of ya!' Olivia thumbed towards the door. 'Go on, get them bags packed and piss off!' she ordered.

'We're not going and leaving you on your own,' insisted Emma.

'She'll be all right, Em,' Dan encouraged.

'I'm *not* leaving my daughter and her bump, while we go off to enjoy ourselves.'

'Why ever not?' he asked.

'*Because*,' she glared with venom. 'That's why,' her heels digging in deeper.

Val thought swiftly, putting her idea to the gathering; and with great excitement from Liz and Olivia, Emma reluctantly succumbed to their cajoling. Dan beamed in triumph, and Val looked forward to spending some time with the daughter-in-law she'd never had.

'You're a bastard, Beech,' Emma told him as he rolled over to cuddle her that night in bed.

'Why now?' he laughed into her back. He knew that something the size of the plight of the Third World was about to be laid at his feet.

'Because I love you,' she began, 'I *won't* go into detail,' an air of haughtiness intoned. 'Let's just say that you're a complete bastard for not supporting me earlier.'

'Okay luv,' he smiled. 'Will this do?' he cupped her breasts from behind.

She *knew* he'd joke his way out of trouble. 'It's an improvement,' she smiled.

'So I'm not a bastard, then?'

'No. We'll promote you to "absolute git".'

'Recognition at last,' he said snuggling into her, his fingers gently wobbling the comfortable protuberances.

A moment later there was danger in her voice. 'Will you stop that?' she calmly warned. 'Or else it won't be a rabid dog that bites your dick off!'

★

The lorry stopped across the driveway entrance and the

driver leaped out, delivery schedule in hand and scruffy flat cap on head. 'I'll wait here, Charlie,' his large passenger called lethargically through the open cab window.

Charlie looked for a number plate to confirm he had the right house, and noting the ceramic '39' tile on the front wall, strode confidently to the door.

A man with bandaged head answered, scratching his rounded stomach.

'Allerdale Nurseries!' said the man with clipboard.

'Hulton Hardware. Your go,' replied Dan.

'Eh?' the caller stumped.

'It's your turn again. Hulton Hardware,' he repeated.

'You what?'

'Oh, I thought we were playing a game – "Name That Store!" or something,' Dan joked without smiling, knowing full well what the man had meant in the first place. 'What about Allerdale Nurseries?'

'That's where I'm from.'

'Grand, I'm chuffed for ya. What about it?'

'Deliv'ry,' persisted Charlie.

'Are we playing again?' Dan asked, making things as difficult as he could until the stranger explained himself, for Dan certainly didn't know what was going on.

'I've no time for this malarkey!' he pointed a blunt finger at Dan. 'I've a deliv'ry from Allerdale Nurseries. Where d'ya want it?'

'What is it?' said Dan, genuine intrigue now holding him.

The man looked officiously at his clipboard. 'One two seatah,' a badly attempted BBC pronunciation commenced, 'screuwll bark bench. Rhosewood. Paid in foowl. Missars Beech, thirty-nine Parkland Drive…' He looked over the board at Dan. 'You're not Missus Beech, are you?' he observed accusingly in his normal accent to the house-holder's shaking head.

'I'm the other half,' Dan replied, hoping his face didn't reflect his 'Are you really such a pillock?' thoughts.

'Don't think you'll both fit on this seat then if there's two the size o' you!' Charlie tried to joke with an overacted laugh, but he didn't see Dan reciprocating, and swiftly returned to his list and terrible attempt at polished accent. 'Herrrr-hum,' his throat cleared. '...Parkland Drive, Hulton. Telephown number...'

'All right,' Dan had heard far too much already. 'You've got the right place; let's see it.'

'Whare?' his voice in turmoil.

'Just get it off the bloody wagon, and I'll *tell* you whare!' Dan's impatience with the man showing.

Charlie whistled towards the lorry and yanked his head backwards, indicating the time for movement from his mate. This wasn't forthcoming. A further whistle received equal response, and Dan implied that Charlie should perhaps consider walking back to the vehicle, ''Cos you'll have to help 'im carry it any road,' he suggested.

Without looking at the customer, Charlie returned to the cab and threw open the door.

'Are you asleep in there, Bob?' he hollered.

From Dan's vantage point, Bob said something to Charlie, Charlie waved his arms around a little, Bob said something else, Charlie grabbed Bob's arm and pulled him down from the cab, Bob was much bigger than Charlie, Charlie poked Bob, Bob punched Charlie, Charlie fell over clutching his nose, Bob said something to Charlie along the paraphrastic lines of 'You silly billy', Charlie rolled around a little, Bob went to the back of the lorry, Charlie rolled around some more, Bob lifted the two-seater rosewood bench with scrolled back from the lorry, and carried it to Dan's feet.

'Where'd you want it, mate?' asked Bob.

'Anywhere you want to put it, Bob!' replied Dan.

Bob smiled. 'Where do *you* want it?'

Dan guided the man and furniture to the back garden, and it was placed on the patio facing the lawn. 'No doubt the boss'll tell me it's in the wrong place,' Dan joked.

'Well, there's more sun over that side,' Bob pointed to the opposite side of the patio. 'Which way's your garden face?' he asked looking toward the cloudy skies in search of the sun.

'Er, south. Could be south-east.' Dan wasn't too sure.

'Well, then. Save you the earache later on,' and the delivery man moved to seat to the sunniest place available on the crazy paving.

'Thanks,' Dan's surprise showing in his voice. 'Thanks a lot. Do you want a brew?'

'No ta,' the man's head shook. 'Better peel that pompous shite off the floor and pick up me cards at the nurseries.'

'Why pick the cards up?' frowned Dan.

'He's the fuckin' gaffer!' Bob grimaced. 'Don't think he'll be too happy wi' me, do you?'

Dan's face was the picture of concern.

'Don't worry,' the man smiled with renewed pride, "e's had it comin' for ages.'

Dan shook the man's hand. 'Good luck, then. Sounds like you're best off out of it,' he laughed in admiration.

'Absofuckin'lutely!' he agreed. 'See y'around!' Bob waved and sauntered down the driveway, aggressively offering a filthy rag to Charlie, who had propped himself up against a wheel arch, blood gushing from his face.

Dan went back into the house and checked on Olivia. She was still on the settee, feet up and eyes closed. She'd be furious that she'd missed all the fun.

'Bit of excitement, Dad,' she said, her eyes still tight.

'How do you women do that?' he puzzled.

'Do what?' her eyes remaining closed.

'You can listen to someone else's conversations when you're talking to someone completely different, you know when a bloke's goin' to put 'is foot in it before he's even opened his mouth, and most annoying,' he stressed, 'you can bloody well see what's going on with your eyes shut! You and your mother are from the same piggin' mould,' he accused.

'The superior sex, Dad,' she opened her eyes to smile at him. 'Quick, come and feel the kick on this!'

He held out his hand and she placed it on to her stomach. 'Can't feel a... oh my God! What a boot he's got,' he gasped gleefully. 'The little bugger!'

They enjoyed the moment together and she took his hand. 'Thanks Dad. You've been brilliant. Mum too. I'm sorry for all the upset,' she smiled painfully. 'And I know things are hardly perfect with this one,' she looked at her bump.

'Stop apologising, will you?' Dan told her. 'I won't lie and say it wasn't a shock when you first told us, but life never turns out how you plan it – doesn't matter how well things are going. Odds are, the better they're going, the harder the knock when it comes. You don't need me to tell you that, your life's been oiked arse over...' she grinned, and he corrected himself, '...turned upside down over the last year or so. You know me, Ollie,' he continued, 'I'm not big on feelings, but we love you more than anything else in this world, and me and your Mum *have* been here before, so it's nothing new.'

'Really?' she quizzed. 'How do you mean?'

He laughed. 'When's your birthday?'

'You're joking!' she was astonished at herself. 'I never knew.'

'Grandad Newton had a shotgun to my back he did!' he fibbed.

'*No?*'

'Well, it was an adjustable wrench actually. Plumbers didn't have much call for guns as a rule in them days,' he smirked.

'I'd have married Ed, you know,' Olivia suddenly turning serious; her eyes welling up with darkened sadness and mouth sinking.

'I know, luvvy. He was a good 'un.' He stroked her hair. 'And he'll live on in Cuthbert,' his voice becoming livelier.

She looked horrified. 'Cuthbert? Not on your Nellie, chummy lumps!'

'That's my girl!' Dan's broad smile told her that he'd once again brought her round to looking forward, and not dwelling on past might-have-beens.

She pulled her tongue out at him in defeated acknowledgement. He blew a victorious raspberry back, and suggested with a chuckle that she get off her fat arse and do something.

'Language, Father,' she warned, pointing to the unborn.

Emma was exhausted when she arrived home from her first day back at work, and flopped straight down next to Olivia on the settee.

'I'm buggered!' she moaned to no one in particular.

'That's fifty pence from you, please, Mother,' Olivia shook an old shoe box under her mother's nose; a slot cut in the lid.

'Eh?' Emma's half-hearted reply.

'It's here on the list. "Bloody", "Bugger" and any derivatives are 50p to the swear box.'

'Bloody big swear box!' Emma choked.

'The rate you're going, it'll be full by bedtime. That's another 50p,' her daughter insisted.

'What's this in aid of?' she peered at the box.

'This baby's not going to be brought up in a swearing house. Dad's already put a fiver in, that's a day's credit for him, unless he uses the "F" or "A" word.'

'"A" word?' Emma queried.

Olivia frowned. 'Nice try, Mother! "Bottom" to you.'

'So "bottom" is okay then?'

'Perfectly.'

'Good. "I'm bottomed", then!' she smirked.

'*In* the right context, Emma Beech!' she kissed her Mum. 'Welcome home, anyway. Hard day for the workers?'

'Don't ask. You?'

'Hectic!' she swooned. 'A bad dose of Richard and Judy this morning, Australian soaps till you're screaming insanity over lunch, then minor celebrities in home-knitted jumpers pretending to be literate with embarrassed members of the public, all afternoon. What more can a girl cram into a busy day?' She pulled her hair in mock frenzy.

Emma laughed. Daytime television was hardly inspiring for the fully mobile, let alone for those wedged in a chair all day. 'You should get off your fat ar... bottom then!'

'That's exactly what brought this about,' Olivia shook the box again. 'I'll drop an "IOU" in there for you, shall I?'

Dan brought in a hot cup of tea, thinking he'd found his new vocation in life – making milky drinks. He welcomed Emma home with a peck on the cheek, and offered a biscuit.

'Isn't tea ready then?' she asked with sarcasm, knowing full well it wouldn't be.

'Not quite,' Dan answered earnestly. 'It'll be about half an hour.'

'Bloody hellfire! What's got into you?' she blurted in surprise.

'50p!' the collector called.

'It's worth a tenner,' Emma confessed, still astonished at his revelation.

'Take your brew and get yourself showered and

changed,' he told her. 'Go on; chop, chop!'

Emma took the mug, and headed for the bathroom. Dan grinned at Olivia and passed her the biscuit he knew she wouldn't refuse.

Washing away the day's problems, Emma was relieved to be home. There had been the obvious questions about where she'd been, and why hadn't she turned into work on Monday? Poor David had got the third degree as he'd opened up on what was to be his day off, and having promised not to say anything, found it difficult to repel Sharon's barrage of pointed questions.

Her on-off relationship with Anthony was back on apparently, following her discovery that he'd got his eye on the plain-looking girl in the shoe shop next door. Emma had not thought of Sharon as the jealous type, but wonders never ceased. Perhaps one day she'd lose her voice; or was that too much like wishful thinking? She, along with everyone else at the shop, was pleased to hear Emma's news anyway, and David even cracked open a bottle of bubbly left over from a weddings promotion night last year, to celebrate at lunchtime.

A knock at the front door broke her train of thought, but knowing that Dan would get it, she soon returned to analysing the events of the day. No one had checked her work over the two days she was away, and the special option held for Mr and Mrs Milne's trip to New Zealand had expired. Luckily they hadn't been in and paid a deposit, and she was able to reactivate the same booking before their planned visit to the shop tomorrow.

If anyone had to be messed around, it wasn't the Milnes. They were regular travellers, and always came to Emma for their reservations which was nice. But they were a proper pain in the arse. No, they weren't. In Olivia's new regime, they were a pain in the bottom. A tolerable pain, though. It was just that everything had to be explained in minute detail, and Mrs Milne was sure to ask the same old question tomorrow – 'How do aeroplane pilots know which way to go? There's no signs up there, are there?' Silly old bat! Oh, the joys of her job.

She decided to wash her hair, and realised that the shampoo was empty. She clambered out of the bath and dashed tip-toe, naked to the door. Scampering along the landing towards the airing cupboard to get a fresh bottle, Olivia emerged from her bedroom with a pile of magazines.

'Something smells good!' Emma yelped to the wide-eyed young woman.

'Yeah, it's ready when you are,' she replied, shielding her eyes in pretence.

Emma dashed back to the bathroom, Olivia watching her wobbling buttocks disappear behind the door once more. The water was cool as she ducked her head into the path of the tiny jets of water, and the shudder made goose bumps rise all over her body. Suddenly, she didn't fancy washing her hair, the smell of history being created downstairs was too tempting.

She dried vigorously, and clothed quickly in tracksuit and slippers. With great occasion she descended the stairs, taking in the aromas of Dan's efforts as she went. Long intakes of spicy essence excited her taste buds, and she licked her lips in anticipation. Was she dreaming? This was an event to write on the calendar in big letters – 'DAN COOKS!'

He met her in the hallway, 'Sit!' his concise instruction.

She obeyed, and went straight through to the dining lounge to take her usual seat by the serving hatch. 'Table-cloth and napkins as well?' she observed.

'Of course, Mother,' Olivia offered her a bottle of wine to check the label. 'To Madam's liking?'

'I'll say!' Emma was savouring this.

Olivia poured a glass of wine each for her parents, and a

large tumbler of grape juice for herself. 'Next best thing,' she admitted with reluctance.

The hatch doors opened and a wonderful cacophony of smells surged through into the lounge. 'I can't believe you've done this, Dan.' Emma was stunned.

'No problems. It's *dead* easy, this catering lark, when you put your mind to it,' he boasted.

'Am I allowed to ask what's first?' she asked him excitedly.

'Of course,' he proudly replied. 'A number 6, number 8 and prawn crackers all round. Followed by 23, 48 and 65 with special fried rice. It came a few minutes early, so get it while it's still hot.'

Dan couldn't understand why Emma was so upset. He thought she'd be pleased – she used to be so fond of Chinese food. That was female logic, though. At least Olivia's swear box was in for a handsome contribution, following the barrage of abuse hurled by his wife through the hatch earlier on. She must have the decorators in, he reflected, with his own unique male logic.

'I T'S RATHER INTRUSIVE all this, don't you think?' he asked uneasily, closing the pages for a moment.

'Oh shut up and read!' Val groaned. 'I'm trying to sleep.'

He watched her roll over, screwing her eyes tight and moistening her lips, ready to sleep. He'd better do as she said.

D. 10 – Wed 19 June: 10.05 a.m. 'Oh what a beautiful morning, oh what a beautiful day!' Phew! It's sunny this morning, and boy, should it be! What a night last night! Livvy's nipped down to the laundry place in the arcade with most of our clothes to be fumigated while we go out of the city today, so I'll catch up with the most exciting part of the trip yet.

After the Chinese last night, we came back and out of the blue, Livvy suggested we go the whole hog for the first time. Jesus! It was Heaven! I love her so much, it was the best feeling I've ever experienced IN MY LIFE! I thought I'd filled that condom. Unreal! Remember 18 June, Sydney for the rest of your life Edward Mallory, or else you deserve to have your balls lopped off.

'Oh Lord!' Adrian cried with great embarrassment.

'Shhhhhh!'

'Sorry,' he whispered.

That's not all though! I'm woken this morning with a warm feeling down there, and I thought I'd pissed myself or something. She's only waking me up by nibbling my bits! I can't cope! She wanted more this morning, and it's such a brilliant feeling being closer to her. I think she might be forgetting the knickers from now on.

We've not had breakfast yet. We decided to get something on our way to Sydney Central railway station, which we think's about a fifteen – twenty minute walk away from the hotel. Viv suggested that we go to a place called the Hawkesbury Museum in Windsor, north west of Sydney. She had a really good time there once with a bloke, so that's where we're off to when Livvy gets back. More later.

'This son of ours was a bit, er…' Adrian couldn't find the words he was looking for.

'Where are you up to?' Val asked sleepily, rolling back towards him and sliding her fingers over his chest, knowing she wasn't going to win.

He checked his facts before replying. 'Day ten; still in Sydney.'

'Means nothing to me. What's happening?'

'They've just… you know…' he struggled again.

'Ah,' she smiled at his discomfort. 'Yes, he was a bit happy after that, wasn't he?' her diplomacy not really aiding Adrian's plight for self-expression.

'Happy?' his surprised eyes telling hers she'd understated. 'Sounds like he was getting an erection just thinking about it.'

'Don't be awful, Adrian!' she told him. 'He was in love. Don't you remember the first time we made love?' her voice softened to a purr; her fingers walking suggestively across his chest.

'Uh-huh,' he smiled. 'You looked delectable; good enough to eat,' he recalled.

'I seem to remember you did,' her eyebrows raised momentarily.

'Those were the… Hey! Liz hasn't read all of this has

she?' his face turning to terror.

''Course she has.'

'Oh my Lord! Who needs *The Joy Of Sex* when you've got your brother's diary to read, eh?' he despaired.

'You're a funny one!' she laughed. 'She's had the birds and bees talk. In fact, she tried giving it to me some time ago. And in any case, her brother's diary is nothing compared to a parental demonstration is it?'

'Oh yes,' he cringed, sliding a little further under the duvet. 'I was forgetting.'

'You read on, and don't worry about any saucy bits. How do you think Olivia found herself pregnant?'

He agreed that he was shutting the stable door a little belatedly, and cautiously turned back to the open pages.

Hmmm. Day 10 started a hell of a lot better than it continued. It's now just before 11 p.m. and it's been a funny old day all round.

Set off for the station at about 10.25 and followed the map in the right direction. Caught breakfast along the way – hot dogs from the place on the corner, where we took a short cut to save us from going all the way to Hyde Park just to double back on ourselves. Anyway, got to the station, bought the tickets but couldn't find where we should be getting the train from. There seemed only to be a dozen or so platforms, and the guide to services said that our train was going in ten minutes from platform number ninety twelve.

Finally found a guard who told us we were on the wrong level – local services went from downstairs. We dashed down the stairs and along the concourse as best we could through the commuters and travellers, and eventually found the huge old board that included Windsor, with little lights next to names of places where the trains would stop on the line to Richmond. We pushed through the gate and up the stairs to the platform, only to see the train pulling away! Next one, 1 hour! Great! It's an hour's trip there, so it'll be after 1 p.m. when we arrive. We waited around on the platform, me reading as per, while Livvy wrote more postcards.

The trains here are different to ours at home. You get on at the door (rather spookily!) and there's a few seats by the entrance, then there's steps up and steps down for you to choose upper or lower deck! We went upstairs and it's all bench seats with a pendulum-type back rest, so you can change the direction you face on the bench. I suppose it's better than our trains with the fixed seats, where you either go forwards or backwards. Having said that, our train seats are a lot comfier! It's a good idea, anyway.

Well, we're sat on this bench, not many others in our carriage. Some bloke with a bunch of flowers, a woman by the door with a pram full of bin bags, and a couple of kids in the nearest thing to a school uniform I've seen yet.

An hour of the New South Wales countryside, more postcards and a bit of reading from the pair of us, and we finally get to Windsor.

Imagine the scene. A bit of twisted Hitchcock. Cary Grant gets off the bus (read 'train') in the middle of nowhere. A dust ball rolls across the road (read 'track') and there's no one around. A car passes (car's all right now, there was a road from the station) but doesn't stop. You wonder where he is. So does he. Another car goes by. You wonder if it'll stop. He hopes it will, he hasn't a bloody clue where he is. So you've got the scene now? It's a thrilling arrival in Windsor.

Into the station building we go to ask where civilisation might be found, and we're pointed in the direction that the cars went. We set off, passing a number of closed shops, houses that seem to be in need of repair, and across what seemed to be a main junction in the road. No one to be seen at the car dealership on the corner, so we continue in the same direction, past a lake on the left until eventually there's a motel-cum-grog shop with a bloke loading half a pallet of beer on to his pick-up truck outside. Hawkesbury Museum? we ask, now gagging for a drink and something to eat. He thinks for a moment then 'Keep on going!' he says. We're given the dot in the distance as the start of Windsor centre. We're here now, so the real temptation to turn round and get on the next train back to Sydney is overcome in our determination to find this place where Viv had a whale of a time. And if she had a good time, it must be good!

The dot becomes a shape. The shape becomes a building. The building becomes lots of buildings, and ultimately we reach Windsor! How do I describe it? Quite quaint – in an Australian kind of way. Nice, pleasant. Nothing obviously wrong but…! I think 'Functional with a Psycho feel' is perhaps the most apt!

We had lunch in a café that doubled up as the local gift shop. We considered the other café that had the town butchers attached, but thought better of it. The thing is, everyone's so very nice and friendly. Is that a good thing, or is it that friendliness that added to the feeling that at any moment, we were going to be eaten by a hungry mob led by the parish vicar?

We asked the woman in the shop, who never stopped smiling, where we'd find the Hawkesbury Museum, and followed her directions – end of the street, turn left down the hill towards the Hawkesbury River and it's on the left.

We reached the river and turned left. Houses. Back to the foot of the short hill. No, not there either. Back up the hill. We're at the main road again. Some bugger's having us on, we say. Back down the hill on the basis that it's got to be here somewhere and lo! and behold, there it is – on the left! A house! A bloody house! We've come all this way to see a house. Very interesting I've no doubt. I couldn't say for sure, we didn't go in! Livvy was in tears, I was up the wall, and God help Viv when we see her!

Ice cream was required! A good $6 triple flavour, full fat ice cream each from the place facing the top of the hill, and a seat outside in the sunshine. Next, a few photos of the place to prove we'd been, and an unsurprising unanimous decision to leave. We first arrived at Windsor Station at 1.05 p.m. We set off for the station again at 3.05 p.m. Super idea – coming here for a day out!

We had to be back at the hotel no later than 6 p.m. anyway, to collect the laundry from downstairs and we did just that. A little before six (good job we found sod all to do in Windsor!), we arrived at the laundry to be given three bags. One of clean but unironed

*whites. The second of clean but unironed coloureds. The third, dry
cleaned denims. Did I say merely 'dry cleaned'? Sorry, I meant to
say dry cleaned with stay-pressed creases.*

*I'm writing this sat here in carefully ironed jeans, the virgin
crease down the front so sharp, the sheets on the bed are shredding
beneath me.*

*The whites have been boil washed so our T-shirts don't come
anywhere near us any more, and Livvy's blue sweatshirt's run into
everything not previously blue. Mustn't grumble though, we're
British! We asked to have clean clothes – that's what we got! So
what if we look like a couple of nerds? We are calm. We are truly
calm. If I say it often enough, we will be calm.*

*Yes. All in all, it's been a funny old day. Tomorrow's got to be
better! Who knows, we may even get mugged. That would be a
small improvement.*

Val was watching Adrian's face as he read. Every now and
again, a brief smile would appear and then an intense
concentration.

'It's good this, isn't it?' he commented, noticing her
gaze.

'Told you so. He prattles on a bit though sometimes.'

'No, he doesn't!' Adrian defended.

'I'm not being nasty. He just goes into detail a bit, that's
all.'

'There's nothing wrong with verbosity, it makes for
fuller reading. I can picture exactly what's going on with
text like this. I think he deserves top marks,' Adrian
challenged.

'It's a diary, dear, not a thesis on everything he sees,' she
pointed out. 'But yes, it's beautifully written,' she agreed.

'Thank you,' Adrian felt vindicated in the defence of his
son.

'Even the waffle!' Val needed the last word, and her
dewy-eyed face was too much for him to argue the toss. He

wished her tight sleep, and marking his place in the journal, rolled over to snore away the remaining hours of darkness.

It was a miserable morning. The wind blew trees at a severe angle, and the rain! Olivia studied the weather from the sanctuary of her bedroom. Downstairs, her mother was getting ready to leave for work; her father having left in the early hours for his first day back after Mum's failed murder attempt. It was Thursday *already*. She couldn't believe how quickly the days had passed this week. Tomorrow was her first appointment with the doctor here in Hulton; she hoped the weather would be kinder – she'd have to walk the mile or so there on her own; her parents being at work, and there still being no car.

Her mother was clomping around downstairs – the sure sign that she was stressed-out over something. Olivia decided to stay put, out of harm's way until the coast was clear. She'd had a fitful night; the baby kicking and punching for all it was worth. She was finding it difficult to find a comfortable position in bed. Thank the Lord she didn't suffer from piles as well.

She heard her name called from the hallway, and considered pretending that she was still asleep, but that wasn't fair. She went to the landing and leaned out over the banister rail. 'Yep?' she responded.

Emma was making the most of her hair in the mirror. 'When did the garden seat come?' She'd noticed it when taking out the now foul-smelling cartons from Wong's Restaurant to the dustbin.

'My birthing stool?' she joked. 'Yesterday afternoon.'

'Why didn't someone tell me?' she pushed at her hair some more. 'I've been waiting for that for ages.'

'You weren't really in that sort of "Oh goody!" mood last night, were you, Mum?' the younger reminded her.

'Well, that's your father's fault!' she replied petulantly,

her locks not doing as they should.

'Apparently so,' Olivia pouted, not sounding convinced. 'Perfect weather to enjoy it today, as well!' she said with great amusement, turning to gaze out of the window.

Emma studied her daughter through the mirror as she came carefully down the stairs. She didn't want to go to work today. She'd rather spend time with Olivia, but with holidays coming up in a little over a week, she couldn't take yet more time.

'Are you sure you'll be okay with Val and Adrian?' she asked the reflection.

''Course I will!' Olivia wondered where the change in topic had come from. 'They're hardly strangers, are they? Look Mum, go off and enjoy yourselves,' she encouraged.

'But what about your birthday?' she persisted.

'Mum!' Olivia was standing firm. 'I've said it's nothing to worry about, haven't I? You deserve a holiday, so damn well go!'

Emma's face wasn't the picture of happiness, but she wasn't going to argue. 'I'll see you later.' She donned her coat and removed her umbrella from behind the telephone table. 'Your dad should be home by mid-afternoon. I don't think he'll be playing trains today – not if this weather keeps up, anyway.'

Olivia waved goodbye from the lounge window, and pottered around in the kitchen for a few minutes, making her favourite breakfast – banana and Marmite on toast. The toast wasn't quite browned under the grill when the telephone rang.

'Hello?' she answered.

'Emma?' the lady's voice.

'No, sorry she's just left for work. Can I take a message for you?' her efficiency amazing herself.

'No, thank you. I'd just heard her daughter was back, and thought I'd make sure it wasn't merely gossip. She's had a terrible time,' the caller continued, unaware of whom she was talking to.

'Yes, I believe so,' Olivia was becoming irked. 'Are you sure I can't say you called?'

'Well, all right then. Have you got a pen?'

'Yes, I have.'

'And a bit—'

'Of paper, yes,' Olivia drew a sharp intake of breath.

'Are you ready?'

'Yes, I'm ready,' her eyes rolling in irritation.

'It's Mrs Toop here.'

'As in "wig"?' Olivia asked with asperity.

The woman clearly sounded offended. 'That's T-O-O-P. Toop.'

'Okay, Mrs Toop. I'll pass the message on for you.'

'Thank you,' the woman's tone was acidic. 'Do you know if that daughter *has* returned?' her tone turning to attack.

'She has as a matter of fact. And it's nice to be home again, thank you, Mrs Toop. Goodbye,' Olivia slammed the phone down, shaking.

She was upset now for her parents. People all over the village must be gossiping about them and their errant daughter. Had they nothing better to do with their tiny little lives? Were they so sad that they had to fill their days with other people's business, and make up what they weren't sure of? 'Bloody vultures!' Oh, 50p to the box.

The telephone rang again. 'Hello!' she replied sharply, still annoyed.

'Olivia? Is that you?' Liz's voice at the other end.

'Oh, hi, Liz. Sorry about that.'

'Sound a bit nowty this morning, luv,' she observed in mock maternal tones. 'Are you taking it easy and putting your feet up? I do hope you're not overdoing it. Are you eating properly? Have you had a shit today? Must make sure you have regular shits, you know.'

'Stop it!' Olivia laughed. 'You'll know what it's like one day, lady.'

'...Nothing like good healthy bowels, I say. How's your tits? Hurting, are they? If they don't now, they will! Ooh yes, you'll know you've got mammaries by the time she's born! Then she'll be wanting to chomp on 'em. That's all right if your nipples aren't cracked, and before they cut their teeth of course. Baby's teeth that is, not the nipples.'

'Will you shut up? What do you want?' Olivia tried to change the subject, her sides aching.

'...And stretch marks. What with them and very coarse veins, you'll look like an A–Z of Manchester by the time you're ready to drop,' Liz continued in full flow. 'Natural birth is it? Not thought of water or riding a Harley David-son over cobbled streets? I'd go with the natural if I were you. Legs in stirrups, and some fella sticking his fist up your muff to have a good grope around. Can't beat it I say! Just as long as they leave your pubes intact. Nothing so scratchy as shaved pubes is there?' she finally snorted laughter.

'What *have* you been drinking?' Olivia chuckled, wiping her face free of laughter tears.

'It's living in this madhouse. Are you sure you don't want to change your mind about stopping here?'

'Has Mum put you up to this?' asked Olivia, desperate to sit down and stretching the telephone's curly cable to reach the stairs.

'No way. I just thought I'd warn you before it's too late.'

'Gee thanks.'

'Hey, that's the kinda kiddy I am. What you up to today?'

'Salvaging my burnt breakfast, but apart from that, not much. Why?'

'Want some company? Me and Carole are bored. We've no lectures till three this afternoon because of some work

they're doing to the heating system. Can we come over?'
she begged.

''Course you can. What time will you be here?'

'I'm meeting Caz in town, so, about ten do?'

'Yeah. Gives me time to haul myself into and out of the
bath. If you don't get an answer when you knock, call the
RSPCA – I'll be beached somewhere upstairs!'

'Get off! You're not that big,' Liz laughed.

'No, but I feel it,' Olivia sighed. 'I'll see you later then,
ya mad cow!'

'Moo!' Liz bellowed and the phone clicked dead.

Olivia wrote a note for her mum on the pad by the telephone:

*Thurs. 8.30 a.m. Mum. Wiggy Woman phoned to be nosy.
Ollie xx*

Liz's manic humour had cheered her spirits, although some
of the things she'd joked about were a little too close to the
truth for comfort. At least she wasn't going to be stuck at
home all day on her own with only the television to keep
her company. She hadn't seen Carole for ages – probably
since last Christmas, so it would be nice to catch up with
her. She wondered if that dishy fella of hers was still on the
scene – Dave was it? He was a bit of all right.

Bathed and ready for her visitors, Olivia had time to kill.
She resolutely ignored the television remote control, and
considered her options. Her music was upstairs in a box –
why did she leave that note for her parents to clear her
room? The radio didn't appeal. She took herself back
upstairs to her bedroom, and picked up the diary that
Emma had returned to her. How embarrassing. Her parents
knew every little detail of her sex life with Ed! She blushed
but smiled at the thought of him. Rubbing her tummy, she
told her passenger that Mummy was going to read him (for

it was going to be a boy, she'd convinced herself) a story about his Daddy and Mummy. 'There's lots of stories in this book about your Daddy,' she told him. 'Happy stories,' and returning to the lounge, she settled down to read, whispering any words that would normally incur a contribution to the swear box.

The doorbell rang, and Olivia heard her name called by two desperate-sounding voices. She got to her feet as quickly as she could, and supported the small of her back as she headed for the door. There stood Liz and Carole, soaking wet through and not an umbrella between them.

They squeezed past her and inside, offering their helloes and leaving a wet trail towards the lino-floored kitchen, where they peeled off their coats and jeans.

'Do you want to borrow some clothes?' Olivia enquired, with an inference that she wasn't going to be sitting with two half-naked girls when her dad returned home.

They both accepted the offer.

'I've got dungarees and a smock, who wants what?' she joked.

Carole looked horrified. 'I'll have the smock, Liz'd prefer dungarees I think,' nodding towards Liz, already stripped down to her bra and knickers.

Olivia laughed and handed them each a towel from the clothes maiden. 'I'll see what I've got.'

They were perched shivering on the edge of the settee when Olivia brought them down a pair of jeans and a jumper a-piece. 'Hope they're okay,' she offered.

'Thanks Livvy,' Liz's mouth chattered. 'You all right?'

'Yeah, fine. Just telling this one a few stories about his dad.'

'Who?' Carole asked, scanning the room around her for 'this one'.

Liz pointed to Olivia's stomach. 'And you want to go into the police force?'

'Oh, fuck off!' she protested.

'Now then, girls,' Olivia established the ground rules regarding the swear box, but was charitable and overlooked Carole's outburst, as she wasn't aware of the penalties beforehand.

Liz was still excited at the prospect of Olivia staying at the farm and was telling Carole just what they'd be up to in the days together. Most of this was news to Olivia too, though she resisted the temptation to interrupt what were obviously meticulous plans. Olivia saw Edward in that planning. What you couldn't plan, wasn't worth doing with him. She fixed a smile on her face and let her mind wander, gently stroking her bump. She had sort of come to terms with him not being there, and taking each day as it came was the best way to cope with her loss. Her dad had been right the other night, he will live on. She felt an inner strength from that belief, and hoped that if there was a Heaven, he'd have a season ticket in its grandstand, watching her now.

Carole speaking her name brought her back into the present conversation. 'Olivia, you with us? I was just saying to Liz: the daft look on your face – you could be having an orgasm!'

'I wish!' she hooted. 'That'll be 50p.'

'Aw! What's wrong with "orgasm"?' she complained.

'Nothing; if you can get one,' Liz chirped. 'Cough up, girl.'

The suggestion of coffee was greeted warmly, but Olivia could really have done with one of them making it for her. Her feet and legs were sore today for some reason, and Junior was bouncing for all his worth. She opened the hatch doors so that she could continue a conversation while she put on the kettle.

'I was trying to think before, Carole,' she called through the aperture, 'when was the last time we saw each other?

Was it Christmas at Liz's?'

'I think it was,' Carole nodded eagerly. 'I asked Liz the very same thing on the bus here before.'

'How's that gorgeous bloke of yours? David, wasn't it?' she asked, moving out of sight to pour milk into the mugs. There was no reply, and Olivia began to think that perhaps she'd trodden into something smelly. She bobbed her head around the hatch door again. 'Not your gorgeous bloke any more?'

Liz shook her head. 'Dodgy ground, Livvy,' she warned.

'Oh! Sorry, Carole.'

'Don't be,' she bravely replied. 'He's still gorgeous – I see him around town now and again with his bit of stuff.'

'I bet she's a fat bitch, though, eh?' Olivia thought the fine worthy of the need to console.

'No, he's quite good looking himself actually. You might know him: Paul Vickers.'

'No!' Olivia was staggered at what her ears had relayed to her brain. 'Paul with Dave? What? Dave and Paul a couple? A bonky-bonky couple? Never!'

'Okay, 'Livia, I think that's enough,' Liz suggested.

'Bleaah, I'm blown away! Paul Vickers? Yuck-ee! I had a crush on him once!' she remembered in disgust. 'Oh God, I'm...'

'So was I,' Carole interrupted, attempting to close the subject for good. 'It's over, anyway.'

Olivia closed the hatch door and bit her fist hard. This pregnancy lark had really scattered her marbles, but Paul Vickers and Carole's Dave? Calm down, she told herself. Carole's obviously had a rough time over this, and you've just stirred it all up again! Let it drop. Forget it. Don't even think about it. She shivered, as though to exorcise the notion of Dave and Paul together.

Carrying the tray of mugs and tin of biscuits into the lounge, she placed them on the coffee table in front of the settee. 'So,' she said, hoping someone would start a fresh topic.

'So,' Liz repeated shrugging her shoulders, desperately trying to think of a suitable diversion.

Carole remained silent, wondering if she should read one of the magazines on the table by her side.

'Well,' Olivia took her seat again, still searching for someone's lead that wasn't forthcoming.

In the silence that followed, Olivia's mind raced. She hadn't *really* just asked that had she? This was surely one of those times when you only *think* your lips have allowed a thought to escape. Please let it be. Carole's reaction and Liz's spluttering of coffee proved her wrong, though. Olivia reddened. It was a normal question, she convinced herself. How *do* you cope, then, finding out your boyfriend's a dung-puncher?

'She's convinced it's a boy,' Emma explained to Mrs Milne. They had been in the shop for almost an hour already, and still not got around to discussing the itinerary for their New Zealand trip. Mr Milne was proud of his grandchildren and liked to chat about them, while Mrs Milne loved the thought of anybody's children and wanted to know the full run-down on Olivia, truly interested.

David observed from behind the one-way glass in his office, and reasoned that the amount of money that the Milnes would sign away at some time today, would more than make up for the time Emma was spending chatting. He supposed that was why Emma was so good at keeping customers – she built up strong relationships with the right ones.

'Was it the same daughter who went to New Zealand last year?' Mr Milne asked.

'Same daughter, but she didn't go to New Zealand. It was Australia with a couple of other places as stopover,'

Emma corrected.

'Australia, eh?' a questioning frown appearing. 'Why are we going to New Zealand, then?' he asked his wife.

'You *wanted* to go to New Zealand!' she told him.

'It's supposed to be wet in New Zealand. Let's go to Australia instead,' he decided.

Emma sighed. It usually helped if the customers knew *where* they wanted to go before booking. At least there hadn't been too much work put into this trip yet, so if they wanted to change their minds, let them get on with it.

'New Zealand is said to be a beautiful country of contrasts,' Emma spoke out. 'You can take in both if you want to,' she suggested to the couple who were imploring one another to make up their mind what they were to do.

'Can we?' the woman looked pleasantly surprised.

'What do you want to do that for?' her husband quizzed. 'No, thank you, Emma, we'll go to Australia this time and we'll do New Zealand another time,' he crossed his arms in defiance. 'That do you, Joan?' he belatedly thought to ask approval.

'Well, put like that – why not?' she settled for his argument, with raised eyebrows and a gratified smile.

Emma put the New Zealand details to one side, making a mental note to cancel the airline seats temporarily reserved.

A further hour passed and the basis of an extensive tour had formed. Emma eclectically drew on her experience in other bookings, and in particular those recounted by Ollie and Edward on their return from their travels, to suggest an itinerary that would suit her rather particular clients.

'Let's run through the air route, and we can build in timings and length of stays later,' she directed. 'Okay, here goes. UK to Singapore...'

'Why did we say not Bangkok, again?' Mr Milne couldn't remember.

'Emma's daughter said it was horrible,' his wife recalled.

'Well, let's say it's not the best all round example of a Far Eastern city for a first visit,' Emma's subtlety allowing for a possible future booking. 'So, Singapore to Darwin, Darwin to Perth, Perth to Alice Springs, Adelaide to Sydney...'

'Wait on!' he interrupted. 'What about between Alice Springs and Adelaide?'

'Didn't you want to take the Ghan Train, Mr Milne?' Emma's assertion best phrased as a question.

'Oh aye,' he raised his thumb, recollecting his agreement to spending twenty hours on a train.

'Sydney,' she continued, 'to the Whitsunday Islands for the Great Barrier Reef. Whitsundays to Cairns, Cairns to Osaka, and Tokyo back home. How's that sound?'

'Bloody expensive,' Mr Milne joked.

'Well, you know what they say,' Emma smiled with a 'you can afford it, you wily old beggar!' glint in her eye, 'There's no pockets in shrouds.'

'That's true,' his wife replied, thumping her other half with a noiseless laugh. 'And even if the' were, notes'd burn where he's going!' she rocked backwards.

'Now, one thought,' Emma resisted the temptation to prolong the joke, 'Olivia enjoyed Brisbane, but I think we're trying to get too much in if we start adding-to now.' They listened attentively. 'Although if you want to fit it in between Sydney and the Whitsundays, we can perhaps pinch a few days from somewhere else.' She provided more options for consideration.

'She liked it, did she?' Joan Milne thought aloud. 'Where didn't she like?'

'She liked it all really, but enjoyed more of some places than she did of others.' You should join the Diplomatic Corps, she told herself.

'All right then,' Mr Milne took up the baton, 'where did she enjoy less than others?'

'Well, and this is only personal opinion, mind, they didn't get to see Katherine Gorge and Kakadu National Park from Darwin because Edward had half crippled himself climbing Ayers Rock, and as they were their main reason for going, that was a disappointment.'

'What's Kakindoos Park about?' Milne's sickle was drawn and ready to sever any unappealing elements.

'Kakadu? It's a National Park area, significant to the Aboriginal people. It's full of wildlife – birds, crocodiles, kangaroos, that sort of thing.'

'Hmm.' He wasn't convinced of its value, and looked at his wife. 'You into all that crap?'

She shrugged her shoulders.

He'd decided. 'Forget Kakindoo, we'll go with Brisbane.'

Emma returned to her computer screen. There was, thankfully, a service from Singapore to Perth. The itinerary amended, Emma turned to the question of lengths of stay in the various places *en route*. The onward travel arrangements were key in this operation. Daily flights and services were no problem, you could pick your day, but when a train or flight had specific days of operation, it was crucial to get everything linked perfectly.

At his desk, David lifted his head to check on the office through the security glass. Mr and Mrs Milne were still sat there in front of Emma. He decided to offer them a cup of tea, and walked down the office to formally introduce himself and make his gesture.

'Hello,' he greeted them both. 'I'm David Green, Branch Manager. Mr and Mrs Milne, isn't it?'

They nodded. 'We don't do surveys,' Mrs Milne explained.

'I'm sorry?' David was perplexed. Emma smiled into the calendar she was referring to.

'We don't like to partake in surveys. Do we Stan?' she

turned to her husband.

'No. Nice to meet you, though,' he offered his hand to shake.

'I'm not conducting a survey,' David clarified. 'I just wanted to make myself known and to offer you a cup of tea.'

'That'd be lovely,' Joan replied. 'Yes, please. No sugar for him though. Does his condition no good.'

'Fine, I'll pop the kettle on then. How's New Zealand coming along?' he asked in anticipation of a large cheque.

'It's not,' Stanley replied. 'Given up on the idea.'

Disappointment adulterated David's voice. 'Oh, I see.' He looked over Emma's shoulder to find out why, in that case, this couple had spent the best part of two hours in his shop, and were now going to get a cup of tea under false pretences. 'Complicated, Emma?' he asked, searching.

'Time-consuming more than complicated,' she gave nothing away.

'Right,' he said. 'I'll put that kettle on then,' and a little disheartened, he headed for the staff room and the kettle.

Emma had broken the back of the phasing for the trip, which came in just under the ten weeks the Milnes could bear being away from their grandchildren. 'Jet lag should bring you to ten full weeks,' she joked, as David returned with two cups of tea.

'No sugar,' he confirmed, the tea slopping over the cups' brim, despite his placing the saucers down carefully.

Emma looked longingly at her boss.

'Sorry, Emma?' he saw that her face was telling him something that words weren't.

She moistened her top lip with the bottom and clacked her tongue thirstily.

He didn't get it. 'How's it going, then?' he tried again hopefully.

'We're going to Australia now,' Mrs Milne told him.

He livened instantly. 'Super!' his soft hands rubbed loudly. 'For ten weeks?' his interest swelling.

'All together,' Mr Milne nodded.

'Grand! I'll leave you to it then,' he said, patting Emma's back. 'Anyone for a biscuit?'

Much discussion ensued, and Emma had compiled a comprehensive schedule with pre-booked excursion packages to Uluru and Kata Tjuta ('Where?' Stan had asked. 'Ayers Rock and the Olgas to you and me,' Emma's reply), the Great Barrier Reef, tickets for the Sydney Opera House, lists of hotels, and a note of all the telephone calls to be made to reserve this Aladdin's Cave of experiences.

With the basic flight itinerary reserved to Emma's planned schedule, Stanley and Joan Milne decided, much to Emma's relief, that four hours in a travel agents was probably as much as they could take. She was desperate for a wee, needed some caffeine, and had missed her lunch break.

She saw the couple to the door and dashed for the toilet.

David wanted an idea of the value of the Milne's booking, and was waiting for them to leave before approaching her. 'Oh, Emma,' he said with high expectation and excited anticipation as she rushed towards him.

'Not now, David. I'm going to wet myself if I'm not careful!' she called behind her on her way to relief.

'Righto,' he shouted after her, hiding his embarrassed deflation.

She sat, head in hands, feeling as though she'd just run a marathon. No one ever seemed to realise just what effort went into a booking like that. The kids joining these days could just about manage something all ready to select from a brochure, but when it came to using their grey matter, they'd rather turn the business away than get involved.

'Emma!' a voice from outside called.

'I've got me knickers round me ankles!' she yelled in

frustration. 'Leave me in peace for a minute, will you? I've just had the Milnes in, for God's sake.'

'It's Mrs Milne. She wants a quick word.'

'Sorry to keep you, Joan,' Emma apologised to the woman who'd returned alone to the shop.

'Don't worry, dear,' she dismissed the delay. 'Just a quick question. The pilot *will* know we're not going to Darwin now, won't he?'

OF COURSE CAROLE understood that Olivia hadn't meant to cause offence. She'd just wanted to go home to collect the course notes she'd forgotten. At least, that's what she told Elizabeth that morning in their first lecture.

'But why didn't you come in yesterday afternoon, then?' Liz asked, afraid that her best friend was going to be avoiding her while Livvy stayed at Wingate Farm.

Carole waffled. Her friend knew that she was still upset about David – even after all this time, and Livvy's outburst was something she could have well done without. She resolved to have a quiet word with Olivia about it.

'Hello, is Elizabeth there, please?' asked the unsure voice on the phone.

'No, I'm sorry she's at college today,' Val answered, not recognising the boy's tones. 'Can I tell her you called?'

'No. No, thank you. I'll try again. Sorry to have bothered you.' The line fell silent.

Val returned to the bureau where she was putting the finishing touches to the arrangements for the presentation to commemorate Edward, and picked up the brass-framed photograph of her son that stood above her endeavours.

She liked that picture. He never did. It made his nose look too big, he said. She'd tell him that he had a fine

Roman nose, and he'd reply, 'Yeah, Roman all over me face!' She thought the photograph made him look like a young, but better looking Tom Cruise. She polished the glass with her cardigan sleeve and put him back to observe.

'Livvy's coming to stay,' she told his likeness. 'Pity you won't be here to sneak into her room in the small hours this time. Mind you, the damage is done on that score, luvvy.'

She marked the large leather desk diary with a thick red star, Friday October 17th – 'Presentation 8 p.m.'. The final total raised in the shops since April would be worked out to the Thursday before the presentation, so there was little more she could do today, and there was certainly no point in completing the giant cheque just yet. She closed the file before putting it safely back in the top drawer of the mahogany unit.

Checking the kitchen wall calendar, she marked the date again and looked at the following week's schedule.

Adrian had booked a weekend away for them, and had told her to be packed and ready for 5.30 this afternoon. She was looking forward to that. Monday afternoon was Mrs Almond's funeral, the doctor having traced the sister and a brother, somewhere in Burnley. The rest of the next week seemed to be free thus far, until Friday when Olivia was coming to stay. She must get the main guest room ready. It was a while since anyone had used that room, it was probably full of cobwebs. She supposed she'd have to ask around or advertise for a replacement for Mrs Almond, too. She made a note on a yellow sticky sheet, and attached it to the fridge door.

Pen still in hand, she thought to leave a note for Liz, too. But wait a moment. Who was this boy? He'd never been mentioned before; what was Liz up to? There was no way she was going to be throwing parties this weekend while her parents were away. Little madam! We'll see about that.

★

It was raining. Not as hard as yesterday, she felt thankful, but it was raining nonetheless. The umbrella she had was as good as useless. It was too small and had already blown inside out twice, and she wasn't even at the main road yet.

Turning the corner towards the main shops, Olivia continued her walk towards Hulton centre, and considered the prospect of being a lone mother to her baby. The thought was scary. She knew that she had the love and affection of her family – and Ed's family come to that – but there was something she couldn't identify that gave her a feeling of not being able to cope. She told herself she was being silly. To focus on the good, and keep taking each day as it came was the way to go on. That's how Jane McMahon had coped in her own hour of need, and it would be how she'd cope, too.

She reached the surgery in a little under twenty minutes. Junior had jogged all the way, her feet were screaming agony, and her back felt as though it were about to break.

The receptionist recognised Olivia and welcomed her home. 'Doctor's running a little late at the moment but he'll be with you soon,' she advised. 'Have you got a sample?'

Olivia always had a sample with her these days. It was part of her handbag now – purse, lipstick, hairspray, tissues, cheque book, diary, pen, keys and morning-fresh piss. She prayed that she never had an accident. She couldn't stand the thought of some religious do-gooder practising a DIY liturgy, thinking that the contents of the little opaque pot was finest holy water.

Putting her feet up on a child-size plastic chair, she surveyed her waiting room surroundings from the seat by the table covered in magazines. They'd decorated throughout, she thought. The ceiling was still Artexed, but didn't the walls used to be plastered? They were bare brick now, a deep red brick with a shiny coating. It looked nice. The woodwork was stripped back to its natural state, and the effect worked well. The panelled doors to the examination room and the nurses' treatment room had been taken back to bare wood too, and the whole thing looked less like a doctor's surgery now, despite the Donor Card posters.

A well-crafted sign on the wall told the waiting assemblage the doctors' names, the practice manager's name, and the names of the two practice nurses who were both honoured with dubious looking photographs as well.

The various success rates of the practice were also displayed for all to see, and Olivia noticed that there wasn't a classification for 'Died Waiting For Doctor Running Late'. Perhaps she should mention it if she were unduly delayed. The old guy slumped in the corner certainly looked a prime candidate for this category, or was he just sleeping? She'd keep her eye out for him.

Olivia had read the 'Life's Like That' sections of all the available *Reader's Digest* issues she could find, and come to the conclusion that people in Toronto obviously had nothing better to do than write three-line letters to the editor. Maybe they *did* have their heads screwed on the right way, though she didn't consider recounting the tale of Edward's Grandma Quirk asking if he'd had all his ejaculations before travelling abroad last year, really worth embarrassing her. Not for the sake of a few quid.

A woman with pushchair and toddler in wellington boots fought her way through the main doors of the surgery and out of the rain. The little girl barked a nasty cough, and led her mummy through the glass door into the waiting room. The man in the corner snorted without warning or apparent reason. What a let-down he'd turned out to be, thought Olivia. The girl stopped dead in her tracks right in front of Olivia's feet, looking her malevolently in the eye. How could a child no more than three years of age make someone seven times her senior feel so pitifully small?

'Hello,' Olivia smiled.

With great performance, the girl thrust forward her shoulders and barked another spittled and unguarded cough in Olivia's direction. 'That's not *your* chair! It's for little girls like me!' she pointed theatrically towards Olivia's foot rest.

'It's for little girls, is it?' she asked. Little madams more like. 'Well, here we are then,' she puffed, lifting her aching feet and offering the chair to the girl.

'Come here, Emilia,' her mother told her wearily without looking up from her magazine. 'We don't talk to strangers, do we?' the article entitled 'How To Satisfy Your Man In and Out of Bed' was pleased to hear, even if Emilia wasn't.

'You've had your feet on it now. Clean it up!' the precocious little girl refused the seat.

'Emilia, lovely,' the mother's droning voice lacked any authority. 'Come here, sweetheart.'

'Yes, go to your mummy,' suggested Olivia, 'and take the chair with you.' She shoved it along the floor and it fell over.

'Mummy!' Emilia tugged at her mother's sleeve. 'She threw that at me! Mummy!'

'Yes dear,' the mother interested only in her magazine.

'Mummeeeee!' the girl tugged harder.

'*What*, Emilia?' she snapped brusquely with sudden impatience.

Emilia's face contorted, transforming instantly into a crimson wrung sponge. The cry was long and high pitched, the sobs that followed dramatic to the point of Academy accolade. 'Arwantiddacher anshethrewitatme andithurted anamgointasmackernowwa!' she wailed.

Shut the fuck up! Olivia wanted to say, the shrill whines splitting her head. What *had* she let herself in for? That's how she'd turn out too if she wasn't careful. A mother, so fed up with her own child, that she'd let it bother anyone else in sight as long as it gave her a few short minutes of breathing space. Who should she feel sorry for? The mother with a little bugger of a child, or the child with a lethargy-riddled and defeated mother? Hurry up Doctor! she wished.

'Olivia Beech?' the welcome call from the treatment room doorway amidst the child's prolonged cries. She entered the room, grateful of its sanctuary, and took a seat.

'That sounds like Emilia Hughes out there,' the doctor sighed. 'You haven't any paracetamol on you by any chance?' he quipped.

Olivia laughed, 'Would you like me to take your blood pressure as well?'

'Good idea nurse, and while you're at it, have I still got a pulse?' he held out his wrist with a warm smile.

Dr Price was a young man, early to mid thirties perhaps, slim build, dark hair thinning from too many long hours in hospitals before entering General Practice, and the sort of natural tan you'd spend an eternity at a health club trying to buy. Olivia could sit there all day trying to find his pulse.

'Now,' he said, looking at her notes. 'Your water sample shows something interesting.'

'Oh?' Olivia listened with concern.

'Yes, Olivia,' his face grave. 'I think you may be pregnant.'

She exploded in giggles. Why did she have to have the doctor with an overactive sense of humour? 'Been in the game long, Doc?' she asked, patting her stomach.

'Ah!' he feigned realisation; his fore finger pointing upward. 'That's the other sign they told me to look out for.' Her posture told him he had successfully put her at ease.

'So, we've established that there's going to be a baby.'

'A *bouncing* baby,' she corrected him, feeling movement beneath the elasticated waistband of the maternity jeans she so hated.

'A bouncing baby,' he conceded. 'And how've you been getting along?'

'Fine.'

'When are we due?' he searched through his papers for the information.

'November 6th,' she told him without hesitation.

'Not long to go, then,' he added to his notes. 'And, as it looks like I haven't had your recent records through yet, any problems?'

'Aches and pains – in the back mainly. Swollen boobs, fussing mother – usual things.'

He smiled. 'Waterworks all right?'

'Yeah, back end too, thankfully.'

The notes continued. 'And how about home? Settling back in okay?'

'Everyone's been really great,' she beamed. 'My boyfriend's family as much as anyone.'

'Good. Let's give you and the baby the once over then shall we?'

Oh yes please! she dreamed.

A thorough examination of Olivia and a listen to the baby's heart revealed no problems, and he wrote down the details of the ante-natal clinic for her to make an appointment during the following week to see the nurse.

'The midwife should be there as well,' he told her. 'It'd be worth your while having a bit of a chat about how you want things to happen on the day,' he suggested.

'Painless?' she asked hopefully.

'I've given birth to loads of babies, Olivia,' his reassuring tones soothing. 'And not one,' he stressed with a handsome smile, 'hurt me a bit!'

He saw her to the door and wished her luck. Taking a deep breath, he called the name 'Emilia Hughes'.

The weather hadn't abated. If anything it had worsened, and Olivia headed for home under sullen skies through torrential rain and road spray. Passing by the grocers, she saw a familiar Range Rover pull away from outside Track & Turf, the bookmakers two doors down. Adrian noticed someone through the corner of his eye, waving as he drove off for his office, but didn't recognise the young woman with the silly little flowered umbrella, and accelerated away down the hill towards the town.

'Ah well, Bump,' she told his disappearing tail lights. 'Wave to Grandad.' And as if to comply, the baby pushed hard on her bladder. 'Thanks, kid!' she gasped.

Olivia was drenched and ready for a cup of tea when she finally turned the key in the front door. She removed her PVC mackintosh and boots, and studied the line of wet between her knees and feet that had been exposed to the elements. She'd better change. In fact, a shower seemed the best way to warm up.

Nicely warmed and in dry clothes, she made herself a tuna-marmalade sandwich, and settled down with a steaming hot cup of tea in the easy chair by the window in the lounge. She hoped that a quiet hour or so might just send the abdominal acrobat to sleep, and began to read him a story about his father.

Thursday 20th June – Day 11: After yesterday's efforts, we decided to stay safe and shop. Yes! Having been over Darling Harbour on the monorail thing on Saturday, we wanted another look and walked there in our spazzy pressed jeans via Hyde Park. Had breakfast in a café when we got there, and went into all the shops in this huge glass-fronted centre. Bought some presents for Mum and Dad, Val and Liz. Ed still can't find anything for his Dad.

'He was a bit useless like that, your father,' she told her still-kicking tummy fondly.

Talk about shopper's paradise in there. Ed had to drag me away before I bought up the entire centre. He wanted to have a look at the Olympic Showcase on some old boat further round the Harbour, so we traipsed around that – talk about wasting valuable shopping time! By the time we'd been Olympic'd, it was time for food again, so we had a gigantic sandwich at the Aquarium there at Darling Harbour, fighting off the bloody birds…

'Oops! 50p Mummy.'

…fighting off the… ('bloody') she whispered… *birds, and rounded it off with a tasty bit of melted chocolate. You know me and chocolate, Diary! It was getting hot (and we were getting funny looks at our razor sharp legs) so we changed into our shorts before heading off for The Rocks. Well, Ed did his usual 'follow your nose' routine…*

'At least you'll be spared that treat!' she chuckled, rubbing Bump in a circling motion.

…and took us down some dock road. Not a decent sight to be seen, let alone shop; just yards and yards of concrete wall and wire mesh. Guess what though? Smart… ('Arse')… *brings us out right beneath The Harbour Bridge at some place called Pier One. There's not much to see, just a few fishermen and a load of hand and footprints set in concrete including Big Bird from Sesame Street…*

'You'd like that one, Bump.'

…Rolf Harris and Normie Rowe. Ed kept on about this bloke. He's supposed to look like him apparently, but no one in England knows what he looks like! Ellen, Mum's friend that we're off to see

tomorrow, told me once that he's the image of him. From what I can make out, Diary, he's the personification of a Terry Wogan/Michael Crawford/Les Dawson mutant, having done everything from fighting in Vietnam, to singing Phantom of the Opera *(while presenting the Australasian Song Contest, no doubt!).*

'We still don't know what he looks like either,' she thought out loud. 'You might be a baby version too, kidder.'

On to The Rocks under the Bridge, and there's a brilliant view of the Opera House. I could keep looking at that place for hours. It's amazing! At The Rocks, there's a big sailing ship and lots of waterfront eateries. I could have eaten something there and then, but Ed reckoned it wasn't that long since we'd had our lunch, so we settled on a can of Coke instead from the terminal used by all the big cruise ships. More shopping and change some dosh at Thomas Cook's, and I finally convinced him it was time to eat again. So, we've eaten tea at Circular Quay and walked back here to the hotel again for a quiet night in bed with the telly on. In ten minutes, it's 'Sale of the Century' and after that, 'The Price is Right'!

Ed's trying to get rid of the luverly creases in our dry-cleaned clobber – you want to see his denim jacket, Diary! It looks like it's been starched and he's not a happy bunny. I'm going to write a couple of postcards now, so goodnight.

The movement beneath her T-shirt had ceased. She closed the diary, allowing herself to drift into a vision-filled sleep, thinking about the fantastic voyage she'd undertaken with Edward. It somehow seemed as if she'd never been to the other side of the world, and it was only the evidence of photographs and souvenirs that proved she wasn't dreaming it all ever happened. Perhaps when she came to, she'd realise it *was* all a dream, and she'd find herself in the middle of her driving test or something. Even the diary recollections had lost their full impact now. They were just notes of a far-off time. Stories of a couple no one knew anymore, who were living a lifetime of happiness in a few short weeks. Life wasn't fair, the voice inside her head said. One day, she'd take Bump to see the sights his daddy had so enjoyed and promised to return to. One day. If it wasn't too painful.

She awoke to clattering in the kitchen and waited, eyes half-closed for her father to come into the lounge.

'Hi, luv!' he shouted, barging through the door.

'Hi,' she whispered sleepily.

'Sorry, am I disturbing you?' the realisation; he'd not thought she might be resting.

'No,' she lied. 'I thought it was burglars. But I bethought myself – they'd not make a noise when they were trashing the place, so then I knew it was just you trashing the place,' she smiled a yawn.

'You've a cheeky mum, you have, Cuthbert,' he told Bump.

'That word's going on the swear list if you're not careful!' Olivia warned.

'What, cheeky?'

'No, Cuthbert.'

'What's wrong with it? It's a smashin' name.'

Olivia's eyebrows reached their upper limit. 'Honest opinion, Dad? Cuthbert Beech sounds like some camp you'd go to for a week's holiday.' Her frankness was wounding. 'I think it stinks.'

His face dropped. 'I've always been good at names.'

'Yeah, so I've heard. Sandie Beech being a prime example!' her arms wrapping her stomach to protect the baby from the horrors of his grandfather's influence. 'You're not going to inflict this one with some film star's stage name.'

'That's it!' he perked up. 'Tarantino Beech.'

'Oh Lord!' Olivia groaned. 'Mother, hurry home and save us!'

Emma returned home a little later than usual; the Milnes had been back in for some information on the places that they'd decided to visit, which had added the best part of an hour to her already heavy workload.

She was pleasantly surprised to see steam coming from the kitchen as she walked into the house, and the table set upon entering the lounge. Dan was in his normal late afternoon state: slouched in the armchair in front of the TV with biscuit wrappers scattered around his feet.

'What's happened to the bandage?' she asked, admiring with a grin the turban effort that had replaced the neat crêpe affixed by the hospital.

'It got wet and unravelled on me,' he sniggered. 'I was walking down Cheapside looking like the Andrex puppy!'

'So who did the headgear then?' she tried not to laugh.

'Ollie did this one. I think she's taking the piss, though.'

'I heard that!' Olivia shouted from the kitchen. '50p!'

'Her and that bloody swear box! I'll be glad to be working double shifts soon,' he muttered, puckering his lips and waiting for Emma to lean down to kiss him. Instead she sat on his knee.

'Oi! I can't see the box now!' he complained.

'Good, you great couch p'tata. Gimme a proper kiss,' she insisted. 'I've been to Australia and back again today, I'm done in. What's your day been like?'

'Jimmy Taylor's still laid up on top of folk going down with the flu, so we had to re-jig the routes and I got the short straw.'

'Jimmy who?'

'Taylor. You know, the bloke in 'ospital at weekend,' he thumbed over his shoulder, as if Jimmy were perched there. 'He's supposed to be back on Monday, though. He better 'ad be, they're threatening to cancel me 'olidays if there's any more go off.'

'Well, that's it, then.' Emma stood and folded her arms,

lowering her voice to stop it carrying beyond the lounge. 'You can't have folk not getting their mail. We'll just have to postpone our holidays till next year,' she whispered.

'Oh no you won't, missus!' Olivia's voice boomed from the kitchen, and the serving hatch doors flew open. 'You're going on holiday whether you like it or not!' she frowned at her mother. 'Right, Dad?'

He nodded towards the kitchen. 'Right, luv.' He daren't disagree.

'How *does* she do that?' Emma asked him in admiration.

In no time, Val had the guest room dusted, vacuumed and aired. With clean linen on the bed, and a run round the en-suite shower room with the mousse cleaner, she was happy that she could leave for a weekend of peace and quiet alone with Adrian without worries. Adrian would be back at around five o'clock now that things were slightly re-arranged, and that would give her time to have a shower, get changed and pack a bag for them, before making a supper to leave.

Liz's Friday lectures finished relatively early, and she arrived home at around four o'clock. She was reading the back of a hair colour box when Val tottered into the living room with the weekend bag packed to capacity.

'Leaving home, Mum?' she asked, seeing the obvious weight.

'Only for a few days, sweetie,' she dropped the bag with a thud by the lounge doorway. 'There was a call for you this morning.'

'Oh yeah? Who?' the box demanding more of Liz's immediate attention.

'He wouldn't leave his name,' Val watched her face closely for guilt, but there was none.

'What did he sound like?' Liz guarded her increased interest.

'Quite nice. Sounded like he was up for a party to me,' Val fished further.

'Great! A bloke *and* a party. Where?' her enthusiasm mounting.

Val was becoming uneasy. She could normally tell when Liz was up to something, and either they were teaching her daughter to bluff very well at this new college of hers, or Val was holding the wrong end of a very big stick. 'He just said he'd phone again,' the truth coming to her rescue. Damn! she thought. I've bloody well gone and done it now.

'Wait till I tell Carole!' Liz beamed. Her face changed and showed serious thought. 'Do you think I'd better dye my hair then, Mum? He might like it the way it is, and I don't want to spoil my chances, do I?' she sought experienced advice.

Val's mind galloped around the room. There was no bluff from Liz. Oh shit! What have I done? 'You don't even know who it is do you? I'd leave it if I were you, luv.'

'Did he leave a number?' Liz's excitement taking over.

'No he didn't. He just said he'd call back,' Val re-affirmed, not knowing whether she desperately wanted him to do so, or that she'd prefer it if he'd forget all about it.

'Did you check the number afterwards?'

'Why should I?'

'To find out!' she tutted. 'God, Mother, I thought you'd have been really nosy, and been grilling me and giving me grief about thinking I'd be having people around while you were away,' her head shaking in astonishment. 'You've been really quite normal, though, haven't you?'

'I suppose I have,' Val's mouth seemed reluctant to speak forth what her brain was screaming.

Liz seized the phone and dialled the four digit code to check the last caller's number. 'Was it about half ten when he called?' she asked giddily.

'About then.'

Liz screamed. 'I've got his number! I've got his number! Mum, should I call him? Should I?'

For once, Val didn't know what to do. 'Why not play it cool and let him call back?' she suggested. 'He did say he would.' She tried to sound cunning to add an element of 'mother knows best', which seemed to work, as Liz agreed with very few 'buts' or 'are you sures'.

'Just *wait* till I tell Carole,' she repeated, light-headed. 'I think I'll call her now.'

Carole was enthralled by the mystery man. The only person she could possibly think it might be, was the one that always smiled at Liz when they were going into the refectory. Yes, it must be him! He was always hanging around the doorway when they were there.

Liz couldn't believe her luck. She thought he was drop-dead gorgeous. She could see him now, moving closer. Their hands accidentally brushing. Their eyes meeting for the first time. He says something romantic like 'I've been waiting an eternity for this moment'. They pause like they do on telly. Their heads tilt – hers left and his right. No, that's wrong – his right and hers right. They move closer still. Their lips finally touching. 'Oh God, Caz!' she yelled, 'Come over. We've got to talk tactics!'

'Carole's coming over tonight, Mum,' she told Val who was making sure that the casserole was okay in the Aga.

'Just Carole?' challenged her mother, hoping for a last minute reprieve.

Liz nodded. 'Why, who else would there be?'

'I don't know,' she shrugged. She thought it best to come clean now, before it was too late. 'Lizzy, this...'

'Is that Dad?' Liz's attention was drawn to the sound of the Range Rover on gravel and she went to the window to watch him draw to a halt by the back door. 'Who's he got with him this time? I thought you were going away on your own this weekend,' she looked questioningly at Val.

'We are,' her voice heavy and sounding a little ashamed.

'But?' Liz's detection first rate.

'But you're not going to be,' the tone unerring.

Liz returned to the window. 'What,' she said slowly and with dread, 'are Grandma and Grandpa doing here?'

'I thought you might like some company,' Val prevaricated.

'Did you now?' Liz's disbelieving eyes bore through her mother's.

'And it's nice for them to spend some time with you for a change. You don't see enough of them, do you?' the justification sounded plausible to Val.

'And this had nothing, *at all*, perhaps, to do with a phone call this morning?' Liz wasn't going to let up.

Val knew she'd been caught out. 'No,' her hole dug deeper. 'Hi Mum, Dad!' she welcomed her parents with a big hug, their entrance timely.

'What's the matter with you?' her ageing father's gruff voice demanded from somewhere embedded in Val's shoulder.

'Just glad to see you. Come on in, Mum,' she ushered the retired legal partner and his wife through the dining room and into the living room.

They were seated by the roaring open fire and, knowing their tipple, Adrian poured a glass of whisky for both. 'Ice?' he asked.

'You know we don't take ice!' his father-in-law responded churlishly. He liked Adrian as much as he'd liked Legal Aid clients in his working days, considering them equally a 'pain in the bloody arse' because in his view, they expected everything for nothing; but they were a fact of life that one had to live with. He'd endeavoured to avoid both whenever he could, and now only one requiring tolerance remained; and *he* was family.

Adrian handed over the crystal tumblers to the guests,

and offered Val and Liz a drink.

Liz was piecing the jigsaw together, bit by bit in her mind. Why would Dad collect his in-laws, the very couple that he would elude at any opportunity, and drive them here just before heading off for the weekend with Mum, if there wasn't a good reason? A short notice good reason at that. 'It's lovely to see you, Grandma,' she said. 'Grandpa too.' She gave them both a kiss.

'You too, dearest,' her grandmother replied. 'It's been too long since we saw that beautiful face of yours. You look just like your mother did at your age. Doesn't she, Arthur?'

'Beautiful, she was,' her husband agreed, leaving Val wondering in what category she now languished.

'And don't you worry,' continued Grandma, her arthritic thumb rubbing away traces of her lipstick from Elizabeth's cheek, 'You and your friends won't *even* know we're here.'

Carole was excited when, in her mother's car, she arrived at Wingate Farm. Not entirely satisfied with her daughter's tale of quiet nights in with Elizabeth, Mrs James just wanted to say hello to Val, and check that it was in fact all right for Carole to stay over. The back door was flung open wide and there stood Liz, her face blacker than the evening sky.

'Hi, Caz,' she muttered. 'Hi, Mrs James.'

'What's up with you?' asked Carole, expecting a quite different welcome.

'Come in and see,' Liz sighed.

Carole followed Liz through the house to the lounge, with her mother bringing up the rear.

'Everyone, Carole's here,' Liz announced to the room, only Val missing. She'd needed to check on something apparently very urgent, a few moments earlier.

Elizabeth stood in the doorway and allowed first Carole

to pass her, and then Mrs James. 'This is Carole's mum, everyone,' she told no one in particular. 'Mrs James, this is Grandma...' pointing to the elderly lady.

'Hello,' the strangers chorused.

'...this is Grandpa...' her arm slowly arcing the room.

'Nice to meet you,' Mrs James mouthed, not really able to see the man's face through the bottom of a whisky glass.

'...I think you know Dad...' she said, watching her mother return to the lounge.

'Hello, Sue. Are you okay?' he smiled to the friendly face. 'You're looking well.'

'Thanks,' she returned the warmth of smile. 'I'm fine, Adrian; you?'

Adrian nodded. 'Fine.'

'...and, oh look, there's *another* person,' Liz pointed to Val, her voice disowning.

'Hi, Val,' Sue waved a self-conscious hand. 'This is okay, isn't it?' her wrist forcing her hand to adopt a circling motion. 'Carole staying?'

'Of course it is,' enthused Val. 'We're off in a minute, but take a seat for a mo' if you like,' she offered an armchair.

'No thanks, I'd best dash,' a look of dread appearing across her slender face. 'I've left Derek with the dishwasher.'

With promises of good behaviour from the house-sitters, and the same from the girls not to lead the grandparents astray, the parents all left the house together. Adrian loaded the luggage into the Range Rover and climbed into the driver's seat, while Val and Sue chatted by the latter's car.

Hoots of laughter from Sue told Adrian that Val was in full flow, and he wanted to get away quickly. The last thing he needed was for Arthur Quirk to come out of the house and delay them further, just for the sake of it. He'd already spent longer than he would have liked in the old misery's company today, and viewed one backseat lecture on bookmaking not being a proper job quite sufficient. He pumped the horn impatiently and Val hurriedly joined him.

'Have they gone yet?' the old man asked Liz with undisguised hope.

She nodded. 'Looks like it. Mind you, Grandpa, they'll be back in half an hour for something they've forgotten. They're useless at going away.'

'Don't you be nasty about your mother,' Martha Quirk warned with the wave of a crooked finger. 'Or your father,' she remembered reluctantly.

'I'm not. They'll be back – guaranteed.'

'Rubbish!' her grandfather dismissed with adamant bluster.

'Carole,' Liz called to her friend seated on the stool by the inglenook, 'throw us Mum's handbag will ya?'

Emma looked at the note and puzzled. 'Who's "Wiggy Woman", Ollie?'

Olivia stopped reading to Bump and looked up from her diary. 'She phoned yesterday.'

'Yes, I can see that. Who is she though?'

'Mrs Toupee,' she skitted with a plumb-in-mouth accent.

'Oh God, her! Stupid old biddy,' Emma groaned. 'What did *she* want?'

'Like the note says, to be nosy. She wanted to know if that wayward daughter of yours was really back like the rumour said, or if she should spread some different tittle-tattle around the town.'

'So who did she think she was talking to?'

Olivia shrugged. 'You tell me.'

Emma shook her head in resignation. She'd learned to get on with her life and not worry about what other people had to say, but now and again there was somebody that would find a chink in her armour. Why was it usually the village gossip called Toop?

'You know, she's on the Parochial Church Council and there's not enough Christian in that woman to make a lion belch,' her scathing prognosis. 'Are there any more messages that I don't know about?' she sighed.

'Not that I know of,' Olivia replied. 'Although, the doctor was asking how your HRT was going today,' she laughed.

'I'll give you HRT!' Emma shook her fist. 'What are you teaching Bump now? Nothing corrupting I hope, like disrespect for Grandma.'

'No, just more Daddy stories.'

'What are you up to?' Emma's interest in the trip was renewed.

'Last full day in Sydney. We've been to see Ellen and had a lovely time with her, haven't we?' she asked the mound. 'She's told us that they're going to have a brothel in shopping centres across Australia – probably to encourage more blokes to go shopping; and we've been down to the beach at Cronulla to see the surfers but there aren't many about; and we're just up to packing the bags ready to go to Ayers Rock, aren't we?'

'Can Granny listen, too?'

'If she wants to,' Olivia smiled. 'It's nice of her to ask this time, isn't it, Bump?' she goaded.

Emma raised one eyebrow, and took a seat next to Hulton's very own 'Jackanory'.

Saturday 22nd June – Day 13: 11.15 p.m. You know you dream about places, Diary? Well, nightmares are kind of dreams aren't they? Today we flew to Ayers Rock. A nice enough flight, Ed played his favourite sport – 'spot the good-looking cabin crew', and must have thought he'd hit the jackpot when the nicest one leant over him to give me something that tasted like dried kangaroo-in-a-bag, and brushed his face with her tits. I'll ask him in a moment if he's ever going to wash again. That's if he's finally calmed down of course.

I'll tell you why 'calmed down' in a minute. Back to the flight, and there was a film shown that someone somewhere found hilarious, but because our headsets didn't really work that well – I got a crackle in one ear and Ed got nothing at all, we couldn't tell for ourselves. The usual slop for food that resembled slugs must have been bad, even Dustbin Mallory didn't eat it!

Anyway, we landed and expected to see an Aussie Meedej with our names on a board like before. The crowds cleared, and there was no one there to meet us. Problems begin! Got on a coach to take us to Ayers Rock Resort, got off here at the hotel and after a bloody long queue...

'Olivia Beech! Get your money out,' Emma held her hand out, open-palmed.

'That's because you're putting me off, Mother!' Olivia smacked her leg. 'Shut up, it's story time; I'll pay later.'

...long queue we checked in. So the hotel was expecting us, but it seemed no one else was. The girl with the big tits and fat... ('arse') she whispered harshly in her mother's direction *...behind the counter, phoned the people that were supposed to meet us and be giving us a tour to the Olgas at 2 p.m. Bearing in mind it's a quarter to two already, it looks like we're not going to see the Olgas. Cutting War and Peace down to just 'War', Ed spent the afternoon in an irate state, phoning round to find out what was going on and booking a trip to Ayers Rock for us tomorrow. Then he booked us a flight, having found out that the next leg of this pre-booked bit of our trip between here and Alice Springs was to be by coach. The five-hour coach fare is $88 each, the hour flight is $108 each. We went for the extra £10 each for a flight, and Ed's going to be claiming the cost back from the tour company when we get home. One for Mum I think!*

'Cheeky madam!' Emma tutted.

Olivia looked sideways at her mother. 'Bump says, "Be quiet Grandma, I'm trying to listen to Mummy's story."'

'Sorry, Bump,' said Emma, forcing her lips tightly closed.

So Diary, we're here at Ayers Rock resort – 20 km away from the Rock, and it looks like it's right next door to us! It's a monster. This bit's been a bit of a let down so far, not being able to see things we'd wanted to, but we've not to let that spoil everything else! We've got to get up at 5 a.m. tomorrow to check out of the hotel, and be ready for the coach to Ayers Rock at 6.10 a.m. I thought this was going to be a restful trip, Diary. It's turning into an endurance test again! The Firm's just starting on TV, so I'm going to see if Ed's all right now and then watch the film. TTFN.

I'm back. He's still chuntering on about missing the Olgas – oops sorry! Kata Tjuta, but at least it's made him forget his stay-pressed jeans for a while! He's had a wash, but says he missed the bit where the girl's nipple stabbed his ear! So he's into stabbing nipples, is he? Bye again!

'You two were terrible, do you know that?' Emma laughed.

'Yeah I know,' admitted Olivia grinning. 'Good, innit?'

'She's grown up so much,' Emma told Dan in bed that night as she stared toward the ceiling in the darkness.

'She's been through a lot, Em. You can't not grow up when you've been through all that,' he reflected, breathless. 'Are you with me tonight?' he demanded.

'Of course I am. Sorry,' she apologised, realising how thoughtless she was being. 'Aaaah. Yes. Oooh. Just there! Yes...'

T HE SUNDAY EVENING light was fast fading as the vehicle turned into the driveway with a familiar scrunch beneath its wheels. They were happier now than they had been for some years; the loss of Edward finally bringing them closer together, having tried to cope with their feelings alone for too long. The weekend away was a success, Val thought. It was a long time since they'd talked about nothing in particular – just the two of them, over a quiet meal or drink together.

Adrian was pleased to find himself relaxed throughout the weekend without prescribed aid. He found to his frustration, though, that the time had passed by too quickly, especially as on Friday night he'd had to turn around after ten miles down the road, so that they could pick up Val's bag. The peculiar reaction when he'd walked back into the lounge had been unnerving – laughter from the girls, and looks of absolute contempt from his in-laws, suggesting he was missing out on something. Never mind, they'd decided to make weekends away a regular thing, and a slight hiccup like that wouldn't spoil this one.

For now, though, he had to look forward to the prospect of taking Val's parents home, which he vowed wouldn't be allowed to nullify the enjoyment of the days away.

Elizabeth was waiting at the back door, the top half open and her arms folded, supporting her weight on the bottom half of the stable-style door. She greeted them with effervescence, her kiss a little too enthusiastic for Val.

'What's happened?' she asked with suspicion.

'Happened, Mother?' the happy daughter replied. 'Why ever should anything have happened?'

Val was not satisfied that all was in order. 'You're very cheerful, how's your grandmother?' They surely couldn't be getting on *that* well.

'Fine!' Liz breezed. 'Probably,' her addendum less assured.

Adrian felt a strange combination of acute apprehension and immense joy. 'Probably?' he ventured.

'Well, it got to the stage where Grandma was missing Felix and Corky; and Grandpa decided that there were none of the boys that Mum had promised would be here for him to give a hard time to. Plus the fact he'd be missing the racing on TV if he stayed any longer...'

'What about my bloody Racing Channel?' Adrian demanded. Who had ever heard of a bookmaker without full racing coverage at home? Okay, he was rarely here to watch it himself, but that was by the by.

'You know what he's like, Dad,' Liz explained, 'any excuse. Anyway, they decided to go home.'

A surge of sheer relief drowned Adrian, while Val looked annoyed. 'So when did they go, then? This morning?'

'No, Mum,' Liz replied plainly, taking the case from Val's hand. 'They took a taxi home on Friday night,' she told her with a wry smile. 'It *was* nice to spend some time with them.'

Val was having a terribly uncharitable thought. This afternoon's funeral – why wasn't it someone closer to home? She'd tried her best with those parents of hers but did they get any better? Did they sugar! She had just about an hour to get herself ready and to get across town to Mrs Almond's house, from where the cortege would drive to St Paul's Church out on the Southport road.

She reached for the black lambswool suit, last worn in March when she said goodbye to her eldest, and it wasn't until she studied her now outfitted self in the mirror that the callous nature of her earlier thoughts came home to her. She'd coped with too much death this year, she didn't want to wish any more on anyone – particularly her parents, however much they tormented her.

The announcement of Gladys Almond's death in the local paper's 'Births, Marriages and Deaths' column – or 'Hatches, Matches and Despatches' as she preferred to call it, hadn't mentioned anything about donations or flowers; so along the way, Val stopped off to collect a suitable arrangement that she'd ordered by telephone.

The young assistant disappeared through the colourful strips of entangled plastic that separated the main shop and back work area, returning only moments later with an ambitious bouquet filled with gypsophila, colourful carnations, spectacular lilies and aromatic roses.

'That's impressive!' said Val, doubting its appropriateness for a funeral.

'Thank you,' said the girl with pride. 'I did it. It's my very first attempt too.'

'It's very...' the words failed Val. Should she accept it and pay the obvious cost of such lavish a display, or flatten the girl's confidence and ask for something a little less ornate?

'Registry office do, is it?' the girl, remembering her customer care training, leapt in, 'Being a Monday and all?'

Val was taken a back. 'Er, no. It's at St Paul's.'

'Lovely! I bet she'll love these,' the assistant gushed, handing over the blooms.

The thoughts in Val's mind were not reaching her

mouth with adequate speed to stop her from stumbling on regardless. 'She would have, but she's dead.'

'Oh my God, that's tragic! The poor woman. What about the husband?' Val could see tears in her eyes.

The thoughts were still being scrambled *en route* to her larynx. 'He's dead, too,' the mouth replied independently of her brain.

'*Both* of 'em?' the girl looked agog. 'But that's just heart-breaking!'

'Well, that's the reason for St Paul's today,' Val tried to explain.

'They're still going to marry *dead people?*' the astonishment of innocence cried.

'Well no...'

'That's not right! I mean, it's... it's... well it's sick.'

'It's not a wedd...'

'How do they expect the congregation to hear the vows for Heaven's sake?'

'Listen to me, it's not...' Val vainly tried again.

'And when they say "You may kiss the bride", what do they do? Shove 'em together face first?'

Val gave up. She should have been at the house by now. 'How much do I owe you for the flowers?'

'Thirty-two pounds,' the look of abject fear on her face. 'I don't believe this,' the girl was in turmoil. 'I *can't* believe it.'

Val prayed that she had sufficient cash in her purse to cover the cost of the flowers, and handed over thirty-five pounds in notes. 'Keep the change,' she told the assistant, leaving the shop in a hurry. Thirty-five flamin' quid! she thought. This had better be some wedding.

There was a small gathering by the gate at Mrs Almond's house when Val pulled up behind the hearse. She looked at the simple floral arrangements already in the back of the sleek black Daimler, and glanced down at her own contribution. Perhaps, she considered, if she wore a red nose and carried a whoopee cushion, people might not notice the full effect of the lilies.

Before having chance to leave the car, Val noticed the pallbearers reach the inner doorway and commence their conveyance of the deceased towards the car. Following on came no one Val knew. An older lady looked to fit the bill as the sister, and the man linking arms with her seemed to be the only serious contender for title of 'the brother'.

The service was a modest affair; no more than a dozen people attended. A stark contrast, thought Val seated at the back of the church – part way through 'Onward Christian Soldiers' – to the congregation at Edward's service of cremation. The passing of time allowed her to smile at his warped sense of humour and choice of music for his own farewell. The number of people there that day who must have thought that she and Adrian had a screw loose when the first bars of 'Wish Me Luck As You Wave Me Goodbye' sent him on his way behind the deep blue velvet curtains. Val couldn't help but laugh into her handkerchief, blowing her nose as poor disguise. One of the few turned, and while enthusiastically miming the words to the wrong verse, adopted a knowing smile as if to share her grief; a sight which made her sniggering worse.

'Gladys was a caring woman,' the vicar told a hushed chapel. 'She loved the simple pleasures of life, but strived hard in everything she did…'

Val blew her nose long and hard, her shoulders and handkerchief shaking long after the noise had subdued.

'…in fact, the Lord called her while she was in the very act of useful endeavours…'

Val coughed politely and bit her hand. I'm at the wrong funeral!

'…So let us remember her as a hard-working, simple woman…', Val's shaking was uncontrollable, silently adjudging the cleric half right, '…as we sing together from the hymn sheet, "Jerusalem".'

The vicar shook hands with the mourners once his duties were complete, and Gladys Almond rested six feet below in the clay soil earth. The older lady was crying, the man of similar age lighting a cigarette, his lighter throwing a dangerously long flickering flame in the wind when Val approached to offer her condolences.

'I thought you were very gallant in the church earlier,' she told the man.

'What do you mean?' he asked with a politeness reserved for a picket line.

'Dashing into the aisle to help the vicar like that.'

'Humph! How was I supposed to know he hadn't twisted his ankle?' he argued. 'Didn't think C of E went in for swinging their smoking balls and genuflecting.'

Val stifled the bubbling titters. 'Yes, some have become a bit "high", haven't they?'

'Bloody religion,' his mumbling tone derisory. 'And you are who anyway?' the quasi- accusation.

'Val Mallory. Gladys was working for me when she passed on,' she considered the loosest usage of the words as not exactly telling untruths in the grounds of a holy place.

'Lazy bitch, never did a day's work in her life!' He blew an arrogant ring of smoke and watched it disintegrate in front of his eyes, before striding off towards the cars.

Val wasn't sure what she should do. She could hardly defend the woman's memory by telling what her brother obviously knew to be lies, but the moment had passed for that now anyway. She stood and thought for while, distracted only by a tap on her shoulder.

She turned around to see the little old lady dressed all in black by her side, handkerchief to mouth.

'I'm so sorry for you,' Val said, the awkwardness of these occasions never relenting. Why didn't someone write a book on what to say in awkward situations? She could do with a copy right now.

'Thank you, dear,' the lady replied. 'Are you Mrs Mallory?'

'Yes, I am,' her mind turning the imaginary pages for the section entitled 'Funerals', subsection 'People You Don't Know Very Well', reference 'Families Thereof'.

'She spoke well of you. Loved your old place, she did,' she smiled with a fondness of a pleasant memory.

Val knew there was no place for her in Heaven. 'I do miss her. Not just as an invaluable help, but as a friend,' she lied.

The woman's smile remained. 'You'll come back for a sam-witch, won't you?' the rhetoric in her voice too natural to be contrived.

'Of course. Is there anyone that needs a lift there?' Val offered.

'No, we'll all fit in the cars we came in I think, 'cept Glad. Thank you anyway.' She held Val's hand briefly, and moved away to greet a group patiently waiting to commiserate.

Val was surprised to find that she was the first to arrive back at the house, and was greeted at the door by a neighbour who introduced herself as Dulcie Toop from six doors down.

Dulcie, she told Val, was not one to boast, but the family would have gone to pieces without her this past week. Selflessly, she'd offered to miss the ceremony (even though, with her standing in the church, she loved a good funeral), manage the refreshments, and arrange the furniture to make sure everyone would be comfortable. Val indulged the woman and made the right noises when required to be impressed.

'They'll all be back soon then,' Dulcie observed.

'Yes,' Val agreed, taking a sip of rather weak looking tea

from the badly-chipped and tannin-ringed china cup offered to her. 'We all set off at a similar time. I must drive a bit faster than everyone else.' She tried to keep the conversation light.

'That's how accidents happen,' Dulcie warned. 'I'd slow down a bit if I were you. That was Gladys's problem – always dashing around.'

'Quite,' Val hid her face in the cup.

'And who'll benefit?' the woman's tone accusing. 'That brother of hers. He'll make sure he gets more than his fair share of what little she left. It's a pity in a way she planned ahead like she did.'

'Oh, in what way planned?' Val couldn't help herself ask.

'They're here now,' she pointed through grubby net curtains at the procession of vehicles drawing to a halt outside. 'Can't chit chat – better get the cling off these sarnies. Give us a hand will you, dearie?'

Everyone had a cup of what they thought was tea, and a plate of sandwiches balanced precariously in one way or another when a nephew broke the silence, and proposed a toast to his aunt.

'To Glad!' the ensemble joined together with greater harmony than they had managed during any of the hymns in church. This somehow signalled the approval for audible communication between fellow mourners and the low, almost ashamed tones of conversation began at once.

'It's been a magnificent send-off,' Val told Gladys's sister, whose name she still didn't know, but didn't like to ask.

'Hasn't it just?' she surveyed the room. 'We couldn't have afforded such a swish do for her,' she replied.

Val was curious. 'So, how *did* you manage?' she asked.

'The Co-op,' she replied with intoned esteem. 'Wonderful, don't you think? That "pay now, die later" scheme.

Lovely bit of crushed velvet in that box,' she admired. 'She always did plan ahead,' the fond smile returning to help her stave off the tears. 'I think I might get some of that velvet for the parlour curtains.'

Val felt the need to excuse herself and went to the kitchen where Dulcie Toop was rummaging in a drawer that appeared to be full of papers. 'Oooh!' the startled woman yelped, 'It's you! I just can't find where she keeps the salt,' she explained with a well-honed conviction.

Val released her harshest glare. 'It's on the table in there,' she tilted her head assuredly towards the room she had just left.

'That's all right then. I'll just put these bills, I mean papers, back in here,' a look of muted confession appearing across her face.

Val remained tight-lipped and watched her leave the kitchen. 'Pharisee,' she murmured. She'd had all the faithless piety she could stomach for one day, and decided to make a move towards home, leaving the family and hangers-on to their own interpretations of grief.

Elizabeth tossed her college bag on to the settee and admired the flowers on the window sill. The perfume was exquisite, and she wondered just what her parents had been up to that weekend to justify such a magnificent arrangement.

'Mum!' she yelled.

'I'm in the kitchen,' was her mother faint reply.

'I know,' she shouted louder. 'Come here a minute! I want you.'

'You come here you lazy sod, I'm busy.'

With a sigh, Liz dragged her feet through to the kitchen where Val was making a shopping list. 'That's better,' she said. 'Now what was it you wanted?'

'Dad must have had a good time this weekend,' the

bouncing eyebrows and cheeky smirk making Val laugh.

'Why do you say that?'

'He's not sent flowers for ages, and suddenly you have a weekend away and *voilà!*' her arms adopting a theatrical wave, 'we have the beautiful blossoms!'

'And you think your Dad's changed the habits of a lifetime, do you?' asked Val, impressed with the idea that he could buy her flowers.

'Well, who else is there?'

'Could be the other fella,' she baited.

'No way! Who'd shag an old biddy like you?' Liz scoffed. 'Mind you, that'd explain the dog hairs on the carpet!'

'You leave Bongo out of this,' quipped Val. 'He's a lovely dog. He can even guide him to the right spot on a good day.'

'Bongo!' snorted Liz. 'Where are they from really?'

Val explained to an hysterical daughter how she'd spent the afternoon, and at times couldn't quite believe the sequence of events herself.

'You're not fit to be let out, Mother!' Liz mocked. 'I'm ashamed. Fancy keeping a funeral wreath to decorate your own home with!'

For a travel agent with many years' experience, Emma was a bad traveller. It was putting her own advice into practical action that she had most trouble with; the actual holidaying was fine.

Whereas she could normally iron and fold a dozen of Dan's collared shirts without much thought or effort, she'd manage three stressful T-shirts when it came to holiday clothes, and be all fingers and thumbs when it was time to pack them in a case. She hated holidays.

This last week had disappeared so quickly, she didn't feel ready for her break and still wasn't happy about leaving

Olivia for over a week, especially so soon after her return home. Her daughter did seem to be pretty settled, though, and it was evident that she was quite looking forward to staying with Val and Adrian – she'd had her bag packed since Tuesday.

With an empty house, Jack could crack on with rewiring the place too. At least that would be sorted before Bump became Baby.

Right now, there was little of Thursday night left; the flight time tomorrow morning meant an early rise, and she was nowhere near ready. She really did *hate* holidays.

Her checklist was full of ticks, crosses and squiggles, the key to which she'd forgotten and given up on. She'd packed sun lotion, but did the cross mean she should have bought some more? Too late now, if it did they could get some at the airport.

The latest advice on electrical goods – was it to go in the hand luggage or in the hold luggage? What the hell. Hold luggage sounds best. She wouldn't have to carry the hair dryer, travel iron and heated brush around Manchester Airport's departure lounge for two hours that way.

'Dan!' she shouted. 'Have you decided what clothes you want to take?' There was no reply. 'Dan!'

'Hello?' he called up the stairs.

'Have you decided what clothes you're going to need?' she repeated, exasperated and ready for bed.

'Those shorts,' he continued the conversation from downstairs.

'*What* shorts?' He wasn't being helpful.

'The white ones with the stripes down the side.'

'I threw them out last year, didn't I?' she yelled.

'You better not have, they're my favourites.'

She could hear him climbing the stairs, the third one always creaked under his weight, and sat on the bed waiting for him to enter the bedroom before continuing. 'I'm done in,' she told him, wiping her brow with the back of her hand. 'Didn't you split those shorts at the barbecue last summer?' she struggled to recall the details in her current harassed state.

'Oh aye. Had me Mr Men grollies on, didn't I? Mr Happy was smiling at everyone when I bent down to light the charcoal!' he laughed. 'Why did you throw 'em out?'

Emma sighed. 'You were too fat to get into them last year, so what makes you think you'd manage this?'

'All right, all right!' he held up his hands in submission. 'So the shorts are gone, along wi' me waistline.'

'What else do you need?' her temper down to a stump.

'What d'ya reckon?' he asked her. She remained silent. 'What are you looking at me like that for, Em?'

'Like *what*?' she huffed.

'Like you're going to stick a knife into me, the minute me back's turned.'

She smiled and tried to laugh. 'How perceptive you're getting in your old age! Now, what do you want to take on holiday?'

Dan got the message. 'Tell you what,' he began, 'you go downstairs and sit quietly while I sort out the packing.'

'No way!' she shook her head.

'Why not?'

'Because we'll arrive there to find you've no shoes, and I've nothing but a basque and suspender belt to wear, that's why not!' she predicted. 'I tell *you* what,' her negotiations opened thoughtfully. 'I'll give you ten minutes to sort out what you need to take, bearing in mind there's a cruise involved with gala dinner – so think Little Chef not Burger King,' she knew all too well Dan's sartorial and gastronomic limitations, 'and I'll come back up here to pack it. Okay?'

'All right, luv,' he agreed, 'if you think that's best.'

'I do. Trust me,' she said, turning towards the door and the chance of regaining a little sanity. 'I'll bring you up a cuppa in ten minutes then.'

She took a seat next to Olivia who was continuing her diary serialisation for Bump, and closed her eyes. 'Tell me when he's gone,' she groaned.

Olivia studied her mother with care. 'Who?' she asked, puzzled.

'Your father. Tell me when he's safely on the flight and I'll come out of hiding.'

'Mother,' Olivia's tone reminded Emma of Hissing Hetty, a school mistress who, at the age of ten, she feared more than the Bogeyman who lived in the pantry himself. 'You *always* do this. You know you'll enjoy it, so drop the melodrama and don't pretend you won't!'

Emma gave her daughter the harshest stare she could muster. 'If you weren't expecting, I'd smack your bottom.' She knew Olivia was right. 'I hate you,' she smirked.

'The feeling's mutual I'm sure,' Olivia replied. 'Now get back up those stairs, and help the poor useless beggar pick out some clothes for his holiday.'

The downward thumping of the stairs told Olivia that her father had been banished from the theatre of operations. Mother, as ordered, was back in control. However hard he tried to be useful, it never worked and Dan always seemed to get in the way. Packing cases was hardly his forte and Olivia felt for him. How different Edward had been to the men she'd encountered before in her life – her dad in particular. She closed the diary and stroked the kicking tummy in the now habitual circles. The baby pressed a strong limb hard from within, and Olivia could distinguish its form with her hand against the taut skin of her stomach. She ran her fingernail across the protrusion and it withdrew. She was delighted. She'd tickled her baby.

'What are you smiling about?' Dan asked as he carried in two cups of tea.

She accepted the daisy-chewing cow mug from him.

'I'm tormenting Junior,' she grinned. 'I've been tickling his little... Ooooof!' her face contorted. 'Little sod!'

'His little sod?'

'No, foot,' she frowned. 'He's just booted me water-works.'

Dan roared with laughter. 'You are *sure* it was his foot you tickled?'

The bedroom was familiar to Olivia. The decor was an image of *Home and Garden* – soft pastel peach and blue shades, with perfectly brushed stencil patterns around the walls by the ceiling. She envied Val's steady hand and patience. Olivia had stayed at Wingate Farm a few times before, and had always been accommodated in this room, with its magnificent views of the north Lancashire fells. She stood by the ornate washstand and basin – there only for effect – and gazed out of the window, admiring the fresh autumnal morning and thinking back to the first time she'd stayed. It was the Christmas before last. Val and Adrian had thrown a huge party for the staff of Adrian's company and Ed's grandparents, some of Liz's friends and herself had stopped over.

A nervous and foreboding smile appeared. She recalled an amorous Edward creeping from his room, down the landing and into hers in the middle of the night; climbing into bed and warming his hands on her bottom as she slept, waking her by gently and slowly teasing his hand up and down her inner thigh, moving his roaming fingers around the front of her stomach, stopping only when his grandmother said she'd scream if he didn't pack it in and get out that instant! How he faced her after that, Olivia never did fathom out. It taught him to count the doors properly, anyway.

She began to unpack her belongings, leaving her ever-ready overnight bag intact just in case it was needed in a hurry. Taking each item from the case with slow care, she found a tidy home for everything. She amazed herself these days. She was never tidy before! Is this what motherhood did to a girl – change her beyond all recognition? Would Ed still have fancied the new Livvy? She feared not. It was their chalk and cheese relationship that kept it buoyant and loving. She didn't particularly like this new persona that seemed to be evolving as a result of her condition. She *loved* being untidy.

Val knocked and entered bearing a tray of tea and cakes. 'Just a little "Welcome to your temporary home" elevenses,' she smiled.

Olivia sat on the bed and checked her watch. 'But it's only just gone nine,' she sniggered. 'You'll have me fat.'

Val settled the tray on the dressing table and opened the drawer beneath the vanity mirror. Taking the two brown envelopes from their concealed resting place, she turned to Olivia with sober countenance. 'Olivia,' her quiet tones a little disconcerting to the young woman, 'Edward wouldn't have been Edward if he hadn't been, well, let's say thorough, would he?'

Olivia shook her head, unsure of what was to come.

Val sat beside the girl. 'He takes... sorry, took after Grandpa Quirk for that.'

'Takes,' corrected Olivia, a cloud of tears forming.

Val smiled a warm and proud smile. 'You're right,' she agreed, 'Takes. And both Edward and Elizabeth were encouraged by Dad from a very early age to have everything neat and tidy,' the words weren't coming easily for Val, 'just in case anything should happen.'

Olivia took Val's hand and with sensitivity, squeezed. She knew that whatever she was struggling to explain, it was causing great pain.

Taking a deep breath, Val continued. 'His eighteenth birthday present from his grandfather was the drawing up of a will, which, under the circumstances and obvious family connections, was read before his cremation.'

A tear crawled snail-like towards Olivia's chin. 'I should have been there, Val. I'm sorry...'

'Don't,' Val wiped the tear from the girl's cheek. 'Don't blame yourself for anything, love.'

'I need to explain...' Olivia cried.

'All in good time,' Val was strong. 'In his will,' she continued, 'he didn't have much to leave, but he did have something for you.' She handed over the smaller, and by far, bulkier of the envelopes. 'I also found this the day he died,' the second, larger envelope was exchanged and Val rose to leave.

'Don't go, Val,' Olivia sobbed. 'Please,' she begged, 'stay. I want you to stay.'

She carefully and timidly opened the first. It was heavy, her finger running a jagged edge through the sealed sheath. She carefully tipped the contents into her open palm and saw a beautiful gold pocket watch. She looked shocked. 'It's Grandad Mallory's watch.'

'He wanted you to have it,' Val's caring smile infused.

'But it was his treasure, I can't!' she cried. 'He wouldn't let anyone else even touch it.'

'I know.'

Olivia leant towards Val and they hugged. 'I like to think I knew my son better than anybody,' Val admitted.

'Know,' Olivia cried.

Val forced a pained smile. 'Know,' she stood corrected once more. 'But,' she continued slowly and deliberately, 'I think that perhaps you hold that honour. I only know about my son that he loved and cared for you a great deal, and if he were alive today, he'd be very proud of you and your Bump,' she held her tighter. 'What he left in his will,' her eyes leaked tears, 'is the item that he felt most valuable, to the person he felt most precious. What he *didn't* know he'd left with the person most precious, will *always* be the most valuable to us all.'

They sat, for what seemed an eternity, and cried together. Bump was distressed at his mummy's anguish and Olivia held Val's hand to her stomach, the pair instinctively knowing what the other was thinking. They offered tissues to one another, and gradually stopped their tears.

Holding the pocket watch tight, Olivia opened the second envelope, lifting from within a notepad.

'I put it in the envelope,' Val said. 'He kept the pad by his bed. You know what he wa… what he's like for making notes.'

Olivia flipped it open, sniffing a knowing laugh at his habit.

'The last entry,' Val suggested.

Turning the sheets, Olivia came to the last entry made the night before he died:

Wednesday 5th March, 12.20 a.m.

Having weird nightmare about Livvy marrying someone else. Someone without recognisable face. I'm not there – just watching from above. Then this poem appears from nowhere:

Beyond Belief

If long ago in days before, these visions I could see
I would have thought without a doubt, my mind was fooling me

You've taken me up far beyond the reaches I foresaw
With open heart I've learned from you, and loved you more and
*   more*

And still in awe I lie here now, your absence deeply wounding
My heavy heart a testament, to love I know enduring

This midnight hour, a lonely time without you here beside me
I wish I knew just how to say, for all you've done – I thank thee

You've taught me much I never knew, I want Love to be free
To lift us up and make it so, for you to be with me

It matters not about the rest, as long as we are true
Our love it conquers over all. My life I'd give for you.

– Don't know where that came from! Just had this compulsion to
write down how much Livvy means to me. I'll send her flowers
tomorrow morning.

A lone tear dropped heavily onto the page, its starburst effect creating flowing ridges in the paper. 'They were lovely, too!' Olivia sobbed, wiping the sheet dry to preserve the text. She drew a deep breath and turned to Val in silence. Damp-eyed, they looked at each other for some time.

'Do you want this tea?' Val finally ventured.

Olivia nodded. 'Yeah,' she sniffed. 'Let's be decadent and eat all these cakes too,' she added with forced bravery, hoping that she could be strong enough to cope during this next week with Edward's presence so evident around her.

Olivia's hand never left the pocket watch as they ate the deliciously sticky cakes, washed down with now tepid tea. The telephone rang, and Val went to answer with a mouthful of iced bun. In her absence, Olivia read again the last lines of her soul mate: '...*Our love it conquers over all. My life I'd give for you.*' You did as well, she thought, raising the watch and kissing it gently, before holding it to her bulging tummy for Bump to listen to the rhythmic ticking.

'That was your mother,' Val announced, returning to the bedroom and retaking her seat next to Olivia. 'She wanted to know if you were okay before they flew.'

Olivia smiled in disbelief. 'I hope you told her I'd popped after eating so much already!'

'I did as a matter of fact, then that we were about to compare notes.'

'On what? You're surely past wanting to conceal love-bites Val,' she managed to joke.

Val lifted her previously hidden hand to reveal a pad that Olivia instantly recognised from her own doodles of Sydney landmarks on the front.

'Hell's teeth!' she exclaimed. 'Where've you dug that up from?' her heart skipping a beat.

'Your Mum came across your diary…'

'Didn't she just!' Olivia's rebuttal.

'Yes, she said there'd been trouble. She came across your diary and had a hell of a time wondering what to do with it. It was me who suggested she read it – or throw it,' she confessed. 'Anyway, sorry if it's caused you some embarrassment, but as you seem to be reading your own to Bump, perhaps you'd like to do the same with her daddy's that I unearthed at a similar time.'

'It's "his daddy", Val.'

'Are you going to be contradicting me *all* the time?' Val quizzed. 'I don't think I can stand it if you are!' she grinned. 'But "his" sounds great to me.'

'Good,' Olivia replied unequivocally, 'you've no choice.' She took the pad from Val and stared at the front cover with a figurative snort.

Val stood and offered her hand to help Olivia rise. 'Why don't we go and sit in comfort, eh?' she asked. 'This could be interesting reading.'

The beads of sweat began to show on Dan's forehead. He wasn't even on the plane yet and he was worrying about it. Emma had never mentioned the fact that this flight was all non-smoking. It's all right for her, he considered, she wasn't dependent upon a regular fix of nicotine. How would she like it though if he stopped her from drinking coffee? Eh? She'd soon crack up. He drew hard on the thinly rolled tobacco, and shook nervously as the smoke emerged from his lungs, and drifted towards the woman in yellow flower pattern dress, reading what looked to be a new Mills and Boon. Didn't they come ready dog-eared and torn? He'd never seen a new one. Not that he read them of course, just he'd always thought... Oh pull yourself together! he told himself.

He watched the woman reading. Her lips moved with the words. They were hairy lips he noticed, very hairy indeed. He imagined her eating a biscuit and never tracing the crumbs in such a dense jungle. Little bugs with tiny machetes, hacking their way through the undergrowth, eagerly striving to reach a morsel first and sticking a conquering flag therein. Still the lips twitched.

He gazed around in search of Emma who was hunting for sun lotion. He could have sworn he saw a carrier bag full of the stuff in the case last night. Ah well, she's the professional.

Yellow flowers continued to read away, Dan's eyes drawn to her again. Her leg had joined the twitching while his eyes were busy elsewhere scanning the departure lounge. Maybe there was a column of little bugs marching from her toes through the leggy forest beneath the American Tan tights, straight on at the knee and up towards the oblivion awaiting them at the knicker elastic. At least, he hoped she was wearing knickers – an ugly bugger of her age. He watched the last of his cigarette burn out and flicked the small tube of paper into an empty soft drink can by his side. Where is Emma?

He felt a hand slide across his back, and he turned to see her face. 'Hello stranger,' he told her, 'you've been ages.'

'Decided to call Val to see if Ollie's okay,' she replied.

'Don't shout,' she saw the warning signs written across his anguished face.

'We only said goodbye to her three hours ago.'

'Yes, but I'm still not happy about leaving her,' Emma's pitiful plea for understanding.

Dan despaired, and reached for his tin of tobacco to roll another cigarette. Turning away, the woman in yellow caught his eye once more. She was scratching her leg, and he smiled.

'What's up?' Emma asked, amused at his sudden change in mood.

'See that woman over there?' he pointed slyly.

'Floral dress?'

'Aye. D'ya reckon she wears knickers?'

He could see nothing but blackness, apart from the white and orange patches that exchanged places when he moved his eyeballs of course. To make matters worse, his cheeks were now beginning to ache. Emma wasn't helping. She normally held his hand and said calming things like 'have a cigarette' or 'there, there, there'. She wasn't talking to him at all though, and his cheeks *really were* hurting. Perhaps if he didn't screw his eyes up so tight, the muscles might relax a bit.

The person in the seat in front wasn't helping either. They kept leaning forward and throwing themselves into the chair back. 'It's in the upright position,' he wanted to tell them, but he supposed it could be because he was gripping their headrest so tightly that they protested so vigorously.

Emma wasn't responding to his calls for commentary. He didn't have a clue what was going on around him in the packed aircraft cabin, only that every now and again he felt the bag or fat backside of an excited traveller knock him. Just sit down, everybody, and don't rock the bloody boat!

He craved a cigarette. It was surely the best part of an hour since he'd had one. The plane's engines whined, and his breathing grew heavier.

'Stop that, you big baby!' Emma told him.

'Oh I see,' he gasped, 'we're talking now, are we?'

'No,' she refuted, 'I'm not talking; I'm telling.'

Dan found the motion a little too much to bear. Why did he ever agree to flying? 'Is it going to be this bumpy all the way there?' his nervous voice escaped between clenched teeth.

She observed his tense expression through a cursory glance. The eyes were still screwed tight, his knuckles white – now clutching the armrest between them, and the perspiration beads again gathered on his brow like migrating starlings. 'I'm afraid it will,' she replied with a touch of condescension. 'It might even get a bit worse too,' she looked beyond him and across the plane, where through the tiny window opposite, she could see the runway apron pass gently by, 'when we've taken off.'

She returned to her book. Not only was she deserting her daughter as she saw it, she was about to spend ten nights away with a whinging lecher.

D. *14 – SUNDAY 23 JUNE: 7.45 p.m. I am knackered! I can hardly walk and my body thinks it's been hit by a tree. We weren't going to let yesterday's problems spoil the entire visit to Aussie's Red Centre, so today the alarm went off at 5 a.m. to signal the start of a successful day. With bags already packed, we grabbed a quick shower and loo (only a six this morning I fear!) and waited in the morning darkness with our carrier bag of DIY breakfast, camera, binoculars and valuables, ready for the coach to collect us. It was still fairly dark when we reached Uluru, just the first signs of daylight breaking through from the east. If Ayers Rock looks big from 20 km away, it's awesome up close! It makes you feel so blatantly insignificant in life, and elucidates without doubt the term 'monolithic'.*

The guide – his name surely wasn't really Bruce? – told us to grab a coffee from the coach in front, and that we could eat our breakfast anywhere but on the coach.

We're in our shorts because we're flying later on and guess what? It's only a few degrees above freezing outside, and the hairs on my legs were creaking as I walked. Livvy's jumper didn't hide her shivers either.

We waited for what seemed like hours in the cold, and then it happened – the sun broke over the horizon, and the colour change in the Rock was incredible. That sudden change in coloration is the most amazing thing I've seen in my life! It looked almost fluorescent against the deep blue dawn sky. I hope the photos come out all right.

No sooner had the sun illuminated the Rock, than we were piled back onto the coach and taken round to the climb site. As we parked up, there were a dozen or so ant-sized beings walking up the side of this gargantuan Aboriginal meeting place, and Bruce suggested we'd have to be quick and join those ants if we wanted to reach the top.

Not wanting to leave anything of value unattended, we took everything with us from the coach and craned our necks to see the top. Fact is, you can't see the top from there, you can see up the steep bit – supposedly about halfway. Believe me, that's a long half way!

There's a stretch of Rock from ground level that goes up for twenty – thirty yards, and to its left is Chicken Rock – so called for those deciding they'd rather not carry on further, to drop out. After Chicken Rock, there's an open stretch of ten yards or so before a chain link rail starts.

'This'll be the best bit Val,' Olivia laughed, pointing at the page. 'He looked so eager, bless him.'

We set off side by side, and Livvy gives me the bag because it's awkward to carry. I'm soon out of breath and really want a rest...

'Cheeky beggar insisted he was all right!'

Val blinked with exaggeration. 'That's our Edward,' she said with a lack of surprise.

...but we carry on a few paces. Livvy says she's okay, so I battle on, moving ahead of her slightly so's to get round an old lady. We've only gone fifteen yards and I've had enough, but we've come all this way, a piece of rock isn't going to beat me!

I'm chattering away, making sure Livvy's okay and I suddenly realise that there's no response. I stop and turn around, only to see her sitting on Chicken Rock, waving at me.

So there I am, knackered already (but not going to be defeated), carrying all our belongings in a silly flimsy carrier bag at the point of no return! On I go, alone.

Well, it's bloody…

'Ooops! Sorry, Bump, can't say that can I?' Olivia corrected herself.

Val looked inquisitive. 'What's that?'

'Can't swear in front of Bump,' Olivia rubbed her wriggling expectancy.

….it's… ('bloody')… steep up that hill, and I'm holding up the entire line of folk behind by clinging on to the chains and hauling myself up. There's little Japanese ladies in dinky white gloves marching, quick as you like, past me as I'm wheezing and puffing my way, pole by pole. God, where's your Ventolin when you need it?

Either side of this chain, there's sheer drops, and the higher I go, the windier it becomes. This piggin' carrier bag on my arm is being blown horizontally, and I suddenly get the urge to drop a 10/10 right there in my pants! Turning round to admire the view though, the fear of falling off is far outweighed by the sheer striking magnificence of the whole landscape. I've seen Lanzarote's Timanfaya National Park, which is eerie. This is just agonisingly beautiful in a kind of endless and deserted way. I really wished Livvy had been able to climb up there.

At the end of the chains, and about forty minutes after you've set off, there's a plateau and I had to stop for a rest. Took some photos from there, and caught my breath before heading on up the last steep section – about a six foot high vertical bit, before following the white lines painted as the route towards the summit on the flatter section. The wind was howling and the bag flying around, so rather than be blown off the top because of our half-eaten breakfast, I decided to head back for the safety of Livvy's arms.

If going up is hard work, it's only to stop you from worrying about coming down! I bet Edmund Hillary didn't descend Everest face first like this. Jesus, it's steep! As I'm walking, my knees were at a 90° right angle, and my bum was scrapping along the 'kin floor!

After ten minutes of this, the right leg has gone to sleep. Nay, the right leg has dropped off! The muscles have gone into spasm, and you catch up to a woman who's …('shit') …scared that she's going to lose her grip, and slide the rest of the way to the bottom.

When the chain stops at the bottom, there's the stretch without support that you've got to cover before falling unconscious on to the floor at the foot of the Rock. It probably took ten minutes just to get from the end of the chain to ground level, the legs felt so badly welded in contorted place.

Livvy was waiting patiently at the Rock base, sitting with other 'chickens' (read 'sensible') amongst a load of dingoes, and applauded my efforts when I'd hobbled to the bench she'd so valiantly conquered. It was all worth the big kiss she gave and her rubbing of my legs – before I might add, showing me the plaques commemorating five deaths on the Rock!

No matter what we did, my right leg just would not straighten, so there we are waiting for Bruce to take us on a base walk, with me one leg shorter than the other! Livvy's rubbing at the top of my thigh didn't ease the stiffness in the leg, just prompted more elsewhere.

Olivia flushed in horror. 'Oh my God,' she moaned. How must this sound to Val?

Val's knowing smile from across the room didn't alleviate her discomfort.

So, Bruce is ready to take us round to some significant parts of the Rock and I've got to get aboard the coach with three stiff legs. On the coach, he tells us that on average, there's about ten people die per year as a result of climbing the Rock, and for goodness sake, don't go anywhere near the dingoes, it's mating season and they're likely to turn nasty! Thanks for the early warnings on both counts, Bruce!

The walk was interesting, plenty of Aboriginal tales and myths. Bruce was a bit of a drama queen though, pretending to be a favoured white man amongst the tribesmen. Yeah, and I'm Ned Kelly!

A quick tour around the visitor centre to grab a few souvenirs, and back to the hotel to collect the baggage and have the certificate signed to say I climbed 'Most of the way' up Ayers Rock.

Transfer to the airport, and a pretty quick flight here to Alice Springs. Livvy made sure that there was no chance of the stewardess sticking her tits in my face this time – she sat me by the window. There was only one worth a glance anyway.

The taxi ride from the airport to the pre-booked hotel was an experience of backward living meets technology. The driver – we'll call him Bruce too for the sake of argument – was telling us in a drawl that was either intoxicated or just severely retarded (either way, Livvy was pissing herself laughing behind her Lady Penelope hat), how there are a massive thirty-two taxis in The Alice to cover the huge 30,000 population. Whether that population includes the sheep, we're not sure. What we've found out though on our expedition for KFC supper, is that The Alice has more than its fair share of inbreds, and very sorry looking Aboriginals.

Message at reception upon our return from the tour operator who's cocked up this portion of the trip says 'Sorry – expect a full refund'. Too right, Buster! And some.

It's almost 9 p.m. now, I'm going to give Sleeping Beauty here a whopping great kiss and go to sleep myself. Tune in next time for more exciting adventures of 'Cripple and Penelope'.

Olivia chuckled. She could picture the scenes he was describing. The Alice taxi driver that Ed seemed so easily to understand. The hotel room overlooking the pool, closed because it was too cold – at 22°! To the rear, the view of the magnificent Todd River – a waterless strip of sandy earth; a short cut for the unfortunate indigenous people whom the white man had so self-seekingly tried to conquer and westernise.

Val was watching, admiring, giving the younger space to reflect. 'Memories?' she asked.

A broad beam, revealing a perfect row of teeth appeared

on Olivia's face. 'Yeah!' she nodded. 'He always had a way of describing things, didn't he?'

Val frowned questioningly and asked her to elaborate.

'Well, why use a sentence when a paragraph will do?' she laughed at her thoughts.

Olivia wasn't sure if she wanted to read any more of the diary. While she felt she had to know everything about Ed, the words were too close for her to get an unemotional view. It hurt to read of his love for her. She sometimes thought it best if they maybe hadn't felt so much for each other. That way, she could just get on with living her life like any other girl in her early twenties. But she couldn't, not fully. She was having his baby, and excited as she was at that prospect, who *would* come running with an overcoat in the rain?

Val observed from the settee. She was full of fear. Fear for what the future held for the young woman opposite and the baby she carried. She worried too that her grandchild would one day be taken away by a replacement father and his adoptive family. She'd be just another old lady that came to visit, the child not knowing who she really was, and her true importance in her (or his, as Olivia insisted) making.

They sat in reflective silence, only the music of the countryside outside to give background to their thoughts. Both considered how potentially difficult these forth-coming days could be.

Olivia studied the woman on the settee. She seemed to be lost in another world, and Olivia had thought better of disturbing her when Val's gaze met hers.

'Sorry, did you say something?' Val asked.

'No. I was wondering if you were thinking what I was thinking.'

'I hope not, luv.'

'Why's that then?' she softly prompted.

'Because I hope you're not, that's all,' Val smiled to cover the tracks of her earlier expressions.

'Now come on, Val, don't be like my mother,' she coaxed the elder. 'Is it Edward?'

'It doesn't matter, really, Livvy.'

Olivia produced one of her stares, the one she was proud of that made Edward fluster and tell all. 'I think it does matter, so please tell me.'

Val hesitated, Olivia willed her stare to have worked.

'When the baby's born—' Val began. Olivia secretly smiled, these Mallorys were suckers for her stare. 'No, that's not right,' Val checked her thoughts. 'It's difficult. It doesn't matter,' she shook her head.

'Oi!' the stare wasn't to be defeated. 'Come on, tell Aunt Ollie.'

Val knew she wasn't going to get away with anything other than the truth. 'I want you to have a full life, Olivia. Will you make sure you do that? For yours and the baby's sake?'

Olivia wasn't sure she understood. ''Course I will,' she replied.

'I mean you won't feel that if the right man comes along, there's anything holding you back.'

'It's too early for that, Val,' her tone adopting an unequivocal expression.

'It is now, I know. But in time, you'll meet someone who loves you as Edward did, and what I mean is, don't stop loving Edward if that's how you feel, but don't let Edward stop you loving someone else, will you?'

Olivia sensed Val's angst. 'No, I won't stop loving Edward. Ever,' she assured his mother. 'And it will have to be someone very, very special to compensate for his loss. No one can ever take his place, and I won't let them. Yours neither, Val, and anyone new will have to understand that,' she felt the top of her nose tighten involuntarily, and she knew that once more, unwanted tears were about to appear in her eyes.

Val dabbed her finger in the corner of her own eye. 'I'm glad you say that. You're too special for us to lose. Both you and Bump,' her unashamed gratitude surfaced. 'We're all pleased you could stay this week, it means a lot to us.'

'Well, if Livvy wasn't staying,' Liz reasoned, 'I could have invited him back to ours for a snog in that double bed.'

Carole wasn't happy with the attitude her best friend had embraced. She'd forgiven Olivia for the outburst last week and now defended her presence at the farm. 'He might be model material, but don't let him do whatever he wants before you're ready.'

'But I *am* ready, Caz! That's the problem, I'm gagging for it.'

They lingered longer in the refectory corridor. He wasn't there. His note, signed simply 'Den', had said to be by the gates at three that afternoon, but Liz was too eager and wanted to catch a glimpse of him beforehand. Perhaps she could fluster him if he wasn't quite ready for the passion-burning lips of Elizabeth Mallory.

Carole had waited long enough and strode ahead to join the queue for food, claiming that they looked suspicious hanging around. No, not suspicious, she corrected; desperate. Liz followed behind, scanning her surroundings for Him. 'Him' wasn't there though; she'd have to wait until three. That is, of course, if the butterflies in her stomach would allow.

'Where've you been to now?' Carole asked, her friend returning to the refectory in a hurry, and retaking the orange plastic seat next to her.

'Needed a wee!' Liz replied.

'Another? What's up with your bladder, girl?'

'I'm excited! Is he here yet?'

'You've only been out of the room two minutes for Pete's sake. Finish your sandwich and think of cold showers or something.'

'Oh we are a damp squib today aren't we?' Liz mocked. 'No time for showers, I'm too busy thinking of his gorgeous cheekbone structure, his swept hair and that almighty bulge in his 501s!'

Carole wrote off the afternoon lecture on Business Administration as a nightmare. She found Mr Jones's Welsh accent too difficult to concentrate on Maslow's Theory of Human Needs, and with Liz straining to see the rear gate through the window every few minutes, she was contemplating emigration.

'I've no watch, what time do you make it?' Liz asked.

'Two forty.'

'Not long now then! I'll check the time again in ten minutes, shall I?'

'Don't bother,' Carole's frustration with the personal, social and intellectual needs of a successful workforce turning to spite in her reply. 'When you think ten minutes are up, it's ten to three.'

A shrill burst of bell signalled three o'clock, and even though she'd been abrupt in the last tutorial, Liz had to ask Carole to do her a favour.

And so it was, that while Liz waited and watched at a discreet distance, Carole stood by the gate waiting for 'Him'. Her gaze was towards the college when she heard a voice behind her.

'Hello,' it said. 'You're Elizabeth's friend aren't you?'

Liz squinted from a distance to see what was happening as Carole froze to the spot, her hips not readily wanting to turn her body around.

When she did, she couldn't look him in the face. Looking towards the pavement, she saw a pair of sensible looking shoes, topped by white socks and the bottom of a pair of chocolate brown slacks.

'I'm Donald,' he told her bowed head. 'When she's not annoyed, my mum calls me Don.'

Liz couldn't make out who it was talking to Carole. What's happening? Who was standing here in front of Caz? Get lost, Den'll be along soon, she thought. Piss off, why don't ya?

Carole straightened up and recognised the spectacles and jacket.

'Is Elizabeth not coming?' the boy asked nervously.

Carole grinned. So this was Den, eh? Or was it Don with the bad handwriting? Either way, it was pay back time.

'So she's coming?' he repeated hopefully.

'Oh yes, she's just along there,' she pointed to Liz's hiding place. 'I'll wave her down in a moment, Don.'

He heaved a sigh of relief. 'I've been plucking up the courage to speak to her for ages – since you told me she'd been watching me that day, in the quadrangle, in fact. Er, I'm sorry I didn't catch your...'

'Carole,' she interrupted excitedly. 'I'm Carole,' she smiled, eagerly giving Liz their pre-arranged signal for 'come and get your snogging gear in action'. 'Look,' she explained, 'she's been dead impressed with the note and looking forward to this afternoon. Call her Liz, and don't be put off by her attitude. If she's offhand with you, it means she likes you.' Her wink gave the boy a much needed boost of confidence.

'Thanks, Carole,' he stuck both thumbs up.

Liz's slow approach was wary. Where was Den? She reached the couple by the gate and ignoring the boy stood there, asked 'What's the crack, Caz?'

Carole grabbed Liz's arm and turned her round to face 'Him'. 'Liz, meet Don. Don, this is Liz.'

Liz stood motionless, her mind vacant and eyes wide. 'Where's Den?' shock and disbelief working her mouth.

'Sorry, it's my pen,' Don explained. 'I'm not used to ballpoints. I prefer ink, but the nib bent whilst I was on draft number six. Sorry,' he laughed nervously, pulling down on the hem of the sports jacket with both hands.

Liz turned to Carole with horror in her eyes. Carole merely smiled warmly, and suggested that the new-found friends walk together for a while – perhaps to the bus station, and she'd tag along as chaperone.

Liz hid her face. 'For who, you cow?' she cried.

In the kitchen, the aromatic scent of curry greeted Adrian. He kissed Val and surprised Olivia by hugging her close. She wasn't used to this side of Ed's dad. In fact, she didn't know it existed. She continued to stir the large pot on the Aga while Val joined him in the lounge, pouring a large drink for him.

'Family meeting tonight, Val,' he told her.

'A what?'

'Family meeting. There's something we all need to discuss.'

'Well, this is new,' she raised her eyebrows in surprise. 'Whatever happened to our private little arguments?' His self-confident smile told Val he was either up to something, or had an announcement to make. 'Well? What is it?' she quizzed.

'Can't you wait?' he gulped the Irish.

'No, I can't. You do know Olivia's here, don't you?'

'Do you think I've just hugged the cat? Of course, I know she's here.' He took her hand and charmingly kissed it. 'You really want to know?'

She withdrew the hand sharply. 'Get it out for heaven's sake!'

'Now, now darling. Control yourself, Olivia's here!' he

joked.

'Well, come on!' she thumped his arm. 'Spit it out.'

'I'm selling up.'

Val was astounded. 'Selling up *what* exactly?'

'Track & Turf. Selling out.'

'The shops?' she gasped. 'But why? Can we afford it? You haven't discussed this with me or anything.'

'Take a breath for God's sake, woman! We're discussing it now, aren't we?' he gulped the whiskey again.

'No, you've just presented me with a *fait accompli* by the sounds of things,' she said, taking a seat. 'Get me one of them, will you?' she nodded at his empty glass.

'I've asked around, and had a nibble from one of the big boys. It's getting too cut-throat, what with the Lottery and not having anyone to hand over the reins to now, I'm getting beyond the age where I want the hassle,' he told her. 'Recently, I've been going into the office with the feeling that I'm simply rearranging the *Titanic*'s deckchairs,' he quipped handing her the glass. 'I want us to enjoy retirement together, not hit an early grave for the sake of a few quid.'

'But what do we live on? You're only fifty-four!'

'I've done the pension bit,' his shaking head assured her. 'With the amounts we've been putting away for over twenty-five years, plus the value of the business and the equity in the odd freehold tucked in there, we've got a little bit for the odd day trip to Fleetwood.'

Val took a large gulp of the smooth anaesthetic. 'You're serious, aren't you?'

'Absolutely, my dear. What do you think?'

'Well, we will have to talk about it properly – the numbers and everything,' she said, the unexpected news throwing her senses into disarray.

'Yes, all right.' He rolled his arm in expectation; he knew the figures would stack up. 'But in theory, what do you think?'

'I'd prefer trips to Skipton or Harrogate,' she smiled at last, 'but I think you're bloody marvellous!' she drained her glass and held out her hand for him to help her up from the chair. Once facing, they kissed.

The lounge door banged. 'What the hell's gotten into you two lately?' Liz stormed past and up the stairs. 'Snogging and shagging non-stop! All I get's some gonk with the hots for physics!' she grumbled.

Olivia considered it none of her business what Adrian and Val did with their shops. She felt honoured that her opinion was sought, but beyond that, embarrassment was more apt. She really was crashing in on their family, when perhaps they needed their own space.

The curry was excellent. Ed always raved about his mother's Indian dishes, but she'd always put that endorsement down to the fact that it was his mother that had made it. After all, no one made trifle like her own mum, did they? Her present abnormal fixation on the curry was probably, she pondered, due to the fact that she didn't wish to be part of the conversation on Track & Turf.

As an outsider, the discussion appeared to have two opposing, though remarkably similar sides, being refereed by someone walking a tightrope somewhere loosely in the middle. In the blue corner, Adrian. He wanted to sell; retire; buy a dog; live a peaceful and relaxing life with his wife; and generally enjoy the rewards of his years of hard work before it all killed him.

In the red corner, Elizabeth. She wanted her folks to enjoy the trappings of Wingate Farm and the security that they could afford to lavish upon her, but couldn't stand the stigma of having retired parents.

In the middle, and preparing to separate the sparring contenders, was Val. She also doubled as second to the blue corner, because she now quite liked the idea that Adrian would be able to spend time with her; and if he was going to be as relaxed as he was last weekend, she was all for it. Her refereeing duties did, however, include the balancing of Liz's arguments that another couple of years would see the pension fund topped up a little more.

So, as honorary ringside observer, and reluctant second to Liz when called upon for a neutral view (frequently provided by Liz herself), Olivia sat and scrutinised her curry.

The longer the debate ran, the more Adrian laughed at the opposition's futile case. The resulting determination of Liz to find more ways around avoiding telling Carole *et al* that her parents were so old, they were retiring, became pettiness in the extreme. The laughter continued, and so the circumference of the circle would be navigated once more.

'Just *don't* tell them,' Olivia suggested, desperate for an end to the bickering.

'Whose side are you on?' Liz demanded.

'Common sense's,' she chuckled. 'Your only problem seems to be what everyone else will think.'

'Only problem?' she choked. 'Don't you think it's a big enough problem to deserve a little more than "only"?'

'Tell 'em that your parents are so bloody wealthy, sorry Bump, that they are sticking two fingers up and just packing it in. Nothing to do with age.'

'Exactly!' agreed Adrian, applauding. 'Well put.'

'But we're not *rolling* in it,' Val protested in her capacity of arbitrator.

'Figurative speech, Val,' Olivia sighed.

'And if you were,' complained Liz, 'I'd be the "poor little rich kid" on a college meal ticket.'

'You are anyway,' Olivia joked.

'Oh, go on then!' Liz huffed. 'What do I care? Make me

a laughing stock! Carole'll have a fit when she realises, 'cause I'm not telling her!' She played childishly with the spicy sauce on her plate.

Adrian smiled sagely at Olivia; he was enjoying this. 'That was a unanimous Mallory "yes" then! What do you think, Livvy?'

He'd never called her Livvy before, always Olivia – certainly to her face. 'Like I said before, you've got to do what's best for you and Val in the long term,' she replied with tact.

Liz grunted.

'Oh, and of course Liz, too,' Olivia added.

'So I *am* here, then?' the teenager moaned to the table's scathing derision.

'Bump must be considered too, you know,' Adrian told Olivia when the jeering had ceased.

That uneased her a little. She couldn't possibly allow the baby to be included in any decision on the scale that they were now reaching, and told him so. He simply smiled and said okay. Like Val, Olivia sensed that his words wouldn't equate to his future actions, but there was nothing she could do about that. The baby wasn't born and the business wasn't even sold. It was all hypothetical, she told herself. If her mum was here, she'd tell her to just relax.

'For pity's sake, relax will you?' Emma told him. 'It's only a boat.'

He was visibly shaking. The plane had been enough for one day, but now he was getting on a cruise ship that floated. He hadn't realised they floated. Well, he realised they went on water, but hadn't thought what that actually entailed – him going on water. At least he could smoke, albeit on deck where he could see the sea. There, and the lounge bar which sounded preferable.

The cabin had a porthole; that was something. He didn't

know yet if it was a good thing or bad thing, but it was something. He had expected to be sleeping on a bunk. He'd not done that for years, and was disappointed in a way that he was to be deprived of the excitement. If he had to sleep in a separate bed to Emma, at least there should be a good reason. Instead, there were two single beds kept a discreet distance apart by a dusky pink melamine vanity cabinet. And, he noticed, they weren't very wide either. They were about par for the cabins though, which the ship's guide described as 'compact'. They were small. It was the occupants that needed to be compact.

It was some time before the vessel would leave Funchal, but Dan was in no state to realise that their cruise had begun from the Atlantic island port when the ropes were finally cast. For over the preceding three hours, he had joined a new-found friend, named Jack, in the bar; Mr Daniel to the uninitiated, according to the barman – whose name badge identified as José.

Meanwhile, Emma unpacked their case and found her bearings. She recognised his form through the lounge bar window, even without her glasses. It was the rounded shoulders and hanging head that she saw as his 'I've had enough; will someone carry me to bed?' pose. He was safe enough, though; propped against the bar while she watched Madeira slowly shrink away into the distance.

The clear evening sky was fast losing its brilliance, as the vessel headed south east towards the easterly Canary Islands of Lanzarote and Fuerteventura, the blues gaining depth as the sun sank steadily into the sea. She stepped inside the warmth of the bar to coax her husband back to the cabin to change for dinner. Not, she thought, that he would probably make dinner after consuming innumerable glasses of spirit, served no doubt the Iberian way – very large and very neat.

His swagger was countered by the swell of the boat, and

of the two, it was he who walked the straighter back along the corridors of steel doors towards cabin 3124, their outside twin.

Theirs was a nine o'clock second sitting in the Juan Carlos Restaurant, one deck up. Dan found himself sitting to a large table of complete strangers when his mind's gears slipped temporarily out of neutral and lurched him into euphoric confusion. Where was Emma? There was an empty seat next to him; he hoped that was hers. He couldn't quite comprehend the environment into which he knew not how he'd arrived. He swiftly gathered however, that there was food involved. The plate of soup, gently swishing around the rim in synch with the rhythmic motion of the supposedly stabilised ship, gave that one away. His eyes followed the crest of the circling wave, his head motionless. Slowly his eyelashes grew infeasibly heavier, forcing the top lids further and further downwards as he rocked backwards and forwards with the ship. Polite conversation, introductions and cruising anecdotes all around, mingled with an inner voice telling him that he needed sleep. He jolted awake. Had he made a fool of himself? 'It doesn't matter,' the demonic brain cells said, 'you need sleep, so sleep.' 'Can't sleep,' the angelic told him, 'Emma will be here soon. Smile and join in the conversation.'

Slipping his shoulders forward felt comfortable. It relaxed his neck. Emma would be back soon from wherever she was, he told himself. The alcohol coursing through his veins weighed down his eyelids once more, and a weary effort to raise them was not strong enough to prevent complete shut-down. 'Sleep,' repeated the soothing voice, 'you need sleep.'

He awoke to the noise of curtains being ripped open and streaming sunlight in his bleary eyes. The ceiling spun and rocked at the same time. Where on earth was he? His body tingled and his limbs felt a weighty ache. His mouth was parched; his tongue senseless from night-long exposure. He wished the ceiling would stop, if only for a moment. Closing his eyes once more didn't seem to work. Instead, it sent an urgent message to his stomach – 'Evacuate!' Suddenly, the heavy limbs were carrying him in search of and through the bathroom door, but he was nowhere near a sink or lavatory bowl when the projectile apostasy was complete. 'You've made a mess,' angelic told him dispassionately. He didn't care. Demonic Dan was in control.

He approached her in the lounge bar. She was wearing a floral print dress, and very nice it looked, too. She didn't seem to hear him telling her that he liked the outfit, so he told her again. Strange, he thought; she just took a sip of the gaily coloured cocktail in front of her, and continued to read her book.

Taking the seat opposite, he sighed heavily and wiped his face with the palms of his clammy white hands. Boy, was he shattered! There was no response. He waved over the waiter and ordered a beer.

'Make that a mineral water,' the face behind the book said.

Dan looked at the perplexed waiter. 'No, a beer will be fine, thank you,' he contradicted.

The waiter moved off and the book lowered, revealing only Emma's eyes. They were cold, and her stare acidic. He didn't like that look, it normally meant deep trouble for somebody. 'You drink that beer,' she snarled, 'and it's your last!'

'Eh?' It was too early yet for him to fully appreciate the situation.

'You heard. You're a bloody disgrace.'

'Me?' he asked, pointing to his chest. 'Why?'

There was mordant hatred in her voice. 'You don't even

know, do you?'

He shook his head. He was in lumber this time. But for what? 'You'd better tell me, luv,' he leant back into the soft chair and resigned himself to a severe ear bashing. Bill would undoubtedly give odds-on for it being a very public humiliation, he thought.

Emma glanced around to check the decibel range that she could possibly achieve without being asked to leave. 'Where do you want me to start, my darling? My sweetness, light of my life?'

He didn't like the sound of this at all.

'Shall we start with dinner?' He didn't have a chance to reply. 'I leave a quite sedate and harmless zombie wedged betwixt table and chair-back, just for a minute, while I go to the Ladies. What do I find when I come back?' Her voice tone changing up an octave. 'The maître d' offering our table companions napkins to clean off their dresses and jackets, while the Cruise Director pulls your head out of your soup.'

'Oh,' he sheepishly lowered his head.

'"Oh"? You might well "Oh"!' she blasted, and he dreaded the thought of there being more. 'As if that isn't sufficient embarrassment for us both!' See, he knew it. 'This morning when I come out of the bathroom – you remember, having just woken you up?' her delivery too sharp for his thumping head, 'I find you've jumped into the corridor bollock-naked, and spewed your guts all over the place!'

'But that was the bathroom,' he cried in disbelieving shame.

'I see. You wanted to cover me in your bile, did you?' Emma's temper bubbled with sarcasm.

'Oh Christ, no!' He couldn't understand what he was hearing.

'Oh Christ, yes, matey!' she continued in full flow.

'Don't you remember banging on the door for me to help you "get out", because there were people in our bathroom staring at you?'

He didn't want to know any more. He scanned the room through painful eyes to make sure no one was staring, or pointing him out to their deck-games partners. 'I feel sick,' he told her as the waiter brought his tray. Dan shook his hand dismissively. 'Mineral water, sorry pal. No more beer.'

Emma placed her bookmark deliberately in the spine of the novel, and closed its cover. She didn't want to show any lenience to the remorseful wreck opposite, but he did look pathetic. She wanted to laugh at the pitiful sight, but dared not. He was to suffer for what he'd put her through, and a short sharp shock was not the most satisfying method. He'd pay all right.

'Lanzarote was nice, Daniel,' she told the hands covering his face.

They slid down, revealing his forehead, eyes and nose. His skin was pale and eyes bloodshot, the perfect horror movie creature, she thought.

'Lanzarote?' he frowned.

'Yes. It was nice, the little bit of it I saw. We'll have to go back there one day.'

'I've missed it?'

She raised her eyebrows and viewed him sternly. 'You might just catch a glimpse if you hurry. What with chucking and sleeping,' her disparaging sigh, 'I'm surprised you've made it up at all.' She checked her watch. 'It *is* nearly time for the gala dinner, sweetness. Do we think we can manage that without incident?'

His guilt grew. He'd lost this battle before he even knew he was participating. Thank goodness there were two beds in the cabin: the floor carpet would have offered little comfort.

Through the queasiness, Dan knew he'd done wrong. He watched his wife getting undressed in the limited space the cabin offered and didn't attempt to move. He would only have been in the way and incurred more wrath. She looked beautiful, and he wanted to stand and give her a huge hug. Should he risk it? He'd ask, that was surely a safer route to take than an unsolicited approach.

'What do you think you'll get out of that?' she replied with feigned indignation, prolonging his hour of atonement.

He looked sorrowful. 'I just wanted to say sorry for mucking everything up.'

She turned away to prevent him witnessing her smile. 'Well, say it like you mean it, then,' she bluffed.

Emma looked and felt a million dollars in her new gown. Dan looked ill, and felt conspicuous in the only suit he owned. She glided into the restaurant in anticipation of the gala dinner. He ambled behind.

The maître d' smiled politely as he showed Emma and Dan to a table of their own by the kitchen doors. 'Your waiter this evening will be Leo,' he said, flicking open Emma's napkin with a loud snap and placing it across her lap. 'And your lifesaver is yet to be decided, Sir,' he added with emotionless humour. 'We shall be drawing lots in the galley, immediately after *entrées*.'

THEIR MEETING SEEMED unnecessarily clandestine as he waited patiently down the alley between the newsagent and florists, by the wheelie bins where she'd said. He'd arrived a good fifteen minutes early; just in case. Just in case what, he didn't really know, but ever since the Cub Scouts had taught him to 'Be Prepared', he had been. He wondered if she'd been a Brownie. He could see her in a Brownie uniform. They were brown in those days. His sister was one, that's how he knew. Brown with a little yellow neck tie. There was the beret too. That was brown as well. It followed he supposed, the Brownies wearing brown. She was a Pixie, his sister. He wondered what Liz had been.

She was late. He would be a gentleman and not mention it, but she was indeed late. By his watch, she was almost three minutes late. He resolved to ask his sister if there was a time-keeping badge in Brownies.

He heard the scraping of feet, and she appeared from behind the largest bin, which was overflowing with floral off-cuts.

'Sorry I'm late,' she said, squeezing past.

He looked at his watch. 'Don't worry about it,' he smiled. 'What's four and a half, no, four minutes and forty seconds between friends?'

She didn't know quite how to take that. Don was certainly different.

They chatted awkwardly by the dustbins and decided to find somewhere for a hot drink: the weather wasn't lending itself too kindly to standing around a draughty alley for too long.

They walked in strained silence the few hundred yards to the nearest café. It wasn't one that either frequented, which Liz considered a good sign. Wearing his chivalry hat, Don queued for the coffee while Liz found a table in the corner with adequate cover, a large yucca tree standing between her and the window.

'There we are,' he said, placing the tray carefully upon the table. 'One cappuccino for you,' handing it to her, 'and one straight coffee for me.'

'Thanks, Don,' she smiled.

'That's okay. We can settle up later.'

Liz was starting to question if this was really a good idea. She was sure he was a nice person deep down, perhaps just not used to girls. But was she *this* desperate?

They sat in resumed silence, the only break being the occasional slurp of Don's coffee. Liz wondered if he idolised the TV tea chimps, but thought better of asking him outright.

'Tell me,' he said without warning, 'were you a Brownie?'

She laughed. That was a line she'd never heard of before. 'Yes, were you?'

He hesitated. What was that supposed to mean? He didn't think boys could join the Brownies, and asked how it could be.

'No, Don.' Liz shook her head. 'That's what you might call humour. You know, ha ha?'

'Ah! Yes, very good. I see that now,' his expression revealing limited understanding; the sort that appears when someone has trodden in dog dirt – they know they've got to get it off, but don't know how to go about it. 'Yes, I like that. "Were you?" Yes. That's, yes, it's funny. I like that,' being the euphemistic "scrape along the kerb" method employed.

Liz's eyes rolled in disbelief. Earth, beam me up!

'No,' Don continued.

Straightening her face in case it bore a gormless fix, Liz wondered what she'd missed. 'No?'

'No,' he repeated. 'You asked me if I was a Brownie. No, I wasn't.'

She decided that if this encounter were to be anything like interesting, let alone a success, she'd have to guide the conversation. He was surprisingly keen to talk about his music interests, and she was relieved to hear that his aural repertoire wasn't completely Brit-Pop challenged. In fact, she thought, once he was talking, he was quite a nice bloke. She'd have to do something about his dress sense, though. The fashion police would have him castigated, and probably charge her with aiding and abetting, she felt sure.

She found herself laughing. She didn't know whether she was laughing at or with him, but did it matter? He was making her laugh. The things he said, however intentionally serious, came over as a bone-dry wit which tickled her. His often-bemused face turned to laughter, too, when she grinned. He hadn't a clue what was so funny, but her good humour deserved accompaniment. He had never made a girl laugh like this. Having said that, he'd never had the chance before, not really. You couldn't count his sister – she wasn't a real girl, and certainly not cousin Jennifer – she was only two-and-a-bit.

They stayed for a second coffee, which Liz bought to even out the finances, and she treated them both to a cake. She couldn't believe how much she was enjoying herself, and suggested they go and have a look around the shops.

'I'm not much of a shopper, I'm afraid,' he told her.

''Course you are! Everyone is at heart,' she replied, nudging his arm across the table.

She'd touched him. He liked that. He wanted her to do it again.

'Where do think we should go first?' she asked, hoping he'd leave the decision to her.

'How about CompMart?' he suggested excitedly. 'They've got a software sale on.'

Her face told him that she wasn't too keen on the idea and he offered the choice to her, remembering his code of gentlemanly etiquette.

'We'll strike a deal,' she said, weighing up the odds in her mind. 'We go to CompMart first to see what's on offer, then we have a look around the normal shops.'

'Done!' he agreed.

And so you have been, chum! she thought with an outward smile.

He was the taller of the two and Liz soon learned that when he was fired-up, Don didn't hang around. He was out of the café and off towards the computer store before she had fastened her coat, and she found herself scurrying after him up the now rainy street.

He lingered by the door, surveying the shop front like a child savouring his selection in a sweet shop. At his side, Liz peered up from beneath her umbrella at his awe-filled face, and followed his gaze to the window. There was nothing exciting to note: posters with ROMs and RAMs, bits and bytes, and mega things. Computers never turned her on. They, she reasoned, were for people who didn't have a life; but it seemed increasingly like his idea of a good night would involve the wrong sort of bits being played with, and any hardware used wouldn't need AA sized batteries.

'Are we going in, or what?' she asked, watching the drizzle trickle from his glasses. He nodded respectfully, and she could have sworn he bowed his head in reverence before crossing the threshold. 'I'll be over here,' she told him, pointing to a computer station with an appealing screen saver melting the page before her eyes. It was as good as anywhere else to be fed up.

He wandered off towards the software, oblivious to anyone or anything around him. Had her bluff been called this time? Would she ever see a clothes or record shop? She feared not.

Having studied the options available to him, Don had selected and paid for his software. Now back in the land of normality, he scoured the store in search of Liz. He considered that perhaps twenty-five minutes was a long time to have neglected her, after all, this was their first 'date' – if you could call it that. It was their first scheduled meeting, at any rate.

He found her, much to his relief. She was sat at a desk, clicking mouse buttons and navigating the latest version of some multimedia package.

'There you are,' he said.

'God, Don!' she sounded thrilled. 'Have you seen this?'

He looked at the screen and recognised its format. 'Yes, it's a good upgrade from the previous attempt.' His knowledge was thorough.

Her face glowed with delight. 'It's brilliant. Have you seen the encyclopaedia thing?'

'Yes, it's very good.'

'It's really good!' she gushed, unaware of his response. 'Just look at this!' She demonstrated a video caption of the Berlin Wall being toppled.

'Yes, it's a good system,' he repeated, slightly wearied by the mundanity of her discovery.

'And just listen to this!' A tune from an African tribal dance emitted triumphantly from the stereo speakers on either side of the screen.

'Yes, Liz.' Don tried not to sound too impatient. 'There's thousands of things on these units,' he told her. 'What about your normal shops now?'

She didn't take her eyes from the screen. 'In a minute. This is absolutely brilliant.'

He thought that another half an hour was quite long enough for her to have been playing on the system, and finally, prising her from the seat with the promise that she could call at his house at any time and use his machine (though heaven only knew what Mum would say), they left CompMart. Him bored, her elated at her new discovery.

'Where to now?' he asked, surprised to find himself relieved at leaving the shop he adored.

'I'm in a spending mood,' she told him. 'How about you?'

'I've just bought these,' he lifted the CompMart carrier bag.

'I fancy a new look,' she told him. 'Let's get some new outfits.'

Her arm around his back pulling him in towards the umbrella excited him. But what if someone was watching? What should he do? Other couples were holding hands. He couldn't do that, not in public. Others were not touching at all – that would be preferable to him, but she was holding on to him. She squeezed him tighter, steering him out of the way of an oncoming double buggy taking up most of the footpath, and whose handler was not looking where they were going. His arm fell around her waist as they stepped on to the road. It felt unnatural, but pleasant. They regained their place on the footpath and she didn't loosen her grip. Oh Lord! He felt a swelling somewhere below. Think of flow diagrams, he told himself. Think of the periodic table. Think of anything but her arm around him. Every step made the feeling worse. He thrust his hand in his pocket to hide his embarrassment. That didn't help too much, the carrier bag over his wrist preventing deep penetration. Don't think things like 'deep penetration', either, he disciplined himself.

She guided him into her favourite fashion store, catering for both men and women. Within seconds she was holding a pair of hip-hugging trousers up against her, and asking for his opinion.

'They're nice,' he said. That *is* what men are supposed to say, isn't it?

'Well, sound enthusiastic,' she replied. 'Do you think they'll suit me?'

He remembered his etiquette. 'I'm sure everything will suit you, Liz.'

'That's a cop-out if ever I've heard one. This way, let's see if they will,' she grabbed his hand and led him towards the rear of the shop. Her skin was soft and he held on to her hand gently, not wanting to let go, ever. This surely wasn't happening to him. She was lovely, he thought, from the land of Beautiful. He was shy, native of the planet Nerd. What was he thinking of, asking to meet her? But here she was, leading him around the shops by the hand. He felt the first signs of renewed swelling.

They stopped by a carousel and she professionally swept hangers aside and back again, pulling out two tops, one fluffy wool, the other more flimsy – both appearing to him to be far too small for anyone Liz's age.

'Right, let's try these on,' she told him, grabbing his hand once more and dragging him towards the changing rooms. 'Wait here for a mo',' she commanded as they reached the girl with the plastic tags by the curtains. 'Don't go away,' she wagged her finger maternally. 'I'll need your opinion. Constructive comments mind, none of that smooth-talking crap like before!'

He stood alone, females by the score around him. His mum never made him stand outside changing rooms when they went shopping. In fact, he couldn't remember ever seeing his mum buy clothes from a shop. They normally came through the post, then went back the week after when the man in the van returned for them.

He felt conspicuous. This was humiliation. She was doing this deliberately, wasn't she? The girl overseeing the changing rooms was looking him up and down with a smirk. Why weren't there any other men stood here? Any that were in the shop were looking at men's clothes, not loitering by the curtain.

He was just about to wander towards the men's section, when he heard his name being called from behind. He turned and saw her head peering around the curtain.

'Pssst! Come 'ere!' she told him.

He sidled towards her, now thankful that those around knew that he wasn't just there for thrills. She threw back the curtain and stood awkwardly in anticipation.

'What do you reckon?' she asked hopefully.

He was dumbstruck. Her figure was perfect. How had she managed to cram all that bust into such a tiny top? She looked gorgeous. Her curves really were curves. 'Oh God!' Serious swelling alert.

'What's up?' she frowned. 'Don't like it?'

'I – er – no. It's – it's – you know,' he mumbled, his hands reaching for the pockets once more, appropriate words evading him. 'Say something constructive,' she said.

'Well?' she urged.

He shook his head in amazement. 'Fantastic tits, Liz.'

He was red with shame when she tapped him on the shoulder, the clothes temporarily back on their hangers before reaching their check-out destination. He turned to face her and she kissed his cheek.

'You're a dark horse, Donald!' she teased.

He rubbed his forehead in anguish. 'I'm so sorry, Elizabeth,' he apologised, wanting to re-live the kiss and enjoy it next time. 'I don't know what I'm saying sometimes.'

'I'm flattered,' she said, seeing the need and now wanting to keep their friendship on the right tracks. 'It was a nice thing to say.'

'No it wasn't,' he scowled. 'It was an unforgivable thing to say.'

She took his reluctant arm and looked him in the eye. 'What are you doing tonight?'

He thought for a second. He was going to send an on-line message to his friends in America, but should he really tell her that? 'Nothing much.'

'Good, do you fancy coming out with me?'

Now this was territory he hadn't come across. Girls asking boys to go out. Was he supposed to accept, or refuse and ask her out immediately? 'I don't know,' he replied with a pained expression.

'Why do you not know?'

'I'd like to…'

'But?'

'I'd rather you come out with me,' he attempted to inject authority to his tone.

Liz laughed. His humour killed her. 'Okay then. I'd be delighted to accompany you this evening,' she giggled. 'Where are we going?'

He hadn't thought of that. 'Where were you going to take me?'

She snorted again. 'How about the cinema?'

'The cinema it is!' he agreed with a deliberate and exaggerated nod. He found her smile enchanting, and tried to fix it in his mind.

'But not dressed like that,' she pointed a derisory thumb towards his striped polyester pullover. 'Come on – make-over time!'

Olivia was resting with her feet on the low stool when Liz

breezed into the lounge. She opened one eye in time to see the younger skip contented towards the stairs with an abundance of shopping. Bump was settled for the first time all day, and she didn't want to break the peace by shouting for Liz now. She'd wait until she'd undoubtedly return changed into her new clobber, parading around the house as if it were a catwalk. She closed her eyes once more.

Upstairs, Liz was in a dream. She didn't know whether she was insane or had just struck gold with Don. He was clever, but was he too swotty? She had laughed today, but was that just nerves? His new clothes really suited him, and she thought he'd been pleasantly surprised at his new-look transformation.

She pictured his face. In the rain with his brand new hairstyle – by Michelle of Head Gear – he'd looked quite dishy behind those spectacles. They'd be next on her hit list; he could do with some trendy wire-rimmed ones. They were on offer in Boots opticians at the moment – it said so on the telly. Smiling to herself in the full length mirror, she tried on her new tight mohair top. Did she really have fantastic tits? Don thought so. She thrust out her chest and turned her shoulders back and forth. Yeah, they were pretty good, even if she thought so herself.

Val knocked and shouted. The voice from inside the bedroom called for her to come in, so she opened the door and admired the new outfit, noticing too the other bags on the bed, as yet unopened.

'Carole phoned before,' her mother told Liz.

'Oh, yeah?' her disinterested reply.

Val found this most odd. Carole, whom she had thought was supposed to be in town with Liz, calling to see if they were still going out tonight, then this reaction? 'You two getting on all right, luvvy?' she fished.

'Yep,' the laconic response. 'Hey Mum, which shoes d'ya think?' she held out two pairs against the new hip-huggers and woollen top.

'The brown,' Val's opinion, still not satisfied that she had solved the conundrum. 'So, you going out tonight then?' she asked her daughter's back, Liz busily rooting in more bags.

'Yes, to the flicks,' her muffled voice coming somewhere from within a carrier.

'That'll be nice. When you phone her back, can I have a quick word with Sue?'

Liz screwed up her nose and frowned. 'Sue who?' she asked, turning to face Val.

'Sue James, you daft bat. Who do you think?'

'Why would I be phoning Mrs James?'

Val sighed. 'You won't. When you phone Carole, can I have a word with her mum?' she tutted. Liz was obviously too interested in her shopping spree to concentrate.

'Oh right. I'd better call her later,' she suggested. 'We're supposed to be going out tonight.'

Val looked at her with curiosity. Had she missed something? 'So who's going to the cinema tonight?' she asked nonchalantly.

With her back to her mother, Liz froze momentarily. She instinctively wanted to say Carole, but she'd surely cooked the Carole goose already. Honesty must be the best policy, albeit a little early on in her relationship with Don. She turned, and holding another new skirt up to her waist, replied, 'Just me and Don.'

Val resisted the temptation to tease at the mention of a new name. 'Don?' she enquired, her face remaining straight, apart from an aberrant raised eyebrow which she soon had under control.

Liz merely nodded, volunteering no additional information. Don was still classified as 'need-to-know', and detail was strictly private and confidential.

'Well,' Val accepted failure. 'I'm sure you'll have a good

time. You won't be late, will you?'

Liz still wasn't to be drawn. 'No.'

Downstairs, Olivia was talking herself out of needing to leave the comfort of the chair, when Val scurried down from the bedroom. She motioned Olivia to follow her to the dining room, out of earshot.

'Who's Don?' she whispered excitedly, when Olivia had finally made it through the doorway having prised herself from between the armrests.

'Don't know,' she shrugged. 'Why?'

Val recounted the tale and urged the still ignorant Olivia to think who it could be.

Almost an hour later, she still couldn't place the name when the telephone rang. Olivia left the ringing for her hosts to answer, and Adrian reached the receiver first.

'Where's Liz?' he asked her, covering the mouthpiece.

Olivia pointed upstairs and he called her name.

'What?' she yelled angrily from above, only half dressed.

'Phone! It's Don, or someone.'

The thumping of footsteps down the landing towards the stairs, was only surpassed by the whoosh of Val's body, dashing past Olivia to reach the receiver and taking it from her husband.

'Hello Don,' she said in her best 'airs and graces' tongue. 'Mrs Mallory here.'

'Oh, hello,' said the voice at the other end. 'I was wondering if Elizabeth is free to speak?'

'Yes, she'll be with you in a moment,' Val continued, any employment application for switchboard operator would surely be successful. 'So you're off to the pictures, I hear?' she pushed on, watching Liz dash towards her and vainly reach for the handset.

'Yes, that's the idea,' his pleasant tones confirmed.

Val raised a 'be patient' finger towards her daughter, who was slowly dying in the centre of the lounge. 'Well, have a nice time won't you, Don?... Oh Don, have we spoken before?' she recognised the politeness of his conversation.

'We might have spoken,' he confirmed. 'I did call one day when Elizabeth wasn't in.'

'Yes,' few people who knew her called her Elizabeth. 'I thought perhaps we had. Well, she's here now, looking as lovely as ever, so I'll pass you over. Nice to talk to you. Bye for now.'

She handed the phone to Liz who glared at her mother's idea of pleasantries, and waved her arms to gesture everyone from the room. Everyone remained, interested. Olivia looked elsewhere while listening in, Val stood mere feet away straining to hear both sides of the conversation, while Adrian simply asked repeatedly, 'Who's this Don, then?'

'Sorry about my mother,' her first words to him. 'She's on day release from the Centre. The men in white coats'll be here with her tablets soon... No Don, that's a joke... No, she's not *really* on tablets...' she raised her eyebrows in heightened embarrassment. Not only was she talking publicly to her 'new man', he was making the task very difficult. '...Yes, that's it – I *am* taking the pith, you're right,' she forced a laugh.

Liz was annoyed when she replaced the receiver. They had all been nasty to her. Only Olivia had shown any kind of tact when, at about the point where Don was explaining what his mother had really meant when she'd said that he looked like a mindless yob with his new haircut, she had eventually struggled to her feet and gone to the bathroom. Liz felt certain that she wouldn't have done that though, had she not actually wanted the toilet. To make matters worse, and despite her protestations, Don was to borrow his mum's car and come to pick her up. That meant the full once-over by the family. She'd never brought anyone back to the house before, and certainly would never have dreamt of doing so this early – she'd not even been out in the dark with him, let alone examined his parts. Well, if her folks were going to assume they were bonking, she'd prefer to have a valid reason to feel guilty.

She dreaded the inquisition that they would subject him to. Would he crack and show his as yet unreformed self? She appealed to Olivia for clemency. "Livia, don't you just remember the rings we made you two jump through when you first came home with Ed?' she begged.

'Too right I do,' Olivia recalled. 'So why should I let you get off so flamin' lightly?' she tormented.

Only Adrian thought she meant the spiteful things Liz said, as she stormed back up the stairs to prepare herself for the encounter. That was if her fingernails could stand three hours of nervous apprehension, she thought.

'What about Carole?' her mother shouted after her, with no forthcoming reply.

He'd said seven o'clock, and it was exactly that as he drove on to the gravel and pulled to a halt by Val's Rover. Liz, still not ready, was watching from the upstairs window, wondering if he had been waiting somewhere down Bent Lane for the clock to strike seven before completing his journey, while Val and Olivia surveyed the same scene from a darkened dining room.

They agreed that he looked quite presentable as he emerged from behind the small Vauxhall car and approached the door carrying a plastic bag. Val, deciding that granting him an audience in the lounge would perhaps be the best format for a formal introduction, rejoined Adrian by the fire when the knock upon the wooden door sounded.

He was met by a beautiful young woman who smiled and introduced herself as Olivia. What was he getting involved with? A house of sirens, perhaps? If there were any more like Liz and this one inside, he'd better keep his overcoat on – avoid any unnecessary embarrassment.

The woman led him through the kitchen and he admired the character of the dining room before venturing into the lounge, where (Olive, was it?) was waiting in the doorway waiting for him to catch up.

A tall man, much taller than he, leant forward and offered his hand. 'I'm Dad,' he said.

'Hello, Mr Mallory,' replied the nervous youth, scanning the room for Liz. He saw only an older lady. That must be Liz's mum. 'Mrs Mallory?' he waved an uneasy hand.

'Hello, Don,' she smiled. 'Come on in. Take a seat,' she offered the settee.

He sank into the cushion, as all who had never before experienced it did, and the carrier swayed.

'Is that for me?' Val asked impudently.

The youth looked shamed. 'Erm, well no. Sorry,' he apologised. 'I should have thought, shouldn't I?'

'Perhaps,' Val agreed in jest, nodding seriously. She could have some fun with a character like this one.

'You ignore her,' Olivia intervened. 'She's a big tease,' she smiled.

Don liked her. He recognised in her a safety belt to rescue him when he was out of his depth. Like now. 'Ahhhh,' he giggled, his eyes widening to show he understood. He was tensely enveloped in the sumptuous settee, reluctant to move and draw attention to himself. They might think he was nervous or something.

'So Don, how do you fill your day?' Adrian asked.

Don remained motionless. Why wouldn't his brain function? Her dad's just asked a simple question – answer it. 'Eh?'

'What do you do?' Adrian simplified the problem.

'College, Mr Mallory. I'm at college,' he stammered.

Where are you Elizabeth?

'Very good,' Adrian over-did his 'impressed' face, making Olivia grin. 'Any interesting subjects?' he continued.

To his alarm, Don's mind leaped not to his studies, but to the changing rooms earlier, and Liz picking lint from the trousers he was trying on. Oh no, not now! he pleaded with his groin. Around him, three expectant faces waited for some sort of reply.

'No?' asked Val.

'Sorry?' Don flapped.

Olivia was suffering quiet hysterics behind Edward's travelling diary, and shook in silent laughter. Where was this one from?

'What subjects are you studying?' repeated Adrian.

'Ah, yes. Subjects,' he tried to regain his composure. 'Physics, maths and computer science,' was the eventual unerring answer, sounding completely and utterly fabricated.

Liz appeared at the top of the stairs to save him from the clutches of her family, and his purgatory was eased when everyone turned to witness her descent. She wore her new, figure hugging outfit and Don's mouth gaped once more.

'Bloody hell, Liz!' Olivia gasped, holding either side of her tummy to cover Bump's ears.

Adrian shuffled in his seat, and Val fixed the best 'I'll look like I approve' smile she could muster.

'I take it everyone's met and been introduced?' Liz asked, knowing full well that she'd heard all that had gone before. 'But just in case,' she continued lifting an open palm in the direction of the visitor, 'this is Don, everyone.'

Olivia found herself joining Adrian and Val in saying hello again for some strange reason, and Don in turn responded with a graceful nod.

He smiled warily at Liz. 'I've brought you something,' he said, struggling to his feet and offering the bag.

Liz beamed and accepted the gift with an excited glow. 'Oh, you shouldn't have!'

'I thought it was supposed to be the mother who got the presents,' Val said, taking a repeated chance to tease anyone that may feel vulnerable. Seeing the bag fall away, she stifled her need to choke. 'Although maybe not,' she quickly concluded.

Liz felt as though someone had turned a spotlight upon her and Don, and wished now to wake up and find this all a perverse dream. 'Thanks,' she simply said, regarding the gift. 'We'll leave this here while we go out, shall we?'

In what seemed an instant, they were gone. Don barely had chance to say goodbye before Liz had him out through the kitchen and into the car, the tail lights quickly moving out of sight of the waving and amused occupants that remained behind.

'Well, he's different,' Adrian judged aloud.

'Mmmm,' Olivia's smirk endorsed.

Val alone stood in his defence. 'He's just a bit shy, I think,' she observed. 'What are you both laughing at?'

Adrian shook his head, unable to reply.

'Well, I think he was very thoughtful,' she huffed. 'Being a gentleman and bringing her a present.' She studied the gift there on the coffee table, and allowed a smile to form. 'Pity it's not a box of chocolates, I could just go a rum truffle.'

'I'm afraid you've come second best to, hang on a mo',' she covered the mouthpiece and checked the label, 'to *Cleisto-cactus Straussii*. If that's how you pronounce it.'

'Beg pardon?' Carole asked.

'A Silver Torch Cactus, luv. She's dumped you for a pot-plant wielding, gibbering wreck.' Val broke the news with subtlety.

'I don't understand,' Carole explained.

Not wishing to incur the future rage of her youngest, Val provided a very vague and broad illustration of the evening thus far, and it became obvious that Carole knew nothing of Liz's plans to meet up with any member of the opposite sex.

'What's his name?' Carole inquired, clearly hurt at the secrecy surrounding her best friend's activities.

'What do you want it to be?' Val laughed.

She could appreciate Mrs Mallory's predicament, and Carole joined in the amusement. 'Well, as long as it's not Don, I don't mind.'

The silence worried Carole. 'It's not, is it?' she implored. 'Mrs Mallory, it's not?'

'I don't think I'd better commit myself, Carole.'

'Oh my God!' she screamed, and Val could hear muffled uproar.

'Carole?' she laughed nervously. 'What is it, luv? Carole?'

The girl controlled herself and told Val, in a strangely broken voice, that there was nothing at all the matter, and that she was sure that Liz would be having a wonderful time.

Adrian sat admiring *Cleistocactus Straussii*. 'Livvy?' he called, interrupting her reading. 'You don't think there's some sort of message for Liz in that thing, do you?'

'How do you mean?' she frowned.

'Not *in it* in it, but,' he became bashful. 'You know,' he grimaced. '"I've got a whopper" sort of thing.'

Olivia hooted. She'd hardly put Adrian down as the phallic association type, and certainly hadn't looked upon the spiky tower as anything other than a strange courtship offering. Her eyes watered at the very prospect of his suggestion, and her expression amused him.

'Or perhaps not,' he retracted the notion. They exchanged a smile, and she returned to the diary. 'Olivia?' he spoke once more after momentary thought.

She drew a long breath, finished the line she had begun and looked up. 'No, Adrian,' she began with a wry grin, 'I don't think she'll be buying him a Venus Flytrap.'

'Sorry, I'm disturbing you, aren't I?'

'No, it doesn't matter. I've read it all before,' she told him. 'I'm just fighting my way through Tokyo's rush hour underground again.'

He blushed at the thought of the contents of that diary, and the vivid descriptions of the young woman sitting in the corner. But it was fitting to his query that it should be that of Edward. 'This presentation that we've got coming up in a couple of weeks, do you think you could do me a favour?'

'I'll try to,' she nodded accommodatingly.

'I'd be really pleased if you could hand over the cheque on behalf of Track & Turf.'

She was taken aback. That was unexpected, to say the least, and her reaction didn't go unnoticed.

'You won't have to say anything. Not if you don't want to,' he assured her, but the stunned look remained. 'Look, don't decide now,' he suggested. 'Have a think about it and let me know, eh?' He winked and put his finger to his lips. 'Expectant mum's the word!' he joked, before Val returned with a tray of coffee and biscuits.

'On what?' she demanded, placing the tray beside Olivia.

'Sorry, darling?' Adrian questioned innocently.

'Mum's the word on what?' she repeated.

'Nothing escapes you, does it?' he bought himself valuable seconds while Olivia buried her head in the text. 'When Liz comes home. We were just saying that we'd let you tell her about Carole's call.'

E VEN THOUGH HE was finally back on dry land, Dan still felt the motion of the ship. Three nights in that torturous steel hull had taken its toll on him. Shaving, he realised, had become a major effort in itself – he found his hand going one way and his face another. How he would ever stop the bleeding from his throat without resorting to tying a toilet roll kerchief, he really didn't know. Even sitting on the lavatory, the swaying from side to side put him off his efforts. He could do with some of Olivia's zoo-poo tablets, he told himself.

Emma was on the balcony, enjoying the afternoon sunshine of the Portuguese island. The cruise had not been the overall success that she had wished for. Dan's antics with the *consommé* had only been the thin end of the wedge, once Geoff and Sheila from West Bromwich had attached themselves like the proverbial leeches. It was the ship-wide story of the fat little 'common man' with the drink problem that had attracted Geoff, a scrap metal merchant by trade, and of course his larger-than-life wife, on Saturday evening after the gala dinner. Their contention of how ordinary, *normal* people had just as much right to be on a cruise as the toffee-nosed gits who'd spurned them upon hearing their thick Black Country accents, had become wearing if not insulting, within the time it took Emma to drink a large whisky and soda.

'Muy Sheela's ginuwine fayk furr wasunt choiyp ya kneuw!' he'd boasted loud enough for all in the bar to hear. 'Nor the diamatey tee-arra. Cost muy at loiyst two owld bangers an' a Nissen 'ut, moitey!' he slapped Dan's arm with a spurious guffaw.

'Aw, stop it, Jiffroy!' his wife screamed in what initially sounded like agony, but quickly deteriorated to a cackle. 'Huys a scroiem, inee?'

'Aye,' agreed Dan in sufferance. 'He's killin' me, luv.'

Emma shuddered in the diminishing warmth of the sun. Thank goodness, they were safely away from those dreadful people. She searched for the shoes she'd kicked off earlier, and returned to the suite that they were to occupy for the week. Dan was whistling away in the bathroom where he'd been for some time now, and she called to check that everything was all right.

'I can't 'ave a decent dump to save me life!' he yelled back.

How charmed she was with his eloquence. Taking comfort on the chaise longue, she laid back and closed her eyes. Just enough time for forty winks, she thought, before getting ready for dinner. She fancied a nice succulent steak dish tonight. The hotel restaurant had international accreditation, and she intended to make the most of the opportunity to feast. Her mouth watered at the images conjured up in her mind. She licked her lips, and smiled dreamily. And the best of it was that someone else would do the washing up, too! This is the life. What a pity it would last only for a week.

''Ere Em? Can you shit, or are you blocked up t'eyeballs 'n all?' Dan's expressive prose shattering the illusion.

There again, she pondered, perhaps a week is plenty long enough. She opened her eyes with a long sigh to see him stood naked, gazing into the wall mirror, viciously scratching his backside. 'Oh Adonis,' she mocked. 'Why, you are *so* handsome!'

'Aye, tell me summat I don't know,' he turned grinning, cupping his private parts in a very unattractive manner. 'Fancy some of this?'

The man in the dinner suit and perfectly appointed bow tie opened the door for them as they left the restaurant, satisfied that the reputation of the cuisine was not merely fable. Descending the marble steps towards the gardens, they agreed that should they ever win the pools, the lottery, or simply rob a bank, they would employ the chef that had prepared their savoured creations.

Emma's senses filled with a chaos of floral bouquet, as she drew a contented breath of the Atlantic evening air. She took Dan's arm and they strolled through the immaculately manicured lawns. She was truly at ease for the first time since the unhappy events of the spring, and possibly some time before that. The imminent arrival of her first grandchild was the jewel of the year. It was only a little over a fortnight ago that they were desperately trying to trace Ollie, and now, they had this sublime expectation to anticipate. She worried about her daughter – how would she be coping at the Mallorys? So far, she'd resisted the urge to call following Dan's insistence that they'd come away to relax, not worry about everybody; but she felt certain that he too was desperate to know how she was. No one would stop her from calling tomorrow though, not on her daughter's birthday.

Dan recognised the sanguine glow in his wife's face, and allowed her the peace of her thoughts. He really could do with the toilet, but she was clearly contemplating something of pleasure and he couldn't possibly break that process – she deserved to be able to relax for once. Severe buttock clenching was required, and if nothing else, he'd have to try and release some silent wind, if these new underpants would let him part his cheeks that was.

They reached the free-form pool, supposedly closed for the evening, but there was a couple enjoying its space in the subtle light of the moon. 'Is that what they call "petting" on the leisure centre pool signs, Em?' Dan whispered through the corner of his mouth.

'Stop looking,' she told him, chancing a furtive peek herself. 'Mmmm, it is,' she confirmed.

He laughed quietly, tripping as he did so over something at the pool side. He stopped to make sure it wasn't anything gruesome or of importance.

'What is it?' Emma asked.

He cautiously bent down and picked up the small material object.

'I sink zat might be mine,' a woman's European accent called politely from the pool, its owner gliding effortlessly through the dimly lit water towards them.

'Put it down!' Emma instructed under her breath, realising that it was the bottom half of a bikini.

'Sorry, luv!' Dan apologised loudly with a smile, making obvious his speedy and careful replacement of the garment.

''Tis okay,' she smiled. 'Per'aps you will pass to me?' putting her feet down and standing in the shallow end to exit by the steps.

'Fuckin' 'ell!' Dan gasped, watching her perfect naked body climb the stainless steel ladder and approach.

Emma picked up the costume and walked hurriedly towards her, garment first.

'Sank you,' the smile never left her face. 'The water is nice,' the French tones advised.

Dan was rooted to the spot in admiration of the girl – no older than Olivia – and her aesthetics.

'That's super,' Emma replied. 'I think we'll give it a miss tonight though,' she laughed, hoping that the girl would please put on the bikini instead of spinning it on her finger.

More splashing from the pool attracted the English couple's attention, and it was Emma's turn to stare as she watched the water drip from the lowest abdominal point of an amazingly endowed Parisian, searching for his towel in a holdall perched high on a wall.

'There's a bus comin' Em!' laughed Dan, pulling her towards the footpath that would lead them away.

'Pardon?' Emma turned to face him.

'Shut your mouth,' he suggested, 'or it'll drive straight in!'

They excused themselves with embarrassed waves and continued their walk back towards the hotel, neither wishing to comment on their discovery.

'You all right, luv?' Emma asked, noticing Dan's awkward gait in the light of a garden lantern.

'Aye, not bad,' he inhaled his freshly lit duty-free cigarette, the first filtered tobacco he'd smoked in over twelve months.

She frowned. 'You seem to be walking funny,' she observed. 'Not got a stiffy, have you?'

'No, my beloved,' he coughed an alarmed laugh. 'But I think from now on, we'll have the lights out when we go t'bed. At least till you've forgotten t'size of that bloke's swizzle stick any road!'

'I didn't need my glasses, either,' Emma flushed at the reminder. 'Well, what's the matter then? You're mincing along like you're carrying a pea between your buttocks.'

He pursed his lips and kissed the air. 'Nothing that a good fart won't cure, sweetie. Get me to the lavvy, for God's sake.'

Suitably relieved and in the safety of the piano bar, they soon struck up conversation with a couple of a similar age, dressed from head to foot in Marks and Spencer summer wear, and looking as though they'd each been cooked unbasted for three hours on regulo 450.

'First day too?' the wiry man asked, after the weather pleasantries and introductions that normally follow 'Brit abroad recognises fellow Brit in bar' smiles.

'First day here,' replied Emma with a nod.

'Fancy a drink?' he offered, his Mancunian accent a welcome sound.

'Not too many tonight, John,' his wife Glenda suggested with a restraining hand on his arm. 'We're here all week, better pace yourself.'

He looked at Dan. 'Yes, dear,' he sighed.

'Drinks sound great to me,' Dan laughed sympathetically. 'I'll grab a barman.'

The good-looking waistcoated bar attendant responded to the wave from the group of four by the grand piano, and was quickly waiting attentively by the side of the thin, slightly balding man with the very red face.

'Two bee-ers,' John began in international English – long, slow and loud. 'One whis-kee and sow-dar, got that young man? One whis-kee and sow-dar.'

Dan daren't look at Emma, her handkerchief was already out to disguise her amusement.

'Yes, sir,' the swarthy man answered patiently.

'...And one Cam-par-ee with plen-tee of ice,' he concluded.

The barman bowed his head courteously and returned to the bar, where he shared a raucous and mocking joke with his older colleague.

The evening was enjoyable. It was, they agreed, a small world with John's daughter from his first marriage – them being childless together – living only a mile or so away from the Beech's home. Dan couldn't wait to tell somebody of the swimming pool beauty he'd experienced and John, lubricated by half a dozen bottled beers, seemed eager to relish the tale whilst Glenda was at a safe distance accompanying Emma to the ladies' powder room. From his enthused reaction, Dan got the distinct feeling that Glenda treated intimacy like post-war tripe – technically available, but strictly on ration and not very palatable when indulged in.

'…She had the most perfect spanner body,' teased Dan with a slow wink.

'What's a spanner body?' asked John with excitement.

Dan's eyes glinted, and he leant forward to emphasise the mystique. 'One look,' he murmured, 'and yer nuts tighten.'

Elizabeth had just about had a day of it. Mondays never were her strong point anyway, but this had been a particularly dismal example. During the morning, Carole had not stopped going on about Don, and how could anyone really contemplate snogging a geek like him? The teasing that Mum, Dad and Olivia had subjected her to all day yesterday was bad enough, but Caz's incessant chuntering had almost resulted in a major fall-out.

At lunchtime, Don was waiting patiently by the gate and Carole hadn't recognised him until Liz kissed him and he'd said, 'Hello, Carole.' From then on, it was a battle to keep him out of her clutches. It was 'Don this' and 'Don that'. 'I like the hair, Don,' 'Great jeans, Don.' It was stomach-churningly sickening, she considered.

Don, however, was a one-girl man, delighted with the little gem he'd found. The fact that Carole was so obviously making a play for him was lost to his naïvety, and as his Boys' Own Guide to Girls didn't cover multiple management thereof, how was he supposed to know that there was a hierarchy of 'Official Girlfriend' and below? Surely all girls were girls, and each knew which was the boy's favourite and chosen one? He relished having the attention of more than one anyway; from monastery to convent, he labelled his sudden reversal of fortunes. Never in his wildest dreams could he have predicted this. So why was Liz, his little diamond, being so nasty all of a sudden?

'I've created a monster!' she told Olivia that evening in hushed tones, as the elder rubbed lotion into Bump. 'All that's missing are the bolts in his neck.'

'Poor sod,' observed Olivia. 'One minute he's a swotty git, the next, you're having a go because he doesn't know how to cope with the fairer sex.'

'There's nothing fair about that cow Carole James,' censured Liz.

'Now come on, Lizzie,' Olivia's advocation intensified. 'You're not going to fall out with your best friend over a fella,' she commanded. 'Just play it cool. Educate Don that he only has eyes for you, and Carole will fall into line without any unpleasant scenes.'

'Do you think so?'

'Trust me,' her tone and smile convincing. *And if that doesn't work, you can always be a bridesmaid at their wedding.*

Liz watched the laborious application of moisturiser, and hoped that she'd be able to have children one day. Olivia invited her to inspect her 'Stilton stomach'. Closer examination of Bump revealed exaggerated vein patterns, and Liz's expression turned from intrigue to terror instantly. Perhaps kids weren't such a good idea.

Olivia too was tiring of the negatives surrounding pro-creation, especially carting around the extra weight that Bump incurred. While she had put on very few additional pounds, the bulbous pouch was exhaustive and cumbersome. For her, it was too late to decide that children were a bad idea, and having come so far, she wouldn't have changed places with Liz for anything.

'What do you think you'll be getting for your birthday?' Liz asked with excitement.

Olivia grinned. It seemed that everyone else was getting

a thrill from the prospect of her birthday, and she hadn't thought anything about it. With being away for the best part of the year, her mind had been far from her true age. The age she felt perhaps, but her true age, no. Her mum had repeatedly asked what she would like, but there wasn't a soul that could grant her real wish. She'd have to reach her own best-before date to have that particular dream come true. In the meantime, whatever kind gift – even the normal useless gizmos and gadgets that came her way – would be accepted gratefully. 'Don't know,' she replied evasively.

'What would you like?' Liz pressed.

Olivia hesitated. 'What I'd really like,' she ventured slowly, 'isn't available.' Her expression told all, and Liz suddenly felt emotional, blinking to avoid any revelation of the glassy feeling that her eyes began to sense.

They sat uncomfortably for a while; neither speaking, Olivia trying desperately not to cry. She reached for the bedside table and picked up the two diaries, both her own and Edward's. 'Come on,' she suggested, attempting to regain equanimity. 'Let's have a look and see what we can read to Bump, eh?'

Liz sniffed and nodded. Taking the diary kept by Olivia, she opened the cover thoughtfully, and looked at the words without reading them. 'Livvy?' she quizzed. 'Did you love Ed?'

Olivia's search for a light-hearted section of Edward's travel notes stopped, and she looked at Liz with conviction. 'I've never felt *anything* like it before,' she affirmed, 'and I still love him dearly now.'

Liz reflected upon that sentiment. Did her brother really mean so much to the pretty girl next to her? She felt proud that he was loved by someone who didn't *have* to love him, but did so because of him. Her hand went out to her companion's protruding stomach. 'Can I feel?' she asked.

Olivia smiled, pleased that she wished to. 'Of course you can, Auntie Liz.'

The sporadic movement beneath the moistened skin was still a source of excitement for Liz, eagerly anticipating the arrival of her nephew or niece. 'He's kicking!' she giggled.

'Oh, is that what it is?' Olivia quipped. 'I thought perhaps that lamb chop I had for tea wasn't quite dead.' She bashed Edward's diary against Liz's arm, and dropping it on top of the first already in her lap, told her to find a funny bit to humour the hyperactive Bump.

'What about the Whitsundays?' Liz asked, the pages falling open at that point.

'Go on then, make us smile.'

D. 20 – Sat 29 June: Okay, we left Darwin today. We'd probably like to say we're sorry, but having seen bugger all of the things we came here to see, our departure is more than overdue. It's now almost nine o'clock (p.m.) and we're sat in Townsville coach station of all places, en route to Airlie Beach in the Whitsundays.

The day goes something like this. Taxi from the hotel this morning at 4 a.m. Yes, a nice leisurely rise with the guy who switches the sun on of a morning. Managed to grab a yesterday's leftover sandwich and coffee at the airport for breakfast. It has to be said, the sandwich was slightly fresher than the coffee, but then hey! It is 5 a.m. – they've not had chance to put the kettle on, have they?

6 a.m. flight that was full, to Cairns via some little place to drop off a dozen people and pick up even more. Breakfast on board wasn't merely eaten; it was inhaled. We were so hungry, even Livvy ate it all! Wonders will never cease.

Got to Cairns at just after 10 a.m., and decided that because we've not done most of the stuff we wanted to so far, we'd not hang around in Cairns, but get straight to the Whitsundays for a bit of sunshine and relaxation. At baggage reclaim, Livvy's rucksack comes out in three pieces – thank God her undies weren't strewn all over the place or else my life would be hell right now! Anyway, we fixed that and made our way to the taxi rank (Livvy walked, I hobbled. Bloody Ayers Rock! I'll kick the bastard next time, not climb it.)

Asked the taxi driver for the railway station, and she said 'why?' Hmmm. Saturday must be brain-out day in Queensland thinks us, until she tells us that the train went yesterday.

The train went? Like the train singular? So, there you have it, the train singular went yesterday and we want to get to Airlie Beach today. Avoiding questions like 'why do you want to leave when you've only just got here?' – not wishing to be nasty about this fine lady's home town without seeing it – we agree to be taken to the coach station.

A Greyhound coach to Airlie Beach leaves at 2 p.m. and so we have three hours to kill around Cairns. Being the nearest international point of entry to Japan, it's pretty well geared up to the Japs, even down to the duty free shops displaying Yen prices next to Dollar. As we've accumulated so much extra clobber along the way, we're in real need of a suitcase…

'Oh God!' laughed Olivia, suddenly remembering the original scene. 'He went looking for one in Proserpine. We'll have to look that up in a second.'

…or something but we can't find one that's going to befit our modus transportus (or whatever the Romans would have called backpackers who stay in 3★ hotels and use supplementary gold visa cards on their parent's accounts), so we must continue the journey south with our collection of plastic and paper carrier bags strapped to the bulging cargo on our backs. Thank heavens we arranged for that didgeridoo and all those boomerangs to be sent home direct from The Alice, and not bring them with us like we'd considered!

Woolworth's provided us with the constituent parts of a picnic lunch for the coach, most of which was confiscated about two hours into the trip by the quarantine checkpoint scouring the area for people taking fresh fruit and vegetables out of this tropical banana growing area. Weird, but bye bye lunch!

If the old couple behind (Sheila and Bruce?) told each other that we'd passed a banana plantation once, they mentioned it every single... ('bloody')... time! It was relief when further south, the bananas turned into sugar beet and they changed the record! I've never been so glad to see night-time fall as today. The silly old biddies couldn't tell what we were passing then and finally fell asleep, obviously tired of providing running commentary based on guesswork as to what sights we were missing.

So that really gets us here in Townsville, moth-eaten. It's dark, Livvy's lolling all over the place and moaning that she's tired, and apart from Livvy just trying to get on the wrong connecting bus, there's little exciting to report.

'He was a sod to me, was your daddy,' Olivia snorted, rubbing her circling hand over Bump's bump.

Liz paused in her recital, pondering for a moment, and flushed. 'Livvy?' she asked coyly. 'Have you read all of Ed's diary?'

The nodding head in reply closed any escape from the line of questioning she'd embarked upon. 'Was it like that?' she continued.

'Like what?' Olivia's puzzlement showing in her furrowed brow.

The younger girl's face deepened to a shade of claret. 'The sexy bits?'

'What sexy bits?' Hadn't they just been hearing about banana plantations?

Liz wished she'd never asked. 'It doesn't matter.'

From across the bed, Olivia studied Liz's face. It told her that it *did* really matter, but the reddened cheeks of abashment – any redder and the smoke alarm would trigger she thought – were stopping her from pursuing the issue. '*What* sexy bits, Liz?' she repeated.

Liz frowned. 'You know!' her hand waving in a hopeful 'please don't do this to me' way. 'When you wouldn't and he wanted to, and then when you wanted to and he couldn't, and...'

Olivia rocked with laughter. Now she was embarrassed. 'Yes, it was more or less like that, I suppose,' she giggled, covering her mouth as if to smother the words of self disclosure at source.

Liz's inquisitive streak now showed itself to be stronger. 'Why do you only suppose?'

Olivia could hear a smoke alarm going off in her own head. Why should she be so bothered? Her boyfriend's entire family had read the words he'd written, and they weren't explicit by any means, but they did reveal a little too much thigh and cleavage for comfort. Perhaps that's why she now hesitated and stumbled a little over the words that whirled around her brain. 'Well,' she began, shrugging her shoulders, 'every story has two sides, and what Ed says is a fair view, from his side, of what happened.' She was relieved to have managed a sensible response. 'Now, let's find the Proserpine part,' she changed the subject.

'Yeah, in a moment,' Liz agreed reluctantly. 'But had you before?' she persisted without mercy.

Olivia grasped that there was reason other than pure mischief for the questions, and replied with a question of her own. 'What's bothering you, Liz?' she was off the defensive at last.

Liz looked around. Quite who she thought was behind her, Olivia didn't know, and it amused her enough to smile.

'What's funny?' asked Liz.

'I'm not laughing,' visions of Liz – MI6 agent extraordinaire, and secret coded messages being passed – flashing across her humoured eyes.

'Yes, you are. What's up?'

'Honestly, there's nothing funny,' she snorted the last of the laughter out. 'Sorry I'm so jolly, I'll try to look miserable for you.'

Liz wasn't convinced, but decided to carry on. It was too late to back track now anyway. 'What's it like?' she asked.

'It?' Olivia didn't want to be difficult.

'Sex!' seethed Liz, flustered.

How should she answer? Does she give the sensible maternal, or the girlie giggle answer? Best get some practice in, she thought. 'It all depends.' Crap start 'Livia! 'By that, I mean you can get a quick grope and a major let-down of a fumble from someone who wants to chalk you up on his bedpost; or you can take your time and make sure you feel comfortable with someone before committing yourself.'

Liz looked mystified.

'Does that make sense?' Olivia asked.

'Yes,' she replied. 'But what if you're desperate to find out?'

This is good practice, Olivia thought. A dozen years or so too soon, but good practice. 'Well, if you're desperate, you either go for option A; or speed through option B, cutting out some of the safety checks along the way.'

'Like what?'

'Like how well do you know him. Like what are his feelings for you, and yours for him. Like if it really boiled down to it, could you carry his child for nine months and love it – and him come to that, until you die?'

Liz appeared deeply pensive.

'Is it Don?' Olivia pressed, suppressing visions of *Cleistocactus Straussii*, and receiving a slow nodded reply. 'Well, nothing's ever simple, chuck. Bear in mind; unless you're careful, life's one long series of disappointments, and there's only you can break that chain. You've got this one chance before you're long-time-dead, and if you think you care for him enough, and want to show him; do it,' she smiled. 'Be careful you don't rush into it all and scare him off though,' she added, a caring laugh in her voice. The smile diminished, and any sign of mirth left her face. 'Listen to your heart,' she implored.

Liz still said nothing, though her expression looked slightly happier.

'I waited,' Olivia volunteered the already obvious information. 'Perhaps I waited too long, looking back. I wanted to shag the balls off your brother the minute I saw him...'

'That's worth at least a pound in the box,' Liz chuckled.

She beamed her flawless smile. 'Too right, and good value! But it's true. The time we spent together before we did was great, but I think Ed says in his diary that we became even closer once we'd actually made love,' her smile became sober. 'I'd agree with that. And then,' she shrugged a resigned pause, 'and then it's gone.'

'Is that what you were doing; making love?'

'Yup!' she held Bump proudly with both hands. 'Had we done it when we first met, it'd have been bonking. The way we were in Australia; it was love all right.'

Liz felt a tear in her eye and wiped it away swiftly.

'What's the matter?' asked Olivia.

'I wish I had someone feel like that about me,' she wept gently, feeling Olivia's arm of comfort around her shoulder.

'You will. Don't worry,' her words were assuring.

Liz blew a large raspberry. 'Cover Bump's ears,' she warned, and Olivia pulled the quilt over her tummy. 'Bollocks!' Liz acquiescently huffed.

'Feel better now?' smirked the elder.

'Yeah!' she wiped her nose. 'Now, what about Proserpine?'

D. 25 – Thurs 4 July: 10 a.m. Livvy's on her scuba diving lessons – day two of five for her. I'm still pretty miffed that the doctor wouldn't pass me fit to dive. These blank spells don't bother me; I've got used to them now. Never mind, I'll get over it. Aussie Doc says I should make a note to see Doc Ainsworth back home, though.

The weather's cloudy again but the forecast is for broken periods of sunshine. Yesterday, Livvy froze her bum off in the pool doing the theory of diving, so I'm glad in a way that I'm not being subjected to that. I'm going to see if I can hire a motorbike to go to the nearest large town – Proserpine (where we fly from when we return to Sydney) – and look for a suitcase. Sheila at reception says I'll find everything and anything I need there.

Watched a bit of TV this morning and I've finally realised what it is about Australia that's so different. Here's a sample news broadcast:

'(A bit of dramatic music to start, eh?) De da der de de, derrrrr de da derrrrr, dum, dum, dum, de da, dum. Dong! Here's the news, cobbers! Dong! The Soviets have launched an all-out nuclear attack on Luxembourg, which is a bit of a nuisance. Dong! The main story tonight, War! Will the Wallabies overcome the All Blacks in Melbourne tonight? Our special report on the colour of the referee's jock strap will reveal the answer...'

Very refreshing! Now, Proserpine awaits.

4.30 p.m... ('Bloody hell')*... fire! I'm back in one piece (I think!). Well, because of my age, I can rent not a Harley Davidson, not a Triumph, not a Honda Goldwing, but a moped. Not even a Vespa, just your common or garden (or scrap yard) moped. The choice of skid-lids is silver-dome nerdy looker, or black full-face thing with dark tinted visor. I'm going to look a complete...* ('dickhead')*... in whatever aren't I, so plump for the silver suppository style, as worn by no one with credibility or pride.*

So, off I go with a rev count and speed that ranges from 'stopped' to full-blown 'moving sedately at pedestrian with leg in plaster' – the latter being accompanied by attention-grabbing screaming engine noises. It must be about 40 km to Proserpine and it took just about an hour to get there with my shirt flapping in the breeze, and my ego under the wheels.

Deafened and knackered, I turn off the main Bruce Highway (real name!) and towards the town itself. Imagine the scene now; the lone rider comes into town expecting to see shops and shopping malls, and is soon weaving down the main street past pub, pub, pub with betting shop, funeral parlour, plant hire centre, pub, food store, second hand car lot, pub. You get the picture? Big city, eh? A must for the Temperance Society recruitment division too.

A kind local, called Bruce probably, directs me to the departmental store. So huge and gigantic is this 'ere shop, I roar past it twice thinking it was a hostel or something. Anyway, parked up outside, removed skid-lid just in case the locals thought I was the man who fell to Earth, admired the sweaty helmet-moulded hairdo revealed in the darkened window, and strode in like the obvious stranger.

Now, how do I do the place justice? Picture any local departmental store – Debenhams, John Lewis, Harrods – you know, any old shop; and as the name suggests, they have departments, don't they? Men's wear – a section of shirts, a section of trousers, underwear and suits. Ladies' couture, hats, dresses, blouses and all, each having its own section within a department? Just like this one really! You wander in and see a carousel thing, four sides of metal frame with hangers attached. That's the men's department. A shirt, a pair of trousers, a choice of two Y-fronts colours, and three sizes of hat to keep away the brilliant sunshine we're not having. Then, there's the same for ladies, children and kitchen utensils and anything else you care to imagine. Really impressive! Each carousel has its own department! Marks and Sparks – you listening?

There's one suitcase in the luggage department and, well, we are desperate. It cost $32 and I wouldn't say it's big, but the best option was to put the moped in it and walk home.

Okay, so I'm out of the shop having finally made Sheila behind the counter understand that I'm not American, and deliberating on how the hell I carry either the moped or the case.

Helpful Bruce, who originally pointed out the store, is walking by having bought his grog for the day, and demonstrates, in his Helpful Bruce kinda way, that I can only just about see over the case myself, let alone load it on to the bike. Thanks, Helpful Bruce, I hadn't noticed.

He minds the mean machine and suitcase, while I go back into the shop to find the camping department and the one 20 metre length of rope in stock. Another $40 for the rope to strap the moped to the case, with the ever helpful advice being offered between swigs of the amber nectar by my new-found friend.

If getting the ropes right was a task, balancing the moped and getting it in motion was nothing short of a white knuckle experience. Things were going all right until I passed the end of the block on which my favourite department store stood. Helpful Bruce is walking alongside, just to make sure I don't fall off, and the whole town is watching the nerd in the silver bullet helmet hold up the traffic that has suddenly materialised from nowhere to form the longest traffic jam ever in the history of Queensland.

The end of the block approaches and suddenly, the cross wind takes a hold of the integral zipper side pocket with double locking genuine Taiwanese padlock. If you've ever aspired to being a kite, forget it. The smell of adrenaline lingers too long!

Leaning into the wind to counter its effect, and with the corner of the case almost touching the kerb; an awe-inspiring 'overtaking the zimmer-frame wielding granny' manoeuvre prompted wild applause from the gathered townsfolk, and my departure from Proserpine will no doubt be the subject of pub quiz questions for decades to come.

The hour-long trip back was condensed to forty-five minutes, the frequent tail wind assisting my land yacht and making the engine yell in terror. Tight corners? No problem! Just shut your eyes and hang on for dear life!

I think the case only touched the road six or seven times per kilometre, so the damage is pretty extensive to both bottom corners, air conditioning not being an original feature of the design.

So, there we are! $72 to get a case and strap it to the moped ($60 plus gas) to end up with a useless piece of kit that will be better *used by some poor sod under Waterloo Bridge than in the hold of a 747.*

The good thing I suppose is that I must have lost half a stone in sweat and full-mark pooability farts. Scuba diving? That's not dangerous! Get a moped, get a life!

The two girls enjoyed the thoughts and words of Edward together, Liz thinking Olivia's waters were about to break if the look on her face were to be an indicator. Bump bounced in accompaniment to the frivolity and his mum decided that it was time to go to the lavatory, just to make sure she didn't embarrass herself further than absolutely necessary.

The telephone rang early the next morning and Adrian's first reaction was dread. Surely not another break-in? He was to finalise the deal today, and the last thing he needed was for the whole thing to be scuppered by an enthusiastic punter who couldn't wait until the result of the steward's enquiry was announced to collect his cash.

'Hello?' his cautious tones answered the lounge receiver.

'Oh, hello,' the woman's voice replied equally cautiously. 'Is that Adrian?'

'Yes,' he didn't place the voice.

'Hi Adrian, it's Emma. Are you okay?'

He sighed with relief. 'I am now, Emma. How's the holiday?'

'Great!' she enthused.

'What can I do for you then?' he asked, his mind on the day's business.

'Is our 'Livia there?'

'Of course she is,' he chuckled at his own stupidity. 'Sorry, not quite with it yet. The brain only gets going at eight o'clock.'

He took the number of the hotel and promised to raise

Olivia immediately.

'Who is it?' Val asked blearily, reaching the foot of the stairs. 'It's not half six yet.'

He raised his eyebrows and gave a knowing nod. 'Emma. Obviously desperate to speak to Livvy. Can you get her?'

'No need,' came an alert voice from the top of the stairs, Olivia having been unable to sleep for some time with Bump evidently excited about Mummy's birthday. 'Was that my ruddy mother doing her usual trick?'

Val yawned loudly and made a noise which Olivia took as a yes.

The waddling expectant tutted, and apologised for her parent's remarkable capacity of being the travel agent able to leave her brain at home with the note to the milkman.

She took the receiver from Adrian who held up the telephone number for her to dial. 'Are you sure you don't mind?' she enquired, conscious of the cost to call international during the week.

'Put her out of her misery for pity's sake,' Val joked. 'And say "Hi" from me too, if you would.'

The barely comprehensible receptionist who answered put the call through to Suite Nine and Emma's waiting ears.

'Hi, luv!' she shouted down the broken line. 'Happy birthday to yooou…' she continued in what resembled drunken karaoke style.

'Thanks Mum, how's the holiday going?' Olivia interrupted the painful noises to protect her delicate hearing.

'Smashing,' Emma replied with verve. 'Your dad's got a rotten hangover again, but we're having fun. Have you got the postcards yet?'

'Don't be daft, we'll see Christmas before any postcards.'

'Well, anyway, let's not waste Val's phone bill. How's my birthday girl?'

'Fat, tired and craving steamed chocolate pudding!' the pretended petulant reply.

'Well, it's almost elevenses time, isn't it? Get some,' her mother suggested.

'No, Mum, it's just gone dawn here – you're ahead of us remember, not behind.'

'Oh bugger! What time is it there then?'

'Well, it's not quite breakfast time, put it that way. You always get it wrong.'

Olivia felt the gaze of Adrian and Val in her back as she listened to her mother's apologies, and promised faithfully to pass them on to the Mallorys.

'So what have you arranged by way of celebration?' Emma asked.

'Me and Bump are being whisked away for a night on the tiles – our choice. Bump really wants to go to Mothercare and me to bed,' she turned to grin at her hosts, 'but I think this lot have other plans.'

The conversation concluded with love and kisses being hurled in all directions. A weary Liz had joined the party by this time, and with a sleepy birthday greeting, handed Olivia a brightly coloured box; its bow impressively and professionally tied. Val had disappeared to retrieve another armful of gifts while Adrian went to make breakfast for everyone – a symbolic gesture of significance, not lost on the three women.

Upon their return, all three sat around the open fire watching an uncomfortable looking Olivia open each present with delight. She was overcome with their generosity – the fine gold bracelet and necklace set was exquisite, and certainly too beautiful to accept.

Adrian agreed and offered in jest to return them to Williams, the exclusive jeweller, on his way into the office.

'Williams? On second thoughts!' joked Olivia, happy to be feeling so at ease. In the back of her mind however, she was longing for Edward to be there. She decided that no matter what, she'd do the thing today she never thought she'd ever feel strong enough to do.

A S THE CLOCK struck ten, the tall man was all smiles. His smaller colleague likewise; he had made a tidy little sum today in just two signatures on that agreement in his briefcase. He couldn't forget though, that the agreement had taken many hours of sweat and tears to conceive, and many more days' hard negotiation to reach this moment. He shook the taller man's hand.

'Adrian, congratulations!' he glowed in admiration.

'Thanks, Sam. Will it be another Constable for the office?' he quipped to the solicitor's apparent discomfort. 'Can I give you a lift? I've got to go and break some news to the staff.'

'No, thank you, I'll make my own way,' replied Samuel Harman, adding, 'It would appear that there is some picture hanging that needs my urgent attention,' in a rare display of satirical wit, that surprised him just as much as it did his client. 'My love to Valerie.'

Liz reminded herself of the conversation she and Olivia had shared the night before. Don was not, she persuaded her doubting mind, about to waltz off with Carole. Neither, although this felt less convincing, was Carole making a determined play for Don.

Of her own fruition, Carole had left the couple in peace during this late morning study period. Tuesday, for Don, was almost entirely study period and he had, quite out of character, allowed himself to be distracted for an hour.

The café in which they escaped the biting wind was not a usual student haunt. There was no particular reason for their choice, it was the nearest one to hand – or foot as the case might be, when they'd decided to find a seat somewhere indoors. The clientele of 'The K r omah', as the establishment's neglected sign proudly confused, was decidedly elderly with its ambience and decor befitting.

Don was in full and enthusiastic narration. He had quickly learned, being the bright spark he assured himself he was, that image really did make the difference. Mum had grown accustomed to seeing the closely groomed hair, and her comments were now far less caustic and frequent than they had been over the weekend. Since he'd realised too that regular shampooing would make the difference, his confidence continued to swell.

Liz was pleased that he was finding post-nerd life as interesting and compulsive as his studies, and decided to ease off the transformation pressure a little. The subtle hints on deodorant had worked, but she'd persist with the hair washing. His idea that once a week was regular must be an improvement on what had been habitual before, but running her hands through an oily rag was not her idea of passion.

She listened attentively to his chatter about real things – music, films and her latest interest, the Internet. She nipped herself to make sure she wasn't dreaming. How she almost passed this one by, just because his packaging was suspect.

'Don?' she asked. 'Can I ask you a personal question?'

He sipped his coffee with a cautious look in his eyes. 'Yes,' he answered, entrusting his sensitivity to her tact.

'I don't know what to say,' she giggled. 'It's a bit embarrassing really.'

'Go on,' he prompted. 'You've started now; don't keep

me in suspense.'

'Well,' she paused for dramatic effect. 'I like you a real lot…'

His heart sank. She's going to finish with me. I knew it! She thinks I'm just a pillock.

She noted the change in his expression. 'What's wrong?'

'You're going to dump me, aren't you?' moisture forming in his eye.

She grabbed his hands across the table. 'No, you daft bastard!' she cried. 'I want to bonk your bloody brains out!' Oh shit, she dropped her head in disbelief of her outburst. That was subtle, Liz!

The sound of crashing china distracted them and bewilderment grabbed him. What was going on? She'd thrown him off balance, and before he could cope with one thing, there he was watching an octogenarian waitress and three Miss Marple customers, clutching various pacemakers and hearing aids in a tabletop sea of tea and milk.

Liz laughed self-consciously and held one hand to her mouth, squeezing the other tight around his. 'Sorry,' she apologised.

He sat bemused. Could he please see the action replay of the last thirty seconds? It all happened so quickly, he missed the lot. 'For what?' he pleaded.

She shrugged and he joined in her amusement, still mystified.

The waitress tottered off at a dangerously fragile speed and returned with a large ragged cloth to mop up her dropped tray's contents. She looked at the young couple like a rabbit watches oncoming headlights, her mouth open and breath perilously unsteady.

Liz viewed Don through eyebrows from beneath a bowed head. He was his shy shade of red. 'What are you thinking?' she enquired solemnly.

'I don't know,' he whispered back, conscious of the

attention they were receiving. 'I suppose I've not known you long, have I?' his face mirrored the copious thoughts filling his mind.

'And?' encouraged the girl.

'And what?'

'Where does that lead you?' she ventured with trepidation.

He opened his mouth but stopped the words. He thought some more before slowly taking great care over each syllable. 'If I'm honest, Liz, I haven't done this kind of thing before, and I don't really know the format,' a grimace concluding the confession.

Liz remained silent, biting her bottom lip. *Fuck!* she cursed herself. *I've blown it. He thinks I'm a right slapper, now!*

He let his thoughts continue aloud. 'Maybe I never thought I'd have someone who wanted me. I'm no catch after all.'

'Don't do yourself down, please,' she begged. 'You know that's not true! I've embarrassed you, haven't I?' she observed. 'I didn't want it to come out like that. But I suppose that's how I feel when you cut out all the crap.'

He clasped her hand around his and smiled benignly.

'I'd really like to get to know you a whole lot more,' she told him. 'And when we're ready, that's me *and* you, we can do what we feel's right. What d'ya say?'

He trusted her judgement, yet knew that she really meant what she'd first said. His courage had never been tested like it was about to be. 'You ready now?' he whispered with leading expression.

She assumed from his question that he wasn't yet completely happy. Licking her lips of coffee, she gulped. Their future was in his hands, and her cards must be laid out if she were to keep him. 'I think that's just about what I was getting at,' she confirmed, trying to remain upbeat.

'Well then,' his normal voice returning with warmth,

'I'd better get down to the chemist's, hadn't I?'

On the hillside at Ash Norton, the wind brought chilling evidence that winter was on its way, and Olivia wrapped herself in the new scarf and hat that Elizabeth had saved hard to buy from the boutique in The Bull-ring/Mall/whatever they called it these days. Across the yard, the wooden gateway creaked as she carefully entered the enclosure of apple and cherry trees at the rear of the farm.

There at the far end, no more than twenty paces away beneath the biggest tree that still sheltered the remains of Edward's first tree house, a simple headstone had been set with the inscription:

EDWARD ALBERT MALLORY
6 MARCH 1977 – 5 MARCH 1997
DEARLY LOVED
ALWAYS MISSED
FOREVER WITH US ALL

She drew a deep breath and slowly, respectfully, walked towards the stone, stopping at a discreet distance to appreciate the carefully chosen script.

'Hello, sweetheart,' she spoke softly, her tears welling up on hearing her own words. 'I've just come to bring our little baby Bump to see you.'

Bump kicked hard from within and months of pent-up emotions swept over her, the conflict of feelings dragging her deeper. She wept openly and freely, apologising uncontrollably to Edward for making a scene. This was more painful than she could ever have anticipated. Her heart was wrenched all over again at her loss, and her ability to cope with the grief ebbed away as she felt Bump's throbbing presence harder and for longer. She sat on the damp ground, wishing for a hole to appear and take her down to be with him.

Time stood still. The cloud cover thickened and the already gloomy skies drew steadily cheerless. She felt scared, uneasy, and cruelly vulnerable. This was the same feeling that prompted her to run before, to become quarry to her past. And yet this time, she didn't want to leave the sanctuary of the long grass. Surely running would help? It didn't last time, she told herself.

Watching from the bathroom window, Val closed her eyes to fight away her own tears, the sight of the distraught young woman distressing.

She wasn't sure from where it came, but a surging confidence lifted her spirits and Olivia wiped dry her face, to meet reality positively. Deep breaths and a slow count steadied her nerve, and she managed to smile at the notion of Bump attempting to communicate with his daddy.

Rummaging in her coat pocket, she extracted a piece of paper upon which she'd copied an amazing profundity that she wanted to read aloud. 'Remember this?' she asked Edward. 'It's called "Beyond Belief"...'

The first spots of rain awoke her from her reconciled thoughts. She took out the pocket watch that still went everywhere with her. The hour or so she'd been sitting there seemed more like seconds, but the feeling of wetness of her legs and bottom proved the watch to be correct. Putting her hand down to aid her ascent, she felt a helping lift under her arm.

'Kettle's on,' said the caring voice beside her.

Val smiled with the understanding that only a grieving mother feels and hugged Olivia tight before leading her into the house. Sitting in the damp outdoors wasn't really the type of pastime she would recommend an expectant woman to pursue, but there was no way anyone was going to begrudge Olivia her mourning, especially Val.

They sat in the kitchen listening to Ken Bruce's 'Pick of the Hits', Olivia now changed into dry clothes – the dungarees that made her feel like Humpty-Dumpty with boobs. 'What do you think of me going back to college, Val?' she suddenly asked.

Val looked up from her cookery book. 'College?'

'Yeah. I know I can't go back to Durham, not with Bump. But locally, or open studies or something. I'd like to complete the course.'

Val was relieved to hear that the discussion revolved around a local issue, not the North East. 'Well, why not?' she agreed. 'It might be best to get Bump settled before you tie yourself to something else equally demanding, but yes, there's no reason why you shouldn't.'

'You don't think I'm being stupid, then?'

'Why ever would I think that?'

'I dunno,' she shrugged. 'Some people might not understand that I'm going to need a job at some stage, and one that pays a decent wage – not just a basic one like Tony Blair's promising us. I'm going to need paper qualifications for that, aren't I?'

''Fraid so,' Val confirmed. 'No, luv,' she patted her fore-arm, 'we'll all be right behind you.'

'What the hell does she want to be doing something like that for?' Adrian gasped.

'She'll want her independence, won't she?' explained Val defensively.

He shook his head in amazement. He could appreciate her need for independence, but being a self-confessed old-fashioned dinosaur, surely the baby's upbringing was most important. It wasn't as if they'd ever go short, was it?

'Just you remember,' warned Val with an acicular finger, 'she's not our daughter. Emma and Dan might just feel a little put out if you suddenly start to hijack their little girl.'

He nodded reluctantly. Perhaps there was logic to the whole thing hinging on Olivia needing to feel her self-worth. That was something he'd lost himself, but thankfully regained, so couldn't, and wouldn't, wish the same fate on the mother of his grandchild. 'To what job does she aspire?' he asked genuinely in what, even to his ears, sounded a trifle lofty tone.

'Don't be such a supercilious git!' Val slapped his backside hard with the tea towel. 'Get yourself changed; we're interviewing in ten minutes.'

He stood with a fish-like mouth, unable to see where he was going wrong. All he wanted was to help out.

'Now!' she yelled.

He suddenly realised why they'd ended up with Gladys Almond. Val's interview technique was purely personality judgement. Not that there was anything wrong with Val's judgement of personality – it was spot-on. No, the problem seemed clearly to be linking the applicant's ability to lift a duster with that undoubted personality.

This was the second person they'd seen and like the first, she wasn't giving the answers needed to form an educated opinion. His remit was 'to sit, be here and keep quiet!' and this is exactly what he was doing. His problem of course, his wandering mind was fully aware, was that he knew that if he spoke up now, he'd be interfering. If he didn't, and they employed Gladys mark two, it would be his fault for not pointing out any glaring flaws in the applicant's figurative make-up. Or actual make-up if that turned out to be the problem. Or genetic make-up come to that. This one was turning into a werewolf, judging by the amount of hormone-induced limb and facial hair she displayed. If she tried shaving, she'd blunt a razor blade or two on that lot, he thought. I've got some hedge-clippers somewhere.

He re-tuned to the interview. The answers to which Val

was being treated seemed to be coming from another dimension in time, as they bore little relativity to the question asked.

'What do you consider to be a thorough cleaning of, let's say, this lounge, Mrs Shuttleworth?' the employer asked.

'It's a lovely room, Mrs Mallory,' the candidate replied.

'Thank you.'

'We used to have a suite a similar colour to that when we were first married. Ours was PVC, mind you,' she smiled with unabashed pride. 'And the inglenook. Just gives it all that farmhouse feeling, doesn't it?'

'Yes, possibly it does,' Val caught Adrian's glare as she turned to view the fireplace.

'But the thing I like the best is the views. Oh, what lovely views you have. You must be proud of your 'ouse, Mrs Mallory.'

'Yes, we are, Mrs Shuttleworth. That's why we're looking for someone to help us with it,' assertion working its way into her voice. 'Now, how would you clean this room?'

The woman surveyed her surroundings and thought hard. 'Pledge, I'd say.'

For longer than he cared to remember, he had been employing staff; but never had three candidates – cleaning ladies at that – frustrated him so much, and straightening the knot of his silk tie, Adrian pleaded to be relieved of meeting number four, scheduled for two days later.

'Why?' his wife demanded.

'Because, darling,' he placed his arm around her shoulder and drew her closer, 'you will find the best cleaner whether I'm here or not,' he patronised, kissing her head. 'Now, are you ready to go?'

'Just let me get my earrings,' she gestured for him to make for the door, 'and I'll be right down.'

Downstairs, Liz and Olivia waited patiently while Bump practised his somersaults and karate. The fact that she'd just less than one month to go didn't impress Olivia. The sooner she could force the baby out and let her stomach turn into a relaxed saggy anythingness, the better.

Liz's mouth refused to obey the mind's instructions in telling Olivia of her morning conversation with Don, and the moment passed when she heard her father descending the stairs.

'Right you two and a half,' he called to the girls. 'Mum'll be down in a minute, where are we going tonight?'

A unified 'anywhere' answer wasn't at all surprising to Adrian, and he suggested that they just drive around a bit to find somewhere.

'Aw, Dad!' Liz complained. 'Can't we decide? I'm starving.'

The mystery tour took them deep into the Lancashire countryside and they pulled up outside the hotel that awaited their arrival for an eight o'clock table reservation.

'I knew all along he was kidding,' Liz lied. 'This place does a mean breaded Camembert,' she added, scurrying into the bar in the vain hope of having a 'proper drink' to celebrate.

The Camembert was indeed delicious although Olivia stayed safe, going berserk as she dubbed it and opting for the vegetable soup. The conversation was lively and the three women noticed Adrian's relaxed disposition. It was a long time since Val had seen her husband like this; Liz and Olivia had certainly never known anything like it, and his daughter felt almost a stranger to the man sat beside her.

She could stand it no more. 'Dad? Are you shagging someone else?' For the second time that day, she sensed a hush around her. 'I mean…'

Val shook her head in disbelief and looked on as Adrian guffawed. 'What makes you level such an accusation on this auspicious occasion?' he chuckled.

'You're doing it now!' Liz responded. 'You're too damned happy! Where's my real dad? The grumpy old bugger that doesn't have time for a dump, let alone fancy sentences?'

He couldn't help smiling. The more he smiled, the prouder he became. He knew for every conceivable reason that the decision to sell had been the right one, and decided that the time was now right to reveal all to those closest to him.

'The deal's done,' he beamed.

'What deal?' Liz asked.

Val knew and grinned. He'd kept that one quiet. The last she'd been told, he was on the verge of settling on a little over two and a half million for the sale of the business – before tax of course. 'So, that's why you were pacing a hole in my lounge carpet this morning!'

'What deal for Christ's sake?' Liz insisted.

Olivia understood too and was pleased for the whole family. 'Well done,' she told Adrian who was attracting the wine waiter's attention.

'More champagne please,' he called, the young man acknowledging with a raised hand.

'What friggin' deal?' Liz's hoarse throat cursed.

Olivia touched her hand. 'Your worst nightmare's come true,' she teased. 'You've got parents on a pension. Oh, and you owe the box 50p.'

Of all the reactions anyone could anticipate, running up and down the restaurant yelling 'We're in the money' wasn't one at the head of the list. Liz was, as the waiter understated, overjoyed at something.

The official announcement was not to be made for a few days yet Adrian insisted, and when her excitement had died down, Liz joined in the general agreement not to tell a soul until it had been. Especially, she volunteered, not Carole.

With calorie-crammed dessert over, and at a time when Val and Liz had gone to 'powder their noses', Adrian apologised to Olivia for temporarily purloining the focus of celebrations.

'Don't think anything of it,' she told him. 'It's worth more celebration than my poxy birthday.'

He disagreed with that sentiment, and having changed the subject in a single breath, was interested to learn what she would possibly like to aim for with her further studies.

'Management of what?' he questioned.

'Anything that needs managing really,' she replied with a self-conscious snort. 'Sounds a bit airy-fairy I know, but I think I've been through enough character-building exercises this year to put it to good use in many capacities.'

Now that, he did agree with. 'Do you know Sam Harman?' he asked.

'The name rings a bell,' she frowned.

'No, that was Quasimodo!' he laughed. 'Sam's our solicitor, though some do say they could have been separated at birth.' With their companions still absent, Adrian swiftly put an outline idea to her that he considered being worthy of further thought and discussion with the legal bell ringer. To his delight, so did she.

The interviewing was over. Val could cope no more with ladies of assorted shapes and sizes telling her of their life stories or medical ailments, if not a combination of the two. She flopped back into the comfort of the settee and held her hands over her weary face. Number four had just left, and was last seen demonstrating her commitment by dragging driveway gravel with her foot into the ridges left by Val's car. The judge's decision? Akin to a wax fireguard – absolutely useless. So it was down to the three seen on Tuesday.

She looked at the notes she'd made at the time. What

had seemed to be the wonderful system of checklists and category scores that Adrian advocated, meant little when she wasn't enthralled by any of them. There must be, she considered, a perfectly sound method of deciding. Where's my pin cushion?

The kitchen felt cold when Don followed Liz through the back door. Holding it open while he waited for the occupants of the Range Rover just turning into the driveway to catch up wasn't going to make any difference to the ambient frost indoors.

He said hello to Liz's dad and sister who were deep in animated discussion, and made his way through the house to join Liz by the blazing lounge fire, and her mother – laid in a strange position on the settee with what looked to be a wet tea towel over her head. He nudged his girlfriend and pointed to the recumbent body.

'*Don't* ask,' she said in a tone meant to arouse her mother.

Val sat upright and whisked away her soothing mask, startled that Liz was not, as she'd thought, alone. 'Oh!' she yelped. 'Hello, Don.'

'Hello,' he replied, the door opening behind him to reveal Olivia and Adrian.

'Where've you all come from?' Val asked, her eyes trying to focus on her watch.

'Was Granny sleeping?' Olivia teased.

'Bugger off! I was resting my eyes,' she sniggered, determined not to show her embarrassment.

Liz excused herself and Don, taking him upstairs to her room to play some compact discs. They were out of sight before Val could even contemplate objecting, and so she turned to her husband. 'Have this lot come in with you?'

'No, only these two,' he thumbed in Olivia's direction. 'Don and Daughter were coming in as we pulled up.'

Val blinked to wake herself. 'So how've you gone on?' she asked, unsure of where they'd been.

'Fine,' Adrian replied vaguely. 'How about you?'

She pulled a face that suggested a distinct lack of success. 'It's got to be one of the three ugly sisters from Tuesday,' she moaned.

Adrian allowed himself a satisfied smile. 'Does it?' he replied, looking at Olivia with a knowing wink.

Upstairs, Don seemed to be moving his foot in relative time to the beat of Liz's 'No Disco Album Ever in the Entire History of the Whole World Has Ever Been Better Than This, Ever! (Volume 5)', which was all encouraging stuff. What she was dying to know though, was had he bought anything yet?

That reddish pigmentation appeared in his cheeks. 'It's a bit of a long story,' he smiled. 'But the short answer is yes and no.'

'Well, you either have, Don, or you haven't.'

'I went to the chemists all right, and even bought things...'

'But they weren't the things you'd gone in to buy?'

'Exactly!' his finger pointed. 'Give the girl in jeans a biscuit,' he joked.

'Sod the biscuit mate; I want a willy!' she protested to his bashfully expressive face. She leant forward and kissed him. She could tell that he wasn't used to the action, but felt confident that there was plenty of potential. She thought it time to let him practise.

Her kiss did things to him that he just could not hide. Why was it that she could move her mouth like she was chewing gum, yet he felt as though his jaws were super-glued? And oh Lord, what now? What the hell was that slimy thing between his teeth? What *is* she doing? It's brilliant whatever it is. Is it her tongue? Surely not.

She forced him backward to lie on her bed and lay beside him, wrapping her arm around his torso, encouraging him to do likewise. Good, he's catching on. Now her hand slid around from his back, over his slim waist until her fingers found the button fly of his denims.

Could the straining in his new jeans really get any worse? He'd thought not, but now that her hands were moving around, her roaming fingers tickling his side on their way to his stomach. Her full palm now rubbed him and he groaned. This is unreal. He anticipated a lightheaded feeling – there was so much blood focused elsewhere; that could be the only inevitable conclusion.

His moaning turned her on. As long as she could stop him being too loud – she didn't want *everyone* knowing what they were up to. She didn't need to ask if that was nice, she could tell from his face that it was. She wished he would touch her. Anywhere, it didn't matter, instead of gripping her back, holding her tightly to him. The restriction against her moving arm made it ache; she'd have to release his hand from her back. Round to the front seemed a good idea.

What *was* she doing? She's never putting my hand on those breasts! The straining intensified. What should he do now? Squeeze. That's what you do; squeeze.

'Ow!' she cried. 'Knead gently,' her patient scholastic advice whispered.

'Sorry…' his apologies smothered by another impressive kiss.

She lifted her head just enough to continue the embrace, whilst coaching too. 'Like bread,' she told him.

'Only granary,' he smooched back, his jaws learning to relax.

She snorted, biting his lip. 'You what?' she giggled.

'I only like granary bread,' he told her, nursing his first injury *d'amour*.

'What've you done to your mouth?' his mother asked when he returned home.

His story of biting his lip when slipping down the college steps seemed to have credibility. He wasn't going to tell her the real cause, nor that Liz's pregnant sister had knocked just afterwards to find out what all the laughter was about, and the ensuing panic to fasten bras and trousers had nearly resulted in two premature heart fatalities.

He told his mother that he would be in his room, listening to his personal CD player and would be downstairs for tea at the six o'clock serve-up time she'd told him.

Sitting on his bed, loading a disc into the portable player, he dreamed of the next stage of romantic encounters with Liz. His education was racing along, and if things continued like this, he would lose his virginity before reaching his eighteenth birthday in December after all.

He laid back and inserted the tiny earpieces to listen to his favourite album. His thoughts returned to Liz's beauty, to her sensual touch, and that almighty erection he'd struggled so much to rid himself of before going downstairs at the Farm.

The swelling sensation returned, and closing his eyes, he reached below and unbuttoned his flies. The rhythm of the music helped him relax and his stroke mirrored the beat. He saw her face, felt her body and tasted her kiss. He was in heaven.

He had already enjoyed the first three album tracks, and the soothing melodies of the fourth accompanied his eventual relief. He opened his eyes and half rising, turned to reach for a tissue. He suddenly felt quite sick. From where, pray tell, had that fresh cup of tea come?

Emma had thoroughly enjoyed their holiday. She still felt guilty that they had deserted Olivia at a time when she really needed her parents, but as Dan and her daughter would both repeatedly remind her, there was no need to worry.

The weather had been kind, apart from the day that Dan had booked a tennis lesson of all things. There was no mystery to his actions; the coach was young, French and had what, on good information, was called a spanner body. The rain dampened his libido however and probably saved him from sampling Madeira's coronary care facilities.

The re-filling of suitcases never worried Emma. No matter how long she'd been away, a cerebral trigger would always tell her two days before departure date: 'You are now ready for a decent cup of tea. You are now ready for a decent cup of tea', and amazingly enough, she always was.

Crumpled and creased, worn and not, all clothes would be bundled into the case with most care apportioned to the souvenirs and duty free bottles that she'd wrap in T-shirts or underwear. For this purpose, Dan's was most accommodating, and any customs sniffer dogs would hardly want to linger around them for too long.

She admired her tan in the wall mirror. She didn't feel much different until she lifted her skirt and compared her buttock with the back of her legs. Very impressive, she thought, but how could she prove to people back home that she *had* caught the sun? Flashing her boobs or backside would make most folk queasy, not jealous. They'd just have to take her word for it.

She shouted through the bathroom door, reminding Dan to put the little soaps, scents and shower cap from the silver tray in between the twin marble sinks, in his shaving bag. No, she replied, not the tray as well. One towelling bathrobe was enough for him to 'borrow for a while'.

Although the suite was luxury itself, Emma was ready for her sweet little home with its moss-filled garden, overdue decorating and of course, safe electrics. The real world awaited their return – moaning, whinging, complaining customers in the shop and the early starts for Dan. She screwed up her face and closed the suitcase lid on its mountain of laundry.

Dan's unusually silent approach startled her as he spoke. 'Tell you what, luv, I'm missing our little 'un,' he confessed.

She took his hand and led him out on to the balcony overlooking the gardens and Atlantic Ocean. He put his arm around her waist and cuddling her to keep them both warm in the cool sea breeze, began a tuneless nasal hum. She looked up at him with amusement.

'*Some enchanted evening...*' he began with a smirk, his dialect flattening every note. '*...you may see a stranger...*'

'For God's sake,' she slapped his stomach. 'They drown stray cats round here!'

He spluttered a smoker's laugh and kissed her. 'Well then, m'lady,' his devoted servant impression being only slightly better than his singing. ''Ow'd you like to accompany me to the bar to partake in a satisfying...' he paused to suppress a grin, '...whis-keeeee and sow-darrrr?'

John and Glenda were in their regular seats by the piano and moved round the table in anticipation of Dan and Emma's company when they saw them enter the bar.

'Do we have to?' Emma whispered through the corner of her mouth, not wanting to spend every night with the same people. She wanted a quiet night alone with her husband.

'Ignore 'em, Em,' he replied, guiding her by the arm to the bar. 'They're nice, like, but I've 'ad enough of 'em for one week,' he told her.

Dan remained standing, but Emma took a high stool at the bar and the attendant moved along the counter; wiping any spills and glass rings as he came towards them.

Dan felt a slap on his sunburned and tender back. 'That'll be one bee-er and one whis-kee and sow-dar!' ordered the Mancunian accent from behind. 'We knew you hadn't seen us,' John told Dan's turning head. 'We're over there, by the piano,' he pointed to Glenda who, across the room, held her hand aloft and waggled her fingers in greeting.

'Actually, John,' Emma spoke, 'we were hoping to have a quiet night together, it being our last.'

'Our thoughts exactly!' he agreed. 'That's why we thought: who better to spend it with?'

Emma's underwhelmed sigh wasn't lost on Dan who repeated their wish for a quiet night, alone. John, however, was not to be fobbed off lightly, and taking the bar receipt, signed for the drinks against his room account. 'Just one drink,' he insisted, taking Emma's arm and dragging her off her perch towards his wife. 'Just one to celebrate Dan's birthday.'

Dan collected the drinks and followed, Emma turning helplessly and mouthing 'Just one!' to his nodded agreement.

At the risk of her sobriety, Emma knocked back her drink with astonishing ease and her expression encouraged Dan to do the same with his beer. His startled eyes refused, and Glenda took up the conversation where her husband had just left off – something about another strike in England; John's daughter complaining that her Giro was held up in a postal dispute.

Dan was intrigued and, to Emma's dismay, motioned to the barman to bring another round of drinks.

The recently all too frequent glassy feeling glazed his eyes, and Dan could tell by Emma's body language that he'd overdone it. He'd only had four bottles, but there must have been so much residual alcohol in his bloodstream, he considered, that he was in fact drunk.

Shaking John's hand and kissing Glenda a little too romantically for Emma's liking, Dan excused them both and wished the couple all the best in Manchester.

'Cheshire,' corrected Glenda.

'They're from bloody Stockport!' Emma fumed as she took up residency at a table of their own, close to the door. 'Anyone would think they're from Alderley Edge or somewhere the way she talks.'

'Don't be nasty, Em,' Dan told her, quietly burping into his closed hand. 'You're only mad at me, and I'm sorry. But it sounds like I'm on strike again for summat. I could do without that.'

Emma agreed it sounded that way, and expressed her thanks to a higher being that this night could only improve.

'Wull Oiy nivah!' a cry from their side. 'Look, Sheela.' Emma was proved terribly wrong. 'It's Dan and Whutsit frum the ship!'

D AN'S POST-FLIGHT recovery technique was taking on unreasonable proportions. It wasn't as though he'd never flown before, Emma considered; he was simply a bad flyer – and getting worse. It appeared to her, that each successive trip brought about more melodrama upon arrival than the previous. Most nervous people shake. Some combine this with an upset stomach. Others pray: some might say they should have been praying when they were that much closer to their maker at 30,000 feet, but they pray regardless.

He *claimed* he was tying a shoelace, but there was no mistaking it; she *definitely* saw him kiss the airport tarmac. Along the baggage reclaim route, he refused to take the moving walkway and his hand never left the concourse handrail, and his gratitude to be stopped by customs displayed the kind of suspicious behaviour which normally guaranteed a full cavity search. Only a cigarette could help settle him and at the first chance he saw, he was inhaling more of his duty free booty.

Any outsider would be hard pressed to tell who was the most pleased to see the other. It was a wonderful surprise to see Olivia standing at the barrier awaiting their arrival, and Emma's reaction, as ever, was to cry.

Adrian shook Dan's quivering hand, welcoming him home and offering to push the laden trolley towards the waiting vehicle, while Olivia tried to prise her mother from around her neck; the taxi, she assured her, was cancelled and wouldn't be charged for.

The Tuesday afternoon traffic was busy along the M60 and Adrian was grateful to see the M61 intersection that would take him in the slightly quieter northbound direction of home. It wasn't long before the excited chatter of the travellers had given way to wide yawns and expressed desires for beans on toast with a proper brew of British tea.

Val had sent, with Olivia, the invitation for her parents to spend the afternoon at Wingate Farm, and to stay for an evening meal; an opportunity to catch up and forget the prospect of cooking. Emma was reluctant, wanting to get home and sit on her own toilet, get the washing machine on, and drink her own tea from a beaker of her own. Ah yes, a beaker of tea!

'Go on, Mum!' Olivia pleaded. 'I've not packed my stuff up yet.'

It was settled, they would accept. Not, Emma believed, that she ever honestly had a choice in the matter.

There were cards dotted all around the lounge when Emma walked through the door ahead of Val. She felt awful that the birthday gifts from Dan and her were still safely tucked at the bottom of her wardrobe. The special card sent from the airport was there though, assuming pride of place. Without asking, she studied each greeting and passed the sort of comment that proud mothers pass. '…Ah. Mrs Solomon remembered. Bless… Ha ha. That's funny. From Janice… Oh! That's a bit rude! Fancy sending a card like that!… Have a happy day in every way, lots of love Val and Adrian. Ah, that's nice…'

Dan, as usual, fell foul of the settee but remained in the position it allowed him to sink into, quite happy that he was back on dry land for good. He rested his eyes and, to Emma's horror, was soon snoring for England.

He was woken when his cup of tea had formed a ring around the rim, and his daughter could take no more of the farmyard noises. 'Did you ever try out for "Opportunity Knocks", Dad?' she asked.

'Eh?'

'You should've. You had us all convinced we were in a zoo.'

He chuckled, and reminded her that she wasn't too old for a smacked bum.

'Well, if we're all awake,' Adrian began, offering Dan a cigar, 'Olivia has something she wants to get off her chest.' He withdrew one for himself and closed the box. 'Have you not?' he asked her.

'Off her stomach, more like!' called Dan.

She glared at him and stuck out her tongue. 'I'm not ready!' she protested to Adrian.

'Get on with it, girl. Make a management decision,' he laughed, leading her into an inescapable alley.

'I've not thought what I want to say!'

Emma and Dan looked puzzled and were both relieved to see that so, too, did Val. 'What have you two been cooking up?' she asked her husband.

'That's what Livvy's going to tell you now. Isn't it, Livvy?'

'Well, I'm not prepared,' she offered mitigation in advance.

'Just shoot from the hip,' he encouraged.

'All right!' She took a steadying breath, and told the assembled gathering of the scheme that Adrian – she'd lay blame at his door – had conceived, and she'd been a party to.

Adrian puffed on the cigar and exhaled with a pride he'd only ever shown for Edward.

'But you're retired!' Val gasped to him.

'Who is?' Emma asked, completely confused. Only a

matter of days ago, she was without a daughter who now was to be a partner in Adrian's venture. But *he* was retired? Since when?

Adrian held his hands up high. 'Let's deal with one thing at a time, shall we?' he suggested.

'I said I wasn't ready,' Olivia reminded him of her initial protests.

He turned to Dan and Emma with a look of sincerity. 'It isn't public knowledge, but I've just sold the bookmakers for...' he considered his words carefully, '...for a small profit. A recent experience led me to think that there may be a gap in the service industry: quality cleaning staff for residential and professional business, coupled with quality repair work: decorating, gardening and the like. With me so far?'

Everyone mumbled their own affirmatives.

'Bear that in mind then, when you consider Livvy's need to find herself suitable future employment.'

'There's no way you're playing bloody char woman, young lady!' Dan roared.

'Hang on, Dan.' Emma held back his attempts to escape the settee. 'What you're saying is...' she thought for a second and drew a blank, '...is what?'

'In simple terms, that Livvy's the boss,' Adrian blew another smoky cloud into the air.

The collective dawning that this was the craziest, most ludicrous, ill conceived, brilliant idea ever concocted brought smiles all around the room.

'Ladies and Gentlemen,' Adrian stood, 'I give you Olivia Beech, General Manager designate of... What are we calling it?'

'Bump 'n' Grind!' Olivia joked to a loud cheer and applause.

He laughed. If that was off the top of her head, he *was* backing a winner, '...of Bump 'n' Grind.'

'It might be a silly question, dear,' asked Val, handing Adrian the cutlery to set the dinner table, 'but where exactly are you going to get these quality cleaners from?'

He shrugged. 'Minor details, darling. But if I can set up a successful bookie's with the kind of support I had from your parents, think what that girl in there can do with the support we can give her.'

They kissed, and she took a pace backward, looking up towards his face with incredulity. 'Do I *know* you?'

He wasn't due back to work until after the weekend, but knowing that there was some form of industrial action, Dan would rather spend his time at home on strike than taken as holiday. Within reason, he could take his holidays whenever he wanted to, strikes were somewhat out of his control, and when the two clashed... well, he'd better find out exactly what was going on.

After his morning's business on the outskirts of town, he had planned to get his overalls on and wander down to the goods shed anyway to do a bit on the train. He made his way then, on a wet Wednesday afternoon, to his favourite retreat in search of someone who could bring him up to date on the situation at work. He was greeted with a full complement of volunteers, running the engine up and down fifty yards of salvaged track.

His heart filled with joy. What a beautiful sight it was. A voice called from the engine and all faces turned to watch Dan's approach.

'Na then lads, you miserable bastards!' he joked, finding his natural vernacular. 'You'll do anythin' t'stop me postcards gettin' there, won't ya?'

'Good to see ya, Dan!' the driver shouted, tooting the whistle and engaging reverse.

'I suppose this strike was because someone had to win t'sweepstake, eh? Who's the lucky bugger then?'

'It's Bill as it 'appens, mate,' a sardonic reply from somewhere in the group.

'Big fuckin' surprise!' Dan slapped his friend on the back. 'Your round then, Billy Boy?'

Bill shook his head. 'Not this time, lad. Jimmy Taylor's been given 'is cards; it'll go in t' kitty.'

'Jim 'as? Why?'

'That's why we're takin' action. He's been pissed once too often.'

Dan scowled. 'I thought that was all sorted?'

'Well,' Bill explained, 'they turned a blind eye at first din't they?'

Dan nodded.

'Then as it got worse, they thought they'd hide 'im in that bloody Pat suit, din't they?'

'Aye,' Dan's impatient prompt for further detail.

'Well, last straw came when he were in 'ospital and said it were Jess had been squeezin' nurse's arse. They've give 'im boot, and we've got engine runnin' as a result.'

'Daft sod!' Dan stamped the ground in anger. 'He knew 'ow stupid he'd been.'

Bill looked sorrowed. 'This walk-out's a token gesture mate. There's no escapin' it this time; 'e's gone all right.'

Dan hung around until 'Chalky' White had returned from home with his Olympus camera with built-in zoom for the official group photograph to be taken; the instant self-developing thing he'd first brought hardly being suitable for the job in hand.

Somehow, the smile on Dan's face wasn't so smiley. He felt a sense of responsibility for Jimmy Taylor, yet didn't know why. He'd promised the bloke a chat and never had it. Perhaps that partly explained his anguish; it was something he could have prevented. He could kick himself. No one had asked Jess to rub up against the nurse though. Randy little moggy. If it was the busty brunette, he wouldn't have minded being there himself. She certainly didn't need a table in front of her to rest her lunch tray on, but there's no call for harassing the little corker.

He wasn't in the mood to take his turn in driving the locomotive, opting instead to return home. As he walked, he considered how he'd often thought that his life had hit rock bottom this year, but looking back, it hadn't come anywhere near. Okay, Olivia went – very traumatic and stressful. The car was written off, so what – it was only metal. The real downer was Edward, but that was, in the nicest possible way, Edward's life that had hit rock bottom, not his own.

He sighed heavily. He'd be forty on Saturday. Wow! What a thrilling prospect that was, his sour thoughts dreaded. Forty years old and a grandad. Oh bugger! That meant, by fifty-six he could be a great-grandfather! Hang on, at this rate, by seventy-two he could be a great-great-grandfather! Double bugger and fuck 'n' all!

He closed his eyes to the fate. Look at the positives, he told himself. There's going to be a lovely little baby in three weeks' time, and he's going to be surrounded by a loving family. First commercial ride of the locomotive must go to Tarantino. He'd sort that with the lads. Bump the train driver – he liked that idea, even though it did sound like a terrorist threat.

'That was quick,' Emma seemed surprised to see him as he removed his shoes at the back door. 'Mind that clean washing!' she warned.

Taking care where he stood and rested his greasy hands, he told her the news; both good and bad, and she sensed that Jim Taylor's dismissal was significant to her husband. 'Was he the chappie in hospital?'

Dan nodded, grabbing a mug from the draining board and shaking off the excess water.

'So what happens now, then?' she enquired.

'About what?'

'The dispute. How long's it to last?'

'They're talking again today. Could be over with and back to normal at any time, the way Bill talks.'

He opened the serving hatch doors to seek Olivia and saw her, feet up on the sofa, arms draped around Bump with her eyes closed.

'Is she sleeping?' he whispered to Emma.

'No,' his daughter's bored voice drifted from the other room.

He groaned and Emma laughed. 'Have you been bitten by a bat at some time?' he asked his daughter, not needing to shout – she was bound to hear him. There was no response.

'Want a brew, city slicker?' he called.

'Go on then. I can't sleep with this one in such a playful mood.'

Watching him settle down with his drink, Olivia winked to her mother and cleared her throat. 'What do you fancy doing on Saturday, Dad?'

He shook his head and gulped his tea to wash away a mouthful of chocolate digestive. 'Haven't thought,' he replied. 'The lads were on about having a celebration drink to christen the engine.'

'That's a nice idea,' Emma suggested. 'We can perhaps have a pub meal at lunchtime to celebrate your birthday.'

'What's wrong with a slap-up meal at night time?' he complained. 'You're only forty once!'

Emma feigned contemplation. 'True,' she agreed. 'But we'll have had a big meal on Friday night at the presentation, won't we?'

'So?'

'Poor old Olivia's going to be suffering, isn't she? Two late nights on the trot, she'll need some rest,' Emma stretched the truth. 'No, I think we should have a quiet lunch at the White Horse,' she was finding it hard to remain straight-faced. 'Or how about The Bell? You like The Bell, luv.'

He never had the final say, so why should he think he would now? It was obviously decided that they'd go to the pub, and perhaps two consecutive nights of rich food would give him enough wind to blow a hole in the mattress. 'Make it The Rat and Drainpipe and it's a deal,' he bargained.

'The Rat and Drainpipe?' Olivia's disgust was vocal. '*That* flea-ridden dump?'

'Oh, all right,' he sighed. 'The Bell, then.'

Behind the cushion and out of Dan's line of vision, Emma's thumbs-up sign confirmed to Olivia the release of a successful smokescreen.

Olivia had been right. Liz was having no trouble at all from Carole, who was giving Don a wide berth and generally allowing her to have time to herself with her boyfriend. During lessons, they were the best of friends and still spoke on the telephone – albeit not as often as before, but then there was Don to think of.

She was pleased that they hadn't fallen out. Friends, she thought, are hard enough to come by; she couldn't just lose such a good one like that. She was pleased too that Carole had accepted the invitation to her dad's dinner and presentation on Friday night. So that she wouldn't feel left out, Val had agreed that Carole could bring a friend. Yes, Liz thought, things are settling down. All she needed now was some condoms.

Don's second expedition to the chemist's – a different one this time – had brought about the purchase of yet more useless goods. Neither of them had acne to the extent that his acquisitions would suggest. If they ever cut themselves, there'd be no worry about plasters, and as for headaches and indigestion, there was no excuse. The one worry, obviously a real impulse purchase, was the home pregnancy testing kit. Having said that, it might come in handy one day.

If he continued in this vein, Liz giggled to herself, she'd be able to survey the layouts of all the local pharmacy counters without actually going to any of them. She daren't think how much this first bonk was costing.

She watched him approach from the science building doors. He was looking as good as ever and, in half an hour, would have his new spectacles too.

'Hi, lover!' she called.

He flushed. It was still difficult for him to show his affections, but he was getting better. 'Hiya!' he dared reply from a distance.

She threw her arms around his waist and kissed him, teasing about a third trip to the chemist's. He was able to joke, thankfully, about his nervous disposition and was relieved when Liz offered to get the necessary party appliances.

'What's this digging in my hip?' she grinned.

'Stop it!' he begged. 'It's hard enough...'

'It's that all right!'

He raised his eyebrows in admonishment, just as her brother used to. 'Elizabeth...'

I'm in trouble now.

'...you know I have trouble controlling it,' he whispered.

She thrust her pelvis forward, pushing against him. 'Mmmm, you do, don't you?' she tormented. 'Are we going to have to walk into town like this?' she smirked.

'No, just let me sit down for a while,' he made for the wall beside them. 'And don't talk mucky!' he warned.

They discussed the weekend as he relaxed, and he

thought that staying at Liz's house on Friday was a good idea, if Mum was okay about it, of course.

'You can have the double room,' Liz's eyes glinted, and he didn't want to respond.

'What about your sister – where will she be?'

'Sister?' she frowned. 'You mean Livvy?'

'Yeah.'

'She's not my sister, you daft sod. She would have been my sister-in-law perhaps. She's like a sister though,' she reflected. 'I wish she was.'

Don was puzzled; I'm missing something here. 'She *would* have been your sister-in-law? How do you arrive at that one?'

Liz hesitated. She hadn't explained, had she? That might be a good idea before Friday, save the poor lad having the fright of his life. She stood and offered her hand for him to take. 'Get up,' she smiled. 'Stiffy or not, we'll go and get your specs and I'll tell you about someone special on the way.'

The telephone message for Dan was that the action was off. Jimmy was taking early retirement and would leave with a nice severance, negotiated by the union on his behalf. Normal service resuming from midday today.

'Okay,' Olivia replied. 'I'll tell him when he gets in.'

'So he'll be back as normal Monday, and we'll see you tomorrow night then, Olivia. Nudge, nudge,' Bill chuckled.

She returned to her bedroom where she'd been busily wrapping the presents bought for her father's big day when the phone rang. She loved occasions like this – Christmas and other people's birthdays. Her mind strayed to just a few hours ahead. What *was* she going to say in front of all those people at the hotel tonight?

As she tore the sticky roll in a jagged and badly angled edge, she began to picture herself speaking, and mumbled a few desperate opening greetings to the carpet. A twinge took away her breath and she blessed Bump for his contribution. This pregnancy game had lost its fun. Everything was hard work these days, even cutting into the colourful paper in front of her. The wrapping, so beautifully started, became a chore and the theory that as long as they were wrapped, the gifts were fine, was soon applied. It was time to take a rest.

She was disturbed by the sound of a car close by, its engine stopping then restarting. Don't come here! she threatened in the darkness of her closed eyes. She hoped that they were going to Mrs Platt's at number thirty-seven. As there was no ring on the doorbell, she allowed tranquillity to flow over her and drifted.

She didn't think she'd slept, but hearing her parents' chatter downstairs, she opened one eye to look at the clock. It was only ten minutes since she'd laid down. She puffed an exasperated sigh and closed her eyes again. There was the sound of footsteps up the stairs and a gentle knock at the door.

'I'm asleep!' she called testily.

Emma entered, smiling. 'Too tired for a surprise, cherub?'

'What sort of surprise?' Olivia snapped sourly. 'I'm knackered.'

'I'll come back later then, luv,' Emma decided.

'And Mum?' Olivia called. 'Will you tell that dickhead outside to stop revving their engine?'

Emma grinned protectively. 'Leave it to me. I'll tell him.'

She returned downstairs and went outside. 'Oi, Dickhead!' she yelled. 'Stop revving your engine. There's a pregnant woman in here wants to sleep!'

Upstairs, Olivia could not believe that her mother would shout such a thing, and was suddenly quite awake.

She knelt on her bed and popped her head between the drawn curtains to see Dan and Emma looking up at her from the driveway, their hands held. There, beside them was a shiny metallic blue car.

The window opened and Olivia's head appeared inquisitively. 'Who are you calling "Dickhead", young lady?' Dan called.

She was lost for words, not completely understanding the scene she surveyed.

'Do you want a ride, or what?' he called. 'You can drive if you want to.'

Her ride in the back of the car was a dream. They'd even arranged to have a baby seat installed in there – but not until after the birth, Emma had insisted. Dan assured her that, unlike previous cars, this one was insured fully comprehensive; and not for the first time in recent months, Olivia's emotions got the better of her. The significance of the car was too much to take on a day that she was to publicly remember Edward. It did, however, focus her mind on what she should say, and her fears about speaking that evening dissipated.

The ride was so smooth that Emma decided not to wake Olivia when they came to a halt at the petrol station half an hour later.

'She looks so peaceful,' she smiled.

'Takes you back, eh, Em?' Dan replied, watching her snooze. 'Our baby's a bit too big for me to carry indoors now mind,' he joked, pretending to attempt a lift.

'Don't worry, Grandad,' she hushed. 'I'm sure you'll have chance for that soon enough.'

Dressing up like a waiter was not Dan's idea of fun. He strained to see the hook behind the bow tie in the mirror. 'What are you ordering a taxi for?' he asked, frustrated at his lack of co-ordination. 'We've got the car now, remember?'

'You going to drive home?' Emma replied, knowing full well that he wouldn't.

He hugged her. 'I knew there was a good reason for me marrying you, my little squdge-bucket.'

'It'll be here in ten minutes,' she told him, wiping lipstick off his cheek. 'Are you ready?'

He nodded, and brushed down the dinner suit, hired especially for the evening, with the palm of his hand.

Emma studied his attire. 'I should have come with you for that.'

'Why?' he moaned. 'What's wrong?'

'Nothing. You just look like a bowling ball that's rolled into wet paint,' she laughed, mocking the waistcoat that strained at his stomach. 'I thought you'd hired one of those cummerbund things?'

'I have!' he whined, undoing his jacket and lifting his elephantine paunch to reveal a band of material acting as a sling.

She snorted a laugh and kissed him again. He tries! she thought with pride.

Olivia's descent to the lounge was elegant. The flattering black outfit she'd selected with Val's help the week before was beautiful. There'd be no other chance for her to wear it, the waist being an amazing feat of expectancy-exclusive design, but she could always donate it to a charity shop, she thought. Either that, or hang on to it in case her dad ever wanted to go to a party in drag.

She looked radiant, and Dan insisted upon having a photograph of mother and daughter looking so splendid. 'Cor!' he mocked, watching them stand together through the camera's viewfinder. 'Couple of stunners out on the tiles tonight!'

'Why, thank you kind sir,' Emma replied with a coy flutter of the eyelashes.

'Lovely dress, Em,' he made sure her head was completely in the frame. 'What colour do you call that?'

She bristled with satisfaction. 'Scarlet, I'd say, darling.'

'Aye,' he admired. 'It matches yer eyes any road! Now say cheese.'

Liz and Don stood by the bar, accepting drinks from anyone offering. Don felt extremely conspicuous in his dinner suit, the braces feeling strange across his back. He thought now how women felt wearing bras. It must be a relief to get it off.

'Hooch is kid's stuff,' Liz told one face she recognised from somewhere. 'I'll have a Holsten, thanks.'

She scanned the room, swigging the ice-cold beer from the bottle. 'Can you see Caz?' she asked Don with a belch. 'Oops. 'Scuse me!'

His advantageous height allowed a greater range to be covered, and he could see her in the corner not far from the door. It looked like she'd just arrived.

'Who's she with?' Liz strained to locate her.

'Don't know,' he shrugged. 'There's some chap talking to her.'

They made their way across the room and Carole screamed hello when she recognised her friend approaching. 'Liz, meet Jason,' she pointed to her escort. 'Jason, this is Liz.'

Liz instantly recognised the face; it was him! Mr Dishy from the refectory himself. She introduced Don to Jason and thumped Carole's arm playfully. 'You little madam! You kept him quiet, didn't you?'

'It's early days yet, Liz,' her face wasn't the picture of enthusiasm.

'What?' she questioned. 'He's bloody gorgeous!' she whispered; not wanting either boy to hear for obvious reasons.

'But doesn't he know it?' Carole confided. 'And the

biggest let-down,' she wiggled her little finger.

'No!' Liz gasped.

''Fraid so,' Carole nodded. 'More meat on a butcher's pencil,' she smiled in resignation. 'How you getting on with Clark Kent?' a discreet finger pointed.

Liz grinned. 'We're getting there all right. No major problems, you know.'

'Brains *and* a decent knob? You lucky bitch! Mine's doing a GCSE.'

'Really?' Liz didn't know what to say. 'How…'

'Clever?'

Liz couldn't help laughing at Carole's sarcasm. 'Yeah, something like that.'

'History,' Carole pushed on in hushed tones. 'He can't read or write properly, so he majors in history.'

Liz fixed what felt like an 'I'm impressed' expression and nodded sagely.

Carole pulled her friend closer and hugged her tight. 'I'm glad we're mates, Liz,' she said. 'I love the way you always let me find the boneheads for myself!'

Liz smiled. 'The right one's out there, somewhere,' she promised.

'Well,' Carole moved free and rested her hands on her hips. 'Just you remember whose fault it is you kissed the mutant frog over there.'

Olivia wasn't expecting anything like the number of guests she encountered as she and the rest of the top table took their seats for the meal. She was impressed that there was an MC to oversee the proceedings, though she'd have preferred him not to house his gavel next to her.

The main course was coming to an end when Adrian leant over to ensure that she was still happy to say a few words before the presentation.

'Yes, no problem. What's the lady's name again?'

He reminded her. 'Add it to your notes,' he suggested.

'I'm "shooting from the hip"!' she smiled, and Adrian patted her hand.

'Good girl,' he winked. He beckoned the MC, who banged his gavel heartily, making Bump kick back equally viciously.

Adrian was introduced to a tremendous round of applause. Olivia hadn't realised, until his opening comments, that there were members of the press there too. This just got better and better didn't it? Where's the door?

He spoke a little of Track & Turf, its efforts to help the community, including the waste paper bin sponsorship with three local councils, and reminded everyone present of the reason for their attendance. Olivia took little in, concentrating on her own thoughts that still needed to be converted into words. Perhaps she should have written it down. At least she wouldn't forget to say the important things she *had* to get over.

She realised that Adrian had finished when there was another, more restrained round of applause and the MC dragged the microphone to rest in front of her.

With a little help from Adrian to draw back her chair, she stood in front of almost two hundred people there in the function room. Staff, family, friends, associates, members of the racing and greyhound fraternity, the press and of course, Track & Turf's new anonymous owners – all watching her.

Tightly holding the gold pocket watch, she took a deep breath and smiled warmly, mentally counting backwards from five as she did so. 'Ladies, Gentlemen, Distinguished Guests,' she copied Adrian's opening gambit. 'Oh, and of course,' she added, 'members of the press.' The empathetic laughter threw her for a moment, but she distanced herself from the audience and let her heart speak.

'…On 17th June, 1995, I was lucky enough to meet a young man named Edward Mallory. He changed my life in more ways than I care to imagine, and it is he who we remember and celebrate tonight. To all who knew him, he was a healthy, fun and loving person with boundless energy and wit. To many of those same people; he still is.'

'Hear, hear!' came a lone voice with table-banging, cutlery rattling accompaniment from the silence.

'...Five months after being confirmed diagnosed as epileptic, and the day before his twentieth birthday, Edward suffered what is thought to be only a minor, though unexpected seizure when he was doing what was natural to him – helping other people.

'Since that time, I have lived with the fact that it was I who should have collected my parents' car from the garage that day, being too lazy to switch off the television and do my own chores...'

Emma wiped her eyes and slowly shook her head, hoping Olivia wouldn't blame herself for ever.

'...Until recently, I wished that, if I wasn't to be in his place, I could have been with him in the car. Perhaps then, he might still be here. Who knows?...'

The man from the local news agency scribbled furiously, his cameraman's Pentax flashing from all angles.

'...However, those observant – and sober – amongst you,' the sound of appreciative laughter bolstered the confidence of the young woman on her feet, 'will have noticed that there will be an Edward Junior in the near future.

'It has often been cited by those closest to me, that if I *had* been with the baby's father on that fateful March day, the world would have been deprived of his child. So then, if Edward Mallory had to leave us prematurely, I am for ever grateful that he left behind within me, his flesh and blood by which we can all remember him.

'Edward's family have been a tower of strength to me, and those around me, in their own hour of adversity. I want to publicly thank Val, Adrian and Elizabeth for all they have done this year; not only for me, but also in supporting my family...'

Dan mopped his brow and took a heavy, steadying breath.

'...Edward was devastated by the discovery of his condition; some symptoms initially identified by a doctor in Australia of all places, who wouldn't let him scuba dive such were his concerns. But he soon learned that the stigma surrounding his illness was so badly distorted – he challenged it, and it was the work of the British Epilepsy Association that helped him come to terms with his condition. He aimed to live a normal and active life, no matter what.

'As we know, something happened that day in March. But exactly what, we will never discover. My own inability to accept what had happened led me to run and hide in a corner – causing only more pain and suffering, simply because I didn't understand. The people whose work can help us understand however, must be able to continue; and thanks to the efforts of Adrian Mallory and his entire staff, it gives me tremendous pleasure to root under this table and find a cheque which I would like to present to Mrs Judy Francis of the British Epilepsy Association.'

There was a further round of applause, with whistles and cheers from around the room. She let the noise die away before continuing with heart-felt pride. 'On behalf of Track & Turf, its staff and customers,' Olivia held up the cheque and passed it to the now standing guest of honour, 'I feel privileged to present you with, hopefully the first of many contributions, £27,500.'

The cameras flashed, and there followed a staged photographed handover for the formal publications and the company's own newsletter.

Olivia returned to her seat, her mother coming to hug

and kiss her, Val and Liz in tears, and Adrian's smile touching each ear. 'Marvellous!' he told her. 'You did him proud.'

She didn't hear the response of thanks and tributes to the company from Judy Francis. She was overcome, and tears of relief streamed down her own face, tracing mascara as they went. She'd finally bared her soul and said her public goodbyes.

S HE HOPED THAT the wine and beer wouldn't affect her judgement. Liz had practised for at least a week, and she knew with her eyes closed where she should walk to avoid the creaking floorboard halfway along the landing. As long as she stood on the complete carpet pattern by the clock and avoided the half pattern next to it, she'd be clear.

He heard the door latch rattle and his heart began to pound. Was this a good idea? Did he want to do this so much that he'd risk her parents' discovery? Yes, was the only and overwhelming answer.

He could tell she was near, the darkness so intense that he could see nothing. The quilt lifted to his left and she slid her body underneath. He felt her hands gently wrap their cold embrace around him and then quickly off again. The mattress rocked and the cover was thrown back, exposing him to the room's chilly air.

'Just let me get this nightie off!' she whispered. There was the whoosh of cotton and she started the whole thing again.

Snuggling up against him, he felt her curves and her hands roaming along his chest and down towards his underpants.

'What've you got them on for?' she giggled.

He thought quickly, and stories overheard in the college changing-room came to mind. 'I've left them on for you to take off,' he lied. He always wore them in bed.

She tried to purr – that's what Honor Blackman always did on telly – and slid further down, sliding the elasticated waist as she went. It snagged on his reaction to her presence, and she sniggered as it twanged back into place with a painful sounding snap against his skin.

He wanted to shout, but bit his tongue, rubbing the stinging ache instead. 'Come up here,' he told her and she appeared at his side on the pillow, blindly kissing his ear in the pitch night. It tickled and he writhed, shivering and feeling sensitive all over. No one ever told him it would be like an endurance test. What would come next – feather dusters on the feet?

He whisked off his remaining clothing, socks as well. They began to kiss, their hands exploring each other. He wished he didn't have to be silent, there was so much he wanted to say. What Mum called his little man had out grown his cub scout outfit tonight. It was into rubber-wear now, if he could get this packet open, that is.

'What do you do with 'em?' he quizzed, whispering excitedly.

'I dunno! Roll it out and stick it on I think,' Liz replied, holding on to him. 'Didn't you do biology?'

'Not practical, no!'

There was the feeling that something was happening beneath the cover, but Liz couldn't tell what. 'What's going on?'

He was frustrated, the open end gripping tight the end of his, leaving a six inch tassel hanging limp. Even *he* could tell that *that* was no good. 'Put the light on!' he whispered.

They blinked in the brightness and Liz choked, taking in what his pride and joy was wearing. 'I'd have knitted one if that's how they're supposed to look!' she tittered.

The burning inside was making him ache, and he snapped off the unravelled device, deciding to start again.

'Don't bother,' Liz begged from beneath the covers. 'Let's just bonk.'

'No,' he remained level-headed, and likening his challenge to another kind of software installation, asked if there was a user guide or something?

Her anxious fingers fumbled over the small box, finding eventually the little slip of instructions. 'Funny lookin' willy!' she observed giddily. 'What's *that* supposed to be?'

Oblivious to her critical analysis of the diagrams, he read the instructions over her shoulder and rummaged for a second sachet. His hands were greasy from the first and in continued frustration, Don bit open the wrapper.

'Shit!' he swore for the first time Liz could recall. 'I've bitten into the rubber.'

They had a third and last chance. She held the shaking leaflet, as he rolled down the sheath, trapping his pubic hairs as he did. 'Jesus! This hurts!' he tried to pull them from their snare.

'Come 'ere!' she grabbed him passionately and kissed.

'Turn the light out,' he hissed, 'I'm being blinded here.'

The darkness returned, their eyes still able to see coloured shapes in the room. He felt her hands run over him, and then her body on top of his.

'Shouldn't it be the other way round?' he questioned. Talk about on the job learning.

She rolled on to her back and he climbed on top of her, banging his head on the headboard as he edged forward. 'Shhhh!' she laughed, biting her lip to remain silent.

He was close to screaming. Where was it?

'Ouch! Wrong one!' she squealed, digging her nails into his side.

'Help me out, for God's sake!' he was desperate now. He felt her hand grip him, a feeling of sheer delight.

'Now,' she cried. 'Get it in.'

He thrust forwards and the heavenly warmth that enveloped him was too much for his straining to handle. It was over.

'Can you hear something?' Adrian asked in the darkness of the room down the corridor.

Val listened. 'Mmmm. I'll have words with her in the morning,' she sighed, rolling over and settling down to sleep.

The Bell was one of Dan's favourite eating pubs. They served the tastiest chips this side of Blackburn and cooked their steaks to perfection. He wanted to drive the new car there himself, Olivia promising to drive them home.

He wore his new shirt and tie – the first presents ever from Bump – his new jumper; one of the treats from his daughter, and a huge badge declaring that his life began today.

In the car park, Adrian's Range Rover was already standing empty out of sight at the far end, the four occupants patiently inside the bar waiting. Locking the car centrally, Dan insisted on checking each individual door handle, then the boot and re-checking them all again before leaving his new toy unattended.

There sounded a noisy welcome from Don and the Mallory family when Dan appeared around the lounge bar door. He smiled sheepishly as they began to sing happy birthday, the other customers looking on at his exposed torture.

The drinks were lined up and presents exchanged. Dan was tearing paper from an engraved crystal tankard – Val's eventual and difficult choice, when Adrian pulled Olivia to one side.

'How you feeling today?' he asked.

'The odd twinge, but I'm okay, thanks,' her tired eyes explained.

'Good. You might be interested in this,' he suggested, holding out a faxed copy of typed text.

'What is it?' she asked.

'It's a write-up of last night by Clive from the Post,' he smiled. 'I think you come across very well.'

She read the headline, referring to the sale of Adrian's business and the links with the charity fundraising. The new owners, the release informed, were to continue the charitable efforts for at least two years, under the same profit based scheme that Adrian had used. He drank from his glass with satisfaction, suggesting she look out for Monday's edition of the paper for the full story in print.

She held her orange juice aloft, her pride again brimming. 'Brilliant!' their glasses clinked.

Don and Dan were agreeing on the quality of the chips. Wide, fluffy-centred slices of potato with a crisp coating, by no means soggy but definitely not hard. Both regarded them eagerly.

Olivia leant over to Liz with a smirk. 'Just what you need to pick you up after a hard night, eh, Lizzie?'

Elizabeth's head spun. 'What do you mean?' she asked guiltily.

'A little birdie tells me you were gliding down the landing in the night,' she teased.

Liz didn't need to say a word, her face conveyed everything that could possibly cover the story. 'Which birdie?' she suddenly thought to ask, astonished.

'I was kidding, actually!' Olivia giggled. 'But now you've admitted it, don't keep it to yourself.'

Liz's heart settled. 'You cow,' she accused, disbelieving of her own stupidity and relieved that only Olivia knew. 'They'd kill me if they found out!'

Val felt in mischievous mood and pressed Liz on her whispered conversation with Olivia. If it was as she said, nothing, then there was no need to be so secretive, was there? So what was it? Oh, still nothing? Was she sure?

Liz hated her mother when she was in such humour, she could be a real loose cannon.

'Are you easily embarrassed, Don?' Val asked openly.

He went red at the thought of being embarrassed, let alone having anything to be embarrassed about. 'Why?' he asked nervously, his complexion deepening.

'Just wondered,' she continued. 'You see I could have sworn that last...'

'Wahhahhh!' yelled Olivia, grasping her stomach. 'Oh, fucking hell!' she gasped, breathless.

Everyone froze, except Emma. 'Luvvy? Is it Bump?' she demanded, jumping to her feet and clearing the table in front of her daughter.

Agony contorted Olivia's face and she managed a grimaced nod, clutching tight her abdomen. Thinking quickly, Val dashed to the Range Rover and arranged the seating to make the young woman's journey to the hospital as comfortable as possible.

Her parents helped her to her feet and walked her to the passenger door. Dan lifted up his little girl and carefully placed her down in the prepared seat, her breathing scaring him. 'You're gonna be all right, Ollie, luv. Everything's gonna be *all right!*' he tried to convince himself as much as anyone.

Leaving the car park, Adrian used his mobile phone to dial the maternity unit and forewarn of the arrival, the entire birthday celebration left in a table of half-eaten meals and an unpaid bill.

Val, Liz and Don leapt into Dan's car, and the Nissan sped after the large off-roader, Olivia's hand gripping that of her mother over her shoulder in the lead vehicle.

The journey around the top of the town took no more

than ten minutes. Olivia, though, felt every single second as Bump continued to move. The entrance to the unit was full of patients' relatives coming and going, or simply taking their nicotine in a mid-visit break.

Adrian barged through to the reception, Emma and Olivia closely behind. A nurse came to calmly assist while Emma completed the questions necessary for admission. 'She's not due for another three weeks,' she flapped.

To the third floor went the lift, and Olivia found herself in a birthing suite with two nurses before she realised that her mother was not there. She called out for her.

The first nurse soothed and settled her, assuring that Mum would be on her way up, and there was no need to worry. The other listened carefully to her tummy, instructing her bluntly to calm down for the baby's sake. Olivia had never felt such pain. She tried to remember her breathing technique. Where's my bag? she panicked. 'My bag's at home! I need my bag!' she called.

'Don't worry about your bag,' assured the kind nurse. 'We have everything you need. Mum's on her way.'

She continued her breathing, repeating her request for painkillers. Where's my Mum?

A third nurse showed Emma into the specialist suite, only minor attempts made to disguise its functionality with a lone picture of flowers and a pink border around its stark white walls. 'Ollie!' she wept, full of charged emotion. 'How you feeling, sweetheart?'

'How do you *think* I fuckin' well feel?' the girl barked. 'Where the bloody hell have you been, Mother? I need my bag!'

Her mother was shocked and looked at the nurse connecting the final monitor pads to her arm. The nurse shook her head. 'Ignore her,' she mouthed, almost silently.

'Don't you piggin' well ignore me!' the patient cried in frustration. 'Gimme some painkillers, for God's sake!'

The nurse looked at Emma and then at Olivia, returning her astonished gaze to Emma. 'How does she do that?' she asked in awe.

Her pain was soon under sufficient control to allow Olivia to sit up and apologise to Emma for the abuse she was handing out. 'I've got to get it out of my system now, Mum while I've got an excuse,' she explained, the beads of perspiration glistening on her forehead. 'You'll smack me in the chops tomorrow if I call you an old bag.'

'That's if he *arrives* by tomorrow, dear,' Emma baited, mopping the fiery brow.

Downstairs, the birthday lunch party was fidgeting. Dan and Adrian both paced like the expectant father; Val remained outwardly calm, while knotting up inside. Liz and Don both privately hoped that last night's condom had done its job, if this was to be the result of such a small amount of spilt milk.

Emma waited until Olivia was resting before leaving the suite and scurrying down the stairs to the general waiting area. All eyes fell upon her; even those of other relatives waiting to hear of their own arrivals, the dark haired father-to-be with his cigar ready and waiting the most eager.

'Well?' Dan asked, desperate for the cigarettes he'd left at The Bell.

'No news,' his wife's unwelcome reply prompting a groan from all but Val. 'She's resting; it's going to be a while yet, I think.'

'In that case, we'd be better off at home,' Val suggested, rising from her seat and slinging her handbag beneath her arm. 'Adrian, Elizabeth, Donald,' she rounded them up like a sheep dog. 'Let's go!'

'Before you do, Val,' Emma walked her friend to the door. 'She's asking for Edward's diary. Do you think you could drop it in?'

Val smiled, and suggested it was the least she could do.

'Thanks,' Emma sighed. 'I'll yell the minute there's some news.'

'You'd better!' Val replied facetiously, kissing her friend. 'And a happy birthday to you!' she called to Dan, his hands running through his hair in nervous exasperation and painfully finding the still-sore scalp.

Emma smiled at her husband. The anguish on his face was love itself. 'You coming up?' she asked.

'Am I allowed?'

'I reckon so, you great lummox,' she held him close.

'I don't think she'll want me seein' the gory end,' he spoke into her hair, desperate not to show himself up by fainting, or having a second taste of his half-eaten lunch-time steak.

She thought his worries tender. 'Very noble, luv, but I'm sure she's other things on her mind right now than her dad seeing her unladylike legs.'

'It's not her legs I'm bothered about,' he laughed. 'It's the bit in the middle!'

'Let's just go and help her through the last, eh?' she replied, happy that he was there at all.

They climbed the stairs together, Emma warning him *en route* that things might be said that Olivia didn't really mean.

'Like being at home then?' he quipped.

When they entered the room, the nice nurse was re-arranging the pillows behind Olivia, and telling her that after the next check – in about an hour if there was no change by then – she could get up and wander around for a while. 'Let gravity help,' she summarised.

Olivia was preoccupied with the thought that it was going to take more than an hour. She snorted when Dan asked what it felt like. 'Imagine having the biggest turd in your life, Dad.'

He frowned.

'Only it's stuck inside you and kicking to get out.'

'Bloody 'ell!' He felt ill at the thought.

'Then multiply it by ten!' She managed a smile. 'And,' she waved a threatening finger, 'that's a pound for the box.'

'Huh?'

'I'm exempt from swearing today, so someone has to make up the contributions. Heaven only knows the first words he'll hear will probably be an 'F' or a 'B'!'

Val arrived back at reception within half an hour. She brought with her a small bag containing toiletries, a towel, the most feminine nightie she could find clean – apart of course from her silk one; she didn't want her own blood on that let alone anyone else's – Elizabeth's monster feet slippers – the only ones in the house that weren't full of holes; some soft drinks; two sandwiches; and, most importantly, Edward's diary.

The nurse on duty behind the desk was sorry not to be able to let her go up to see Olivia, but would let her parents know that she was waiting.

'No, don't bother,' Val insisted. 'They've enough to think about. Can you just get the bag to Livvy for me, please?'

The nurse was good to her word, and the bag arrived in the suite soon after Val had departed for the second time. Emma rooted through the contents, touched by the kind consideration of a true friend.

'Great!' Dan enthused, trying on the slippers and noticing the sandwiches. 'I'm starvin'!'

Emma smacked his hand away, telling him in no uncertain terms that Val was *not* thinking of him when she made them. 'Go to the vending machine if you're that hungry,' she scolded.

He made for the door, and Olivia suggested her mum go

with him, to take a break and stretch her legs.

'No, I'm all right, luv,' she replied, screwing up her nose and shaking her head.

Olivia mimicked the face, telling her to bugger off and leave her in peace for a while. Reluctantly, Emma withdrew from the room but not before placing the call button right beside her daughter's hand on the bed.

'Will you *please* go?' Olivia wanted to be alone.

She waited to make sure that her parents wouldn't burst back in for a wallet or handbag, and when she was satisfied that Dan must be happy to wander around in green clawed slippers, took out Edward's diary and searched for a piece that she'd been picturing all afternoon.

D. 41 – Sat 20 July: Nearing end flight BA 008 – Tokyo to London Heathrow. Well, we're on our home-leg good and proper now. How can I sum up the past forty-odd days? Well, they've been the best of my life. There's not a single thing I'd change – not even our first humdinger of an argument.

From the choking heat of Bangkok at midday, to the freezing knees of Ayers Rock at dawn. From the horse racing in Brisbane, to the mean-machine moped in Airlie Beach. Viv's toilet roll and thousands of postcards. Kyoto's tradition and Tokyo's hysteria. It's all been a scream!

And what's the best part for me of this trip, as I sit here on a Jumbo somewhere over Europe? It's sitting next to someone I can call my true soulmate. She won't let me read her diary, but so what? I know what she thinks. I don't need to see it written down. Right now, she's asleep and whistling nicely! I'm going to miss that at the Farm when I'm all alone at night.

Friends have said me and Livvy are crazy wanting to spend so long together. I think Mum considers this 'make or break' time with us. There ain't no way we're breaking. Wherever she goes, I go. I'm so glad we've experienced this trip, no one can ever take away your memories. If there's one thing that's become apparent during this wonderful adventure, it's that life's no rehearsal. Do it today, tomorrow may never come.

When I have kids, I'll make sure of two things. 1) they're Olivia's; 2) they grow up with a sense of being. A sense that they have the right to question and explore. More importantly, that they exercise that right. There's a huge world out there, I want them to see what I've seen, and the so much more that I've not yet seen.

I think, with this trip, my life's only just started. From now on, every day will be a new adventure. I'll enjoy every one, loving Olivia till the day I die.

The telephone rang once, and Val had the receiver to her ear.

'Val?' Emma's shrill excitement. 'Get your arse over here!'

The Mallory house was delirious. For five hours they had sat on tenterhooks, and they scrambled for the car to make the short journey back to the Royal. Even Don was excited to be seeing the new arrival.

The man with his cigar still on alert, was looking deflated as they fought to be the first into the waiting area where Dan was to be found, perfecting his Cheshire Cat impression. There was a clamour to congratulate him, kisses and handshakes, hugs and tears.

'She's having a bath while Em looks after the little 'un,' he told them.

'What about the details, then?' Adrian demanded.

They knew already he was a healthy 6lb 5oz at birth – timed as 6.10 p.m. (and a few seconds), but Dan filled them in on the latter stages which were, the nurse had told him, quite quick for a first born – especially one so early. 'But what d'ya expect?' he grinned with pride.

Liz turned pale on hearing the sequence of events from

the baby's head first coming into view, to the 'Whoosh! Splat!' as he launched into the world – his mother teaching his grandparents a few new words, many worth remembering, Grandad thought.

'And how did you feel?' Don asked, getting into the swing.

'Me?' Dan swaggered. 'I knew he were a Beech when I saw the size of his tackle,' he laughed. 'But then the nurse told us that was the umbilical!' he joked, unable to hide his delight. 'I were chuffed to little fluffy chips, mate!'

'What about a name?' Liz wanted to know.

Dan smiled and put his arm around her shoulders. 'I'll let her tell you that one, luvvy, but don't guess too hard is all's I'll say.'

They waited for more than an hour, the stranger joining Dan and Adrian in the doorway of the unit to smoke his cigar to celebrate Olivia's new arrival; Don declining the offer of tobacco on grounds of his asthma.

'Think my missus needs some dynamite,' the man moaned. 'Been sat here since eleven last night I have,' the cigar glowed as he drew breath. 'Then you buggers come in and only have to wait a few hours! What's she got; a Velcro fitting?'

Emma turned the corner and flopped down beside Val with a tired smile. 'Next!' she called. More congratulations, hugs and kisses were shared all round – even the dark stranger found himself covered in lipstick, before Val and Adrian were allowed to go and see her for a few brief moments before her transfer to the ward.

They entered slowly and saw Olivia sat upon the bed, hunched over a bundle of white blankets. She turned to see who was at the door, and quietly beckoned them closer.

All babies are beautiful, Val believed, but there was her first grandson, and he was perfect.

'He's got his daddy's eyes,' the fatigued mother described what was hiding beneath the closed lids.

'But your nose,' Adrian smiled. 'Lucky beggar.'

Grandma Mallory couldn't wait to get her hands on her grandson, and rocked him gently in her arms. 'Hello!' she beamed as he opened his blue eyes to take in the blurred visions of a life outside. 'Hello!' she repeated. 'You're beautiful, aren't you? Yes, you are. You're beautiful.'

'We can't call him Bump now, can we?' Adrian ventured, leaving his wife to the gooey Grandmaspeak. 'Dare we ask?'

Olivia's exhausted eyes smiled. 'Do you really have to?' she hugged him. 'His middle name's Sydney,' she blurted, clinging tight, wiping her face on his shoulder.

Like Emma before her, Val joined in a chorus of tears. Adrian fought stay calm, acknowledging the nurse who had entered with a wheelchair, ready to transport Olivia to the private side ward that he had arranged only minutes before.

They watched her being wheeled towards the lift, a second nurse carrying a screaming Edward alongside. The chair stopped and was turned around. 'Hey! What time is it, again?'

Val checked her watch. 'Just before eight o'clock,' she announced.

Olivia nodded. 'I thought that's what you'd said. What's happening about Dad's party?'

The guests at The Rat and Drainpipe were beginning to think it mighty strange that there was no sign of Emma or Olivia. They were making the most of their party spirit, when the crowd of supposedly celebrating steam enthusiasts arrived, minus a should-have-been-surprised Dan.

'Where's the principal guest?' Bill asked a balloon-bearing bystander, obviously there for the same function.

'Don't know,' replied the brassy young woman. 'We

work with Emma, don't we, tiger?' she asked her young boyfriend. 'She's not 'ere either,' she told Bill. 'Our manager's just gone to phone their 'ouse.'

David returned with a blank look and shrugging shoulders. 'No one home,' he told them, taking his pint from the bar where he'd left it and enjoying a refreshing mouthful.

The party continued in buoyant mood and few worries regarding the whereabouts of the birthday boy or his family. The more time passed, the more boisterous the throng, and when the buffet was revealed, a hoard of hungry guests devoured the pies and vol-au-vents set amongst bowls of salad and plates of pungent smelling egg sandwiches.

They had left Olivia to catch up on her much needed rest, and Emma held Dan's hand as they returned downstairs to the main waiting area to find Adrian sat chatting to the only other person waiting – the dark-haired man on his now cigarless vigil.

Adrian bade his farewells and wishes for an expedient birth and stood to greet his friends. Emma yawned and fell jocosely into Adrian's open arms. Dan, desperate for the toilet, excused himself and agreed to meet them by the doors.

'Everyone gone home?' Emma asked.

'To the pub actually,' Adrian corrected her.

'Wetting the baby's head *already*?' her tired mind in only first gear.

'Yes *and* no,' he grinned. 'To celebrate Dan's fortieth birthday, really.'

Her jaw visibly dropped. 'Oh bugger!' she laughed. 'So what now?'

He had it all under control, and primed her on the revised plans.

In the car, Emma all but choked when Dan said he

could kill a pint of Boddingtons. He still wasn't sure why Adrian had stayed behind when Val and the kids had gone home, but he was glad that his stinging eyes didn't have to concentrate on the road. He just prayed that Adrian was better at driving his car than he was at juggling his plates. He still hadn't forgiven him for his Zorba impression on the patio, all that time ago.

As planned, Emma sighed and asked Adrian to find somewhere that they could take a drink.

'There's the…' he strained to read the name of the sign ahead, '…Rat and…'

'Drainpipe!' shouted Dan. 'Aye, we'll 'ave a pint in 'ere mate!' he instructed, right on cue. 'Pull in!'

Hiccup. He fought to remove his underpants. Why, he wondered, when you've had a few drinks, do your underpants insist on sticking *right* up the crack? He still couldn't get over tonight. Fancy all those people he knew being in The Rat! Bloody brilliant. After the most amazing sight of his life too. His little girl having a little boy. *Hiccup.*

He called loudly for Emma.

'Coming!' she replied from the bathroom.

Sniffing his socks, he decided that there was another day's wear in them yet. 'I've had a brilliant day, Grandma!' he yelled.

She entered the room, and his eyes were wide. 'Bloody 'ell!' he gasped.

So, he was forty, she thought. Was that inches round as well as years? It looked like it; his shoulders arched and stomach bulging as he sat slumped on the bed. She loved him though.

His huge frame swayed as she approached, her new night-gown entrancing his inebriated brain. His glazed eyes followed her seductive crawl on to the bed, her hand reaching for the light and turning the dimmer switch down low.

'I want you,' she purred.

'Bloody 'ell, Em,' he blew a short sharp breath of realisation. 'I'm pissed!'

'So?' her tempting tones deliberately dismissive.

His mind went through its own distinctive sober-up
programme: talking gibberish nonsense.

'Shhhh,' her finger pressed to her lips.

'Thanks for a brilliant party, luv!' his eyes a fixed blur on
her cleavage. 'I'm pissed!' he told her again with a snigger.
Hiccup.

She slowly made for him to lie down, her hands caressing his body. 'Oh God,' he spluttered.

'Shhhh!' she told him again, drawing closer to his face
and biting his bottom lip.

'Oops! Sorry,' he apologised, grabbing his stomach.

Don't you worry, chuck; I've a real thing about farts.
'Kiss me Dan,' she tempted.

They rolled around the bed, arms and legs everywhere,
hands moving freely when she stopped abruptly. 'You know
what I want you to do tonight?' she panted.

He thought hard. He hated quizzes this late at night,
especially after drinking. It couldn't be the washing up; he
hadn't noticed any dirty dishes. 'Go on,' he prompted.

She whispered her desire, nibbling his ear lobe.

'What, *now*?' he looked surprised.

She nodded a slow and sensuous wink.

Oh shite. Really? 'That's what you *really* want?'

Again she nodded, even slower, licking her moistened
lips. 'Right now.'

He cracked his knuckles and apologised for unleashing
more malodorous wind. Kissing her with beery breath, he
slid down beside her. Caressing her smooth skin as he
went, he travelled the length of her body, reaching her feet.
She giggled, his warm breath tickling her sensitive toes. She

arched her spine as he began to move back up along her, the opposite side enjoying his touch. Reaching her inner thigh, he took a deep breath and remembered the advice he'd been given on Emma's wildest fantasy:

'Just you nip the bugger… Nip it quick.'

For help and advice, the British Epilepsy Association
may be contacted at:
Anstey House, 40 Hannover Square, Leeds, LS3 1BE.
Telephone helpline 0345 089599.